"What a joy to have this in Eng[lish]
Dimitri's fantastic fantasy novel has everything I like.
A sensation of damp shadows moving just out of
sight, and a slow, joyful, and mysterious unravelling
of events. I can't recommend it too highly."
Joe R. Lansdale, author of *The Thicket*

"Francesco Dimitri's first novel in English is a wonder and
a revelation. Hidden within this gripping, frightening story
about an arcane manuscript is a deep, clear-eyed, and
compassionate meditation on friendship as it evolves over
time. *The Book of Hidden Things* is fantasy at its best: using
magical tropes to illuminate real life."
Terri Windling, author of *The Wood Wife*

"*The Book of Hidden Things* is both a mystery and a map.
Follow the clues along the trail in Francesco Dimitri's
dazzling debut and you'll be ushered into a hidden world of
magic, not only within these pages, but also within your own
life. Be prepared to be transformed."
Mark Chadbourn, author of the Age of Misrule series

"What a glorious read! This sun-drenched fantasy is a feast
for the senses, reflecting on the value of friendship and what
it means to finally grow up. If you loved Neil Gaiman's *The
Ocean at the End of the Lane*, this book is for you."
Helen Marshall, author of *Gifts for the One Who Comes After*

THE
BOOK
OF
HIDDEN
THINGS

FRANCESCO DIMITRI

TITAN BOOKS

The Book of Hidden Things
Print edition ISBN: 9781785657078
Electronic edition ISBN: 9781785657085

Published by Titan Books
A division of Titan Publishing Group Ltd
144 Southwark Street, London SE1 0UP

First edition: July 2018
2 4 6 8 10 9 7 5 3 1

A CIP catalogue record for this title is available from the British Library.

Printed and bound in the United States.

Did you enjoy this book?
We love to hear from our readers. Please email us at
readerfeedback@titanemail.com or write to us at
Reader Feedback at the above address.

TITAN BOOKS.COM

For 'that' Paola.

When the storm comes you are the eye,

When the sun burns you are the shade,

When it is all kind of good, well,

You are better.

She held herself not in the way of a mortal,
but in the shape of an angel, and her voice
had a sound which was other than human.
A spirit from Heaven, a living Sun,
that was what I saw.

Francesco Petrarca, Canzoniere, 'Sonnet 90'

FABIO

1

Sitting at the table next to me is an elderly German couple. When the waiter recognises my accent, still local despite my best efforts, he winks and says, 'They're from Berlin. Moved here last month.' He is thrilled that someone has taken the trouble to move all the way from Berlin, no less, to dump their bones in this pit. I wonder what the pull of Casalfranco is for them. So what if it is sunny down here? They have sunlamps in Berlin. I glance at the couple; they look happy. Give them time.

No, I don't like it here. I don't mean the pizzeria; the pizzeria is fine. I mean this town, this part of the world: Puglia. Oh, I'll grant you that in this season it hits you with a heady scent of rosemary and lemon and flowering thyme. When I got out of the cab on this warm June night, I had to close my eyes and drink it all in, like sweet wine on a date. But it is a honey trap. Another three weeks and the summer sun will evaporate the scent and burn the land to a cinder, and what little life there is left will have to start a war for the last drops of water left deep underground. I didn't trust Casalfranco when I was here, and I trust it even less since I got out. This place is feral. I am only back for tonight, for the Pact. And I am unsure, to be honest, if the Pact still stands. It is a miracle it lasted this long.

I am at a corner table; not any table, but *the* table, *our* table. It was free straight away. I am alone, surrounded by three empty chairs, wondering if the others will come. In front of me is the wood-fired oven, a cavernous mouth of white stone. A dark-skinned *pizzaiolo* is working a ball of dough with jerky movements, while another handles a pizza overflowing with Parma ham, rocket and parmesan shavings. I think I know the dark-skinned guy: Guido or Gianni or something like that. I was at school with his second cousin.

I came to American Pizza (their pizza is as Italian as it gets) direct from Brindisi Airport. In the authentic southern tradition, the car I had booked was nowhere to be seen. It took me two hours to get another, so when I finally reached Casalfranco I was twenty minutes late for what had been since time immemorial (or secondary school anyway) the hour of the Pact. I called the B&B to tell them that I would check in after dinner. I had forgotten that being twenty minutes late, in Southern Italy, means being anywhere from ten to thirty minutes early. I forget every time. Art says I do it on purpose, but I don't think so.

Maybe the Pact has fizzled out.

They will come, I say to myself. *They will come*. I have been repeating this all the way from the airport. *It's the Pact; they won't break it.* The Pact was Art's idea – hence the capital P, because Art always puts capitals on words, multiplying their power, transforming them into Words. The Pact is a silly game which I swore I would stop playing last year, and if the boys don't show up (I am by now almost sure they won't) I will feel like a complete idiot. I could have put to better use the money I spent on this trip – the flight and the B&B were dirt cheap, but lately for me *dirt cheap* has become synonymous with *stupidly expensive*. And yet, here I am.

I am nibbling a bruschetta heavy on garlic, washing it down with what is left of a glass of Primitivo, the strong local red, when I see Mauro enter the pizzeria. So one of them has come after all. With his cream chinos, white shirt and navy-blue jacket, Mauro plays the part of the grown-up with a grace I can only dream of. In keeping with the Pact, I acknowledge his presence with a small nod, as if I see him regularly. He nods back and comes to the table. He's put on some weight since I saw him two years ago, but he's got a better haircut. Both things please me.

'Been waiting long?' Mauro asks, sitting down.

'Less than the last time.'

'Making progress.'

'Baby steps, Mauro, baby steps.'

He cracks a smile and pours himself a glass of wine. 'I wasn't so sure we would see you again.'

'Neither was I.'

'When did you fly in?'

'Just now. I'm here straight from the airport.'

'You didn't swing by Angelo?'

'He doesn't know I'm in town.'

Mauro undoes his smile. We've been friends for too long to hide our feelings, and right now, he feels I'm a jerk. He doesn't understand my relationship with my father, and I can't blame him; most of the time, I don't understand it either.

'I'm not staying at his,' I explain. 'I've booked a B&B. I'm leaving tomorrow early in the morning, and I thought it wasn't worth the hassle to stay with him.' *Stop that.* I don't have to justify myself – I am a grown-up.

'Say we bump into someone you know and *they* tell Angelo.'

'Let's hope it won't happen.'

Mauro raises his hands in surrender, and says, 'I arrived yesterday.'

'Have you seen Art?'

'What do you reckon?'

I reckon not: it would feel like a breach of the Pact. Silly as it is, we are serious about it, or have been. Either way, I have let it draw me back to Casalfranco, inexorably, once a year, for seventeen years, with the exception of the last one. What my eighty-year-old widowed father can't accomplish, the Pact can. I reckon this is our last hurrah; I'll make the most of it.

'Art is bonkers,' says a voice behind my back.

Mauro stands up. 'Tony!'

I turn my head to see Tony make a bow and a flourish. 'These days I go by *Tony the Mighty*.'

Tony is not tall, but he is so muscular and compact, in his sleeveless shirt, you only need a quick glance to decide that you are too tied up right now to mess with him. He always was physically imposing, and a bit of a buffoon too. He was the main reason why bullies, after some half-hearted attempts, gave up on Art – though Art could be scary in his own right. We thought Tony would become, say, a professional boxer, or perhaps an enforcer for the Sacra Corona Unita, Sacred United Crown, the local mafia. He ended up a surgeon, and a good one at that. Some months ago, he managed a particularly difficult heart transplant, which gave him his fifteen minutes of fame. We were often wrong, back then. Take Art, for example. All the expectations we had.

Tony rests a hand on my shoulder. 'You graced us with your presence, I see.'

'I'm sorry I couldn't make it last year.'

'You will be, man,' he says, as he sits down.

Mauro tells him, 'I've read of your master stroke.'

'It was impressive,' I say, grinning. 'I mean, I didn't think you could tell a heart from a kidney.'

Tony says, 'I got lucky. I happened to be holding a heart in my hands and I tripped and the heart flew up and landed snug in the right place. Only,' and he lowers his voice, 'between you and me, I'm not sure it was a *human* heart I was holding. Could've been a dog's.'

'As long as it works,' Mauro says.

'The fellow isn't barking. Yet. How are you guys doing, anyway?'

'Fine,' Mauro says.

That is an understatement. Mauro is not exactly *modest*. It is the other way round. His approach is more like, *If you don't know about me, then you can't afford me.* Mauro is a lawyer in Milan, a specialist in taxes and finance. He lives where money lives, and when you live where money lives, a part of that money is bound to come and live with you too.

As for me, 'Can't complain,' I lie.

'Of course you can't,' Mauro says, with a wink. He thinks I'm doing grand, and why shouldn't he? He doesn't know, none of them do, and that is fine by me for tonight. Plenty of time tomorrow to face the bucketload of mess I made of my life.

I check my watch. 'Where's Art? It's getting late.'

Tony says, 'Hey, *I* just arrived.'

'Yeah, and you were late even by local time.'

'Fabio, my dearest friend, are you hungry? 'Cause you're a bitch when you're hungry.'

'I'm kind of peckish,' I admit. I barely registered the slice of bruschetta I'd already had; southerners can eat, and it is a mortal offence to imply otherwise. Casalfranco has this power, when you step into it. You revert to old habits.

Mauro waves to attract a waiter. 'Antipasti please,' he says, 'while we wait for our friend.'

2

Art has big ears and a big nose, the blackest eyes you have ever seen and bottle-bottom glasses. In the mid-nineties nobody would have considered him attractive; nerd fashion was yet to become a thing. Not that Art was so easily classifiable. His marks were high, his social grace disputable, yet there was something about him – an intensity, a *magnetism*, for want of a better word – that set him apart from your run-of-the-mill geek. Part of it was that he wasn't intimidated by girls (or bigger boys, or priests, or professors); it was him who brought Anna into Mauro's life, when we were fifteen.

Anna and Rita went to the beach at the same spot we did, in Portodimare, a village less than ten miles from Casalfranco. The beach was smooth white sand, fading into water just slightly less clear than air. When tramontana, the northern breeze, blew, the sea was still *come una tavola*, like a table. Look at it from the seashore, and you would see the sand and rocks on the bottom, with banks of *cazzi di Re* (King's cocks, brightly coloured fish) swimming by. They're so called because, local wisdom has it, the cock of a king has more colours than yours.

We were used to fish, less so girls. We had noticed Anna and Rita; their accent marked them as Milanese, and thus deserving awe. We had no clue how to approach cosmopolitan, sophisticated, world-weary *Milanese* girls. They had noticed us (out of boredom, I would say) but it was the boys' job to make the first step. It was a Mexican standoff: we eyed them and they eyed us, and everybody kept their positions, until one day Art said, 'Enough.'

We had been playing football on the boiling-hot beach, hoping the girls would take heed of our athletic feats. They hadn't. We had cooled down with a swim, emptied two bottles of ice tea from Mauro's bag, and now were sitting on the sand, sulking.

'Yeah,' I replied, annoyed, 'because *you* know what to do.'

Art tilted his head towards me and brought two fingers to his eyes, as if to say, *Watch me*. He jumped up – and almost tripped over the ball. We chuckled. He was unfazed. He straightened his glasses and walked, in his trunks that were too large for him, to where Anna and Rita were lying on their beach towels. When he got there, he hunkered down beside Rita and asked her, 'May I bother you one sec?'

Rita scoffed, 'If you really have to.'

'I noticed your hands.'

'My hands?'

Art nodded, and in all seriousness he said, 'My mum's a gypsy. She taught me how to read hands.'

'No way.'

Art laughed. 'I'm not saying I believe it works.'

'And why do you want to read *my* hand?'

Seamlessly, Art took Rita's right hand into his own. She let him do it. Bending over her like some goblin from a book of fairy tales, Art traced the contour of her palm with the index finger of his left hand. Coming from anybody else, that gesture would have been downright creepy, but Art was so disarming that even I would have fallen for it, and I knew perfectly well that his mum was as much of a gypsy as I was a Swede.

'Your hands have a special shape,' Art said. 'Mum would say it's the hand of a dreamer. You're quite a sensitive young woman, aren't you?'

16

Rita opened her mouth, amazed. 'How do you know?'

'It's all over here. And look at this line! The line of relationships, can you see it? All windy and dramatic. People just can't get you; your special sensitivity singles you out from the crowd. You feel lonely at times, even though you've got plenty of friends.'

'That's... that's right,' Rita said.

Then Anna intervened. 'Bullshitter,' she said, pushing Art, amused more than annoyed. Art lost his footing and his goblin-like pose, and we all guffawed. It didn't happen very often that Art was called on his bullshit.

Art laughed too. 'Yeah,' he said, 'maybe.' Ice had been broken, his point had been proven, and he had already lost interest. That's Art, that's always been Art: easily intrigued, easily bored. He sticks to us, and to the Pact, and that is all the stability he needs in his life.

3

Art doesn't show up.

We make our way through the antipasti (warm bread, Parma ham, deep-fried calamari, oven-baked mussels, hard cheese, grilled vegetables, and olives – everywhere else it would be a complete meal; here, it is a warm-up), pizza and two bottles of Primitivo wine, and Art still doesn't show up. Even Mauro looks disappointed, and Mauro is the unflappable one. On the night of the Pact we show up. You might go abroad and get married and become a prince in a foreign land, but on the night of the Pact, you show up. There are no *ifs* and no *buts*. That's the theory – and we carried on the practice for a surprisingly long time. The first time, during our first year of university, none of us were really expecting to find the others, but there we were, all of us. After that it became sort of a game to hold on to the Pact and see who would drop out first.

The longer we respected the Pact, the more important it became to us. Art said, four or five years ago, that we were caught in a well-known psychological loop: you start believing that your actions matter just because they are your actions. The longer you continue doing a thing, the more important it feels, the less you feel you can stop. *It's called cognitive dissonance*, he said. *Sit at a desk every day and you'll convince yourself that your job makes a difference, and that you like it, even. Drink a priest's wine long enough and you'll be ready to buy that it's a god's blood.* I asked him if that meant he didn't believe in the Pact anymore. He answered, *I do. I really do.*

Last year I broke the spell. I didn't feel like talking about what was going on in my life, and I didn't feel like facing Mauro and Tony's success. I had been unsure whether to tell the others I wasn't coming, and in the end opted not to, because I knew Tony would complain, and Mauro disapprove, and Art would twist my arm to go after all. I told myself that talking openly of the Pact meant breaking it anyway, and it was better for everybody if I just gave a no-show.

I received a frantic call from Tony's phone in the course of the night; surely something terrible must have happened. After I made it clear that I was alive and well, Art shouted *Traitor!* over the phone, laughing, and made me wish I was with them. I was thinking of that *Traitor!* three days ago, when I resolved, against my better judgement, to come.

Mauro says, 'And this time it's Art blanking us. You started it, Fabio.'

'I was busy.'

'One is never too busy for the Pact,' Tony says, in the pretend voice of a professor.

'How many times will I have to say I'm sorry?'

'Many. But blanking your mates is like you, it's not like Art.'

I pick up my phone. 'Let's get done with it.'

'That's a breach of the Pact.'

'Tony, the Pact is a children's game.'

'So what are you doing here?'

I ignore him and dial Art's number. My call goes straight to voicemail. 'His phone's turned off.'

Mauro gestures the waiter to bring us the bill. 'He's staying at his old place, isn't he?'

Tony says, 'Yep.'

Nine years ago Art's dad died, and two years ago his mum too, and at that point Art decided to move back to Casalfranco, from Prague, where he had happened to be at the time. It took all of us aback, considering how profoundly he hated Puglia, and Art offered no explanation to speak of. My secret fear is that it wasn't an entirely sane choice. He was falling apart by then. When I saw him he was gaunter than ever, and spent most of the night talking of the *uniquely fascinating*, in his own words, nature of drystone walls.

Mauro says, 'We should go and check on him.'

'That's a *huge* breach of the Pact,' Tony says. He's only half fooling.

'You said it yourself, this is not like Art.' Mauro stands up. 'I've got my car parked outside.'

I'm about to object: *We've been drinking all night, we can't drive.* Then I remember where I am. Not in London, but in Salento, the heel of Italy, where nobody thinks twice about drinking and driving.

We pay our bill – ridiculously cheap – and leave, to find ourselves in a small, circular piazza paved in stone. White houses with flat roofs surround it, and two palm trees sit comfortably in a flower bed at the centre. A rusty drinking fountain stands in one corner. Someone has broken the tap, so the water is gushing out uninterrupted. It is the loudest noise I can hear in the soft southern night. We take a dimly lit alleyway, scaring away a lonely cat. I come here rarely enough not to be used to the architecture anymore, the narrow paths and the ramshackle doors, an odd mash-up of Arabia, Greece, France, and entirely local shabbiness. Casalfranco feels smaller than it is; at a population size of around thirty-five thousand people, it still pretends it is a village. When I was growing up there were no bookshops, no cinemas or theatres. I had to take a one-hour bus trip to get my book fix. A local historian found that all the townsfolk are related to one another. Inbreeding explains a few things about this place.

Mauro's car is a five-door Ford; nothing flashy, but in mint condition. Tony runs to the right-hand door, crying, 'Shotgun!'

I find a spot on the back seat between a child's car seat and a squeaky dragon. 'Are you here with Anna?' I ask, as Mauro starts the engine.

'Children and wife, the whole crew. We decided to make a holiday of it, before the bulk of the tourists arrive.'

Not my problem, thank goodness. I'm flying out of here at five-thirty a.m. The last thing I need is to get stuck in conversation with Anna.

Tony takes out a packet of cigarettes and offers one to me and one to Mauro. We share a silent smoke as Mauro drives out of town and into the countryside. Art's place lies around six miles south of Casalfranco proper. Each of us could do the journey with our eyes closed, after all the times we travelled it when we were kids.

Art will be fine. When you worry about something (your lover being late, your medical check-up) it almost invariably turns out fine. But the night is spoilt anyway. The *Pact* is spoilt, and it is all my fault. I know it had to happen, sooner or later, but that doesn't make it better. The part of me that indulges in self-pity says, *You ruined another good thing, Fabio, that's my boy.* A pocket-sized double of myself claps his hands sarcastically in my mind.

The town fades into open countryside, until we find ourselves driving on a narrow, dark road, and I mean *dark* – with no lampposts, no roadside bars, no hint of electric light whatsoever. The land surrounding us comes into existence only for the fleeting time our headlights touch it, and it is flat as the sea on one of those tramontana days. Vineyards first, the plants all bent, and then thick olive trees, bent too, and twisted. Things that grow here must make do with very little water and too much sun, as well as wind, hailstones and storms. Only the strong survive, and even those come up wizened and scarred. It is a timeless landscape, not in a way I like. It makes me feel very frail.

Mauro turns into a lane, cutting through a new area of vineyards. The grapes, still young, shine under the headlights. They are sided at intervals by the oval shapes of prickly pears, with their colourful fruits already ripening among the thorns. Art comes from a peasant family who have been living for three generations in a house Art's grandfather built with his own hands. It is a sturdy square building at the end of the lane, a white cube in the middle of nowhere. Back then there was no plumbing or electrics. Art's dad installed them, but they are not in use right now. The house is pitch black.

'He's not home,' I say.

Mauro pulls up next to a battered old Fiat Panda, which I suppose belongs to Art, and we get out. With the engine killed, the ceaseless song of crickets fills the air.

'Art!' Tony shouts. 'It's us.'

The crickets make the quiet more striking. A dog barks somewhere far off, but that is all.

'Fabio's right. He's not home,' Mauro says.

'What about his car then?' Tony asks. 'Art!' he calls again. He tries the buzzer. Nobody replies.

Mauro says, 'That's odd.'

'It's possible that he forgot it was today,' I try.

22

'Is it?' Tony asks.

I shake my head. Art doesn't believe in forgetting.

Tony says, 'We should take a look inside. He could be hurt. Or...'

He stops before saying what we all think: *high as a kite*. We don't know for sure if Art is using hard drugs, but we have talked about it in the past, and we agree it would make sense. It wouldn't be all that surprising, considering what he went through – but *that*, we never talk about.

I lift a ceramic pot (it contained geraniums once, before Art let them wither) sitting just beside the door. Art, and Art's dad before him, used to hide a spare set of keys beneath it. 'No joy.'

'Remember, pal?' Tony says. '*I* don't need a key for a crappy lock like this. I haven't forgotten my old tricks.' He puts a hand on the flimsy door handle. 'Oh,' he says.

The door is open.

4

We formed the Pact in American Pizza seventeen years ago, on the night Art threw his life down the drain. School was over, and we would soon sit our finals. We were all leaving for university: Tony to Rome, Mauro to Milan, and I had set my mind on London, that reservoir of exotic dreams. Art was going to Stanford, California, thanks to an unconditional full scholarship which had been the talk of the town. A scholarship was Art's only chance to go to a decent university, and when he was pondering where to apply he had thought that he might as well aim high.

He was aware that Stanford wouldn't give a second look at an application coming from a below-average Italian school, so he embarked on one of his projects: in eight months of ultra-intensive work he wrote and illustrated a two-hundred-page graphic novel based on his own translation from Latin of Lucius Apuleius' *Metamorphoses*, a trippy story of magic, shape-shifting, and mystery cults which had been his latest obsession. Art translated the story into English, wrote a script, and made the illustrations, in a style drawing on influences as different as Steve Ditko and Francis Bacon. He packaged and sent the originals to Stanford – he couldn't pay for full-colour copies. It was an unqualified success; the letter he received back was almost pornographic in its praise. Art's parents were beyond themselves with pride, and we were too. We were never jealous, I think, of the things Art could do. We knew he existed on a level of his own.

None of us planned to ever come back to Casalfranco. Art and I shared a white-hot hatred for our hometown, Mauro had plans with his by-then-girlfriend Anna (all of them came to pass), and Tony had discovered things about himself that would have made life in Casalfranco highly unpleasant, though it would be some time before he confessed that to us.

Against all odds, my father didn't flinch at the idea of me leaving town. He was confident it wouldn't last. 'You'll come back,' he said. That's what everybody else said too. It was normal for young people to want to go and spend some time away, but invariably, they returned. *Ti Casalfrancu sinti*, the wise folk would remind you in dialect. *You're from Casalfranco*: your birthplace was your destiny, so you better not put on any airs. And it was true that growing up between thirsty soil, King's cocks and the Corona didn't equip you very well for the big blue world out there. Casalfranco was like a rubber band: you could stretch it, but sooner or later it would snap you back in place. Of all those in our year at school, only Mauro, Tony and I did get away and stay away. Even Art ended up moving back. It is sad. Unfair too; without his influence, I am not sure the rest of us would have resisted Casalfranco's gravitational pull.

American Pizza was grim in that distant age before holidaymakers and retirees: a few shabby tables with red-and-white checkered cloths, a faded picture of a local football team, and in the corner a yellowish, sick plant we called Audrey, after *The Little Shop of Horrors*. It was a dump with an embarrassing provincial name, but their pizza was good. More to the point, it was cheap, the only pizza in town Art could afford.

It began with him saying, 'I'm not going to Stanford.'

'You decided to go into fishing instead?' Tony joked.

'I'm serious.'

Tony and I exchanged a look. Mauro cleaned his lips of melted mozzarella and said, 'Are you?'

'Entirely. Something happened.'

Tony asked, 'Are your parents okay?'

'Something *good* happened.' Art made a theatrical pause, looked at each of us in turn, then announced, 'I have a book deal for the graphic novel. Someone in Stanford's admissions committee has a brother who is an editor. One thing leads to another, he wants to buy it.'

'Art, this is great!'

'I know, right?'

Mauro asked, 'And why is this a reason not to go to Stanford?'

'They're paying me an advance. It's enough to take a year off, with the odd job here and there.'

'Which is better than a full scholarship at one of the coolest universities in the world because…?'

'It leaves me more time to pursue my interests.'

A silence followed. We knew Art too well to think he was joking. 'I hope you thought this through,' Mauro said.

Art dismissed his words with a gesture. 'I got the scholarship this time, I can get it again whenever I want. It's only a gap year, boys. It's normal in other countries.'

I asked, 'And where are you going instead?'

'Turin. There's two or three libraries I want to check out. And then Volterra. Fascinating town, that one.'

Tony said, 'Let's talk again after the finals.'

'I already wrote to Stanford,' Art said.

There was another silence, heavier than the first one. Something had happened to Art when we were fourteen, which had left him more damaged than anybody thought, but that was the first time I truly questioned his sanity.

'I'm leaving. That's what I wanted,' he went on. He bit into a slice of pizza and said, with his mouth full, 'And *this* is all I'm going to miss about this shitty town.'

'Casalfranco is not the worst place in the world,' Mauro said.

'Don't be so sure about that,' I said. 'This place is a monster sucking the marrow out of your bones.' We were all grateful for the change of subject.

'It has good pizza though,' Tony said.

'Sure,' Art conceded. 'But, honestly? In a year's time, we'll see this pizza's not even *that* good. We like it because of all the memories we attach to it.'

'Meaning, we have good memories. Meaning, it's not all doom and gloom down here in the sticks,' Tony said.

Art made a brief nod. 'Not all. I'll miss the pizza and I'll miss you guys.'

It wasn't a thousand years ago, but it was before Facebook, before Skype and before mobile phones became ubiquitous – down south anyway. Distance still mattered.

'It's not like we're never going to meet again,' Tony said.

'Actually, yeah, it kind of is,' Art said. 'We're not planning to visit a lot, right? Christmas and summer, if that.'

'So this is, what, the Last Supper?'

I held in front of me a slice of pizza with anchovies and capers, and said, in a deep voice, '"I tell you the truth, one of you will betray me."'

Art said, 'We'll all betray each other. We'll make new friends.'

'Girlfriends too, lots and lots of them,' Tony said. 'Don't take it personally, guys, but I'd sell your skin in a heartbeat for the right pair of boobs.' He cupped his hands on his chest, to

27

make the point clearer. Then he took off a hand. 'For *one* boob, too, provided it's nice enough.' Tony went to great lengths to hide he was gay, and he succeeded, mostly because it was impossible then for us to think that *gay people* could walk in our midst. Mauro and I would find out two years later, when Tony came out to us and Elena, his sister, to muster courage before coming out to his parents. Art had known all along, though he never told us.

'Girlfriends, jobs, don't get me wrong, it's all going to be great. But *this*?' Art touched the table. '*This* is over. The end of our life as we know it.'

We let his words linger. Art had this way of talking, combining the insight of a wise hermit with the bedside manner of an eight-year-old. There wasn't a doubt in any of our minds that he was destined for great things.

'That sucks,' Mauro said.

I shrugged. 'There's nothing we can do about it.'

'Says who?' Art asked.

He got on my nerves sometimes. 'Says the real world…?'

'Let's stick our middle finger up to the real world! Let's keep the dream going.'

I used my chin to point at the owner of American Pizza, who was sitting behind the till, immersed in a black-and-white porn comic book with a vampire on the cover. *Jacula*, an Italian classic. With his round belly and his overgrown chest and back hair, sprouting from the grimy vests that were his uniform, you'd be forgiven for thinking he was a gorilla (he was known in town as Kong). '*That* dream?' I said.

Art raised an eyebrow in mock seriousness. 'I am a man of varied taste. Listen: we'll make a Pact. Every year on this day, we're going to meet.'

'Mate…' I tried.

'Ssst!' Tony said. 'Let the wise one talk.'

'Thank you, my friend,' Art said. 'As I was saying: we'll meet once a year, every year. Whatever happens, wherever life will lead us, we'll meet in this place, on this day, at this time. It doesn't matter if we never see each other for the rest of the year, or we're in touch regularly. We'll never mention the appointment. We'll never try to cancel it or reschedule it. On the tenth of June, we'll just come to Casalfranco from whatever corner of the world we happen to be, stroll into American Pizza and take our table, and pretend time never passed. Fuck the real world.'

I could see the idea working, but I could see its problems too. 'It'll bind us to Casalfranco.'

'It'll bind us to each other,' Art said. 'I'm willing to do that. Aren't you, *mate*?'

'What if we're busy?'

'Then we *un-busy* ourselves. It's a Pact with a capital P — hardcore shit.'

'It's awesome,' Tony said. 'Deal for me.'

'*Fuck the real world*, now and for ever,' Mauro agreed.

It meant I would have to come back to Casalfranco at least once a year, which I didn't want to do. But keeping my friends would require effort, and I wanted that, very much. The price was steep but it was worth paying. I, too, agreed to the Pact.

And Art — he never went to university.

5

The moment I step inside, I know the house is empty. Empty houses give off a peculiar feeling. It's not a lack of noise or movement, it is subtler than that; it is the lack of a sense of presence. I can smell old books, and dampness. Tony makes a show of sniffing the air, then proclaims, 'No rotting bodies. It's a start.'

Mauro clicks a switch on the wall and, to my slight surprise, the lights do turn on.

The first thing I notice are the books. It's a small square room, with a table and a couple of straw chairs, and there are books everywhere – on IKEA shelves, against the walls, stacked on the floor, thrown with their spine open on the table. Art got me into most of my favourite writers. Not that I have much time for reading, these days.

'Art?' Tony makes one last half-hearted attempt.

'He's not in,' Mauro says.

'I know,' says Tony. 'We should check, just in case.'

I am already moving towards the kitchen, passing under a tufa archway. I have a feeling of temporal displacement: the place is right, the timeline all wrong. The last time I was here I was nineteen, and I was saying goodbye to Art's mum and dad before leaving for London. We didn't even speak the same language. I would speak Italian and they would answer in the local dialect, as different from Italian as Welsh is from English. They were kind people, and I liked them much more than I liked my own father. They were aware that their son was not cut from the same cloth as everybody else, but never made a big thing of it. How is it that seventeen years have passed? Surely there is a mistake. They are dead and I am a grown-up who has wasted his best years following pipe dreams, squandering what little talent he had.

There is something wrong in the kitchen.

It is a comparatively large room, where once all the family would gather. Again, there are books everywhere, but that is not what strikes me. What strikes me is the table at the centre, the same table I remember from back then. There is a plate on it, with a fork, a glass and a bottle of wine. The plate is dirty with leftovers of mouldy pasta with cheese and tomato sauce. A fat fly is taking a lazy stroll on its rim. The bottle is half full, but it has been left open, and the wine smells foul. There is wine left in the glass.

This is *definitely* not like Art. Art would finish his pasta and his wine, then put the cork back in the bottle and do the dishes straight away; you could never accuse him of being tidy, but he is as clean as a cat. Also, he would never waste half a bottle of wine. I hear Mauro and Tony behind me, and I hear them stop. I know they are thinking what I am thinking.

'Shit,' Tony says.

He is taking out a green bag of dog food from one of the rickety cupboards. 'This is *tailored* dog grub. I know the brand. It's the same stuff one of my exes gave to his darling fox terrier. It'll turn your dog into a scholar, an athlete and a politician, and they charge you accordingly.'

Beside the fridge are two shiny metal bowls: one with some

water left, the other with dog food leftovers. They are sturdy, good quality, expensive. 'Since when did Art get a dog?' I say.

'And since when does he go on spending sprees?'

'I'll go check the rest of the house,' says Mauro.

I open the fridge: half a salami, some more cheese, two peaches rotten black. Not like Art, not like him at all. I walk to the garden door at the back of the kitchen. I find it unlocked. I open it and a breeze lets the fresh air inside, carrying the familiar scent of marijuana. It brings a smile to my lips. I make out a row of healthy plants at a short distance from the house. Art started growing his own weed as a teenager and, from what he told us, he kept growing it on and off, whenever he had a chance. Clearly, when he got back to Casalfranco he set up a small production line – marijuana grows fast in this climate. In the old days he would hide his pots from his mum and dad. Now he doesn't need to bother with hiding, or potting for that matter; the plants stand a couple of metres tall, large enough to be visible in the moonlight.

On second thoughts, that's a hell of a lot of weed for one person.

My smile freezes. I knew that Art had dealt weed, as a side job, in the past. He'd dealt in Turin, Paris and other places, but here? Only the Corona has the right to deal in Casalfranco; it is a fact of life, not up for discussion, no more than the brute force of the sun is, or the change of seasons. However strapped for cash you are, you keep your weed to yourself.

'Fabio,' Mauro calls. 'Come.'

I follow his voice to a door leading into another room.

32

'Welcome to the jungle,' Tony says. 'The *book* jungle.'

The room is filled with books: the piles are so high I can't see the walls. This used to be the living room. There was a TV at the far wall and a sofa in the middle of the room. Now there are only books. Even with the light switched on, it is a dark, foreboding place. Tony's right – it's like a jungle. I wouldn't be surprised to find ink anacondas crawling towards us, and paper monkeys throwing their hardback poo at us.

'Not to mention the bedroom,' Tony says, moving to another door. There are no books here, only crumpled sheets on the bed and an open wardrobe full of clothes. The walls are covered in drawing pins and traces of Blu-Tack, with patches of lighter colour, as if someone had been pinning on the walls a sizeable number of papers, left them hanging for a while, and then decided to take them down all at once.

'Art was collecting clippings on the walls,' Tony sums it up. 'All serial-killer style.'

Mauro brings a hand close to a blue dot on the wall, without touching it. 'We don't know what he's doing.'

'Just kidding,' Tony says, in a lower voice.

'Don't.'

'I'm not surprised though.'

'Why?' I ask.

Tony says, 'You didn't come last year. You didn't see him. Art was… Art, but even more so than usual. A lot more.'

'Mental health issues?' I ask.

'He's Art. He lives in his own world at the best of times.'

We wander back to the kitchen, where I let myself fall into

a chair. With everybody else, I'd take out my phone and check their recent activity on Facebook to see what they have been up to. But Art is not on Facebook, because he doesn't care for Facebook's ever-changing privacy policy, thank you very much.

Tony takes out his phone.

'What are you doing?' Mauro asks.

'Calling the Carabinieri.'

'Why?'

Tony makes an exasperated face. 'Because Art's missing and his posh dog is missing as well and we're worried?'

'We don't know Art's missing.'

'He'd never leave the house in this state!'

'It's not nearly enough to file a missing person's case.'

His phone still in one hand, Tony touches the back of his neck with the other. 'We could give the Carabinieri a heads-up…?'

'Believe me, we don't want to. For a start, we will have to explain why we thought we could break into Art's house in the dead of night. We don't live in Casalfranco any longer, we're not regularly in touch with Art, and we know nothing about his current life.'

'We're *mates*.'

Mauro shrugs.

I say, 'Also: the weed.'

'What weed?' Tony asks.

'Art's got a little plantation outside.'

Mauro goes white, which would be funny if there was anything funny about tonight. 'A *plantation*?'

34

'Not a *plantation* plantation. Eight or ten plants. Large plants.'

'We could dispose of them before we call the Carabinieri,' Tony says.

I say, 'And when it turns out we're panicking over nothing, Art will be delighted about that.'

Before Tony can reply, Mauro pushes, 'At any rate, are any of you guys a criminal mastermind? Because I'm not. When the Carabinieri start the investigation, I can assure you, they *will* find out that *eight or ten* plants of marijuana were just made away with. Doesn't take a genius. We'll be in shit deeper than you can possibly imagine.'

Tony says, 'Hold on, what *investigation*? I'm just saying we should tell the Carabinieri that we're concerned.'

'And you think they're going to leave it at that? Any other person, yeah, but this is Arturo Musiello we're talking about. The Carabinieri will break into a sweat at the first mention of his name. Journalists will flock to Casalfranco.'

My tired brain takes one or two seconds to make sense of Mauro's words. When I finally get them, I gape at him. The thing he's talking about – we never talk about it.

Tony says, in a sombre tone, 'You mean…'

'Yeah, I mean that.'

We don't talk about that, partly because Art doesn't talk about it, and partly because it's better this way. I too had boxed up those days in a dark and dusty corner of my mind, where I never go. It still gives me the creeps, twenty-two years later, even though I don't have a clue what happened. But I knew Art before and I knew Art after, and I swear, he was not the same. I don't have a clue, and I am not sure I ever wanted to.

6

When I try to explain Salento to Lara, my English girlfriend, I say: Italy is a long peninsula, and Puglia is a peninsula at the end of it. Puglia is a long peninsula, and Salento is the peninsula at the end of it. The world does continue beyond its crystal-clear sea, but it doesn't feel like it. It feels like Salento is the end of the line, the end of it all. I promise her that one day I'll show her, if she is so eager. We'll drive down from London, and she will notice the landscape change, the urban civilisation of Europe and Northern Italy give way to the wilds of the south, and then the real wilds of the real south, this flat, lawless land, where on a bad year people still offer sacrifices to the saints begging them to make it rain, just a little, if they please, just enough for the cattle and the grapes to pull through. And then Lara and I will sit on the beach, and look at the Mediterranean, and she will feel what the locals feel: that this land is indeed *finis terrae*, the farthest end of the world.

That will happen in summer. I would never bring her here in winter. Winter in Salento makes you wish you were dead, with everything turning cold and bitter and even more hostile than usual. The wind, in particular, behaves like a psychopath. It bites and lashes at you, and when it blows from the sea, it crushes you with the stink of dead fish and a dampness that weighs you down like clothing when you are drowning.

It was winter, and we were fourteen, when something happened to Art.

At that age we weren't spoilt for choice as to what to do with ourselves on long winter nights, other than watching horror films on telly or going to American Pizza. Our interest in girls was getting to its peak, but the girls our age were too busy with older boys to notice us, so we killed our time, like the other kids in town, walking up and down the main street, soldiering on with the cold seeping through our bones. The *struscio*, it is called, one of the bits of southern culture none of my English girlfriends ever got. *So what do you do?* Lara asked me once. *You just walk back and forth?* She couldn't believe the answer was yes. You walk back and forth in a small pack, and every now and then you stop and talk to an acquaintance, or play with one of the stray dogs that seem to forever haunt Salento.

Art had got a telescope for Christmas.

It was entry-level, but good quality; his parents had saved for a while to buy it. Art was going through an astronomy phase, and they did what they could to support him, as always. After that, he went through his photography phase, which had such a momentous impact on my own life. Art went through more phases than I care to count, and I guess he still does. It is not that he gets bored with his old toys and shouts 'Next!' in a spoiled way. He *does* get bored, but only once he understands how those toys work (which, admittedly, happens quickly). When he takes a fancy to something new, be it astronomy or pick-up techniques, he gathers all the books, the tools, the knowledge he can put his hands on, he squeezes the juice out of them, and once he is satisfied that he has sucked the topic dry, he moves on. He would say, *Specialists stick to one line, but I'm after patterns.* I never knew if that made sense. Trying to understand Art has always been frustrating.

Anyway. He had this new telescope and he planned to christen it with the easiest target in the sky, the moon. Finding a bright night in Salento is easy – you just pick a night and it's almost certainly going to be bright. Art picked the first Saturday after the Christmas holidays. 'It's a full moon,' he said. 'It'll be grand.' He wanted us to be with him. At the time, I didn't understand why; none of us cared about astronomy. Now I realise that the telescope was the most precious thing Art had ever possessed, and he wanted to share it with us, for all the times we'd pay for his drinks, or his coffee, or cigarettes. None of us were bothered by any of that, not even Mauro, but Art is the sort of person who doesn't like to be in debt, even if the debt is in his mind.

A normal boy would have just stuck the tripod in the fields behind his house, but not Art. Art had worked out, through some maths that was well beyond my grasp (and might easily be bullshit) that the best moon-gazing spot around Casalfranco was an area a few miles inland. From there, he assured us, the visibility was optimal, and we were bored enough to actually let him drag us there. We brought with us a bottle of wine, tobacco, weed and some food. The weed was a recent discovery. Art hadn't started growing it yet.

We got there on Mauro and Tony's Vespas, Art and me

riding on the back, awkwardly balancing the telescope. With no helmets, of course, because in the nineties you wouldn't be caught dead wearing a helmet down here. Tony had been driving a Vespa since he was ten, well before the legal age of fourteen. Mauro had just started and was still thrilled by the novelty of it.

The spot Art had picked was in the back of beyond. The last proper house was a good ten minutes from where we eventually stopped. We had passed by a few dark, solitary huts, blocks of bricks with no heating, electrics or water. Almost nobody lived in those huts anymore. Almost.

We found ourselves in an expanse of scrub – clay-red earth and spiky bushes, criss-crossed by drystone walls marking the boundaries of fields. We were surrounded on all sides by the gnarled silhouettes of olive groves in the distance, as if the trees trapped us in the middle of a secret henge. It was a desolate, unforgiving place.

'We're lucky the wind calmed down,' Mauro commented.

Art whispered, 'Look at the moon.'

The moon was immense. I am aware this is in part my imagination. Memory is like Alice's medicines; it makes things bigger and smaller at whim, and that night looms so big that everything is oversized. But part of it is true. By some trick of perspective the moon did look immense, a luminous hole in the night sky. Mauro and Tony left the Vespas at the edge of the unpaved road and we walked on into the open countryside.

There are no marked paths in Salento, no kissing gates or gracious stiles, only drystone walls, with occasional openings in them, either made on purpose or caused by a collapse. This countryside is not made for walks. It ravages you with wind in winter, it burns you down in summer, and the only reason why one would possibly want to walk here is toil – or to follow a crazy friend with a telescope. It had not rained for almost two months, and what little moisture there was in the dirt came from the sea. The moon gave the thirsty land a purple hue. Art had forbidden the use of torches (he said our eyes had to get accustomed to the dark, to make the most of the telescope), so we had to rely on moonlight to negotiate our way between brambles and rocks. It was easier than I thought it would be; I hadn't realised how bright a full moon can be.

Tony howled.

It made me jump. 'Fuck you.'

'Why, don't you want to call in the werewolves?'

I was uneasy. Without factoring werewolves in, Casalfranco had its share of flesh-and-bone unwholesome characters, and, honestly? That night, in that place, I wasn't so sure I would count them out.

'Here,' Art said.

We were on a comparatively elevated position. Ahead of us, after miles of scrubland and drystone walls, was a little deserted road, the only sign of the modern world in sight. After that was the sea, moonlit and speckled with waves. Art and I started immediately to assemble the telescope, while Tony and Mauro rolled a joint, opened the wine and got out the food. The joint had been smoked and a new one had been rolled by the time the telescope was ready. It was a stocky white tube on a tripod, with a smaller tube on top of it, and a panoply of wheels.

'The small tube is the finderscope,' Art explained. 'It has a broader field of view than the main body. By rolling this wheel, you see, you align the finderscope with the main body. Then you use the finderscope to find what you want to look at, and only then do you look into the telescope.'

Tony said, 'The moon is bigger than Mauro's mum's ass. Can't be that difficult to aim at it with the big tube.'

'Yeah? Here, try without the finderscope.'

Tony plastered his eye on one end of the telescope. He shuffled it around a bit, then said, 'Okay, I give up.'

Art took his place. 'An object as big as the moon, you *could* find it, but it's quicker with the finderscope.' He shuffled the telescope towards a clump of olive trees. 'To align finderscope and telescope, you aim them at a terrestrial object and…'

Art lifted his head, still looking at the olive grove, and frowned.

'What's wrong?' Mauro asked.

'I thought I saw something.' Art squinted into the telescope again. 'A movement.'

'It's the weed,' I said.

Art shook his head and drew back from the telescope. 'I'll be right back.' He started towards the olive grove. 'You guys stay and watch the gear.'

None of us went with him. *Why?* I have been asked over and over again. Isn't it obvious? We were all too scared. Three is company. Two, not so much. Art didn't mind being alone, but Art was used to living in open countryside. We considered ourselves townies.

41

'Go!' Tony shouted behind him, as Art half walked, half ran towards the olive grove. 'Show the werewolves who's boss!' His quips fell flat.

Mauro was trying to adjust the telescope. 'This damn thing,' he muttered. 'Can't make it work.'

I didn't need the telescope to see Art get to the tree line, hesitate one moment, and then step into the grove and out of sight. I squinted to make out what he could have seen. I have gone through those moments a million times, both on my own and during the investigation, but honestly: I only saw Art, until I didn't see him anymore.

Art shouted.

We all sprang back.

Then – silence.

'Art…?' Tony said.

'Art!' Mauro called.

Art didn't reply.

Tony said, 'What the fuck…?'

We looked at each other. My skin was turning into scales. If I was uneasy before, I was rapidly sliding down towards full-fledged terror. 'We should…' I started, then I stopped. *We should go and see what happened*, I was going to say. We all knew that, but no one wanted to make the first step.

Tony whispered, 'He'll get bored.'

'You think it's a prank?' Mauro asked.

'What else?'

I was tempted to call out Art's name one more time, but I didn't. I didn't want to call attention to myself, even though

42

I didn't know *whose* attention I didn't want to call. If only we were braver, or more generous, we would have moved sooner, and perhaps we would have found Art before it was too late. We were very young, that is all I can say. As you grow up, you stockpile a lot of *if onlys*.

Eventually we managed to unfreeze. Tony put the cork back on the wine bottle and brandished the bottle as a club, and, thus armed, we walked cautiously towards the grove. Olive trees live for centuries, and the older they are, the more twisted they get; these ones were positively ancient. Thick and warped, they looked like the damned in Gustave Doré's illustrations to Dante's *Inferno* – one of my father's favourite books.

We stood on the tree line, as on the threshold of a temple, not daring to enter.

'Art?' Tony called. 'We left your telescope behind. *Unattended.*'

Mauro gestured for him to shut up. *Listen*, he mouthed.

I could hear my heart thumping. I could hear my friends breathing. But no noise came from inside the grove. In that perfect silence, I would have heard Art, or anybody else, in there. Or would I? I had no inclination to step inside and see for myself. The grove gave off a sense of danger, and not the sort of Hollywood danger you defeat with some wit and a brawl. It was a stranger crawling into your bedroom, a priest forcing a boy to his knees and not to pray; it was real danger, the one that takes something away from you.

And suddenly I couldn't stand it anymore. I turned around and dashed towards the Vespas, running with all the energy I could gather, running running running. Mauro and Tony ran behind me. We arrived at the mopeds short of breath. While Mauro and Tony fumbled for the keys, I cast a glance at the olive grove: it was motionless; not bigger, not stranger, not darker than any other clump of trees. I have been asked by so many people to explain what happened that made us run, and I always give the same answer: nothing. We didn't see anything, we didn't hear anything, and yet we were afraid. *No, not of ghosts*, I had to say endlessly to smart-asses with or without a uniform. Whether ghosts exist or not, you know what they are supposed to be; they have a name, a definition. But we didn't know what we were afraid of; we were just afraid, and our incapacity to put a name on that fear made it infinitely worse.

I don't know the reason why we were afraid, but I will swear, until the day I die, that it was a good one.

We rode back to the last house we had passed, and called the Carabinieri from there. They thought it was a prank at first, but finally they accepted they had to move their ass out of the station and come have a look. They wouldn't find Art that night, or the next day – or, in one sense, ever. The world as we knew it was turned topsy-turvy. Casalfranco was on the news; townsfolk discovered a hitherto unheard-of reserve of love for Art; and when the hope of finding him alive started dimming, a local crook hinted not so vaguely that we, his friends, might have killed him. It was madness.

It lasted seven days.

7

Those seven days were the sort of real-life horror story that pops into your mind when you are in a particularly low mood and you want to hurt yourself a little more. The guys and I would rather forget about it, but considering that is impossible, not talking about it is the next best thing. We never talk about it. Never, ever. I curse Mauro for digging it up.

'This has *nothing* to do with that,' Tony says.

Mauro shoos away the fat fly that tried to land on his forehead. 'Try and convince the journos.'

'So what do we do?' I ask, to steer the conversation away.

'It's very possible that Art's crashing somewhere and he left the kitchen in that state because that's how he rolls now.'

'Or he's stoned in a field with his dog.'

'Or that. I say we wait a little, and if Art doesn't reappear, we go to the Carabinieri. But it won't come to that.'

Mauro doesn't want to land Art in trouble, and he doesn't want his own name to get attached to that old freakshow. It crops up on crackpot websites as an *unexplained mystery* and the like; the official version is not convincing, they say. Must be some sort of cover-up. Thank goodness our names aren't part of the story. That's because in the early nineties the Internet was still graduating from American computer freaks' pastime to global revolution. But now? It would take all of five minutes for us to get famous, which would do no good to Mauro's career.

Tony says, 'Last year Art mentioned he was seeing Carolina. Maybe she knows where he is.'

'Carolina Mazziani?' I ask. Once she would have been out of our league, but time passes, and someone goes up, someone goes down.

'Her. He called her *la Madama*.'

Art's touch is unmistakable; in medieval times, *madama* was what you called a noblewoman, or alternatively, a brothel keeper.

Mauro says, 'Why not? We'll talk to her tomorrow.'

I say, 'She won't like it.' The thing with Carolina is, she is married – to a pharmacist. By Italian law, there are a set number of pharmacies in a certain area; you can't just open a new one. So pharmacies are passed from father to son, like feudal titles. On a small-town level, pharmacists are well heeled, and well connected.

Mauro says, 'Too bad for her.'

Tony brushes his hands. 'We're playing *True Detective* then. Is it now that I blather on about the meaninglessness of life?'

I check the time on my phone. I hadn't realised it was this late. 'Guys, I'm not joining the party. I've got a flight in, uh, six hours.'

'Stick around one more day,' Tony says.

'I really can't. I've got a mountain of work to do.'

'Oh, come on,' Mauro says. 'We all have jobs.'

'You're on holiday!'

'I've got my little girls with me. Trust me, that's harder than being in court.'

I shake my head. 'I won't play third wheel to your bromance.'

Tony punches my shoulder lightly. 'All those ladies won't photograph themselves, eh?'

'Exactly,' I say, and it comes out far less convincing than I would have hoped.

8

Mauro drops me off at the B&B well after midnight. It is a detached house on the way to the sea, with a Greek-style arched portico and a huge Mediterranean pine in the front garden. When the car stops, a toothy bulldog runs to the gate, barking furiously. We already said our goodbyes and our let's-be-in-touch-more-often, so I wave to Mauro and Tony and they drive off. There is a doorbell next to the gate, and I press on it, twice, while the dog keeps barking. At last the front door slams open and the landlord comes out, pointedly cross. With his sandals, his large belly and a bald patch on his head, he looks like a dodgy Friar Tuck.

'Sorry,' I say, as he calms down the dog. 'I said I'd be late.'

'Not *this* late.'

I refrain from saying *sorry* again. In the south you must never apologise twice. Once is fine, in the right context, but do it twice and you'll come across as a pushover, and, consequently, fair game. Not even your friends and family will pity you if you get screwed. *Però te la sei cercata*, they'll tell you. *You went looking for it.* You deserved to be overcharged, insulted, beaten up. Swim or drown, boy, that's the way it is.

'I'm here now,' I say.

On entering the garden, I make a point of petting the dog –

47

look, I'm not scared. He licks my hand; he's a softie, to his master's disappointment. The man's mood manages to turn even sourer. He pulls me inside the house with all the grace of a dancing hyena, shows me my room and shoves a set of keys in my hand. 'Mind the front gate,' he says. 'Arnie'll clear off at the first chance.'

Arnie being the dog, I suppose. I can see why he is eager to skip. 'I'll be leaving early tomorrow morning, and don't worry, I'll be careful with the gate. If Arnie'll let me go,' I add, pretending for his master's benefit that Arnie is a bad boy.

'He legs it, you're paying for a new dog, *capito, sì*? Leave the keys in the room, and pull the gate behind when you leave. Breakfast's already in the room.'

I would love to be locked somewhere with this man and a hammer. I suppress my homicidal fantasies, wish him goodnight and close the door. The room is smaller than my first bedsit at university, with no hints of local charm. There is a pixie-sized fridge with an open carton of milk in it, and two stale croissants on the top of it. (Fabio, meet your breakfast. Breakfast, meet Fabio.) I see no kettle, and, consequently, no tea or instant coffee. You never find them here in the south. There is a tiny en suite though, so I guess I shouldn't complain.

Art is all right, I say to myself, as I brush my teeth. But I'm lying and I know that. The state of his house, the weed, his ditching the Pact: it looks bad. The fact is that Art has disappeared for seven days before, and we still don't know what happened then, so what hope is there of us understanding what is happening now? There was the wildest speculation at the time (my personal favourite: UFO abduction, because there was a telescope involved, and telescopes plus teenagers equals aliens), but after his return, everybody in town convinced themselves that it had been a juvenile attempt to run away from home. Tony, Mauro and I knew that everybody in town was wrong, and our wildest speculations never stopped. Mine were probably the wildest of all.

Art is all right, I repeat. I am being a shit, leaving my mate like this, but I won't allow Casalfranco to suck me in. A girlfriend waits for me in London, and a life which is a mess in urgent need of sorting out. I won't get stuck in this godforsaken corner of the world. *Art is all right*, I repeat as a mantra.

Art is all right.

9

Art got me into photography. My motivating force was a burning desire to see boobs, in general and, in particular, Marta D'Antonio's boobs. Marta was a redhead, a year younger than us, with freckles all over her face, her arms, and (I fantasised) the rest of her body. I would have committed unspeakable acts to confirm those suspicions, but I couldn't think of any unspeakable act that would actually help me.

I used to be helpless around girls. I was comparatively smooth as long as we stayed friends, but when the moment came to make the next step, the moment to ask them out, or try and kiss them, I would freeze, and become unable to act. I could hear my father's stern voice saying, *Don't be ridiculous*. A proper, polite young man didn't do that sort of thing, though it wasn't clear how proper, polite young men were supposed to reproduce. I was stuck.

Art suggested photography. Since the end of the summer before he had been testing a theory, namely that you can get girls to undress more or less as you like if you tell them it is for artistic ('artistic' was the key word) purposes. Like that Helmut Newton guy (he had to tell me who Helmut Newton was). To demonstrate that it was more than a theory, Art showed me one of his photographs – only one, because he had an understanding with his 'models' that his artistic *oeuvre* would stay private, and Art was a man of his word. In that photograph, though, was the nipple of Gina Ostuni, one of our classmates. She was covering the other breast with her hand, and pursing her lips towards the camera. That photograph made me feel like an archaeologist who has just discovered a lost civilisation. It also gave me an immediate hard-on. (This was before camera phones, selfies and Internet porn; we were way less used to nipples than the lucky bastards born in the next decade.) Art's theory worked. Art's theories almost invariably did.

'The secret is,' he explained, 'that we all, boys and girls, think we are the centre of the universe. We think we are significant. You make someone believe that you think that too, that you think *they* are significant, and they'll do whatever you want, just to please you and confirm your belief. It's as simple as that.'

Every now and then Art's cynicism made me uneasy. But not enough to beat the indisputable reality of Gina Ostuni's nipple.

I borrowed a third-hand camera from Mauro and, my heart

beating like a marching soldier, I approached Marta D'Antonio, telling her that I meant to take a few portraits of her, like, for an artistic project of mine. In keeping with Art's instructions, I used the word *artistic* at least three times, and I didn't mention the nude thing, yet. You had to build up to that one.

'I thought Art was the photographer,' she said.

That caught me by surprise. The next moment would be a defining one for my life. If I had caved to my first instinct (blush, stammer out a lame answer, and split), I don't think I would be a photographer today – which wouldn't necessarily be a bad thing, considering. I didn't cave though. By miracle an answer came to my mind, perfectly formed, the only answer that could save the situation. 'Yeah,' I said, in a jaded voice. 'I'm teaching him the basics.'

It was pure Art; he loved it when I told him.

And it worked. It took me three Kodak films (which were expensive, but well worth it) and around eighty poses before Marta D'Antonio agreed to drop her bra, that last bastion of virtue, and show me her boobs, for my purely artistic purposes, giving me proof that, yes, she had freckles all over. I was in heaven. It was a strictly see-don't-touch basis, and nothing ever happened between me and Marta D'Antonio, but I learnt that naked girls *did* happen, and that gave me the boost of confidence that would lead, in time, to real girlfriends and actual sex. And it made me fall in love with photography – I felt a burning gratitude towards the camera, that magic gizmo, to the point that Mauro granted me an 'indefinite lease' on it.

My first camera; I still have it, in my London flat.

10

I wake up with the sun.

The sun.

I jump out of bed, cursing myself, and grab my phone to check the time. The phone is out of juice. I look out of the window. The sky is cloudless, clear and ruthlessly blue. It is nowhere near an early morning sky. *That fucking phone.* Old as Yoda and I can't afford to replace it. Its battery has the lifespan of a haiku, and yesterday I was too strung up to remember to charge it. The phone died so the alarm didn't ring and the cab driver couldn't call me when I didn't show. *Of course* he didn't try the doorbell; you never expect a southerner to do more than strictly necessary. The booking was on my card and he would get the money one way or the other. Fuck him, fuck this phone, fuck my life.

And fuck this town. I sit on the edge of the bed with my head in my hands. I'm not in the best of places, financially. Another plane ticket, even low-cost, and another night in a B&B, even a cheap one, are a strain I could do without. 'Fuck!' I shout. It is this cursed town. It never eases its grip on you. It never lets go. When Casalfranco decides that you will stay, you stay. Sometimes I fear that the rubber band will have its way and pull me back. That I will never manage to break free for good.

I plug the charger into an adapter and the adapter into a socket, and when the goddam phone comes back to life, I dial Lara's number. She doesn't pick up. I text her:

> I overslept & missed my flight. I'm a moron. Coming back tomorrow. Call me when you can.

It is half past ten. I have an entire day to spend in town, and I won't bloody spend it in this shoebox.

I call Tony.

11

Carolina was one of the Beauties — Art's capital — of our generation, the aristocracy of school. The Beauties were all good-looking, there is no denying that, but no more so than so many other girls (fabulous women being the only good thing Southern Italy ever gave to the world). What set them apart from us members of the peasantry was their ancestry; to qualify as a Beauty you had to come from a notable family, one which had been in town long enough for at least one or two cases of incest in their tree. The Mazzianis, Carolina's family, had money once, and then, after copious amounts of drinking and gambling, no more. Their surname still carried some weight, of history, if nothing else. I once managed to get one of the Beauties, Gemma Pizzi, naked for my camera, but that's as far as any of us went, until many years later, when Art came back to town and started banging Carolina. I have not seen her in maybe ten years, which suits me fine. Her voice had always grated on me.

Tony knocks at her door, under a fierce sun. It is only me

and him; we told Mauro we would handle this, so he could stay with Anna and the girls. I hope I will be spared Anna. This trip has already turned ugly enough.

It takes me a moment to recognise Carolina when she opens the door. Her beauty is gone. She's put on some weight, but it's not that – in a different world she would still be very attractive, in a more mature way. In this world though she has lost her magic, that elusive spark that made her a Beauty. Everything about her – her looks, her hair, her eyes – is dull. Carolina has fast-forwarded from teenager to middle-aged housewife, without the charisma of wisdom.

A kid is crying inside. 'Come on in,' Carolina says, not pretending she is glad to see us. We take off our sunglasses and let her lead us to the living room. A cream leather sofa and a white cot stand at the centre of the room, facing a plasma screen. A gory crucifix hangs on the wall above the screen, and, if that wasn't enough holiness for this household, the patronising face of Padre Pio stares at us from the wall behind the sofa. I have little sympathy for the saints, even less for the hip ones. Just below Padre Pio is another framed picture, in which Carolina and her husband, dressed for a boat trip, exhibit a rictus which is supposed to be a smile. Carolina is living the dream: she doesn't work, spends her day at home taking care of her baby, alternates her Sundays between parents and in-laws, never forgetting, my dear, to go to mass and take the host, so that townsfolk can see how chaste is the heart beating in her chest. When my English friends ask me why I ever left this sunny, food-filled, wine-fuelled heaven, I would like nothing better than to shove their head into a life like hers, and keep it there until they gasp for breath.

Carolina scoops up the baby from the cot. The baby, unimpressed, pushes on with his gig. 'I should've known Art is one of those who kiss and tell. Who else knows?'

I am going to say, *You should be the one bragging that Art, a sodding genius, was ever between your legs*, but Tony rushes to answer before I have time to. 'Only our gang: me, Fabio and Mauro. We won't tattle.'

'As if anybody would believe you.'

I say, 'I'm famous. They will.' Which is, depressingly, true, inside Casalfranco's borders. People here divide into two camps: either they go out of their way to ignore the fact that I am a slightly well-known fashion photographer, or they believe my fame is hot shit, rather than the small beer, soul-crushingly poorly paid affair that it actually is.

'And that means what exactly? Is this some sort of blackmail?'

'You know Fabio,' Tony says, 'he's a joker. No, Carolina, listen, we only want to know if you've seen Art lately.'

'Why?'

I have to raise my voice to cover the kid's wailing. 'We had an appointment and he didn't show up.'

'What are you doing in Casalfranco anyway? I thought you were in London.'

'Just taking a couple of days off.'

'Must be hard work, snapping photos of all those *models*,' she says. It is all poison, no trace of actual sarcasm. With her free hand, she imitates the gesture of taking a photo. 'Click, click, click.'

'It's all digital now. Clicks are gone.' I'm fucked if I'll let this idiot get to me.

'About Art,' Tony gently says. 'Is he all right? He's not picking up his phone.'

'Not my problem. I dumped him, dunno, six or seven months ago.'

I am sure she remembers month, day and hour. 'What happened?'

'He was creeping me out.'

We are still standing. Carolina didn't invite us to sit and, even worse, she didn't offer us a cup of espresso, which in the south is tantamount to shouting in your face, *Go fuck yourself with barbed wire*. I make a show of sitting down on the sofa. 'Care to elaborate?'

Carolina is rocking her baby up and down, which doesn't stop the baby from crying. 'How come *you* need *me* to explain Art?'

'We've not been in touch, lately,' Tony says.

'Did he tell you of his Project?'

I can hear the capital P in the word. No, Art didn't mention it.

Carolina savours the look of surprise on our faces. 'That's why he moved back to Casalfranco. For his Project.'

I ask, 'Which would be…?'

'It's about that time he vanished.'

For a moment the stifling heat disappears, and a cold wind blows on my neck. 'The time he was supposed to have run away, you mean.'

'Maybe he ran, and maybe he didn't.' Carolina pulls back her lips in what she must think is a sly smile. 'Actually, he told

56

me one thing about that time.' She savours each word as it rolls off her tongue; she knows something we don't, which gives her a small amount of power over us. That must take her back to when, at sixteen, she had reached the high point of her entire life. 'A secret.'

'Please, Carolina...' Tony says.

'He took *me* into his confidence.'

'Please. He's our friend and we're worried about him.'

She shakes her head. '*I* can keep a secret.'

Someone should remind this waste of space that her high point is well past. That someone being me. I take out my phone and tap on it.

'What are you doing?' she asks, amidst her kid's howling.

I finish and turn the screen. I have written a Facebook post.

> My best friend Art slept with a married woman, Carolina Mazziani! Go Art.

Carolina is tagged, and so is her husband, and so are a few common friends from that time.

Carolina's eyes go wide. 'You...'

'I haven't published it yet, but I'll do it in three, two...'

'You're a bastard,' she spits out.

'And you, my dear.'

Carolina takes a deep breath and looks at Tony. 'Art said only one thing.' She pauses, but her attempt at drama is spoiled by the kid, who doesn't get his cue to stop crying. 'He said that he'd been shown *opportunities*.'

57

Tony and I exchange a look. I feel an echo of the eerie sensation I felt when Art disappeared – a creeping uneasiness, my skin turning into scales.

'Did he explain?' Tony asks.

'You know Art. He said that his Project was all about grabbing those,' one-handed air quote, 'opportunities.'

'And you don't have a clue what he was talking about.'

'It involved an awful lot of research.'

'About?'

Carolina grabs the remote and switches on the gorilla-sized plasma TV set. She points the baby at the TV, like a gun. The baby keeps crying. 'Religion, I guess.'

'Religion? Art was the least religious person I ever met,' I say. I vaguely recall that he did have a short brush with spirituality a while ago, in Paris. My opinion was, and still is, that he was in it for the girls.

'Seriously, I didn't care enough to listen.'

Or you weren't clever enough to understand.

'May I ask, why did you dump him?' Tony says.

'He was so obsessed with his Project that it wasn't possible to have, like, a normal *conversation* with him anymore.' She shows her tongue at her baby, in a gesture of motherly affection, which makes the baby cry louder. 'We weren't serious anyway. Just having some fun.'

'Have you seen him lately?' I ask.

'What is this, an interrogation?'

I shake my phone. 'Humour me.'

'Yeah, I think so,' she says, receiving my threat with a

58

disgusted face. 'I bumped into him once or twice. He barely said hello.'

'And the last time would be…?'

'Last week? Three weeks ago? Why should I remember?'

I can't wait to get out of here, but I have to ask one last question. 'Do you know where he gets his cash?' Lately the value of money has been made clear to me.

And there we go, I finally have Carolina's interest. She snaps her head towards me. 'Cash? What makes you think he's rich?'

'I'm talking basic living expenses, for books, bills, car insurance…'

Her interest evaporates quicker than water in August. 'He's got savings I suppose. And every now and then… he's not a dealer, like, proper, but he sells a little weed on the side.'

Art deals weed. In a small town with a strong Corona presence. I don't need Mauro to tell me how quickly this could have escalated. If the Corona finds out there's a dealer in town who is not on their books, they ask him either to get on their books or shut down shop. They ask gently, at first. The dealer being Art, his answer is long-winded and filled with detailed anatomical theories on where they should put their books. Badness ensues.

This is Casalfranco, a voice inside me says. *This is Casalfranco sucking you in. This is Casalfranco.*

Get out while you can.

12

And I won't be spared Anna.

Tony calls Mauro, and Mauro asks us to join him with his family on the beach. Casalfranco definitely has it in for me – nothing new there – and it is hitting me from every corner. *Bring it on.*

Being a sensible man, Tony is staying at his parents', who, before retiring, had run a grocery shop for fifty years. He is driving now on the Litoranea Salentina, a long, winding coastal road. It runs through dunes on both sides, peppered with tamarisk trees, juniper bushes and wild flowers. The sight of the sea on our right, beyond the dunes, is breathtaking. You never get used to this sort of grandeur. The sea and the sky are matched shades of blue, reflecting each other, making you think you could swim in the sky or fly in the sea. The water is as transparent as lacy lingerie. Even from this distance, from a moving car, I can see the rocks at the bottom.

Tony pulls up by the roadside, behind Mauro's car. In two weeks the road will be lined with cars, but it is early season now, so there is only us. The few holidaymakers who are already here don't make it this far, keeping to the beaches of the villages. This means there are no illegal parkers yet; those guys who ask you for one euro to 'guard' your car – that is, not scratch it themselves. In the south, you need to bribe someone even to be able to park your car.

Facing the sea is a ruined *torre Saracena*, a Saracen tower, one of the many watchtowers built along the coast as sighting posts against Saracen pirates. It is a sturdy white block with a door halfway through its height, and an arched stone staircase leading to it. I take off my shoes and socks and leave them in the car. Saracen pirates ceased to be a thing a long time ago, and the towers are informally used as signposts for stretches of beach. I wish I had my trunks with me; I would love to take a dip. In jeans and shirt, the attire I was planning to wear on the air-conditioned flight back home, I am sweating like bacon on a grill.

Mauro sits under a large red umbrella with his daughters, reading today's *Corriere della Sera*. The beach is largely empty, except for another umbrella, so distant that it looks like a parasol. Anna is floating far away from the shore. When she sees us, she starts swimming back towards terra firma.

'Uncle Tony! Uncle Fabio!' shouts Ottavia, the older girl, at five years. She is well trained; her enthusiasm at seeing us is not justified by the two times she has met me, and the three times, as far as I know, she has met Tony. When we get to the umbrella, Ottavia throws her arms around Tony. Rebecca, her little sister, snoozes on a beach towel.

'Anna and the girls are leaving,' Mauro says. 'The sun's getting too strong for children. Would you drive me home after we talk?'

'Sure,' Tony says.

'And here come the boys!'

Anna drips water on the volcano-hot sand as she walks to us. The last time I saw her was three years ago, at Tony's sister's wedding, but I got drunk quickly, and we barely exchanged

61

any words. I have been avoiding a moment like this, and even as we drove this way, I hoped against hope that it wouldn't come. But then, so many of the moments we dread do come. We pay taxes, we overdraft, we lose friends, we die. We have our hearts broken.

'Hi, Anna,' I say.

She was gorgeous when we were young, and she is even more gorgeous now, two decades and two kids later. Her boobs are full, her hips large without being fat, her long, wet hair gleams in the sun as black as a total eclipse. She has cellulite on her bum, light wrinkles around her eyes, and she wears these signs of time proudly, as marks of honour. Anna doesn't cast her beauty in amber; she lets it grow and change. It is one of the things I like about her. I'd tear off my clothes and tear off *her* clothes and fuck her silly in the sea right now, if I had a chance.

'The three musketeers, minus D'Artagnan,' Anna says, and why does she have to bend that way to get her towel? She wraps it around herself and, more or less covered, she undoes her bikini top to change into something dry. The top falls on the sand in slow motion. My mind stops processing everything that is not Anna: images of Anna's breasts, bare under that fucking towel, keep coming at me, graphic, powerful. She is killing me. I don't know if she is doing it on purpose or it is Casalfranco finding new ways to mess with me. I know I should avert my eyes, but would you? Lucky me, I have sunglasses.

Tony says, 'Well, Art is…'

'Art is missing again,' Anna says, as she raises a foot to take off her bikini bottoms. 'Mauro told me.' I have seen women changing under a towel since I was a little kid. It is not supposed to be erotic. *It is not supposed to be erotic.* 'I'll leave you handsome men to talk while the ladies go home and spin silk.' She can afford jokes – none of us are a patch on her. Anna is a professor of philosophy in Milan; the *New York Times* called her work on artificial intelligence 'paradigm shifting'. Once she gets started on her theories, only Art can follow her.

When she packs and leaves with the girls, I feel like I just lost something precious. I am drenched in sweat. I take out a cigarette and light it, saying, 'We've got bad news. Art's dealing.'

'As in…?'

'As in.'

Tony and I bring Mauro up to date with our conversation with Carolina. It ends with Mauro shaking his head. 'Fuck.'

'Fuck indeed,' Tony says.

'That definitely rules the Carabinieri out.'

'Wait. What?' Tony asks, with an edge in his voice. 'That makes it more urgent to talk to them, if anything.'

'Art's a *dealer*, Tony. That's an order of magnitude worse than growing weed for yourself. We were at *his house*. Nobody will believe we weren't there to buy.'

It is the seashore sun; it scorches you, it makes you edgy and unreasonable. We are locals; we should know better than to talk under this sun. You wait for it to set before discussing anything that matters.

'Art's supposed to be one of your *best mates*!' Tony says, raising his voice. 'And, oh, sir, I apologise if that looks bad on your CV.'

Mauro, too, raises his voice. 'It's not only about me! Do you think Art'd be happy to have the Carabinieri on his doorstep?'

'Art is fucking missing,' Tony half shouts.

'*Is he now?*'

Tony makes to answer, then shuts his mouth, shuts his eyes, and takes a long breath to chill out. 'Peace,' he says, in a quieter tone.

Mauro lifts his hands. 'Peace,' he agrees. 'Might be nothing, do you see what I mean? The first time, he came back unscathed.'

Tony says, 'Not unscathed.'

'He was healthy and…'

'And whatever happened to him was so bad that he had to come up with a ridiculous lie.'

Mauro doesn't reply. None of us ever bought Art's story. We were young, we were naive, but we were not stupid. 'Right,' Tony says. 'You know what? Let's put it to vote. I want to have a chat with the Carabinieri, Mauro doesn't. Fabio, it's down to you.'

I am sure I am going to say, *Carabinieri it is*. If Art comes back in one piece, we will have landed him in a lot of trouble, but how can we be sure he will come back in one piece?

I am still thinking of Anna though.

I am still thinking of her breasts under the towel, of the stupid things we have done, which a part of me, a nasty, brutish part of me, wishes to do again, repeatedly. Every grown man carries a dick-driven teenager inside, and we have to be careful not to unleash him; but I can't be careful under this sun. The teenager in me knows that if we go to the Carabinieri now, I will have no reason left to stay in Casalfranco, and no reason to meet Anna again in the foreseeable future. Not that I would ever make a move on her, because I wouldn't.

I know I am digging myself into a hole when I say, 'I'll tell you what: we stick around two more days. If Art's not back by then, we go to the coppers.'

13

Lara called me while I was on the beach, where there was no signal. I find a voicemail when I check my phone, at the exit of a small rental where I asked Tony to drop me – you need to get your own mode of transport around here. The rental is a block of bricks by the roadside, surrounded by empty fields. I don't know how customers are supposed to get here in the first place, if they don't have Tony carrying them around.

'Hey, dumbass,' Lara's voicemail says. 'Planes are huge. I thought it was difficult to *miss* one.'

I call her back, and when she picks up I open by saying, 'Don't rub it.'

Lara laughs. She has a beautiful laugh, my Lara. She asks, 'Did you get thoroughly pissed with your mates yesterday?'

'Not really.'

She pauses, then says, 'What's wrong?'

The faint trace of a West Country burr in her voice makes her sound rougher than she is. I love that. 'Art didn't show.'

'Why? What happened?'

'I don't know. His phone is dead.'

'Have you tried his home?'

'He wasn't in. Tony – do you remember Tony? – is going there again, to see if Art's back.'

'Are you worried?'

'I don't know.' I can't explain the situation to her, not on the phone. In the three years I've been with Lara she's never met the guys. I only came to Italy for the Pact, and none of them ever swung by London. Mauro was busy with his family, Tony with his surgery, and Art with whatever his obsession of the moment was. I told her about them, I told her about the Pact, but I didn't mention the time Art disappeared. I let that story lie in its dark corner.

'Did you talk to the Carabinieri?'

'Not yet. We want to be sure it's necessary.'

I know full well that Lara is picking up from my voice a lot more than I am saying. Falling for women smarter than me is my damnation (or is it possible, as Tony once jokingly pointed out to me, that *all* women are smarter than me?). She doesn't press me. She says instead, 'Are you sure you want to fly back tomorrow?'

I pause, feeling like a Judas. 'Actually, not so much. I was thinking, I should stay for two or three days, just in case.'

'I'd say that's sensible. Do you need me there?'

'Don't worry, I'll be all right.' I am disgusted by my words, as though I were planning on cheating on her, which I am not.

'Okay then, let's Skype later.'

'Yup,' I say.

We say goodbye, we say I love you, and we end the call.

I sit on a blue Vespa. I told Tony I wanted to rent one for old times' sake, though the simple truth is I can't afford a car. I had to rent a helmet too – the days of easy riding are over. I turn the key and the Vespa's engine purrs. I haven't heard that sound in fifteen, sixteen years, and it hits me so hard that it sends me flying, not through space, but through time, to travel back to when I was a teenager, to when I knew beyond doubt that I was going to do brilliantly in life, that I had my friends on my side, and I was immortal. I start the Vespa on the large unpaved road, under a blinding sun, alone.

14

The plan was to head to the B&B. Tony would spend the rest of the day arranging a longer leave from the hospital and enjoying some quality time with his parents, Mauro would do the same with his family, and I was going to extend my booking again, Skype Lara, and then pretend to work a little. I am doing a book, in theory – a personal take on non-conventional (by fashion industry standards) beauty. My agent thinks it is well timed, and I hope that he is right, because something needs to rescue my finances and my career from the black hole they are falling into. The Vespa throws the whole plan into the bin. I ask myself, *Why?*, and I don't have a better answer than, *Because I'm back in the saddle of a Vespa*. We think we are in control of our lives, but we aren't. Most of the time we don't know what we are doing and, sheeplike, we follow *something*, call it fate, or the subconscious mind, or the whims of a dumb moped.

The countryside has not changed. There are one or two new houses, and some of the old ones have crumbled, and that's it. This land hasn't changed in centuries, and I wonder if there isn't a magical inertia at work, a long-forgotten curse which makes change, any change, impossible. I pass the house from where we called the Carabinieri twenty-two years ago, and a mile further on I pull over to where we parked our Vespas. The sun is setting, but it is still high enough to trace the contours of the olive trees with razor-sharp clarity. This sort of light simply doesn't exist in England; even on the brightest days, the English landscape has a mellowness, a misty blurring on the edges which makes features merge into one another. Here, boundaries are defined, and each object is very much itself. That tree is only *that* tree; it has nothing to do with the earth it grows upon or the rocks surrounding it. This light has no patience for ambiguity. In its way, it is a great backdrop. I should take some pictures for my book, before I leave. Provided I find the right model.

I see the olive grove. I have never gone inside, not once. It is time to do just that. I am thirty-five and the sun is up; I flat-out *refuse* to be scared. I take off my sunglasses and stick them in the collar of my shirt, and stride towards the grove, the helmet in one hand. Then I get to the tree line and stride no more. The cicadas are chirping madly, and it is only an impression, surely, but when I rest a hand on a tree, their chirping reaches a crescendo.

Sod that.

I enter the grove. I would love to say that to my grown-up eyes the trees look smaller and harmless, but they don't. They are every bit as threatening as I remembered. Their twisted trunks still make me think of the damned in hell. An eerie drumming will start at any minute, and they will take life and start dancing around me – and I will be their lunch. I wipe sweat from my forehead. You don't have to believe in ghosts in order to know that some places have an atmosphere, that they retain, if not a memory, at least an echo of what happened in the past. The atmosphere here is gloomy, the low angle of the sun only making the gloom stand out more. What happened that night? How is it possible that we didn't hear or see anything, in this desolation? *And where is Art now?* Talking to Carolina has somehow convinced me that the episodes are, indeed, connected, that Art has vanished again, and he has vanished now because he vanished twenty-two years ago. I stop at a big white rock jutting out from the ground. 'What happened here?' I say aloud.

The answer is a smell.

It is bittersweet in a way that makes me sick. It brings back to my mind Tony sniffing the air in Art's house yesterday night, proclaiming, *No rotting bodies*. But that is exactly what this smell is, a rotting body's. I hear a different humming on top of the cicadas'. It ties a knot in my belly. It comes from a point ahead of me. I walk deeper into the grove, and I see it.

A body.

From a noose hangs the body of a dog, a shaggy white mongrel. The rope is tied to a sagging branch. The poor creature's hind paws are swinging a hair's breadth from the

69

ground, slowly rocking back and forth. I bring a hand to my mouth and hold my breath. I look around, I stretch my ears, but I can't hear or see anyone. I am alone in this grove, or if I am not, then whoever is hiding is smarter than me. The air is motionless, without the faintest hint of a breeze. Then how is it possible that the dead dog is swaying? The branch on which it hangs is the only thing I see moving.

I hesitate, then move closer. The dog's fur is matted with spots of mud. His eyes are vacant. One of the spots moves.

I recognise the humming at last: flies. Millions of them are tucking into the corpse, hungry like sharks in a feeding frenzy, so forceful in their assault that they make the body swing. It is them, not mud, matted all over the dead dog's fur.

Art has a dog. Had *a dog?*

My lungs give up: I breathe out and in again. The stench is overwhelming. My head spins. To avoid crashing down, I lean on an olive tree, and I close my eyes and catch my breath as I hear the buzz coming closer, the sharks rushing to me, attracted by the smell of my fear.

My phone rings.

15

Seven days after Art disappeared, my doorbell rang.

I don't have a clear recollection of those days; they are a blur of activities I didn't particularly care for (talking to the Carabinieri, avoiding the journalists, talking to the Carabinieri

70

again, banding with Tony and Mauro to cuss at the people who were suddenly Art's best friends and Art's mentors and Art's fans). I did them on autopilot. My real energy went into not giving in to the fear that Art was dead. The most difficult part was the allegations that we were responsible. Up to the moment Art returned, the guys and I were *suspected*. Of what wasn't clear, until Concetta Pecoraro, a local charlatan who had made a business of talking to the Virgin Mary, declared that Mary had told her that Art was dead, and heavily implied that the three of us got him killed. You would think that nobody could believe this story, and in fact, nobody did. Not openly.

My father, on the other hand, didn't think for a moment that we had killed Art. He thought that we were covering for him, that Art had run away and we were pretending we didn't know out of a misplaced sense of friendship. While Art was missing, my father's was the least dramatic and therefore the least popular theory, but once he came back, everyone in Casalfranco would declare that his had also been their theory all along.

I was nauseated by the freakshow, and worried beyond words for my friend, when, on a rainy Saturday afternoon, my doorbell started ringing. My father was at school for a teachers' meeting on the topic of Art (there were a lot of such meetings all over town. I didn't understand their point, and neither, I think, did those who organised them), so I was alone, my head buried in the *X-Men*. I let the doorbell ring. Whoever it was (journalists, Carabinieri or, the worst of all, do-gooders from church) would soon get bored and be on their way. They didn't; they just kept pressing.

I put my comic book away and stomped to open the door. 'Yes,' I grumbled with bad grace.

'Hey, man,' Art said.

I took a step back. For a moment, a very brief moment, I was *terrified*. Art was only Art, but his presence there was so unexpected that he was like a monster, like a werewolf. I swallowed and found it in me to say, 'Art?'

'Yeah, I know.'

'What…?'

'I'm starving.'

In a daze, I followed Art to my own kitchen, where he fished from the fridge some Parma ham and cheese, and stuck them in a piece of ciabatta.

There was something off about him.

'What happened?' I asked.

'When?' Art said, his mouth full.

'Art, you *know* when.'

'May I get some milk?'

'Knock yourself out.'

Art gorged on a carton of milk, then wiped his mouth with a sleeve. He noticed that he still had his coat on. He took it off and placed it on a chair. 'It's warm in here.'

'Art…'

'I don't know what to tell you.'

'You were gone *seven days*.'

'Was that seven days?'

'What happened to you?'

He scratched the nape of his neck, looked at the empty

carton, at his sandwich, at his coat on the chair. 'I ran away from home,' he said. 'I should've told you guys, but I knew you would have spilled the beans.'

'What? Why?'

'I wanted to see if I could outsmart everybody in town. Well, I could.'

I knew there and then that he was lying. He didn't make the slightest effort to lie convincingly. His voice said, *I'm telling you I ran away, and you might buy it or not, but you know what? Frankly, I don't give a damn.* That attitude was, I think, the main reason why everybody was so quick to believe him. They didn't like Art's attitude and they didn't like him, and they were all too happy to brush off his disappearance as a cry for attention. 'Are you all right?'

Art showed me his sandwich. 'Now that I'm getting some food, yeah, I'm fine.'

'Okay then, let's try it again: what happened?'

'I ran away from home.'

'You ran…' It was such an obvious lie that it made me angry. 'Fuck you, Art! We've been through the mother of all shit-storms because of you.' I slammed my hand on the kitchen table. '*What happened?*'

He stopped munching then, and looked at me, without *really* looking at me. His gaze was lost somewhere else. 'You don't buy it?'

'No.'

He shrugged and got back to his sandwich. 'The town will.'

'Do you have any idea of what's happening out there?

You're a nationwide story. Half of the country is convinced we bumped you off, the rest can't decide if we were covering your ass or you were abducted by aliens. The Carabinieri have given us hell, and the journos, and our families, and the teachers at school. I have a *right* to know.'

After a pause Art said, 'Yeah, you do.'

I was going to shout at him again, but I stopped, because I finally realised what was off about him. His clothes. They were the same clothes (the same jeans, the same shoes, the same sweater) he had on when he disappeared, last Saturday. He had spent seven days in them. He should have smelt bad, but he didn't. His clothes were clean.

'Art,' I implored him, 'what happened to you?'

He said, 'I don't know.'

16

Back at the B&B, I throw myself under the shower and wait there until deep canyons open on my fingertips. Tony checked on Art's place; he told me over the phone that it is still empty, though there are things we need to discuss in person. He sounded upset enough, so I saved the story of the dog in the olive grove. That, too, is the sort of story you tell in person. The dead dog's stench haunts me. I use up all the shower gel, and the shampoo, but the stench is still with me, as if the dog is hanging in this tiny cabin with flies doing the *struscio*, back and forth, between us.

What the hell was that? There are plenty of strays around here, and in the not too distant past people would eat dogs when other sources of meat were scarce. I wouldn't be surprised if that still happened. But *hanging* one, to leave it to rot? What for? In that particular olive grove, of all.

Art kept a dog.

I don't want to go there. It might all be a coincidence, but Art taught me not to believe in coincidences. *What we call a coincidence*, he would say, *is a system we don't understand yet.*

It is out of the question that I will stay in tonight. I need fresh air and a drink. The stench still lingers after the shower, and when I close my eyes, I see the dog. I should have taken it down and buried it. *It's only a dog.* It has a meaning though, it must have, and that meaning is bothering me.

I am on Skype with Lara. 'You sure you're okay?' she asks.

Her voice brings me back to reality. In moments like this I resent video calls. My generation still remembers the world before cams, when you could hide behind a phone. My generation – already old codgers in our thirties. 'It's the heat, and this town.'

'You can't stand hot weather, you don't like your hometown – you're a faulty type of Southern Italian.'

'Return me to the factory then.'

'Nah, I'll keep you. Out of pity, you know.'

In my darkest moments I think, *Yeah, I know.* Lara is a web designer employed by one of the major agencies in London, and makes in one month what I make in six (providing they are six *good* months). At twenty-seven, she has *time* and *options*. And she is beautiful, with her ash-blonde hair and her small, slightly pointed ears. She is not model material (too short for the industry, her boobs are slightly irregular, and her attitude in front of the camera just too goofy), but when you snap for enough time, you learn that real beauty is very often not model material. Which is, by the way, the theme of the book I should be working on.

'Fabio…?' she says.

'Sorry, I got distracted.'

'I don't know what's wrong with you, but when you want to talk, I'm here.'

'There's nothing wrong with me.'

Lara blows me a kiss and says, sweetly, '*Never* BS me, darling.'

I am on my feet the moment we close the call. I need to get out of here *now*, in my sweat-stinking shirt.

A northerly breeze cools down the air, making the night pleasant. The Vespa brings me to Portodimare, whose transformation from a fishing village into a tourist village was completed a few years ago. We used to spend all summer here, back in the day: the beach in the morning, playing table football late into the night, drinking cheap beer that grated our throats, and shoving coins into the last coin-operated, non-ironic jukeboxes this planet would ever see. In high season, Portodimare has shops and stalls open until late, and I am hoping some of them have started the season early, because I need more clothes.

I get lucky, if you can call it that: I find socks, boxers, and two garish t-shirts, one of which I wear immediately. I LIKE BOOZE, it reads, and the two o's are the bottoms of beer glasses.

What a crazy laugh. It is nine-thirty, too early to go back to the B&B. I need drinks, and food.

I stroll to the small piazza where most of the bars are. In my days, this piazza was the picture-postcard perfect *rotonda sul mare*, a round space with a view of the sea and a small harbour. Now, after a renovation project which bitterly divided the village, harbour and piazza are sleek monstrosities of concrete which a provincial kid would have found hip in the late nineties. None of our hangouts survived the transformation. New ones took their place, identical to the old ones, only without any jukeboxes and with a wider choice of drinks. At the plastic tables of these new bars, new teenagers sit, identical to us. They scare me. They rub my nose in how disposable we all are.

I pick a random bar and sit al fresco. I buy a stale sandwich and a bottle of beer, and light a cigarette. A bunch of teenagers at another table burst into laughter. Their heads form a halo around a phone on which – let me use my telepathic powers – a cat video is playing. I miss my friends. I wish I wasn't alone tonight. I am still rattled after the dog in the grove. *It's this fucking place*, I think for the hundredth time, when I pick up, in the background noise, a voice I know.

The voice halts.

It is an *oh shit!* moment. I screwed up. I waltzed around as if I were in London, where you are just another face in the crowd, but here, in this network of small towns and villages, every face has a name, and the sheer force of statistics will make you bump into people you know. Also, statistics play dirty.

'Fabio?' my father says.

17

My father looms over me. His lips are a thin line, which is the closest he will ever get to crying. He is fifty per cent hurt, fifty per cent furious. I struggle with the desire to recoil – he is not a violent man, but he is a southerner, and boxes on the ear were part and parcel of my education.

'Fabio,' Don Alfredo says. 'Is that you?' This smirking bastard is the senior priest in Casalfranco, a friend of my father, and a powerful old shit.

I ignore him entirely and look at my father. 'I guess we should talk.'

We have nothing to talk about! a lesser man would shout. My father nods and turns to his friend. 'Alfredo, if you'll excuse us…?'

'Of course, of course,' Don Alfredo says. Slightly stooping, with a big nose and a bald lumpy head, he could be a vulture drawn by a Disney artist on a bad trip. He nods a goodbye, which I don't answer, and makes a show of shifting to the furthest table. The show is useless; I am certain he won't snoop. He doesn't need to. My father will tell him everything, either later tonight or in confession.

'What is he up to?'

'Who?' my father says.

He used to be dead set against stock phrases and useless words. *Who? Who do you think?* 'Don Alfredo.'

My father sits down, with movements more cautious than I remember. 'There is some trouble with the Ferragosto procession.

We need to organise a few details before the season begins.'

The Ferragosto procession is a procession of ships, held along the coast on the fifteenth of August. The tourist crowd find it oh-so-picturesque. Don Alfredo must want a piece of it.

'Portodimare isn't part of his parish.'

'Portodimare has a new priest, a good man, but he does not have his finger on the pulse. Don Alfredo is lending a hand.'

'Or, he's after the spotlight.'

My father opens and closes his hand, once. If I were fifteen, he would have hit me. 'What are you doing here?' he asks.

It is the same question I am asking myself. 'I am sorry I lied,' I say.

'You lied?'

'When I said I wasn't coming again, this year.'

His hands lie flat on the table, both of them, in a slightly unnatural pose. He is big on composure. 'Did you?'

I hate it when he does this: when he pretends that what I say isn't real. The implication being, as his son, my duty is to obey and behave and shut up. I comb a hand through my hair. 'Sorry, I'm not in the mood.'

'You are *never* in the mood.'

'Something came up! Something serious.'

'Serious how?'

I glance at Don Alfredo. 'Will it stay between us?'

'I will be the judge of that.'

'Fine,' I surrender. 'Yesterday Art didn't show up.' *Why are you talking?* I wonder. *Why are you telling your father what happened?* Twenty-four hours in Casalfranco is long enough for me to decrease in size, shrinking to be a little kid who thinks his daddy has all the answers.

'So?' he says.

'So, it's strange. What with what happened to him when we were kids…'

'*Nothing* happened to him when you were children. He ran away from home to play a prank, and he came back when he'd had enough. That is the end of it.'

'That's not true.'

'We were all worried sick, Fabio. Do you remember the state his poor mother was in? And why? Because Mauro wanted to show, what, that he was *better than us*?'

'It's Art, not Mauro.' This is odd: my father never gets names wrong.

He pauses for a moment. '*Arturo*. That is what I said.'

'Art didn't run away. I don't have a clue what happened, but I know he didn't run away.'

'You will never grow up,' he scoffs.

I slap a hand on the table. 'And you'll never stop thinking you know better than everybody else!' I half shout.

'Don't make a scene.'

'Okay.' I take a long breath, imagining the title for a book: *The Zen of Surviving Your Parents*. 'Back to square one. We're worried for Art, so we're sticking around for a couple of days. If we don't hear from him, we'll call the Carabinieri.'

'You should call the Carabinieri *on* him.'

'Dad…'

'No, Fabio, listen to me: you left Casalfranco. You're not

in town, *I* am. And I've met your *friend* a few times since he moved back. Art was always a bad egg, but he got worse.'

'What's that supposed to mean?'

'He has issues. Dishevelled hair, long beard, he looks like a madman. He spends *days* at the library, instead of looking for a job. He is so self-absorbed that he doesn't even say good morning when he meets you.'

The picture makes me smile. 'That's Art through and through.'

'He dotes on his dog more than is natural.'

His dog. I smell the rotting stench again; I hear the flies buzzing. 'What dog is that?'

'One of the strays. Arturo adopted it, which would be commendable if the circumstances were different, but he behaves as if it were a… person. He talks to it in the streets. I heard him once, telling it how beautiful it was, how intelligent and bold.'

'Would that be a big, shaggy white dog?'

'Why are you asking?'

'Dad, please…'

My father closes his eyes and brings the index and middle finger of his right hand to his temple, making an effort to remember. 'A brown Pomeranian cross,' he says eventually.

The dog in the olive grove is not Art's. I hope I don't show how relieved I am. I make to sip my beer, with an unsteady hand, but the bottle is dry. 'From what you're saying Art seems more insane than bad.'

'Arturo comes from a hard-working family, and he is not

stupid. He had all the chances to make something with his life. No, your friend was always a selfish boy, with a sense of entitlement even bigger than yours, and finally God is making him foot the bill. *Quisque faber suae fortunae.*'

Every man is the architect of his own fortune: one of my father's favourite mottos. What he does not say is that he blames Art for being the architect of mine too. 'We have different opinions,' I repeat. 'I won't argue with you.'

'As you wish. At any rate, what are you doing here?'

'I just…' I stop in my tracks. I just told him; he doesn't remember, and he is not pretending. I feel like the sea swept over Portodimare, transforming the land into water, and the very grounds on which I am seated, on which my life rests, are being swept away. My father is a classicist, fluent in Ancient Greek and Latin. His brain is his pride. He is never unfocused, never forgetful. 'I just told you,' I say.

'Told me what?'

I try to swallow, but my mouth is dry. I turn to look at that sodding priest. His eyes are pinned on our table, with a pious understanding as false as my triumphs.

'Dad,' I ask, 'are you all right?'

TONY

1

You know what? Mauro can fuck off, massive jerk that he's become. On our way to Carolina this morning Fabio said we've got to cut him some slack, that the guy has a wife and two daughters to think about. Point taken. Still a jerk. Fabio, that's a good man. He deserves all the luck he has and then some.

This car smells like Dad's aftershave. A deal is a deal and it's not cool to break it, but all the same I am driving to the Carabinieri. Mauro could talk round Fabio, not me, with all that *we can't be sure* and *we should wait* bollocks. Mauro's good with words, but what good are words? I know in my gut that Art is *gone* the same way he was *gone* the first time. I also know, we *all* know, that that time Art didn't run away from home and didn't spend seven days on his own, no. *Art was taken and bad things were done to him.* They didn't leave physical traces, but, fuck me, not all traces are physical. I mean, look at his life after that! The bad guys were never found because the Carabinieri got in their mind that there were no bad guys. So, the bad guys are still out there. And my buddy's missing again.

The phone rings: my little sister Elena. Great. I've been avoiding her so far, and I wish I could keep it that way, but I won't be able to just not answer. I'm not Mauro. I take the phone and wedge it between my cheek and shoulder. Last Christmas I got Dad a hands-free set for the car, but he managed to lose it within two weeks. Dad has no beef with technology, as long as technology keeps its distance. 'Hey, Elena,' I say.

'Where are you?'

'Driving.'

'Are you dropping by later?'

'No, sorry, I promised Mum and Dad I'll have dinner with them.'

'Tomorrow, then. Come for lunch.'

I'd rather have a dust-up with Conor McGregor. 'Sure.'

'You *have* to see my belly; it's bigger than it looks on cam.'

Elena is six months pregnant. Three years ago she married Rocco Fistetto, an old acquaintance of mine. If it weren't for Mauro stopping me, at the wedding I would have done something stupid (something like having a swing at the groom). Fabio and Art got pissed in the first half-hour, but Mauro wasn't drinking and took care of me. I should remember that, when he makes me mad. 'Wow,' I say, 'can't wait.'

'Rocco is grand too. Business has been very good lately.'

My little sis. She likes nothing better than winning and gloating. 'Yeah, Dad told me. Is one o'clock fine with you?'

'Let's do one-thirty.'

'Okay. Listen, the signal here is terrible.'

'No worries,' Elena says. 'See you tomorrow.'

If only I could stop loving her. But you can't, can you? Family and mates, they're all that matters. Whatever they become, they're all that matters.

2

On the night before Elena's wedding, Mum said, 'You should talk to her.'

'Mum…'

'It's not too late.'

We had had a family gathering to whet the appetite for the Big Event. Nothing major, only fifteen people or so among uncles, cousins and Elena's closest friends. Dad had been a happy puppy all day, and now he was sleeping off a few too many glasses. Dad didn't get the problem with Elena and Rocco, he still doesn't. Mum has been very good at keeping him in the dark. 'There's nothing he can do,' she says. 'At least he's happy.'

Mum and I were in the garden, going through an old ritual of sharing a drop of bold yellow Strega liqueur before going to sleep. She knew she'd catch me off guard.

'Elena's stubborn,' I said.

'She's your sister, Tony.'

I finished my Strega, parked the glass on the table with more force than necessary, and stood up. 'It won't do any good,' I said, to no answer.

I pussyfooted inside and up the stairs, even though probably I didn't need to be that careful, with all the booze Dad had in his bloodstream. Light framed Elena's door. I knocked and she whispered, 'Come in.'

Dressed only in a t-shirt of mine, she was sitting in a swivel chair at her desk, the same desk she would sit at when she was at school and I helped her to do her homework. Her wedding dress was hanging from the top of the open wardrobe door.

'What are you doing?' I asked.

'Going through old pictures. Come.'

I got nearer. She was looking at a pic Dad had taken during a Sunday trip to the zoo, a long time ago. There was me, ten years old and trying to look tough in a reversed baseball cap and with the sleeves of my t-shirt folded to the shoulders, holding hands on one side with Elena, cute as a button in pink dungarees, and on the other side with a chimp in denim dungarees. Elena said, 'Do you remember? You insisted you didn't know who was who anymore, that your sister and the chimp were dressed the same, and they looked pretty much the same, and you got confused.'

I chuckled. 'Yes. I made as if I wanted to leave you there and take the chimp with me.'

Elena was laughing. 'God, you made me cry.'

'And I felt bad for the rest of the day.'

'Yes, well, you shouldn't have. It was fun.'

I tilted my head at the wedding dress. 'Can't sleep?'

'I'm excited. What about you? Had your drop with Mum?'

'Yeah.'

'And did she ask you to come?'

Caught wrong-footed again. 'Sort of.'

Elena put back the photograph on the top of a neat stack and sighed. 'I'm getting married tomorrow, Tony.'

'It's not too late to call it off.'

'You and Mum should put this in your head: *I love Rocco.* I love him.' It wasn't true; I believed that then and I believe that now. She went on, 'Couldn't you be happy for me? At least a tiny smidge?'

'He's no good for you.'

'Who are you to decide?' she said, raising her voice.

I wasn't looking for a fight, not on the eve of her wedding. 'I just want what's best for you.'

'I know you mean well. But that doesn't give you or Mum any right on my life.'

'Are you pregnant?'

'What…' Elena laughed quietly. '*Am I pregnant?* Is this what you think?'

'It'd explain all this hurry to get married.'

'What hurry? Rocco and I have been together seven years.'

'You were children when you got together.'

'I'm a woman, Tony, a grown-up perfectly capable of making her own decisions. Anyway, no, I'm not pregnant and I'm not planning to have children for a while, if you want to know, not before Rocco's position is more secure.'

I held out my hands. 'I had to give it a try.'

'Tell Mum to stop fighting this,' Elena said, kindly. 'It's all good, we're happy, there's nothing to fight against.'

'Just do me a favour: whatever happens, remember you've got a brother. I'll look out for you, no matter what.'

Elena stood up and kissed me on my cheek. 'That's so sweet,' she said.

3

The Carabinieri station is a three-storey yellow-tinted building. It's way too big for Casalfranco, a place where petty criminals are in short supply and the professionals will never see the inside of a prison. The building was started in the early thirties, when the mayor decided that a big-ass Carabinieri station would make Casalfranco (and by reflection, him) look good in Mussolini's eyes. When they finally got around to finishing it, in 1939, Mussolini had a world war on his hands. Il Duce never got to see the station, the mayor's only son was killed in a battle against Allied troops, and the mayor shot himself when he heard the news of Mussolini's execution. The station remains.

I park cautiously and look around before I get out of the car. Mauro's family home is not far from here, and it'd be awkward to bump into him. He's got nothing to worry about though; I won't grass on him and Fabio. I'll say to the Carabinieri that I went to see Art on my own, and I'll take whatever grief there might be.

On the inside, the station is haunted by the smell of burnt sausages. Someone had a late lunch. A fan whirls tiredly somewhere, without getting even close to cooling down the room. A man in a blue short-sleeved Carabinieri shirt sits behind a Plexiglas screen. The top three buttons of his shirt are open, letting a fair amount of chest hair show. He watches hip-hop on his laptop, using (to his credit) a pair of earphones. The fan is with him, beyond the Plexiglas, pointed at his face. Fair enough. He takes out the earphones and greets me with a '*Salve.*'

'Oh, good afternoon, sir.'

'How can I help you?'

'It's about a friend of mine. He… uh… he might be missing, I think.'

The man crosses his fingers on his globe-shaped belly and shifts his bum right and left, aiming for a more comfortable position. 'He *might*, you say.'

'I don't know for sure. He didn't show up for an appointment and isn't answering the phone. He's not home either.'

'Do I know you?'

'Excuse me?'

'You're Tony, aren't you?'

I give the man another look. Yes, I know who he is: a third cousin on Mum's side. I struggle to remember his name. 'Cosimo!'

'Yeah! Didn't you move to Bologna?'

'Rome, actually.'

'Yeah, that's what I meant, *Rome*. And what brings you to Casalfranco?' he asks, much more interested in gossip than in a possible missing persons case.

I keep my good face on and say, 'I was here to meet this friend of mine, the one who didn't show and might be missing.'

'When was that?'

'Yesterday.'

Cosimo sucks air between his teeth, and shakes his head as if I'd just said something incredibly stupid. 'Too early to start an investigation.'

'It's Art. Arturo Musiello.'

Cosimo sucks air again, harder. '*That* Arturo Musiello.'

'The one and only.'

'Too early to start an investigation,' he repeats, slower.

'I get it, but you guys could ask around…?'

'I said it's *too early*, Tony, way too early.'

At last I get the message. I've been living in Rome too long, and I'm not as used to a certain kind of local finesse as I would be, a way of telling things without speaking. Let's see if I remember how it's done. 'Will it ever be…' I hesitate, '*not too early?*'

'No,' Cosimo says, glad that the discussion is over. 'How's your sister?'

'Brilliant.' I go with his change of topic.

The Carabinieri don't want to talk about Art. Which means one thing – Sacra Corona Unita.

4

Art, where the fuck are you?

I kill the engine, leaving the stage to the cicadas. I'm back at Art's house. The red fields are dead as the planet Mars in a

90

NASA pic. 'Art?' I call out, as I get out of the car. He doesn't answer, of course he doesn't, because he's not fucking here.

I enter without knocking. It is much cooler inside than outside. Art's granddad built this house with thick walls to keep at bay the extremes of the seasons, the summer heat and the winter wind. Everything is as we left it. I should leave a message for Art, just in case, and go. Mauro's right, in that we should keep a low profile: the first time Art disappeared we found ourselves suspect number one even though we were just boys. Now we're grown-ups and Art's a drug dealer, it's going to be a million times worse. But five minutes won't hurt. Cosimo's reaction to Art's name pushed me up all the way from worked up to disturbed.

I do a quick survey of the kitchen, but except for the posh dog food and the books, there is nothing to see – not a computer to hack, not a clue to investigate with a jumbo magnifying glass. I feel halfway between a burglar and an ass. Seriously, I should leave. Make it an early night so that I'm ready for lunch tomorrow with my pregnant sister and her lovely husband. One more thing first. Last night we checked only the house. There is another building in this field. Two decades play strange tricks on your memories, and it is not that you forget some things, but you stop thinking about them.

I exit the house and head to the vineyard, while cicadas play their gig. The grapes are in a wretched shape. It's going to be a poor harvest this year. Art's dad would hate to see his son neglecting the family land. I walk on red dirt, under the red light of dusk, until I reach a trullo, a drystone hut in the shape of a cone. Art's grandfather used to live here before he built the new house, and Art's dad kept it for memory's sake, until a young Art reclaimed it as his hideout. He dried his weed in here (it's not ideal, but kids must make do with what they get). He *smoked* his weed in here. We had a lot of fun in here. It's good to see it's still standing; time can ruin many things, not all. Its door never had a lock.

I step in, and halt.

At the centre of the trullo is a cage, a squat cube of steel bars. There's a leather whip on the floor, a bundle of ropes in a corner, a ball gag, a chain dangling from the roof. Pushed against the wall is a large crate. I open it, and the first thing I see is a black leather mask, shaped like a horse's head, with a zip where the mouth is. I bring it to my nose and smell sweat – it has been used, a lot. The crate is full of sex toys: a shedload of dildos and butt plugs and advanced BDSM gear – a long metallic thingy which looks like a cage for dicks, small clamps for your nipples, stuff I don't have the mileage to put a name to. My least favourite is a plastic gag connected to a long tube, whose other end, I get after some consideration, is supposed to go into a vagina. *Yuck.* No judgement here; I've got friends in the scene and all that, but it's not *my* scene. Must be one of Art's phases. In the post-*Fifty Shades* age, everybody fancies a bite from the forbidden apple. Art, though, was never one for bites; he'd gobble up the apple with skin and seeds.

There's nothing wrong with a spot of rough fun, is there? Nothing wrong with books stacked in every nook and cranny of a dark, dusty house. Nothing wrong with dealing a little weed. Nothing wrong with treating a dog like royalty, or with that dog vanishing, or with vanishing in general, or with the Carabinieri not caring about that. There's nothing wrong here, nothing to see.

The bad guys are still out there.

Fuck them. I too know bad guys.

5

I was fifteen and 'Wonderwall' was playing on the jukebox, on a July night as hot as Satan's armpits. It was the summer after Art went missing. His parents were finally starting to let him off the hook, and they allowed him to go out again, but only on strict orders to come back too early to have any actual fun.

We were in Portodimare's piazza. Mauro had put a coin in the jukebox and chosen 'Wonderwall', but in July, with the village full, you never knew how long it would take before your song played. When Liam Gallagher finally started singing that the day of *something something* had come, our table-football tournament was almost over, with Art and Fabio thrashing me and Mauro. Art was helpless at table football, but Fabio was good enough for three. He had this special move of his wrist that made the little plastic footballers jerk forward in an almost sexual way, sending the ball speeding like a rocket. Now that I think of it, I'd like to play him some day, see if he's kept his form. I get training in the hospital cafeteria.

Anna and her friend Rita (who knows what she's doing

now?) had been following the match, each of them shouting encouragement to one team and booing the other. We were the champions, they were the hooligans, and by the end of the third and final match, we were all dripping with sweat.

'Hey!' Mauro said. 'The Gallagher brothers are here!'

Fabio took advantage of the distraction and used his signature wrist movement to send a fireball beyond Mauro's hapless goalkeeper. Anna clapped her hands, and Fabio and Art exchanged a high five. 'Three matches out of three,' Fabio said.

'Losers,' Art added, with mock contempt.

Anna inched closer to Fabio. 'For the hero,' she said, pecking him on one cheek.

I brought my hands to block my eyes. 'Get a room.'

'They're just friends,' Rita said.

And Anna immediately confirmed, 'That's right.'

I didn't care for Rita. She was from Milan, as was Anna – their families were the advance troops of tourists to come. Anna and Rita were the textbook definition of cool, even better than the Beauties. They were not local yokels, no sir, they came from *Milan*; they'd seen things, they'd gone places. Anna played it fair, but Rita made it her life mission to ensure you never forgot she was an urban gal. She would cram into one breath the story of a lunch at McDonald's (terribly exotic to us), a trip to a multiscreen cinema, an amazing hip-hop gig. Us, we didn't have stories. Stories didn't happen much in Casalfranco, and those that did, you knew better than to tell.

'Ice lollies?' Fabio suggested. They were the cheapest way

to cool down; you could get six of them for little more than the price of a bottle of beer.

'I don't think so,' Art said. Then, to me, in a posh voice, 'I apologise, dear sir, but if I'm not home in twenty minutes Father will blow his top. I will take you up on your kind offer of a lift.'

I checked the time on my Swatch. 'Isn't it early?'

'Nope.'

It was, but Art must have had his reasons to say otherwise. 'All right.'

Mauro said, 'We'll catch you guys tomorrow on the beach.'

Summer was like that: three full months of nights at the jukebox and days on the beach. I wonder if I will ever be that free again.

Art and I left the others and mounted my moped. 'What was that about?' I asked, starting the engine.

'Fabio and Mauro could do with a little space.'

'With the girls?'

'Yeah. Mind, I'm not saying they'll get laid.'

'Give them some credit.' I was a bit jealous of them – not for the girls (none of them were my type, I thought), but for the general notion of *having a date*.

'If Fabio was alone with Anna, maybe. But Rita? She'll ruin it for everybody. She's more into drama than into people.'

'Because you're such an expert.'

He didn't reply. It'd turn out he was spot on: Mauro tried to kiss Rita, and, at that, she screamed and accused him of being *like all other men* and left, and Anna had to follow her.

We thought we'd never see them again, but next year Anna returned, and the rest, as they say, is history.

When we turned into Art's lane, Art said, 'Stop here.'

'Why?'

'So that Mum and Dad won't hear I'm back. You're right, it's early.'

I killed the engine and pulled the moped into a field. We left it there and walked on, accompanied by the soundtrack of crickets. 'We should've bought a couple of beers.'

Art produced from a side pocket of his cargo shorts a sizeable bag of grass. 'This is better.'

'Hey, that's *a lot* of weed. Where did you get the cash?'

He smiled smugly, opened the bag and passed it to me. 'Smell it.'

I obliged and said, 'It's good.' I couldn't have told good weed from bad more than I could have told a Montepulciano from a Chianti.

'Isn't it?' Art said. 'It's mine. I grew it. Rocco got me the seeds. It's cheaper this way, and you get better quality.'

'Your dad will…'

'I hid the pots behind the trullo, and I'm drying the weed in there. Dad knows that's a no-go zone for him. And besides, what he *doesn't* know is what marijuana looks like.'

I let him guide me through the dampness of the night. Sweat had plastered my t-shirt and my shorts to my skin, and I'd rather have had a gelato than a joint, but I couldn't admit that. We entered the trullo and Art turned on a torch he kept there. He pointed it at a line of marijuana branches hung upside down to dry. 'I took down one batch. I couldn't wait.'

'Did you try it?'

'I don't like to smoke alone.' He really didn't, back then.

I'd never be as ballsy as Art. And I'd never be as self-assured as Fabio, or as calm as Mauro. I thought I was lucky they wanted to hang out with me, and, all in all, I haven't changed my mind about that.

I watched Art roll a gigantic joint and take the first drag.

'How is it?' I asked.

He handed me the joint, saying, 'Try it for yourself.'

I smoked and said, 'Wow. Good stuff.'

'Could be better.' Unassuming and modest Art was not, but he was big on self-improvement.

'Is this your next project?' I asked. 'Weed?' His interest in astronomy was pretty much gone. He had tinkered with some new hobbies recently (sleight of hand, ancient history) but nothing that stuck.

He shook his head. 'Photography.'

'Why?'

'Have you ever seen a naked girl?'

'Unfortunately, no.'

'Me neither. And I'm thinking, photography could do the trick. You tell a girl you're going to take a *portrait*, an *artistic* thing, and she'll get her boobs out; not for you, for... posterity.'

'It's a theory.'

'I'm going to test it.'

My head was light, very light. Art's weed was way more powerful than what we were used to.

Art asked, 'Do you ever think about sex?'

I laughed. 'Just about every day.' Midway through the joint, I was as stoned as I'd ever been.

'No, I mean, *seriously* think about it. You, me, Fabio, Mauro – we're best mates. We love each other. So how come we never fuck?'

I had a fit of laughter and coughing simultaneously. 'Because we're not poofs?'

'*Poof!* That's only a word. It means bugger all. How does that work? A girl gives you a handjob, and that's cool, but a guy does the same and it's wrong?'

'That's pretty much how it works.'

'Oh yeah? And what if you're blindfolded and don't know who's giving the handjob?'

'You'd better bloody get rid of the blindfold then.'

'What for? Once you've got a boner, what does it matter if it's for a guy or a girl?'

'It matters because I'm not a poof,' I insisted, laughing. I was laughing a lot; Art was making me uneasy.

'That doesn't make sense,' he said. Then added, 'Are you high?'

'Yeah.'

'Close your eyes then.'

'Are you going to give me a handjob?'

'Close your fucking eyes, dude.'

I did. To this day I couldn't say if I was expecting what was going to happen. I'd never thought I could like men; I wasn't gay, that wasn't an option. You were supposed to *respect* gay people, but also never forget that they were at best sick, and at worst, callous sinners. You didn't mix with suckers signing up for Hell.

I felt wet lips touching mine.

I opened my eyes and made to draw back, but Art pushed my head against his own. I was stronger than him and I could have pulled back if I wanted, but I didn't. I was enjoying the kiss and I was stoned enough to ignore the fact that I wasn't meant to enjoy it. Art's tongue touched my teeth, and sent a hot shiver down from my mouth to my groin. I was getting a boner.

Art pulled back and watched me in my eyes, with his insufferable smirk. 'You liked it.'

'Fuck off,' I sniggered.

He took off his t-shirt. His scrawny chest was almost beautiful among the long shadows. I stared in amazement while he got to his feet and kicked away his trousers and boxers, and was naked in front of me, his eyes on mine, his boner coming up.

'What's next?' he said.

I reached out with my hand, and grabbed his dick.

6

Thank God for Mum's cooking. For dinner she made orecchiette, the ear-shaped pasta, with tomato sauce, deep-fried aubergines, steak, fresh fruit, and a tiramisu, all washed down with strong Primitivo wine. Where I live in Rome, meals this big went out of fashion, but I'm glad they're still popular in the deep south. Not that I could eat like this every day; my metabolism isn't a teenager's anymore.

Dad is over the moon about his grandson – he was happy when Elena found she was pregnant, doubly so when she found it was a boy. He'd be even happier if *I* had a son, because that would mean the surname would live on. Mum is worked up about the baby too, or, at any rate, she pretends well. They make a fuss about not telling me the baby's name, to leave the honour to Elena. We're drinking an after-dinner Fernet, the bitterest liquor in the universe, when my phone goes *dling* with a text. It's Fabio.

> Crossed path wit my father.

Fabio only uses the word 'dad' to refer to other people's dads. I text him back.

> How come?

> Portodimare driking and e wos tere with the blody priest.

> How pissed are you? You're texting like a lolcat.

> Pissed.

For Fabio to admit to being drunk, he must be off his face. I dial his number.

'Where are you, mate?' I ask.

'Bar Aloha,' he answers in a slurred voice.

'I'm coming to get you.'

'No need…'

'I want a drink too.'

I end the call before he has time to object. Fabio and his dad, Angelo, never got along. Fabio is an only child. His mum died of breast cancer when he was ten. If you think that brought father and son closer to each other, think again. Angelo is old school, straight back, chest out, iron discipline, God and family, which Fabio is so not, and mixing them together is like dropping water on frying oil. The fact that Fabio makes a living taking pictures of scantily dressed ladies doesn't help – once I overheard Angelo say to a friend that *Tony, bless him, didn't choose to be sick, but what is my son's excuse?* For real.

I make it to Portodimare just after midnight, to find Fabio emptying what must be the latest of many glasses of rum. In Salento, they don't believe in shots – you drink like you eat, like it's a competition. 'Tony,' he welcomes me. When Fabio gets pissed, he does his best to put on the dignified face and voice of a schoolteacher.

'Let's go home,' I say.

Fabio uses my arm to prop himself up. 'I'm on my Vespa.'

'I won't let you drive, buddy.'

With him leaning on my shoulder, we totter away from the bar. 'You *can* drink and drive here,' he mumbles. 'This is Southern Italy, where men are real men and they drink and they…'

'What do you know about real men, dude? A couple of glasses and you're pissed.'

He pushes me back. 'Hey! I'm the *realest* man of all, am I.

See? I can stand on my own feet.' He staggers. He stumbles. And just like that he throws up. The vomit gets all over his trousers. I spring back too late. Some of it lands on my shoes.

'What the fuck,' I laugh.

Fabio isn't laughing. His eyes are welling up. He lets himself fall to the ground, ass on the dirt. He takes his head in his hands and starts sobbing.

I'm not sure what to do. I never know what to do when people start crying. I can slice their chest open, no sweat, and clean up their arse, but I'm useless at wiping tears. I sit at Fabio's side, in the dirt, and wrap an arm around his shoulder, kind of. 'What's wrong?'

His voice is a little firmer when he says, 'My father.'

'What's his problem?'

'Alzheimer's.'

Bam. I wish I wasn't a doctor. That way, it's possible I wouldn't know how exactly final a diagnosis of Alzheimer's is. I might believe cancer is worse, or HIV, but I don't have that luxury. Angelo will die a ghastly death. He will lose his mind, and soul, and it might take years upon years before he's lucky enough to flatline. I know shit happens, but it doesn't make it any easier to take it when it happens to a friend. 'I'm sorry, man,' I say, fully aware of how little help that is.

'He's still lucid, more or less. He was waiting for me to come this year, to tell me in person. And I didn't…' he stops. 'I'm a fucker.'

'It was never easy between you two. At least you can afford to give him all the help he needs.'

Fabio scoffs. 'My ass.'

'Your job…'

'I've got a bit of a name, doesn't mean I've got cash.' He pauses. He jerks his shoulders. He looks like he's going to be sick again, but he manages not to. 'I'm *broke*. You know how much a photographer makes? Think a very small sum and halve it. Then halve it again. Every brain-dead kid with an iPhone can take photos.'

'*Crappy* photos.'

'Magazines will eat crap as long as it comes cheap. Fuck, fuck, fuck. I've got enough cash for the next four months, if that, then I'll need to serve tables or I don't know what. All I have in my name is Google hits, and that means *fuck all*.'

My mouth goes slack. I wish I could make him stop. To me, Fabio is a symbol of the things you can accomplish when you've got brains and guts, which he has, in spades. Every last person in Casalfranco went out of their way to convince him that being a photographer was a stupid idea, that grown-ups need real jobs, with sick leave and steady pay cheques. My mate didn't yield, and he came out on top. That story was important to me. It meant you can take a stand against what people say, and do your thing. Turns out maybe you can't.

'Oh fuck, why are we doing this?' he says, between sobs. 'Don't tell Mauro. Please, don't tell Mauro, no, don't tell *anybody* that I…'

'It's all right, man,' I say, tugging him tighter. 'It's all right.'

'Don't tell anybody,' he mutters. 'Don't tell.'

7

Elena lives in a newly built house. When we were small the roads in this part of town weren't paved; now there's a tobacconist and a grocer, and some villas. Elena's sits in a wrap-around garden larger than she'd need, with palm trees, fruit trees and prickly pears, scattered in a studiously casual way. It gives off a new-rich vibe, in a style that came into fashion in the noughties and Art dubbed *Narco-Chic*. I hate to say that in my sister's case that is not wide of the mark. Elena buzzes me in.

Her husband Rocco is waiting in the garden, his arms open wide, a bright smile on his face. 'Hey, Tony!' he welcomes me. He kisses me on both cheeks and gives me a bear hug. He's my age, leaner than me, but as strong. When we were boys we fought a lot, playing, sort of. Behind him is Elena, with long chestnut hair and the exuberant figure of the women in my family. Her belly is round as a football. Both her hands rest lovingly on it. Three years of marriage, a baby on its way, and she has lost nothing of her shine; another thing I hate to say is that she's happy with Rocco. She too hugs and kisses me.

'My handsome brother. I'm so happy you managed to come!'

I touch her belly. 'I tried torture on Mum and Dad, but they refused to tell the baby's name. I had to come.'

Elena pulls me by the hand to the back, where a table is set under a canopy of scented wisteria. In Rome, I'd wait a couple of months before eating like I had last night, but this is not Rome. Antipasti are laid out on a bright blue tablecloth: courgettes, deep-fried calamari rings, a wicker basket of warm bread giving off a delicious smell, and a bottle of white wine in ice. I pick a wisteria flower and bring it to my mouth; nowhere else in the world do wisteria flowers taste as sweet as in Salento. I take off my sunglasses and sit down. 'I missed your cooking, Elena.'

My little sister offers me a smile. 'You'll get plenty.'

'Are you supposed to fuss around the kitchen?'

'Boredom is more dangerous than work.'

I turn my attention to Rocco, to show respect to the man of the house. 'I *need* to hear the big secret. The baby's name.'

Rocco lights a cigarette for himself and offers me one, which I accept. 'Guess.'

Oh, come on. The guess is so easy it isn't even a guess. But I play along. 'Stefano?'

Elena is pouring wine for all of us. 'Wrong,' she says. 'Try again.'

'I don't know,' I say, to cut it short.

'Let's raise a glass.'

We all do.

'The name's Piero,' Rocco says. 'To Piero.'

We clink our glasses, looking each other in the eye, as you do when you toast here. 'Like your dad,' I say. Big whopping surprise.

'And the next one will have *your* dad's name,' Rocco immediately points out. 'Or your mum's, if she's a girl. And I promise you one thing, Tony.'

I raise my glass once more, to invite him to go on.

Rocco says, 'I'll never let this boy be ashamed of his uncle. You'll see him whenever you want.'

'That's… that's great. Thank you.'

'You're cool, whatever some folks say. You know I don't have problems with what you… do.'

What *Rocco* does with his life, in my book, is far worse than anything I might remotely think to do with my dick, but this isn't the moment to take offence, so I nod non-committally. I try a calamari ring. God, is it delicious. It gives way under my teeth like a charm, and my taste buds sing at the light aftertaste of olive oil in the batter. I ask Elena, 'How do you do that?'

'Mum taught me.'

'Don't tell her I said this, but you've surpassed the mistress.'

She smiles. 'What's up, Tony?'

'What…?'

'You've got something on your mind.'

That's my little sister for you. Beautiful and clever and pitiless. I guzzle a good swig of wine. 'I'd like to have a word with Rocco.'

'I'm happy to hear that.'

'Elena…'

Elena shakes her head slowly. No, she won't leave.

'It's okay,' Rocco says. 'It really is, Tony.' Rocco is, to put it mildly, a complicated man. He owns a small building firm which is doing great. It's doing great mostly because he has the right sort of connections, of the Sacra, Unita and Corona kind.

I sigh and say, 'I've got to ask you something.'

'A favour?'

'No.' I pause. 'Not exactly.'

'We're family, Tony. Ask away.'

'It's about Art, Arturo Musiello, a mate of mine. Do you remember him?'

Rocco is motionless. The only movement around him is the smoke billowing out of his cigarette. 'Yes. Yes, I do.'

'He disappeared.'

'What do you mean?'

'We have this thing, with the old gang: we meet once a year in Casalfranco.'

Elena says, 'Yeah, Rocco knows.'

'This year Art stood us up. He's not home, and doesn't answer the phone.'

Slowly, Rocco brings the cigarette to his lips. 'It's not the Corona.'

I would give an arm – my *right* arm – not to be having this discussion in front of my little sister. 'I suppose you know he was dealing weed.'

'Yes.' Rocco takes a few drags from his cigarette. He doesn't speak, and neither does Elena. Finally, Rocco asks, 'How much do you want to know?'

'Everything I need.'

'Be careful.'

'I know.'

Rocco nods. 'Fine then. Art had the Corona's blessing.'

'Did he work for… them?' *For you*, I almost say. I pray Rocco isn't better connected than I think.

'No, he's small scale. We're talking a handful of plants. Excellent quality though.'

'Since when does the Corona allow competitors, big or small?'

'They don't. I said Art had their *blessing*.'

'I don't follow.'

'He did a service for the Corona, and in payment he asked for a… how can I put it? A licence.'

This is getting worse by the minute. Mauro's voice in my head insists, *Stop talking right now, jackass. Stop talking and walk away. The less you know, the less trouble you are in*. 'What did he do?'

Rocco stubs out his cigarette on a wooden ashtray. 'He didn't run away from home, did he? When he was a boy. Elena says you guys never believed that.'

'He didn't. Before you ask: no, I don't have a clue what *really* happened.'

Rocco distractedly reaches out to a calamari ring. 'He's a weird man, your friend.'

'Rocco, please. What did Art do?'

'He healed a girl.'

'How do you mean, *healed*? Art's not a doctor.'

'He didn't heal her that way.'

'What, he worked a miracle?'

'Yes,' Rocco replies, simply.

I don't know what to say. It doesn't happen very often; usually when my brain blanks, my mouth takes over and goes on blabbering on its own. Not this time. 'May I have another cigarette?'

Rocco hands me the packet. 'She had leukaemia. Eight years old, and at the end of the line. The doctors' only doubt was whether she had two weeks to live or four.'

'Crap.'

Elena is taking small bites from a slice of bread, with the silence of a perfect wife. She breaks it to ask, 'Have you seen cases like that?'

'Some.'

Rocco says, 'This girl, though, she wasn't just another girl. She was the daughter of a very powerful man.'

'Powerful, how?'

'Let's put it this way: in Salento, he's the head on which the Crown sits. The King, if you want.'

No, I don't want. I don't want to know, I don't even want to have asked. But I have to, for Art, for my mate. 'Do I know him?'

'Don't ask that sort of question, Tony, don't *ever* ask them. Names don't do any good.'

I shouldn't have had a drink; my head feels dizzy. 'Course. So Art got in touch with this… King.'

'Art came to me asking to be put in touch with him.'

'How long ago would that be?'

'Two years ago.'

'Just after Art moved back to Casalfranco?'

'More or less.'

'And you did as he asked.'

'I've known your mate since we were boys. He talks a lot, but he puts his money where his mouth is. I've got friends of friends who work for the powerful man, so fixing a meeting was easy. Art promised he would heal the girl, if he was left alone with her for, and I quote, a night and a day, no questions asked.'

'And the *powerful man* allowed that?'

'You'll never be a father, Tony, you can't understand. The girl was as good as dead. The powerful man, the King, would have done everything in his power to save her. If Art were a charlatan, at least the man would have had someone to take revenge on. He checked her out from the hospital, just before sunset, and brought her to Art's house.'

'Then what?'

'The powerful man left, and after a night and a day, he returned. He found his girl sleeping. Art said to let her sleep, and that she'd be fine when she woke up. The man took her home and did exactly that; he let her sleep. The girl woke up a couple of days later.'

'And she was fine.'

Rocco nods. 'Peachy. Art refused payment. He only asked to be allowed to sell his produce in Casalfranco, promising he'd never turn that into a full-scale operation. He also asked not to be bothered by the Corona again. He made it very clear that healing the girl had been the one and only service he'd ever do for them. I received a nifty sum for my services, the girl lived, and as far as I know the powerful man kept his promise and hasn't been in touch with Art since.'

I mull over the story in silence. It's not that I don't believe in miracles, because I do. What I don't believe is that *Art* could work one. I've seen pigeons more spiritual than he is. 'But now Art's missing and my friends want to go to the

Carabinieri,' I say, massaging the truth a little.

'Not Fabio, I'm sure. Is it Mauro?'

I nod. 'You know him.'

'You can tell him not to waste his time. The Carabinieri know that Art is involved with the Corona; they won't charge him for dealing, but they won't start a search party for him either. They won't give a fuck either way.'

'What about the Corona?'

'They might be interested,' Rocco says, after a pause.

Elena says, 'Rocco could spread the word and see what happens, if that's what you want.'

I look at her. 'I'd appreciate that.'

Rocco says, 'Brother, mind a piece of advice?'

'Sure.'

'Be careful with your friend. There's something funny about him.'

I joke, 'But you said he's a miracle worker. Like Jesus.'

'Jesus, or the other guy,' Rocco says. 'I wouldn't know.'

8

Art didn't cry for the death of his dad. 'I had plenty of time to get used to the idea,' was all he said, and actually his dad had had cancer for the better part of three years and he had made peace with the fact he was shuffling off the mortal coil. His mum died without notice. She was making orecchiette for the first communion of the granddaughter of a friend, on her marble working table, just beneath a socket. She was very proud of that table, which was a gift from her husband for their twenty-fifth anniversary. To make an orecchietta, you take a tiny piece of dough, you fold it in the shape of an ear around your thumb, and you leave it on the side. And then you make another one, and another, for as many pieces of pasta as you need, in a work that can go on for hours. When my mum does it, she enters into a sort of trance. That is what must have happened to Art's. Her husband had installed all the sockets in the house way before anything remotely similar to health and safety entered into the picture, and like many old things in town, those sockets were at the end of the line. She didn't notice that the one above the table was dangling, just slightly. She didn't notice the naked cable hanging too close, and didn't notice the back of her hand touching it. It was a bad way to go.

When Art called her, as he did every day, and she didn't reply, he immediately alerted the Carabinieri, who went to check on her and discovered the body. Art was in Prague at the time. He found a flight to Brindisi Airport the next day. Mauro and I were there for him, waiting with a car. I'd driven from Rome, and Mauro had taken a flight from Milan. Fabio couldn't come. He was tied up with a photo shoot, or something.

Art came out of the gate and he reassured us, 'I'm fine.' We got a quick coffee, then drove to Casalfranco's morgue for the identification of the body. Art asked Mauro and me to go in with him. When the shy, young doctor showed us the body, I felt a lump in my throat. Art's mum was small and she had died as she had lived, clad in black; she took to black when her husband passed and never stopped. She was a sweet woman, always kind to us. Other mums would have been disappointed in how Art was throwing away his gifts, but she never complained.

'It's her,' he announced, and the doctor duly took note.

In the parking lot of that dreadful place, Mauro asked, 'Do you want to get some rest? We can talk to Don Alfredo for you.'

It was February, bitter cold. Art lit a cigarette with a match. 'I can't go home just yet.'

Art's mum very much wanted to have a good Christian funeral, and Art was strong enough to swallow his opinion and accept that. In the past hours Mauro and I had liaised over the phone with Don Alfredo, to organise the function. There are other churches in Casalfranco, but Don Alfredo's is the *chiesa matrice*, the main one, and there was no higher honour for the old woman than to have her funeral there. The trouble was, honour costs money. Don Alfredo asked for a thousand euros, cash, plus three hundred for his *trusted* florist. Business as usual. That was far more than Art could afford, but not a big dent on mine and Mauro's finances. We would pay everything, and we would pay for the undertaker too. Art would have done the same for us.

Don Alfredo's office was inside the church, at the back of the left nave. Mauro knocked at the door, and the priest's voice invited us, 'Come on in.'

When we entered, he was switching off the TV. 'Art,' he said, standing up from his leather armchair, 'my son, I am sorry for your loss.'

Art didn't answer.

113

'Your mum is in a better place now,' Don Alfredo said. 'She's happy.'

Art said, 'When are we having the funeral? I need to put up the notice.' When someone dies in Casalfranco, the family posts a funeral notice on walls in different parts of town, so that people know where and when to go. Art's mum had been very insistent that the notice should be up as soon as possible and on as many walls as possible; she wanted all the townsfolk with her on her last trip. God, I loved that woman.

Don Alfredo raised his neck in a stiff pose. 'The day after tomorrow, at three pm.'

'Couldn't we move it to the evening? More people would come.'

'That's the only slot available, I'm afraid.'

'Fine,' Art cut it short. 'Is there anything you need?'

'There's the matter of the payment.'

I took out a wad of notes and handed it to Don Alfredo. 'Here. Thirteen hundred, cash, as you asked.'

'Cash,' Art scoffed.

Don Alfredo ignored him, licked the point of his index finger, and set out to count the notes. 'There's everything,' he said. 'Not that I doubted it. You're an honest man, Tony, your… condition notwithstanding.'

I let that go. I didn't want to have an argument with a priest in his own church. I didn't have a lot of respect for Don Alfredo as a person, but I did for his office.

Don Alfredo went on, 'That condition is a problem, as I hope you understand.'

Art said, 'I'm not sure I do.'

I said, 'Art…'

'Your suggestion,' Don Alfredo interrupted me, 'was that the three of you should be the pallbearers, along with a cousin. That can't be done, I'm afraid.'

'Can't?' Art said.

'I cannot allow a man in a state of mortal sin to walk down the central aisle of *my* church, in such a pivotal role. It is nothing personal, Tony. You know there will always be a place for you in the House of God, when you decide to amend your ways. We hate the sin, we love the sinner.'

After a moment of silence which seemed to stretch out for one or two ice ages, Art said, 'So I guess you're going to pay taxes on that *cash*. Stealing is a sin too, Father.'

Don Alfredo narrowed his eyes. 'I'm doing you a *favour*, do not forget that.'

'A favour? I wouldn't say that, no. You're selling your services.' Art raised one finger and moved it in a small circle. 'All this – the church, the pomp, the bread and the cheap wine – is a fancy dress party. And you? You're the third-rate clown whose job is to entertain the kids with some fanciful bollocks and jump when he's told *jump*, that's all you are. So, Father: suck it up, and *jump*.'

Don Alfredo gaped at him. Then he closed his mouth, and curled his lips in half a smile. 'I'm calling it off.'

Art's reaction came out of nowhere: fighting was not his strong point, and he tended to avoid it. But that time he clenched a fist, drew back his arm, and punched Don Alfredo.

I felt a jolt of excitement, and I didn't pray to Jesus for forgiveness, 'cause I was sure Jesus felt the same. Art's blow was feeble, but then again, so was Don Alfredo, and he stumbled and almost fell. At the last moment he caught a corner of the sofa, and pulled himself back up. Mauro caught hold of Art's arms, from behind, to keep him from hitting the priest again. Blood was pouring from Don Alfredo's nose. 'Don't you dare use my mum's funeral as leverage!' Art shouted, wriggling to break free. '*Don't you dare!*'

'Art, calm down,' Mauro said.

The priest shouted back, wagging his finger like a censer during an exorcism. 'You filth! You can forget the funeral and—'

I interrupted him, 'We did pay.'

'I don't care for your money!'

'Yes,' Mauro said, in flat voice. 'Yes, you do.'

And boy, was he right. We had to fork out three hundred more to calm him down, but in the end Don Alfredo accepted our apologies and clutched his talons on our notes. When we drew Art away, Art apologised, 'That cost you.'

'Totally worth it,' I said.

Mauro laughed. 'Agreed.'

We drove to Art's. When we got inside, the familiar scent of his house enveloped me. Meat hung to cure, young wine, boiled greens, that was the scent of the last peasant households in Casalfranco. With Art's mum gone, this was one more place from where that scent would disappear forever.

The dough was still on the table. Some orecchiette were neatly lined, until the lines became a mess of squashed pasta.

Art's mum jerked and jolted in her last moments of life, while high-voltage electricity burned her from the inside. She'd left on her prized table a physical trace of her death.

That was when Art started sobbing.

It took me a little while to get it. *Art was crying.* I'd seen him swimming in a storm, giving his middle finger to an entire town, organising with cold efficiency his dad's funeral. I didn't think he had it in himself to cry.

'Hey,' Mauro said. 'Do you want a moment?'

'No, please. Stay.'

Mauro filled a glass with tap water, while I stood transfixed, and Art cried, standing at the marble table. Mauro said, 'Here.'

Art sipped his water. 'What you guys are doing for me is… beyond words.'

'Stop it,' I said.

'I hate crying. It's pointless.'

'Your mum died. Crying is just normal.'

Art looked at me, puzzled. 'But I'm not crying for Mum's death.'

'You aren't…?'

'I'm crying for her *life.*' He took an orecchietta between thumb and index finger. 'She died while making *pasta*, for Christ's sake! That was the last thing she did, rolling out dough in the form of an ear, the last actions her brain thought of, her muscles carried out. *Rolling out dough in the form of an ear.* How's that for a meaningful life? And what was her biggest dream? Having an asshole muttering empty words over her body!'

'She was happy with her life,' Mauro said, quietly.

'Her life was small. So small! This house, this town, this fucking *world*, everything's so incredibly small. Mum let that asshole tell her how she should behave, how she should dress to get to *Heaven*, as if he knew jack shit about the Hidden Things. Mum spent her life doing as she was told and accepting being… small. So clever, so smart, and small as fuck.' He paused. 'Like mother, like son. I've been small for too long. It's time to…' He stopped.

'To?' Mauro prompted.

'Rise.'

After the funeral, Art didn't return to Prague. He stayed in Casalfranco and never moved out again. I should have known that he was cooking something up.

He always was.

9

'Rocco is a moron,' says Mauro.

We're sitting in the porch of a roadside bar on the Litoranea, snacking on pistachios and black olives, and drinking Campari. The bar is built, for reasons I can't begin to fathom, in a style reminiscent of an alpine lodge. We face the beach, on the other side of a narrow two-lane road. A shrine to the Virgin Mary, comprised of a statue with vacant glass eyes and offerings of flowers and candles, lies half-hidden in the broom on the border where sand and tarmac meet. 'I agree.'

Fabio's pale, and, behind his sunglasses, he looks like he

doesn't want to talk, or listen, or live. He has told Mauro about his dad's Alzheimer's.

'Do we have a way to verify the healing story?' Mauro asks.

I cast a glance at the barista, who sits inside watching TV. He's tall and wiry, and he has skin like leather. It's not that he'll keep what he hears to himself; he won't hear anything in the first place. 'It's tricky. Rocco didn't name names. But I've got an acquaintance who works in surgery in Casalfranco and he's asking around. I told him it's for a paper I'm writing.'

'Your working hypothesis being…?'

'Unexpected healings do happen. Art might have got lucky somehow.'

'Art had dealings with the Corona,' Mauro says. 'That's *huge*, even for him. How far can we trust Rocco that they're not involved in Art's disappearance?'

'Fifty-fifty. He's right that the Carabinieri won't give a shit, though.'

'And you know that because…?'

'I've talked to them.'

I'm prepared for a telling-off that doesn't come. Mauro calmly pries open a pistachio and brings it to his mouth. 'You didn't even pique their interest?'

'Not in the least.'

'It's like the other time,' Fabio says, the first words he pronounced since we ordered our *aperitivo*. 'Art's gone and we're left to wonder where he is.'

For a fleeting moment Mauro looks like the teenager I used

to know. There is a shade of that boy on his face – he was the quietest of us, the one who thought before acting. Then his lips curve down in a weary expression and he's a grown-up again, a man in a line of work entirely made of grey areas. He says, 'Let's lay all our cards on the table, shall we? At fourteen, Art was kidnapped. Do we all agree on this?'

I do. Fabio makes a gesture with his chin that might be a nod.

'Those who kidnapped him, whoever they were, they had good reasons to trust Art wouldn't talk, even to his family and closest friends. Otherwise, they would've simply killed him. Making away with a body is easy: you tie a big rock to its feet, load it on a sailing boat, and chuck it into the waves. No noise, no trouble, no leftovers.'

I'm dazed. We're opening up a twenty-two-year-old can of worms, and the worms had time to rot and putrefy and generate worse creatures.

Mauro goes on, relentlessly, 'My feeling is that Art's abduction was a case of sexual abuse.'

Fabio says, 'They didn't find any trace of violence.'

'Seven days of blowjobs might leave little trace,' Mauro says. 'Especially if you don't look very hard.'

I ask, 'What are you getting at?'

'We know for a fact that Art was kidnapped as a boy. We know for a fact that, after his mum's death, he decided to stay in Casalfranco. It seems reasonable to suppose that he dug up his kidnapping from wherever he had blocked it for the last two decades, and that became his new obsession. Then –

he vanishes again. Maybe he caught up with the kidnapper, maybe the kidnapper caught up with him. Either way, there was a showdown and it didn't go down well.'

And at last I put all the pieces together. Shit, how *dense* I am. 'You think Art is dead.'

Mauro says, in his deadpan voice, 'Art *is* dead. Probably killed by the person, or persons, who abducted him twenty years ago.'

'But he had… he *has* the Corona's protection!'

'He had a *business licence*, that's all he had.'

'Why must he be dead? They might have kidnapped him again.'

'Yeah, to ask for a ransom from his rich relatives. Tony, get a grip. They killed him, they killed his dog, and they found two big rocks and two pieces of rope.'

Fabio says, 'The story of the little girl is really odd though.'

'Jesus could resurrect the dead, and he still ended up on a cross.'

I know death; I meet it every day. I've had patients dying in my hands. I've used scalpels to cut human corpses. This is different though. This is a part of me, of my youth, leaving forever. I know in my gut that Mauro's theory makes sense. 'Art is dead,' I force myself to admit. 'Mauro is right: Art is dead and no one will look into it.'

Mauro's voice is bitter. 'I've seen that a lot. It's easy for lonely people to slip under the radar. Then, one day, a distant cousin comes knocking at my door, wondering if their relative had a stash of money under the mattress, and if I could find it for them, please. Art has nobody, and it takes nothing for one like him to be lost.'

'Art has *us*,' I say, looking Mauro in the eyes. I pray he's not going to say that we should calm down and return to our lives, because in that case, honest to God, I will head-butt him.

'Yes,' he says. 'Yes, he has us.'

Fabio says, 'I went to the olive grove yesterday.' He's locking eyes with the statue of the Virgin in a staring contest he can't win. 'There's a hanged dog down there.'

10

Mauro and I make our way to the olive grove through a red, rocky field, at sunset. We want to see the dog with our own eyes. I'll snap a photograph too – I don't know what for, but it might come in handy. Fabio excused himself and went back home (in his words, *to my father's place*), mumbling about a Skype date with Lara. We'll catch up for dinner.

'What's wrong with him?' Mauro asks. 'He's got the face of a man on the verge of a breakdown.'

'Angelo's Alzheimer's…'

'Must be more than that.'

'I promised not to tell you.'

'You're going to do it anyway.'

Yes, I am. Loyalty is one of those tricky things which you have to stretch, every now and then, in order to preserve it. 'He's broke.'

'Wrong investments?'

'No investments *at all*. He actually never made it as a photographer.'

'But I thought…'

'His name returns a few hits on Google. That has nothing to do with having money, as he made abundantly clear just after shooting the cat all over my shoes.'

'But he shot high-profile stories! Stuff for *Vogue*, if I remember.'

'Some. Enough to build a name, not a bank account.'

Mauro stops. He's a difficult man to read, but I can see he's surprised. 'Why did he never tell us?'

I don't answer.

Mauro looks at the olive grove, then at me. 'Don't you hate it sometimes? Being a grown-up. Get a job, get a better one, pay taxes, pay more taxes, same old, same old. We are only alive at weekends; the rest of the time, we're hamsters in a wheel. And we can never quit spinning, 'cause there's always another bill, another mortgage, another… what the hell, another *brat*, to keep the wheel turning.'

'It is what it is. Once upon a time you had to go get mammoths, now you go get credit cards. On the plus side, we don't have to risk our neck every day.'

'Yeah, but at least with hunting you knew what you got.'

We enter the grove. There is a rotten smell in the air, very much like work. Like the morgue. This place triggers bad memories, but that's all they are – memories, things in the past, holding no power anymore. It's the present that can jump up and bite your ass.

'Do you see any dogs in here?' Mauro asks after a while.

We scoured the grove twice. If there was a shaggy dog hanging from a tree, we would've seen it. I take off my shades – it's getting dark – and scan my eyes around one last time. '*Nada*.'

Mauro bends his neck upwards to look at the olive branches. They might as well be sculptures for how little they move. 'Do you believe Fabio had an hallucination?'

'No, of course not.'

'Me neither.'

I say, 'I don't like where you're going.'

'Again, me neither.' Mauro makes a weary smile. 'Someone took down the dog.'

'They stumbled upon it? They took pity and…'

'*By coincidence* a dog ends up hung here, of all places, just when Art vanishes again, and *by coincidence* someone takes it down exactly when we start looking? As Art used to say, a coincidence is…'

'…a system we don't understand yet.'

Mauro nods. 'There's a system at work here.'

'And we're far from understanding it.'

Mauro rests both his open palms on the bark of a tree, like a hippie trying to commune with its spirit. He sighs and turns to me. 'I'm thinking we should search Art's house.'

'Changed your mind?'

'Let me be clear: this is not a TV series. We won't find the bad guys on our own, we won't trap them with a cunning plan cooked up amongst buddies, in a crescendo of emotions.

That's not how it works down in the gutter of the real world.'

'There's no need to be patronising.'

'Just want us to be aligned. Amateur sleuths don't solve crimes.'

'Why go back and search then?'

'Because Art's only got us.' Mauro pauses. 'And because we've only got us, too. Getting a rough idea of what's going on might be the prudent thing to do, for us, for the living.'

In a dark blue sky, a white moon rises beyond the trees.

I'm starting to understand why Fabio is so scared of this grove.

11

We have dinner at a beachside restaurant, a type of eatery which was once very common. The front is a regular fishmonger. You pick your choice of fresh fish from a stall, where it is still squirming over layers of ice, and the cook grills it for you. Nothing's fancy, but everything's delicious.

The cook is a tanned bald man, with a belly as huge as Elena's. We have our dinner with the murmur of waves in the background. The tables and the chairs are plastic, but there is a touch of dolling up − fairy lights have been strung from the wooden staves holding the pergola above our heads. It always starts with fairy lights, and ends up with another good restaurant transformed into a tourist trap.

I have a good time, considering. Art might be dead, but

tonight we're alive and we're together and he'd love to see this. Some colour has returned to Fabio's cheeks. After a few drinks, he and Anna kick off their shoes and go on the beach for a walk and a cigarette. They come back announcing that Fabio will take some photographs of Anna for his book. Mauro is happy about that. Fabio loves Anna as a sister, and right now he needs every last friend he can get.

After the dessert, Mauro clears his throat, and raises his glass of Fernet. 'To Art,' he says. 'A great man.'

We all say, 'To Art!' Even Anna, and Ottavia and Rebecca, who toast with Coca-Cola. I will mourn my mate, but not now. My brain accepts he's probably dead, the rest of me hangs on to that *probably*.

I drive back home pleasantly fuzzy. I find Mum waiting for me in the living room, lounging in her rattan armchair in front of the TV. She used to do the same when I was at school; at whatever time I would come back, she would be there, waiting. She used to curl up, but arthritis doesn't allow that anymore. She was once a figure of power, and now she looks so frail, with her white hair and her face cracked like a broken windscreen. She sits in the same spot, in the same chair, and it's like she is a rock and time is the sea, washing her away wave after wave. I pray it won't take her from me too soon.

'Hey, Mum,' I say.

She turns off the TV. 'Elena left a note for you.' She points her chin to the table, where a closed envelope sits.

'Thank you.'

'Is this something to do with her husband?'

I freeze. 'Mum…'

'Just answer the question, Tony, it's not that hard.'

'No: it's not about Rocco.' Stretching loyalty again.

Mum exhales. 'You should talk to her.'

'Mum, we had this discussion a thousand times.'

'How could my daughter marry *that* man?'

'He loves her, she loves him.'

Mum scoffs. 'I wish he would die,' she says, her voice stone cold. 'I can't sleep at night when I think that *my grandson* will be raised a…' She stops, and sighs. 'I wish he would die,' she repeats.

'Me too,' I say, sincerely.

'Will you talk to her?'

'Sure.' It takes so little to make Mum feel better. I kiss her on her forehead. 'Go to bed, Mum.'

She closes her eyes and smiles, and I figure that, when she does that, she imagines that I'm still eleven, and Elena is five, and everything is easy, and that blessed moment of her life will never pass. 'Good night, Tony.'

'Good night.'

She shuffles to her bedroom, and I open the envelope, my good mood crushed and buried. There's a slip of paper, with a time and place written on it. I memorise them, then take a box of matches from the kitchen, go to the fireplace, and set the paper alight.

12

Fabio and Mauro promised they will come to the appointment Rocco gave me. That's tonight, though: the day is all about searching Art's house. We are taking a moment to look at it before heading inside, our eyes shielded behind sunglasses. It is just in front of us, at the end of the lane. Surrounding it on all sides is Art's family plot, roughly half of which is the unkempt vineyard, while the other half is just wild plants, rocks and red dirt. At the back is the trullo, as small as a toy from this distance. The brutal sunlight makes everything tremble, as it did when we were little, as it will do long after we're dead and gone.

'Let's get cracking,' Mauro says, opening the door.

The plan is to search the house and the fields. I get a pot of coffee going, while Fabio hits the books in the kitchen. A lot of people are converting to electric coffee makers, but Art stuck to the old ones, those that you fill with water and powdered coffee and put on the hob. Soon enough the sound of the pot, like a person gargling, fills the air, together with the heartening aroma of coffee. Mauro and I leave Fabio at the table with a cup of espresso.

'Shall we start in the bedroom?' Mauro asks.

'You're the expert at investigation.'

'In finance. I'm an expert at spreadsheets.'

We start in the bedroom. The bed stinks of stale sweat, and the stains on the linen leave nothing to the imagination. 'Art has been seeing a lot of action.' That cheers me up. If you're going to die, better if it happens after a good fuck or three.

'It'd be interesting to know with whom,' Mauro says, distractedly, while he rummages through the mess of clothes on the floor.

'Always the romantic.'

'This is the least romantic place I can imagine.'

We move on to the book jungle. Getting inside is not easy, with the columns of books blocking the way. Most of them are practically floor to ceiling. I bow to Mauro and gesture to him to go in first. 'Where's your trusted machete when you need it?'

Mauro makes a perfunctory chuckle and starts wading through the books, moving an encyclopaedia out of his way, kicking away a coffee-table book on Saracen towers. 'Look,' he says.

We come across what I can only call a *glade* in the book jungle, small and Art-shaped; the columns encircle a cushion on the floor, an Olivetti typewriter and a pile of blank paper. We stare at the tableau. A *typewriter*. I feel something close to awe for the mounting strangeness of this house.

'My God.' I drop to one knee and brush two fingers on the typewriter's ribbon. My skin gets smudged. 'How did we come to this? Art is, gosh this is hard, he's a… hipster!'

'What do you think he was writing?'

I stand up again, spreading my arms wide to embrace the room. 'The truth is out there.'

Mauro glances at the books, dubious. 'What do we do now? Fields?'

'Hang on, didn't there used to be a basement?'

'You're right. Where Art's dad kept the wine.'

'I bloody loved making it.'

Every year Art's dad made wine for his family, and we helped, by squashing the grapes with our naked feet, jumping inside a wooden press. It was messy and noisy, the only good thing about the end of summer.

'The door was outside, right?' I say.

'I think so.'

It's at the back, close to the kitchen door. It doesn't have a lock, or any electricity, just a torch on a nail at the mouth of the staircase. Mauro picks up the torch and we go down stone steps, worn and slippery. It's positively cold, a stark contrast with the burning heat outside. I take a long breath, hoping to find the smell of grapes I liked so much. I gag and cough. Rather than grapes, I inhale a stink I know all too well, of blood and shit and bacteria gone nuts. It's how bodies smell when you slice them open.

The staircase ends in a simple square room, with a table at the back wall. On a rack are neat rows of sharp-edged implements. Some are butcher's tools, others are smaller; at a glance, I make out three surgical-quality scalpels. Dark stains are splashed on the table and the floor. An apron, covered in more brown splashes, hangs next to the rack.

I close my eyes and pinch my nose. This can't be happening. This can't be Art. This is a place of hope, laughter and sweet grapes.

'It's a slaughterhouse,' Mauro whispers.

13

In the trullo we don't find anything remarkable that I hadn't already seen. Mauro knows even less than me about BDSM (I wouldn't necessarily have bet on that). He's not shocked; after the slaughterhouse, what's in the trullo has all the emotional impact of a stamp collection. As for the slaughterhouse, I don't know. It's common enough for country folk down here to butcher their own animals. Admittedly, it's far less common to drag them down a staircase and use surgical implements on them. I refuse to think about that right now. I can't afford to freak out.

We search the car, where the only thing of interest is a fat bag of weed stuck in the glovebox. I pocket it – Art wouldn't want to see his produce go to waste. Then we move to the fields, the part we're dreading. We start from the tall marijuana plants. They're green and strong, even though they've not been attended for a while (Art always said that marijuana is easy; a five-year-old can grow it). From there we move to comb the vineyard. When we finish it's mid-afternoon and so hot I could melt. Mauro and I are shirtless and sweaty.

'Nothing here,' he announces.

I shake my head. We don't need to add what we both think – *thank God*. When you find a slaughterhouse in your mate's basement, you kind of expect to find, on top of that, a mound of freshly dug dirt in his garden. It's one of those cases where no news is good news.

'Gelato run?' I suggest.

'You serious?'

'Sure.'

'You're a god among mortals.'

I leave Mauro and Fabio at the house and drive to the closest gelato parlour, a few miles towards town. I buy a tub of chocolate gelato with three paper spoons, and head quickly back to Art's, racing against the inexorable melting of my cold, sweet booty. A Mercedes slows me down. I curse it. This lane is too narrow for me to overtake, and all I can do is make puppy eyes at the polystyrene tub and pray the gelato won't be a puddle by the time I arrive.

The Mercedes turns into Art's lane.

All the alarms in my head go off. I fumble for my mobile, then I remember there's no signal here. I follow the car into the lane. The sun beats on my face, blinding me. Even with my shades on I can't see who's driving. I press on the pedal – let the fuckers know I'm on them. They might be random guys who took a wrong turn. Well, a little scare won't hurt them.

The Mercedes stops. I stop too, unsure of what's next.

Suddenly the Mercedes comes back to life – in reverse. A scenario goes through my mind: the sturdy Mercedes hitting my parents' humble Fiat, making an accordion of it and squashing my body like a mosquito. I press on the pedal and yank the wheel to the right, and I get out of the lane and into the field. The Mercedes misses me by a whisker. I hit a rock, hard, and something in my poor car makes a loud noise, and I come to a sudden halt.

'Fuckers!' I shout, turning my head and unlocking the belt, ready to fight.

The Mercedes doesn't stop. It continues its run in reverse, and it's gone.

Fuckers.

I have their number plate.

14

My front right wheel is wrecked. I note down the plate number on my phone before I forget it, then I leave the car and run down the lane. Mauro and Fabio come to meet me midway, both shaken. I guess theirs is the grown-up reaction, not mine. If it weren't for the damn wheel, I'd chase the Mercedes and beat the crap out of whoever is on board. I shake the polystyrene tub. 'Those assholes were after our gelato.'

'How's the car?' Fabio asks.

'We've got to change a wheel.'

Mauro starts, 'What the hell…'

'Gelato first,' I stop him. 'You gotta know your priorities.'

'We'll eat while working,' Fabio says.

'No hurry.'

'Say the Mercedes guy comes back.'

'I'm counting on that.'

'Say he comes back *with friends*.'

I pause, then concede, 'I don't like it when you're right.'

'Yeah, me neither.'

While I open the boot to get the jack, Fabio and Mauro throw themselves on the gelato. I set the jack under the car, recounting the details of my brief rendezvous with the Mercedes. 'I took the number plate, for what it's worth.'

Mauro hands me the gelato tub and a spoon, saying, 'I can trace the vehicle's owner.'

'That easy?'

'I have a guy.'

'You couldn't wait to say that, could you?'

'Guilty as charged,' Mauro says. I can't believe I wrenched half a joke out of him. I pass the tub to Fabio, and Mauro helps me to take the new wheel out of the boot.

Fabio scoops gelato saying, 'I've seen the typewriter.'

I start to dismantle the wrecked wheel. Fabio and Mauro aren't any good with cars; I'll do this quicker on my own. 'Did Mauro tell you about the… basement?'

'Yeah.'

'Fortunately, we found nothing else in the fields,' Mauro says. 'No trace of Art's dog, either.'

I ask, 'Any wisdom in the books?'

'Some,' Fabio replies, and his voice means, *a lot*. He takes a piece of paper out of a pocket and holds it out. I stop what I'm doing to look at it. At its centre, it's typewritten:

THE BOOK OF HIDDEN THINGS

A FIELD GUIDE

I seize it and turn it over. The other side is filled with Art's minute handwriting. I need to bring the piece of paper closer

to my eyes to discern what's on it: a sequence of numbers and
brief notes, separated by small dashes.

27: the dunes on that beach are especially rich in broom. –
32: see if it's true that salt marshes were already there in the
 XIst century. I should touch upon that in TBOHT.

'Art's note-taking system,' Fabio explains. 'Not exactly user-
friendly. He'd write down on a piece of paper the numbers
of the pages of a book that caught his interest, with either a
quote or a brief note, and then keep the paper inside the book.
There's a piece like that in almost every book in this house.'

I pass the paper to Mauro and go back to the wheel.

'And *The Book of Hidden Things* is…?' Mauro asks.

'Something Art was writing. He took an awful lot of notes,
like, "Good for *The Book of Hidden Things*", or, "Remember this
for *TBOHT*."'

'So Art's Project is a *book*?'

'Might be.'

'Like when he did the *Metamorphoses*?' The comic book that
convinced Art to screw up his big chance with Stanford. It got
him rave reviews but the money wasn't great. Not that Art had
any fucks to give about either.

'It's not a graphic novel. It's non-fiction this time.'

'About *what*?'

'Art didn't leave any drafts lying around. I can only go by his
notes, and from that, I guess…' Fabio's voice trails off. '*The Book
of Hidden Things* is about Casalfranco's countryside, plus religion.'

I'm screwing in the bolts – ten minutes and we're good to go. 'Art loathed both.'

'It's a good theme for a book. This countryside is overflowing with churches, chapels, shrines, so on and so forth. Art was focusing on a handful of places, which he was using, if I get it right, to illustrate a general point about the connection of physical spaces and, ah, spirituality.'

'You're telling me Art moved back to a place he hated to write a book on *folklore*? While setting up a torture chamber in his trullo and a God-knows-what in the basement?'

'Art wasn't well,' Fabio says.

'Carolina said the Project was related to the first time Art disappeared.'

'Ah, but there *is* a connection: the olive grove. I found some old registers Art borrowed from the town library and never returned. You guys want to guess who owns the grove?'

I say, 'Not particularly, no.'

'It's *the Church*, Casalfranco's *chiesa matrice* to be precise. In practice, Don Alfredo.'

I bury my head in the work I'm doing, to hide my surprise. 'With all the things people said at the time, nobody talked about that.'

'Well, of course the Church didn't want to be involved with Art's disappearance.' He pauses. 'Or Don Alfredo is more involved than we think.'

'I know where you're going, Fabio, and I'll stop you right there. I don't care for him either, but he's not a child fiddler.'

'Yeah, because a paedophile priest would be totally new.'

'Don Alfredo never…'

'Don Alfredo was *never found out*, which is different. A hell of a lot of priests all over the world weren't, until a little time ago, and there's many more who never will be.'

'That's a strong allegation,' Mauro says.

'Look, I'm just saying that a kid went missing in a priest's property in a period when we know for a fact priests were using kids as their playmates. Art's family could have told Don Alfredo all sorts of things in confession, or other people told things about them, it doesn't matter. He's the senior priest, he knows *everything*.'

Mauro says, 'He might have had something which kept Art's mouth shut.'

Fabio nods. 'Then Art's parents died and Art came back to Casalfranco, to have a go at him.'

'And he started writing a *book*?' I ask.

'He wasn't well!' Fabio repeats. 'How many times do I need to say that? *Art wasn't fucking well*. He kept a slaughterhouse in his basement, for Christ's sake! He was looking for a way to get back at Don Alfredo, and he got sidetracked, discovering an interest in landscape and religion. A new phase began. That's Art through and through.'

'He healed a girl,' I say. 'Supposedly.'

'It's religious obsession all the way down. I'm sure Jesus meant it when he proclaimed himself as a messiah, and I can see Art climbing on a soapbox in a piazza and proclaiming that actually, now that he thinks of it, he's one too.'

Mauro says, 'It doesn't explain the abattoir, the dungeon.

Or what happened to Art this time.'

'It explains what happened *then* and that's a start.'

I stand up, covered in grease and dirt. 'We're good to go,' I say. 'Are you still up for tonight?'

15

I walk to the church through stone alleys, all crooked, with their uneven pavement and their white houses that seem forever to be crumbling down but never do. The church itself is a tall Romanesque building in a tiny piazza, with a front rose window and two lions guarding the door. Before entering I pat the head of the lion on the right, as I've done since I was a little kid. I step inside, into the silence and darkness, and inhale the smell of incense. It never fails to make me feel safe. I dip a finger in the holy-water stoup, trace a cross on my forehead, and bow in the direction of the tabernacle.

The church is nearly empty; my only company is two elderly women, small and withered, with black shoes, black gowns, black cardigans, and black veils over their heads. The House of God belongs to them more than me. Until I reconsider my shagging choices, I'm not allowed to receive Holy Communion – I'm excluded. It hurts. It's a beautiful thing, to know that the son of God accepted incarnation, suffering and death for us, and that we can share His body and blood. *His body and bollocks*, Fabio would say. He's at ease with Mauro's faith, but not with mine, first, because Mauro's is more superficial than mine, second, because of where I stick my penis. He says, *Priests go on preaching that you're a perv.* I know, I know. Many priests are like that. Not all though. The Church is not about priests, anyway, it's about Jesus Christ, and I could share a couple of ideas about how he and his disciples entertained themselves on Palestinian nights.

My Lord, I pray. *Is Art with you? I'm sure You opened to him the doors of Heaven. He was a good man, You know that, of course You do. He was always there for his buddies. Always pushing us to be the best we could be. He didn't believe in You, but You don't mind, do You? All that matters to You is what lies inside our hearts, and Art's heart was gold. He was too smart for his own good, but isn't it sad, my Lord, that Your children made a society where being too smart is a bad thing? My Lord, I promise that I'll do my best to give Art the justice of men, the only justice in our hands.*

Speaking of which.

I hope I'm doing the right thing tonight. I'm not condoning evil, my Lord, I'm only trying to do good. Lend me Your strength and let me keep my moral compass. You know how lost I can be, without Your hand guiding me. Protect me and my friends tonight, my Lord. Protect us.

Protect us from evil tonight.

16

The fires blaze in the distance. They shine yellow and orange beyond the olive trees, in the absolute darkness and flatness of the land. The moon is a sharp-edged crescent; the flames reach out to it, like hands striving to grab it for savage purposes.

'Kill the engine,' Fabio says.

'We're not close enough.'

'Kill it!'

I pull over at the edge of a field of olive trees. Ours is the only car for a good few miles, and when I turn off the engine and the lights, we might as well not exist either.

'Can you hear that?' Fabio whispers.

A rhythm of drums and human voices, faint, as if coming from another world.

'Holy fuck,' Mauro says, under his breath.

I say, 'You guys can still sit this out.'

'Don't be stupid. But what the hell is that?'

'No idea. Fabio, can you reach in the glove compartment? I brought a pick-me-up.'

Fabio fishes out a bottle of rum. He takes a sip and hands it to me. I drink a little and turn towards the back seat, to hand the bottle to Mauro.

'It's going to be fine,' I say, starting the car again. 'Rocco wouldn't send us here if it wasn't safe.'

I take one or two wrong turns, lanes giving on to open fields, and have to double back. I tried to convince my mates not to come with me, honestly, but they wouldn't hear reason. 'What did Anna say about tonight?' I ask.

Mauro replies, 'She's understanding but not *that* understanding. I cobbled together a story about an acquaintance of Art we wanted to talk to.'

I bite my tongue. Lying to your partner? Not good.

I finally find the right lane, an unpaved stretch of road

cutting through barren fields. The drums are so loud now I can hear them over the engine. Two men are standing at the end of the lane. One gestures us to stop. They both carry guns, holstered, but in plain sight. Another field behind them has become a temporary parking lot. I stop the car, kill the engine, and roll down the window. I put my hands on the wheel. Fabio and Mauro take my cue and keep their hands visible too.

The men approach us from both sides of the car. '*Ccè bbuliti?*' the one on my side asks, in thick dialect. *What do you want?*

'I'm Rocco's in-law.' I hope it's the right answer.

'Elena's brother?'

I'm a little taken aback by my sister's name. 'Yeah.'

He looks in the car. 'And you guys?'

'I'm Fabio.'

'Mauro.'

The man seems satisfied. 'Elena wasn't sure you were all coming.'

'They wouldn't miss it for the world,' I say.

The men let us pass, and I park the car next to a grey BMW. They search us, with detached competence, then point us towards the fires. 'Have fun,' they say.

17

The music is a *taranta* played on tambourines and harmonicas. The fields beyond the car park, Mediterranean scrub with occasional olive trees, are ablaze. Three bonfires burn tall, at a distance from one another, forming a large triangle. There's a lot more fire than that; everywhere I look, I see oil lanterns on bamboo sticks. The flames are the only source of light for miles. They throw shadows around, of people, shrubs and knobbly trees, and those shadows twirl with the shifting of so many flames. The shadows grow big and small. They change. They melt into one another, skimming across human skin and vegetation, only to move away soon after. They are a living duplicate of our world of flesh and bones, a duplicate which is no less real, and no less able to reach out, and hurt, than the original.

The air is thick with smoke and the bitter aroma of *jummarieddi*. A short man with a sunburnt face sits at a huge pit filled with burning coals, where he is roasting meat on long skewers. *Jummarieddi* are the most intensely scented thing humankind has ever put on a grill, with a flavour to boot. They are among the last survivors of a less tame age. To make them you take the entrails (kidney, liver, everything goes) of a freshly slain lamb, or a goat as a second choice, wash them with water, salt and lemon, and season them with more salt, pepper, bay, parsley, and basically whatever herb you happen to have in your back garden (where chances are you've just killed the animal). Then you roll everything in the lamb's peritoneum, stick the roll on a skewer, and put the skewer on hot coals. *An acquired taste*, people not from here define *jummarieddi*, but only when they're being polite. You don't find them much in tourist restaurants. They make my mouth water.

Next to the coal-filled pit is a table loaded with paper cups, and next to it, a row of wooden wine casks. There's not a drop of water in sight; the notion of teetotal never made it this far south.

Give or take, there are a hundred people in the field, maybe a few more. Men outnumber women ten to one. Maybe a few more. Some are crowded around the pit, drinking wine, chatting in small knots. The majority of them, though, are gathered in the space between the three bonfires. Their backs move excitedly, and when their shifting and rocking offers me a glimpse of what lies beyond, I see a *ronda* in full swing.

It is made of three concentric circles. The outermost is a circle of spectators, watching the show. Inside that is a circle of oil lanterns, and inside that, the third and last circle, is a circle of men, only men, making music with tambourines, harmonicas, or simply clapping their hands. At the centre of the three circles, at the heart of the ritual, two men are dancing, and fighting.

'The Dance of the Swords,' Fabio whispers.

Mauro adds, 'The unabridged edition.'

One of the men at the centre must be in his forties. He's bare-chested and covered in sweat. His skin sparkles in the flames. His opponent – his *partner* – is barely in his twenties, skinny as a dead twig, with his white shirt flapping out of the trousers. Each of them points two fingers towards the other, pretending the fingers are knives. They use the fingers to thrust, cut and block, exactly as if they were knives. It's not just a dance, and it's not properly a fight.

I've seen a Dance of the Swords in the past, in a sanitised form. It's a strange dance, born in the criminal underground of Salento, and protected, so the legend goes, by none other than San Rocco, a popular saint among peasants. The dance was

143

supposed to be how criminals kept their fighting skills honed in prison. The dancing part is more than a little misleading though; the fighters do follow the rhythm of the *taranta*, but, at the same time, they also try to outdo their adversary. They have to keep track of both things at once: the dance and the fight, the music and the bloodlust. I can't move my eyes from the *ronda*.

'I'd kill for some *jummarieddi*,' Fabio says.

'We're at a Sacra Corona Unita get-together; mind the words you use,' Mauro finds in himself to joke.

Their words snap me out of the dance's spell. While we gravitate towards the burning coals a happy voice shouts, 'Hey!'

Elena is waving at me. *What the fuck?* Rocco should be here, not her. She should be safe at home, not in the fields among criminals. We need to talk, me and her.

'Easy,' Mauro murmurs.

I force my facial muscles to fake a smile, and wave back. I point to the *jummarieddi* with an enthusiasm I don't feel, and pat my belly saying 'Good food!'

'I'm so glad you came!' Elena says.

'So would I be if I knew what we'd come to.'

'Oh, come on. Mum and Dad brought us to see the Dance of Swords when I was… what? Seven?'

I pay for a plate of *jummarieddi*. 'Six. But that was in the centre of town and well advertised, not in the middle of nowhere and secret.'

'This is the real thing. It's like *jummarieddi*, you know? Too strong a flavour for the tourists. Mauro! Fabio! Long time no see.'

'Since your wedding,' Fabio replies. He points at her belly. 'Oh, and by the way, congratulations.'

'Thank you. Do you guys want a rundown of what to expect?'

Mauro says, 'Please.'

I know how Mauro's mind works. He's taking in everything about the situation, the people involved, already thinking of ways to get out of trouble in a court, if we end up in court. Which is unlikely. What trouble arises here is sorted far from the prying lights of civilisation.

Elena points at the *ronda*. 'They're only warming up. When they're ready they'll get the blades out.'

'For real?' I ask.

'Sure.' She points to a poised man in his fifties, with a flat cap and a denim jacket. 'That's Gianpiero. You want to place a bet, you talk to him.'

'A bet on a dance?'

'A bet on a fight.'

'How do you tell who the winner is?'

'The dance stops at first, second or third blood. Before entering the *ronda* each two dancers decide how far they'll go.'

Elena is in her element here. I could cry – or, even better, smash things and faces. It is all I can do not to shout at her to run back home immediately, to Mum and Dad and an honest life, and be the good girl she was raised to be. I don't have that authority anymore, if I ever did. 'What are we doing here? Me and my mates, I mean.'

'Someone'll talk to you.'

'And where's Rocco?'

'At work,' Elena replies.

18

My little sister returns to the crowd after buying us three cups of wine. Nothing for her, because she's pregnant and she's a good mother. I follow her with my eyes as she makes herself busy smiling and waving and talking to people. She has a lot of friends. They treat her like a man, the highest accolade there is.

'I'm sorry,' Fabio says.

'She's not a bad person.'

'Of course.'

The *jummarieddi* are a thing of awe, bitter in an absolutely delicious way, like I hadn't tasted since Art's dad got ill. We wander to the *ronda*, to follow the dance, or the fight, or whatever it is. The pace of the music becomes faster, and after draining my cup and polishing off the meat, I find myself tapping a foot to the beat. Elena, Art, all my worries fade away; the drums and the dancers' movements pin me to here and now, to the circle, to the blades. I recognise the hypnosis for what it is – sure I do – but I won't, or can't, resist. It's like being possessed by some spirit who heard the call of the *taranta*, the knives, the entrails on burning coals.

Fabio leaves his empty cup on the ground and starts clapping his hands. We're joining something bigger; we're part of the music now, part of the dance. The dancers wave their arms and shift their feet to the music, and the music is the rope bonding us to them, bonding all bodies sweating together in the circle, the fighters and the musicians and us common mortals. Clapping my hands feels almost like being at the centre, with a blade in my hand and another man to bring down. Who knows how it would feel to really dance. I would have a great time.

I glance at Mauro, beyond Fabio's laughing face. Mauro is motionless, his wine barely touched, his eyes attentive.

The dancers merge back with the circle, and two new dancers step forward, both bare-chested, both glinting with the reflected light of the fires. They are more or less our age, one of them with raven-black hair tied in a ponytail, the other completely shaved. I root for ponytail guy. He's hot.

'Second blood!' Gianpiero shouts in the booming voice of a ringmaster.

These dancers don't waste time on heating up. After a few perfunctory steps and moves of their fingers, they draw out two nasty-looking boot blades, without stopping their dance. They start to thrust and dodge, and the smiles never leave their faces. I can't tell if they're actually trying to hit each other or just playing, where the dance ends and the fight begins. Ponytail guy suddenly plunges forward, and he seems to penetrate shaved guy's guard – only, shaved guy is dancing sideways, and ponytail guy hits air. Shaved guy doesn't: he lets his knife drop on ponytail guy's cheek, opening a gash. Blood pours all over his face. That's me: always betting on the hot guy, never the good one.

A hand taps my left shoulder.

I turn. A man stands there, a little shorter than me (and I am no giant). He might be in his seventies, and each of his years is a stone making him sturdier. He's in a pair of corduroy trousers and a white shirt, open on his chest to show a shiny golden cross. More gold – a wedding band – is wrapped around a finger. His face is marked with two scars, one on a cheek, the other on his upper lip. This guy's so dangerous that he doesn't need to show it; he has no guns, no blades, and his face wears a plain expression, not the tough-guy act you can see on the other faces here. He's the sort of man holidaymakers would find *quaint* and we locals know better than to find anything at all.

He makes a curt gesture with his head, inviting me and my mates to follow, and we oblige without saying a word. He leads us away from the *ronda*, back to the burning pit, where he gets a plate of *jummarieddi* without paying. He shovels one in his mouth and asks, 'Is it the girl?'

I say, 'Excuse me?'

'Is it the girl, that put Art in trouble?' He points at Mauro. 'Hey, Serious One. Get me a glass, *sì*?'

Mauro nods and hurries to fetch him wine. If this man wants us to be his minions for tonight, we'll be his minions for tonight, and say thank you for the opportunity.

I ask, 'Carolina, you mean?'

'That bitch counts for nothing. I'm talking about the other girl, the one Art was in love with.'

We answer with silence. *The one Art was in love with*. Mauro returns and hands the wine to the man.

Fabio says, 'We never heard of another girl.'

The man tastes the wine, looking thoughtful. 'I'm Michele,' he introduces himself. 'Don't bother with names. I know yours. Art talked about you every other day. He was always, *My mates this, my mates that.*'

'How did you know him?' I ask.

'He came to me a couple of years ago.'

'After…'

'After healing the little girl,' Michele says.

'It's true, then.'

'Yes,' Michele says. 'Yes, it's true.'

It doesn't matter whether I believe that or not. Folks like Michele are always right, in practice if not in theory, because they have the means to enforce *how* right they are. When they say you're their minion, they're right. When they say your mate is a miracle worker, they're right again.

'Oh, and by the way,' he adds. 'Rumour has it, you guys want to know her dad's name.'

Danger, my instinct shouts. 'I—'

'You'll stop that,' Michele interrupts me. 'You'll stop that immediately.'

I nod. The King wishes to stay private, he will stay private.

'Good. We can talk, though, the four of us. Art's my favourite boy. I wish him only good.' He drains half his glass of wine in one go. 'When he healed the girl, he asked her dad three things: to deal a little weed in Casalfranco, to never be bothered again, and to be put in touch with me.'

I say, 'We didn't know this part.'

'Rocco is not at liberty to discuss it. I am.'

'With all due respect, sir,' Fabio says, 'who *are* you?'

Michele touches the scar on his cheek. 'The dancing master.'

The more I find out about Art, the less I get him. 'Art wanted to learn the Dance of the Swords?'

'He learnt it all right. Best pupil I ever had; he entered the *ronda* like nothing could hurt him. He went for third blood, always. Won more than he lost.'

'I never pegged Art for the sporty type.'

Michele dismisses my comment, annoyed. 'The dance is not a *sport*. It requires skill, sure, and for most dancers that's all there is. But every now and then – very, very rarely – one like Art comes along.'

'One like Art, that is…?' Fabio asks.

I glance at Mauro, who's too intent on listening to speak.

Michele says, 'A man blessed by San Rocco. Or a saint, himself.'

I move my eyes from Michele to the *ronda*. Second blood – the dance is over. Two new dancers, younger than the last ones, are entering the circle. They can't be more than twenty, tops. The crowd cheers even more loudly. 'First blood!' Gianpiero shouts.

I say, 'I never pegged Art for the saintly type either.'

Michele scoffs. 'And what would you know?'

'I'm a good Christian.'

'Good for you, boy. You still don't know the first thing about the dance. You think it's just a bunch of thugs waving knives at each other, *sì*?'

There's no polite way to answer that, so I don't answer.

'You don't know the first thing,' Michele repeats. 'The dance belongs to San Rocco, and we dance to honour him. The moves, the music, the blades and the blood – that's how we call San Rocco upon earth, that's how we *talk* to him. The Dance of the Swords is a *prayer*, boy, and I've seen nobody pray like Art.'

For a few moments, no one speaks. The *taranta*, the cheers from the crowd, it's difficult to think of them as a prayer. The boys in the *ronda* are not signing themselves with holy water, they're drawing each other's blood.

Fabio breaks the silence, using his I'm-better-than-this-religious-hogwash voice. 'So, what did he pray for?'

Michele stares at him. 'You don't believe.'

'I'm afraid not,' Fabio says, refusing to divert his eyes. 'It doesn't change what I'm saying. Never seen a happy man praying. Those who do, they ask for something.'

Michele grimaces. 'You're going to Hell, that's your business. You're right though, we turn to the saints when we need their help. Isn't that selfish? We all pray for what we don't have: money, health. Love.'

'The girl?' I say.

'Yeah.'

I ask, 'Does she have a name?'

'Art wouldn't say. He's a prudent man, when he wants to be. He calls her *La Madama*.'

La Madama. I remember Art using those words. We all thought he was referring to Carolina. Will we ever stop being wrong about him? 'Then he danced,' I say, 'and he… prayed for the love of this woman?'

151

'For San Rocco to help him with her, *sì*.'

I let the news roll inside my head. The bottom line is, Art was sleeping with a married woman while in love with a mystery lady. Nothing strange on that front; all of Art's appetites were insatiable, until they came to an abrupt end. What surprises me is the *in love* part. I didn't think Art was wired for love. I say, 'You and Art were close.'

'I like to think so.'

'Do you know he was writing a book?'

'*The Book of Hidden Things*. He didn't show it to me. He promised he would, but he never did.'

'And when was the last time you saw him?'

'Last week,' Michele says, without hesitation. 'Eight days ago. We had coffee together.' Michele looks at the *ronda*, making it very clear that he doesn't want us to distract him now. He follows the dance with the eye of an art collector in a gallery. After a while he turns his attention back to us. 'You think Art is dead.'

It's not a question, so we don't answer.

'You're looking in the wrong place,' Michele continues. 'Art could be cocky, and not everybody got on well with him, but the boys wouldn't have lifted a finger against him. He saved an important life.'

Fabio asks, 'Is Don Alfredo on your payroll?'

My stomach leaps. This is one of those questions you never ask. Michele looks at Fabio in the way men like him look at men like us, when they are pondering what's less hassle – let your tongue blabber on, or cut it off and be done with it. 'No,' he says.

'Then he's involved somehow.'

'He's a man of the Church.'

'He's a prick.'

It's a sudden gesture, quicker than my eye. Michele raises a hand and slaps Fabio, with a downward movement, hard enough to crack Fabio's lips and spill blood. I clench my fist, ready to go. You don't leave your mates on their own in a fight – for all the good it would do. We wouldn't last two minutes out here.

A flash of anger goes through Fabio's eyes. He dabs at the blood with a hand.

Michele folds his arms and stares at him, as though challenging him to react. 'You *must* respect a servant of God,' he says.

It looks like Fabio might be stupid. He's not. He says, 'I apologise,' and I can start to make plans for the future again.

Michele ignores him and turns to me. He pats me on a cheek, amiably. 'You find anything out about Art,' he says, 'you run it through me, *sì*? Elena has my number.'

19

I drive back to Casalfranco and the modern world, my mind filled with Elena, saints, drums and blades. Fabio, riding shotgun, looks out of the window, a dark expression on his face, while Mauro, on the back seat, checks his phone.

'If I get what just happened, we're working for the Corona now,' Fabio says.

I answer, 'I wouldn't say that. We're only being friendly with a, uh, *dancing master*.'

'We don't have any choice.'

'That's also true,' I admit.

'In the parking lot I looked for the white Mercedes. It was too dark to be sure, but I don't think it was there.'

'It wasn't there,' Mauro says.

'Hey,' I say. 'Look who found his voice again.'

Mauro didn't move his eyes from the screen of his phone. 'My guy just emailed me back about the Mercedes. I don't think it's Corona.' In the back mirror, I see him frowning. 'No, it's definitely not Corona.'

FABIO

1

'I'll never forgive you for messing with my Plan,' Art said, putting his hands on Mauro's shoulders.

'Which would be?' Mauro asked.

'Sitting out the Mass. There's a nice little bench behind the church. A perfect spot for reading, that one.'

'You're not *really* planning to miss my wedding.'

'Oh, come off it, the reception is the real McCoy. In years to come, people will tell stories about what we were eating, who got drunk, and who made a pass at whom. Nobody will remember the *Mass*! They're all the same. Priest, rings, kiss, ready to go.'

Missing the Mass had been my hope too – but Mauro was adamant: he wanted Art, me and Tony to be his best men. Mauro's brother was let off the hook, officially because he'd converted to an obscure school of Buddhism in Milan, but actually because Mauro couldn't be one hundred per cent sure that his brother wouldn't drop acid during the ceremony.

That's how I found myself a stone's throw away from the main scene, dressed in a black suit, a white shirt, and a skinny black tie, when Mauro slipped a golden ring on Anna's finger and kissed her. Anna's white dress was a simple thing, with flowers embroidered on the top, a long skirt, and no veil. It was indisputably chaste, but it wrapped around her body in a way which set my imagination on fire. Graphic images kept rushing to my mind of all the things I would like to do to the bride, on the altar. I've had sex in a church once (I was shooting a catalogue in a picturesque village in Tuscany, where I met a witless, talentless, good-looking twenty-year-old student of photography, whose mother happened to have the keys to the local church), and it was delightful. But with Anna? Nothing would beat sex on an altar with Anna. Even though she was getting married to a guy who chose me over his brother as his best man.

And I found myself there, in my black suit and my Wayfarer sunglasses, when the newlyweds came out of the church, under a shower of rice thrown by their friends and family. I threw especially hard, whether to show enthusiasm or to vent my frustration I don't know. After the service, I shepherded the guests to the cars, and sat in Tony's with Art and two teenage cousins of Mauro who spent the entire trip glued to their phones. Somewhere between the church and the restaurant I managed to stop thinking about me, Anna and the feeling of a marble altar on a naked ass.

Anna and Mauro had chosen a beach restaurant, The Acacia – one of the many new places that were opening on the coast. It was a comparatively cool July afternoon, blessed by a tramontana breeze. With the waves barely moving, the sea looked like a glass showcase for the treasures of sand, rocks and fish beneath. The tables were laid out partly on the sand, partly on wooden platforms under pergolas. Everything was painted white – the tables, the chairs, the platforms, the pergolas. Surrounding the restaurant on all sides except the one facing the sea were the acacias that gave the restaurant its name, as well as juniper bushes and intensely coloured bougainvillea.

We arrived late afternoon, with the sun already giving an orange hue to the water, the sky and the white furniture. The men were dressed more or less the same as me – black suit, white shirt; most still had their sunglasses on. The women showed a little more imagination, though I missed the forest of hats I had come to expect from British weddings. I was thinking that it was the sort of setting that would inspire a hack photographer to bag some cheesy snap, when the hired photographer started doing just that, urging guests to stand with their shoulders to the sea, or to look at the sky with a raptured expression, as if they'd seen the bearded face of God blessing the marriage. *Thus dies beauty*, I thought.

'You need a drink,' Art said. He'd gotten hold of two glasses of white wine, and was offering me one. An intact roll-up dangled down from his lips.

I took the glass. 'I need *drinks*, plural.'

Art put his wine down on the white tablecloth of a white table, and produced a box of matches. He lit his roll-up, then waved the match to extinguish it. 'How're you doing?'

157

'Why do you ask?'

'No reason.'

'Bored. And happy.'

'Teenage sweethearts getting married. Oh my, that is lovely!'

'I detect cynicism.'

'Anna is cool.'

'But?'

Art took a drag. 'But Mauro will fucking hate being married. Anna too.'

'You always have an opinion, don't you?'

'You know that.'

I took out a cigarette. My financial situation wasn't as grim then as it is today, but it was on a quickly descending slope, and I was already pondering whether to switch to roll-ups or quit smoking altogether (I did neither). 'You think Mauro made a wrong turn way before this.'

'He shouldn't have gone into law. It's not him.'

'You know better than him about his life?'

Before Art could reply, Tony plunged into our conversation, wrapping his arms around our shoulders with a Joker-sized grin. 'The antipasti are out. And Lordy, do they look good.'

Art had been right. Italian weddings are all about the food. Yes, there's the Mass; yes, there are long-forgotten friends and rarely seen relatives; there might be some dancing too, and wine flows liberally. But really, it's all about food. I have been to receptions which were binge-eating orgies lasting six, seven hours. The dishes follow one by one, and after a while they merge into each other, and you are too high on nutrients to distinguish between them, to actually taste their flavour. This one wasn't quite so bad, thanks to Anna's touch. She had agreed to get married in the south, but in exchange she took a stand on the reception: abundant, yes, but not coma-inducing.

Maybe it is because of that, or perhaps because of my state of mind, but I can remember every dish on the menu that day, and the order they came in. To drink we had water, Primitivo wine, and Pinot Grigio. For antipasti we had Parma ham, white melon, aubergine roulades, a whole Parmesan cheese with a knife to carve it, raw anchovies in a marinade, beef carpaccio with chilli, a salad of octopus, prawns and celery, and a never-ending supply of *'mpepata*, that is, mussels sautéed with black pepper. Then we tucked into a beautiful homemade pasta with scampi, a fish soup, lemon sorbet (the secret ingredient of weddings, since it cleans your belly and allows you to keep eating), a choice of grilled tuna or grilled prawns, deep-fried seafood (squid, baby cuttlefish, shrimps), and grilled vegetables (aubergines, peppers and courgettes, seasoned with olive oil, salt and mint). Finally, the dessert: a self-service selection of locally made almond sweets, gelato – and the wedding cake. A restrained event, like I said.

Mauro and Anna had placed the three of us on a table with a gay male cousin of Anna's and two of her friends. We had met the month before, for the Pact, but even so, we had a lot of catching up to do, we always did, so we were barely civil to the strangers and spent all the time talking amongst ourselves. In June I'd learnt that Art was living in Paris, working as a dish-washer in a strip club (not a fancy one: Titty Twister, not

Moulin Rouge). He had joined a commune led by a self-styled punk poet, loosely inspired by the works of a French socialist mystic of the nineteenth century, Éliphas Lévi. When I'd asked why, he'd answered, *Why not*. Now, in typical Art fashion, he had grown bored with it, and he was thinking of coming back to Italy, to Naples, a city where he'd never lived. A friend of a friend could (probably, possibly) get him a job as a bookseller. His career choices, or lack thereof, had been a source of equal parts amazement and worry for us for the first few years, until it, too, became just another fact of life.

The cake was a three-tiered sponge affair soaked in rum and coffee, glazed in white icing. On top was a small statue of a woman reading an old tome, and a man in a lawyer-esque black robe. The real Anna and the real Mauro took their place behind the cake. She put her hand over his. He cut the first slice, the audience whooped, and Anna and Mauro kissed again.

'Now,' Tony said.

Art stood up. 'Ladies and gentlemen!' he called.

Anna and Mauro, still entangled, turned to him. The crowd fell silent.

Art opened his arms wide, as if to give a blessing. 'Our friend here, Mauro, is getting married today, which is what mates do when they hit a certain age. All well and good.' He lifted a glass. 'Also, that lucky bastard landed a girl way out of his league.' The crowd laughed. 'And we rightly toast him, them, and their future together. But. Splendid as their future might be, we should never, ever forget the past. Because the future starts here and now, but it's the past that led us to here

160

and now. It's the past that makes the future possible; the past is our *map* to the future.'

On cue, two waiters stepped closer to Mauro and Anna, bringing a box wrapped in black paper with a giant red ribbon.

'So this is our gift to our friend. Anna, we're not leaving you out; I'm sure you'll enjoy it too.' He paused as the waiters put the box on the table in front of Mauro. 'It's your past. And, we all wish, a part of your future.'

Mauro smiled, mumbled, and opened the box.

It was an electric guitar, a red and white Stratocaster. The idea had been Art's, and Tony and I had put in most of the cash (I couldn't really afford it, but they didn't know that). You wouldn't think it, seeing Mauro now, but he used to be quite a guitarist in his day.

He took the guitar in his hands, stunned. 'Guys...'

'Play it!' Tony said.

'I haven't touched a guitar in...'

'Play it, darling!' a drunk aunt shouted.

'Play it!' I joined. And the crowd started chanting: *Play it, play it, play it.*

With a shrug, Mauro put the strap across his shoulder and picked up the plectrum. Leisurely, theatrically, he walked to the small stage set for the band he and Anna had hired, connected the guitar to the band's amp, and tried one note. He adjusted the guitar, tried again, adjusted again.

A half-hour later he was playing with the band. People were dancing on the beach, in the moonlight, all drunk and happy. Tony was in a corner, telling tales to a young male relative of

161

Anna's. Art danced with ungainly jerks, as if unsure of what to do with his hips, his arms, but not giving a shit about it. I sat at a table, alone, smoking, sipping Fernet and watching the scene.

'That was a wonderful present,' Anna said. She'd managed to untangle herself from the attentions of her guests, mostly because at that point said guests were more interested in music and spirits than in complimenting the bride. She sat down at my table.

'Art's brainchild,' I said.

'Of course. Is it true that he's leaving Paris?'

'That's what it looks like.'

'Why aren't you dancing?'

I flicked ash from my cigarette into one of the half coconut shells they'd given us as ashtrays. 'I'm not a joiner.'

She took me by the hand and stood up. 'Come.'

'Where?'

Anna laughed and repeated, 'Come.'

We moved away from the madding crowd, towards the seashore. Anna was barefoot. I took off my Church's shoes and Paul Smith socks, memories of better financial places, and rolled up the legs of my trousers. We walked on the shore, leaving The Acacia behind. The water was pleasantly warm. The music carried in the night, but now I could hear, beneath it, the repetitive sound of surf. There were no waves to speak of; the sea was as calm as the starry moonlit sky. Anna let herself fall on the damp sand, and I sat beside her. 'God, I needed some silence,' she said.

'Married life is tougher than you thought?'

She laughed. 'Noisier.'

I extracted a bag of weed from my pocket. 'Art's supply. He says that the weed he grows in Paris has a Pastis aftertaste.'

She pointed her chin to the distant restaurant. 'My husband gets the rock 'n' roll, I get the drugs.'

'But you both miss the sex,' I said, and immediately regretted it.

'We'll get that later,' she said. 'Anyway, I'm not smoking tonight.'

I rolled a joint with shivering fingers. A wiser man would stand up, find an excuse and leave. I wasn't shaking with cold or drunkenness; my shaking was due to the struggle going on in my body, between sexual excitement and the necessity to contain it.

'We didn't have time to talk much, you and I,' Anna said, as I smoked.

'That comes with a wedding.'

'How's life in Fabio's world?'

'I found myself a new girlfriend.'

'Did you?'

'She's Indian. Well, born in London, actually. Her name's Ruhi.' That was before Lara. Ruhi was a model I'd worked with; relationships between models and snappers happen often, and rarely last.

'Good for you.'

I smiled and held out the joint. 'For *her* too.'

Anna gave me a light push. 'I said no, thanks.'

I took the joint back to my lips. 'Except for that, there's

'nothing new.' Nothing that I cared to tell. Nothing that would make me look accomplished, and important, and worthy.

'I do have news.'

'You got married?'

'I've got *more* news.'

'You're pregnant,' I said.

She was taken aback. 'How…?'

I shook the joint. 'Never seen you refusing a drag of Art's produce,' I said, with a lightness I didn't feel. 'And you only drank a glass of Prosecco tonight, that I could see.'

'Were you watching me the whole evening?'

'I had my eyes pinned on both the stars of the show. How did Mauro take it?'

'He doesn't know yet.'

'You think he'll freak out?'

'Oh, no, no. We were *planning* this. It's going to be my surprise for the after-party. Though he'll probably have noticed I wasn't drinking, so, it's a surprise only in name.'

'Happy?'

'A little scared too.'

'You'll be great. The ultimate Yummy Mummy.'

'It's not going to be easy to juggle a career and a baby.'

'For you and Mauro? A piece of cake.'

Anna stood up. 'I want to swim. This sea is just too perfect. Help me out.'

I walked to her back, and pushed down the zip of her dress. It was like a perfectly made ribbon. Once the zip was down the dress came undone at once, slipping down Anna's shoulders,

164

arms, bum and thighs. She wasn't wearing a bra, only white knickers. Anna didn't have qualms with being naked. She'd spent the first twelve years of her life in Germany, where her dad worked in an engineering firm, and grew up considering nudity completely normal. She had started sunbathing topless at eighteen. We all had seen her boobs; this wasn't the first time for me, or the tenth.

'Thanks,' she said, and ran into the sea.

I stood there, transfixed, watching her enter the water and dive in.

Then I brought my hands to my buckle. I knew that if I gave my brain any time, my brain would stop me, and I didn't want that to happen. In a rush, I got rid of my black suit, skinny tie, my white shirt and my boxers. Buck naked, I dived into the sea.

The water was warm as soup. I went with my head down, to let the sea embrace the whole of me, and swam towards Anna. She was in up to her chin, but still in her depth, her feet on soft sand.

'Welcome,' she said.

I grabbed her by her hips, and pulled her to me. Not for a moment did she try to draw back; she offered me her lips wide open and welcomed my tongue. I touched her teeth, and felt her tongue searching for a place inside my mouth. She placed her palms on my shoulders, and leaned on them, lifting both her legs underwater, to wrap them around my hips. The pressure of the soft tissue of her knickers on my erection was everything I ever wanted from a woman, from life. Using two fingers, I pushed her knickers to one side. I thrust my middle finger inside her, curving it into a hook. I could detect the different kind of wetness inside her.

'Ah,' she moaned.

I fucked her with my fingers until I couldn't anymore, and then, when my fingers were too exhausted to move one more time, I let her go. She held me tight, her perfect ass propped on my hands, as I brought the tip of my dick to the side of her knickers.

She nodded.

I entered her, pushing my hips towards her, and using my hands to pull her to me. She was weightless, suspended in water. I was fucking Anna and that was magnificent, but it wasn't enough. I wanted to fuck her more, I wanted to fuck her as much as possible, I wanted to bring this one chance to its utmost limits. I slipped a finger down her ass, to her anus, and I traced little circles with the tip of the finger. Then I pushed it inside. Anna bit my shoulder not to cry aloud, and I pushed the finger further in, while thrusting with my hips, while sucking her earlobe. She tasted of sweat, skin, and salty water.

I refused to come until she came; or she pretended to.

And when I came, I was sad, because I knew that was the end, and I wished I could start immediately all over again, and fuck her until the first light of the day, and see the sun rise while her naked body was one with mine.

When we went back to the reception, our hair was wet, and we confessed we'd been swimming. Nobody suspected a thing, not even the older, drunker aunts. They all knew I was like a brother to Mauro.

That was six years ago. It was the last time Anna and I were alone. Today, because Art disappeared, it's happening again.

'Is this remote enough?' she asks.

She jolts me awake from my reverie. Here I am, in the sun-dried countryside of Casalfranco, with that woman – that extraordinary, mind-blowing woman – who is ready to get naked for me once again.

'Yep,' I reply. 'Yep, it is.'

2

This harsh light of midday is more than I could wish for. Our ancestors from classical times believed in the danger of *demoni meridiani*, the midday demons – when the sun is this strong, the middle of the day can be as scary as the dark of the night.

The sky is stark blue, the earth stark red. We pull over in the dirt, at the border of an empty road, to enter a red field. We both wear sunglasses and hats – mine is a battered baseball cap I found at my father's home, where I decided to stay after learning of his Alzheimer's, Anna's a large-brimmed hat that gives her the air of a diva from a Fellini film. There are sparse olive and carob trees, and occasional prickly pears, but apart from these, the vegetation in this field is just low bushes and brambles. There are no barriers between us and the photons exploding from the sun, smashing into Spaceship *Earth* with the weight of cannonballs.

'Photo shoot first, or picnic?' Anna asks.

'Shoot, if that's okay with you.'

'Sure.'

The land slopes slightly – *very* slightly – but in this flatness it is enough to make a difference. When Anna walks towards the top of the slope, I recognise the perfect frame: the contrast between earth and sky, and Anna creating a bond between them, in a light which caresses her body and makes it redolent with a deeper shade of reality. She is a goddess of the land.

'How do you want me?' she says.

'Do you need to ask?'

She smirks, and takes off her hat, and I remember how I felt that first time, when Marta D'Antonio dropped her bra. Anna slips out of her long, gypsy-style gown and pulls off her tank top. She is in a bikini now, the same she was wearing on the beach the other day, with her husband and children; but here, even that bikini has a touch of the forbidden.

'I *am* going to use these pictures in the book, you know that.'

'You can stop saying that.'

'I worry for your career.'

She brings her hands behind her back to undo her bikini top. 'The rector is a sexist pig, but he's not stupid enough to say so much as a word about a full tenured professor doing what she likes with her body.'

How can you not fall in love with such a woman?

Her bra drops to the ground. Her nipples are only slightly

darker than the clear skin surrounding them. I have seen hundreds of naked girls, and I have seen Anna naked, but there is always something magical about the moment when your eyes touch nipples running free; nipples are a door from one world to another, from the grey of the everyday to a place of enchantment. Anna wiggles out of her knickers, and now she is naked, with that eternal smile on her lips.

'You're ravishing,' I say. I lift my sunglasses onto my head; I need to see the natural colour of the light.

She replies, 'I know.'

I'm aroused. That happens often when I work. My love for boobs, and bums, and legs, has never waned. Beauty is not something you get accustomed to, and no beauty in the universe is a match for a naked woman's. I say this with no shame or guilt. I admit that I became a photographer to get girls to undress, but I grew up into a professional, and I learnt (though not without mistakes) where my responsibility lies: I am the one who *communicates* that beauty, the one who makes it eternal and mobile, transmitting it to other places, to future generations. I *want* to be aroused when I see my models naked. I channel that energy through the camera, and I fix it forever in my work. Arousal is a natural answer to beauty, it is a beautiful thing in itself.

After what I found out about my father, having Anna naked with me, and a camera in my hands, is like finding a pool of fresh water when you have lost your way in a desert.

'Turn,' I say. I don't waste time with *please* and *thank you* on set; I'm not a dick like some other snappers, but I convey empathy through my movements, not my words. The less we speak, the more the model and I can focus on creating something together. A good session is a lot like sex; you don't want to talk much.

We go on for more than an hour, with some short pauses to refresh ourselves with ice tea. Seen through my camera lens, Anna is even more beautiful than I remembered. The small stretch marks on her belly and bum talk of a life fully lived; of wine and dinners with friends, of her children, and of the effort she made to get back in shape after having them. Anna is a woman who values her beauty without being obsessed by it. She should be on the cover of my book. She should probably write the introduction.

At one point, I know the session is over; I can't explain the feeling but I have come to respect it. And yet I don't want to stop. When I say those words, *We're done*, Anna will put her clothes back on, she will cover her nipples, and I will feel like all magic has been drained from the world never to come back. Anna is Mauro's wife. Lara waits for me in London.

Two simple truths I must not forget.

'We're done,' I say.

3

We sit in the shade of one of the lonely carob trees, its thick trunk exposing its old age. Anna has put her bikini back on, and only that; even under the shade, it is too hot to get dressed. I have my jeans on, but have abandoned my t-shirt.

'Did you get any good shots?' she asks.

'Some are going to be brilliant.'

'Your modesty is impressive.'

'I was complimenting the model.'

We sit on a towel, eating sandwiches with Parma ham and mozzarella. Anna brought an ice bag, which stood against the attack of the sun and kept the bottles satisfyingly cold. Drinking beer under this sun is not wise; it will only make us feel even warmer and sweat more. But right now, it is too intensely pleasurable for us to care.

'To Mauro,' I say, clinking my bottle against Anna's, 'for taking care of the girls this morning.'

'Considering how often he's left me alone with them during this holiday, it was the least he could do,' she says. 'This was supposed to be a *family* trip, not a mates' week away.'

'We kind of ruined it.'

Anna shrugs with a small laugh. There are at least three layers to what she's saying. Superficially, she is complaining, and on a deeper level she is just kidding. There is a third layer, though, one only visible to a person who knows her well, where real anger lies. While I was snapping, I noticed something in Anna which I didn't remember ever seeing in her before. A discontent. A trace of disappointment.

'Mauro thinks Art…' her voice trails off. 'I'm sorry, perhaps you don't want to talk about it.'

'It's on my mind too.'

'Mauro thinks Art is dead.'

'I tend to agree,' I say. 'Though I still hope for a miracle. It might end like last time.'

'But *how did it* end last time? Art told a story to the town, a different one to you guys.'

'I reckon he was lying in both cases.'

'I always wondered why you didn't press him for the truth.'

'We didn't want the truth.' I swallow a good mouthful of beer. 'Once we knew it, we would have had to do something with it, and we were too scared to go there. We should have.'

'You were kids.'

'If we'd been better friends, Art would be with us now.'

Sweat glistens on Anna's skin. 'Mauro told me about the *healing* too.'

'What do you make of it?'

'I consider myself a rationalist, but it is strange. The way Mauro talks of the night Art disappeared, it almost feels like it was… supernatural, can I use that word? Not that he puts it like that, but the sense is there. And now, the healing.'

'Said the rationalist.'

She shrugs.

I say, 'To be honest? I've played with the idea that there could be something *not of this world* about Art's vanishing.' It is a relief to say it out loud, without worrying about being laughed at. 'Did Mauro tell you of the cry Art made as he went into the olive grove?'

'Yes.'

'We could never agree on what it meant. I thought it was fear, Mauro thought it was anger, and Tony…' I shake my head. 'Tony thought it was, hear this, *joy*. How odd is that? There were other things too. When Art turned up at my door, his clothes were clean. The kidnapper took the trouble to do his victim's laundry? And Art, after he returned, he was every bit as clever as before, but even more... self-absorbed.' I pause to finish my sandwich. 'So, yeah, I played with the idea of magic. You know what happened that changed my mind?'

'What?' I have Anna's full attention; it is a deeply erotic feeling, one that, if I were Master of the World, I would rule never to end.

'I grew up. And I learnt that devils, and ghouls, and all the things that go bump in the night, are excuses we make up to tell ourselves that there is something worse than us, something darker than human beings.'

'How very angsty of you.' Anna sips her beer, gracefully lifting her neck. 'You suspect the priest.'

'It's him.'

'May I ask you something personal?'

'You and I just went as personal as it gets.'

'Why do you hate religion so much?'

She doesn't ask, *Did something happen with Don Alfredo?* But I know that is the question she is really asking. 'Don Alfredo never got close to my willy, if that's what you mean,' I say, getting a laugh out of her. 'No, it goes back to when my mother died. I was ten, and desperate. It was so sudden – she was diagnosed with breast cancer, and four months later,' I snap my fingers, 'she was gone.'

Anna knows this story. What she doesn't know is what happened next.

'There was one day when I was crying, not making a scene,

mind, just crying in my room, and Don Alfredo came around, entered without knocking, with my father, and said, *You shouldn't cry, because your mother is with our Lord Jesus Christ.* And my father said, *Listen to Don Alfredo.*'

'They were trying to help.'

I scoff. 'And then Don Alfredo added, *If you keep on crying, that'll be a sin. Jesus Christ called your mum and you shouldn't question the will of Jesus, or he'll send you to Hell.*'

Anna opens her eyes wide. 'Son of a bitch.'

'I was speechless. I was so surprised I did stop crying, for the moment. I looked at my father, and he was staring *adoringly* at Don Alfredo. That gave me such a shock, like an electric shock, you know? I found my voice again, and you know what I said? I said, *Better in Hell than with Jesus and you pricks.*'

Anna bursts into laughter again. 'Sorry I asked,' she says.

But I am laughing too, opening another beer. 'My father never forgave me.' *My father.* Who was expecting me to come this year to tell me he is dying. 'I don't believe in God, Anna. If he existed, though, I'd rather be damned in Hell than spend eternity with a smug, omnipotent bully.'

'Mauro didn't tell me this story.'

'I only ever told Art. Mauro and Tony wouldn't have understood. Not that I'm saying that your husband is stupid or...'

'I know what you're saying.'

She bends to get another beer from the ice bag, and I have a flashback of her body, naked, swaying for my camera, and I struggle to refrain myself from making another terrible mistake.

'A secret for a secret,' she says. 'Do you remember the first time we dated?'

I smile. 'That night when Art and I *crushed* Tony and Mauro at table football, before you made the clever choice and picked Mauro. You and your mate… what was her name?'

'Rita.'

'Rita, yes. You guys said you'd be our *hooligans.*'

'It was Art's idea. He'd sensed that I found you cute, and told me that you were too dumb to make the first move, so I should. And I protested that it didn't work that way, that it had to be the boy. Art replied, *What does it matter?* She makes a pause. That *what does it matter* changed my life, in more than one way. Actually, what did it matter? Being a boy, being a girl, doing girl's things – it was all rubbish. I could ask out Fabio the Hot Southerner if I wanted to. I could study physics. I could do whatever I wanted. To make my plans less obvious I asked Rita to root for Tony and Mauro's team. She agreed – for a strawberry lipstick. Funny I still remember that.'

'So that's how everything starts,' I say, shaking my head. 'Art and Art and Art again.'

'I hope Mauro's wrong. Art deserves better than dying crazy and alone.'

I don't speak for a while, basking in the presence of Anna, and the comfort of the beer. 'Do you ever wonder what would have happened?' I say. 'If that night Mauro had succeeded in kissing Rita and…'

'Yes. Yes, I do.'

'I don't feel bad about what we did,' I say, and it's almost as if someone else is speaking, a creature made of fire.

'Me neither,' Anna says, after a while. 'We needed to get it out of our system.'

'I'm not sure I got it out of mine though,' I say, ignoring my better part, which was shouting at me to shut up, to not go into the most dangerous territory there is.

Anna looks at me. 'Me neither,' she says.

MAURO

1

I am having the time of my life.

There, I admitted it, thereby certifying myself as a bona fide Dreadful Person. It had to be done. I have learnt from bitter experience in court that you can lie to everybody but yourself, because when you lie to yourself, all you do is train yourself to believe in lies, which makes it easier for your opponents to feed you theirs. Honesty, like sex, is a private affair. I am sad for Art, of course, and I try not to think about what might have happened to him. Notwithstanding: great time. For once I have something that goes beyond taxes, nappies and Peppa Pig. I feel like an old trinket which was gathering dust on a shelf, until someone bought it, and dusted it, and gave it a new lease of life. That someone being Art.

I asked him once why he doesn't believe in God. He said, *I don't like the idea of a being more powerful than me.*

I wonder what Concetta Pecoraro would make of it. She

was famous for a while when we were children, and that peaked during Art's disappearance, but then his reappearance put an abrupt end to her career. She must have saved something from her salad days though, because her older son still drives a Mercedes – a *white* Mercedes. It is parked in front of the house where mum and son live cheek to cheek, in the middle of a small vineyard at the edge of Casalfranco.

'Yeah, that's the car,' Tony says. We left ours at a little distance to walk here – the road is not exactly isolated, but it is not very busy either, and we didn't want to alert Concetta to our presence.

Tony, hands in his pockets and aviator sunglasses on his nose, is looking at the Mercedes. Everybody in town knows that his brother-in-law has *friends*, which should discourage people from acting hastily. Or not, depending on how clever said people are. What Tony refuses to understand, even after it was spelled out at the Dance of the Swords, is that it is not his brother-in-law having friends, it is his sister. Elena is the boss of the house, and also, she is more than 'well connected' with the Corona, she is Corona herself. I can't say I'm surprised. From what I remember of Elena, the sweet little girl Tony fondly looks back on never existed in the first place. She is only slightly less dangerous than Michele; but I guess we can count on her being on our side.

Fabio pushes the gate open. I have vague recollections of seeing the vineyard on TV in the late eighties, when I was little and Concetta was a local celebrity. It is tiny, just a glorified garden, really. It was known then as the Blessed Vineyard; they said that each of its grapes contained the blood of Christ. The grapes didn't need a priest, and not even to be made into wine, to be transubstantiated. You could just pluck one, gobble it, and there you go – you had your communion, and a special one at that, for the grapes were supposed to taste like true blood. The Virgin Mary in person had granted the grace. She had appeared to Concetta bringing some major spiritual messages, and the two of them had got along like a house on fire, so much so that Mary promised to come back regularly. That's how Concetta cobbled together a mystical start-up. Once a month Mary would appear in the vineyard, making herself visible only to Concetta, and give Concetta platitudes about peace on earth and the necessity for people to donate money to Concetta herself, for the greater good. The money would allow Concetta to pray full-time, and so bring peace on earth sooner rather than later (apparently the Father, Son, and Holy Ghost all held Concetta's prayers in the highest regard). Concetta would repeat Mary's words verbatim and cash in. On the evidence of Concetta's visions the Virgin had a shaky grasp of theology and grammar, and was quite mindful of the state of her friend's bank account. The clergy wasn't impressed; a lot of folks were.

The bishop issued a statement declaring that Concetta wasn't, in fact, seeing the Virgin, or anybody else for that matter, and that she would be excommunicated if she were to continue to say otherwise. There was nothing miraculous about her grapes, and moreover Concetta was committing mortal sin by giving communion to the faithful without properly blessed wine, and without being a priest, and without an ecclesiastical authorisation.

Concetta replied that she got her authorisation directly from the Virgin Mary and carried on unfazed.

It was kind of fun, except for the poor gulls who became poorer because of Concetta. Don Alfredo did his best to back the bishop, but a lot of people in town took Concetta's side. They kept eating her grapes and throwing their money at her. At the height of her success, a single grape from Concetta's vineyard would set you back as much as a dinner in a good restaurant. Concetta paid her fees to the Corona, and nobody bothered her. She would have lived happily for ever after, if it hadn't been for Art.

2

A TV is playing at full volume inside, a talent show in which a man with no talent is mauling 'Stand by Me' in a Venetian accent. I knock politely. The show goes on, nobody answers.

'Excuse me,' I say. I try the door, which is open. 'Signora Pecoraro?'

A few coughs, then a croaky voice. 'Yes?'

I walk in, followed by Tony and Fabio.

'Who's there?' the voice asks.

We follow it without replying. Concetta sits in a square living room, which is clean and tidy, except for the thick cloud of cigarette smoke. She looks a hundred years older than in the pictures I googled this morning, and at least a hundred kilos heavier. What little is left of her hair is dyed an artificial brown and backcombed to make it look bigger than it is. It gives her the appearance of a decaying prop from the set of a low-budget horror film. She doesn't seem to recognise us. I would pity her if I hadn't met so many hustlers of her kind.

'We are friends of Art,' I say.

Concetta opens her eyes wide, coughs, and takes a drag from her cigarette. 'Art who?'

'Arturo Musiello: you know who.'

'That little shit.'

'He's not little anymore.'

'A big shit then.' She coughs. 'I know who Art is and I know who you are.'

I fold my arms. We have agreed that we need to look like we mean business, but it is an old lady we are dealing with here. Tony and Fabio are queasy. I am not. I am a lawyer.

'We're here to talk about yesterday.'

'I don't know what the fuck you're talking about.'

'Signora Pecoraro, you almost killed one of us.'

'To be precise, *me*,' Tony says.

She cackles, 'I don't *almost* do things.'

A smile comes to my lips in spite of myself. The woman has spirit, you have to give her that. 'Is your son home?'

'Saverio!' she shouts. 'Saverio!' she shouts louder.

That makes Fabio jolt. He is in much better shape today – the photography session with Anna did him good – but he is still on edge. His father's condition and his hatred for

Casalfranco make this even harder for him than it is for Tony and me.

'I'm coming, Ma!' a booming voice answers. After twenty-odd years, it still stirs unpleasant memories. Heavy steps come down a staircase, each one a forceful beat on a drum, announcing a beefy man with a pissed-off face. Barefoot and bare-chested, he only wears a pair of shorts. Saverio was big when we were boys, and he's got bigger. A curling tribal tattoo spirals up from his right side to his arm, ending in a circle of blades surrounding the wrist. A scar cuts through his left eyebrow. Oh yes, I remember that. Tony made it.

When Saverio sees us, he stiffens. I can see his muscles tensing, and there's a lot of them, so it takes a while to tense them all. I glance at Tony. He is cool as a cucumber. Saverio is a good head taller than him, but Tony thrashed him once and I bet he could do it again. Tony is like a terrier; you can pit him against an adversary twice his size and he will come out on top. He says that is because he loathes violence, so when violence starts, he is in a hurry to end it.

When Concetta looks at her son, she does so with a pride which could be put to better use. 'You remember Art's friends?' she says.

'Yeah,' Saverio says, his eyes fixed on Tony.

'Hi, man,' Tony says. 'How you doing?'

'Get the fuck out of my house.'

'I don't think so, no.'

Saverio steps forward, threateningly.

I say, 'Do you know what I do?'

He has a puzzled look. 'What you…'

'What my job is.'

'I don't give a fuck.'

'You should, Saverio, because I'm a lawyer, and a pretty good one at that.' I step towards him, my belly showing from under my shirt, my arms one third the thickness of his – physically harmless, I know. I also know that we are not in the Middle Ages, and this guy needs a reality check. 'You remember what happened when your mum ended up in court, *sì*? Be my guest, hit me. Kick me, for all I care. Next thing you know, I will sue your ass, and I promise, you and your family will lose your fancy car, your house, your vineyard. I won't stop until I have squeezed every last penny you've got squirrelled away under the mattress.' It's bollocks, of course – that is never going to happen, not for a little brawl between friends. But Saverio doesn't know that. That's the thing with men like him; when they were boys, their size and the sheer intensity of their meanness made them terrifying. They cling to that, then they hit twenty and real life begins, and one day they wake up and find themselves utterly powerless. In the grown-up world, brawn is futile. So is brain, ultimately. The one and only thing you need, the ultimate strength and source of power in this country, is an understanding of how to make bureaucracy work for you. No matter how much I find this depressing, I have been shown over and over again that it is exactly the case.

'You're in my house,' Saverio repeats.

I roll my eyes. 'Only yesterday, you attempted to cause Tony grievous bodily harm.' I pause, then lie some more. 'We have photographs of your car, your number plate. We came here for old times' sake, because we have known you since we were kids and we thought we could talk this out.'

Tony chips in, 'Personally, I wasn't that keen on *talking*.'

Saverio pretends to be on the verge of hitting one of us, but I know he won't. I bet he has had his run-ins with lawyers, and he is scared enough of what we can do. I have seen men like him – I have seen them a lot – when I was a rookie, before I started dealing with the real scum, and hard as they beat their chest, they know that their place is at the bottom of the food chain.

'Shut up or move, boys,' Concetta croaks. 'I'm watching telly.'

She is smart. I get now why she made such a splash as a crook. She does not want to hear what could pass between her son and us, just in case things do end up in court after all.

Saverio exits the room, and we follow him to the kitchen, another neat and tidy space. A scent of tomato sauce and basil, with just a hint of cigarette smoke. I notice an original fridge from the fifties, with its rounded shape, which I'm sure never moved from this kitchen since it was first put here.

'So,' I say immediately. 'Yesterday at Art's.'

'I talk, I never see you again – is that the deal?'

'Cross my heart,' I lie.

Saverio walks to the fridge and takes out a bottle of beer, which he opens. 'Art's my dealer,' he says, after making a show of drinking in our face without offering. 'He has good stuff. I was there to buy. I saw a car was chasing me, I freaked out. Thought you were Carabinieri.'

184

Tony says, 'And it seemed like a good idea to go head to head with a Carabinieri car?'

'Seemed good at the time,' Saverio says.

Which is a badly delivered whopper. I move my eyes to my friends. Tony is not buying it either. Fabio doesn't care. Sweating even more profusely than this muggy weather would account for, he ignores us, his eyes transfixed by something on the wall behind my back. I don't want to be obvious and follow his gaze, so I turn to Saverio.

'Art has disappeared,' I say, trying to gauge his reaction.

'He did a runner from the cops?'

'He's got friends in the Corona,' Tony says. 'So no, the Carabinieri aren't really an issue here.'

Saverio's hand shakes at the mention of the Sacra Corona Unita, which goes to show that he does, indeed, know his place in the food chain.

I say, 'We're looking for him. Do you have any idea where he is?'

'I'm a buyer, not his mate.'

'When did you see him last?'

'A month ago? I don't keep tabs.'

'Do you know his girlfriend?'

'What girlfriend?'

'Maybe not his girlfriend, but there was a girl he fancied.'

Something passes through his body – a quick reaction, swiftly concealed. He shrugs.

I pinch the top of my nose. 'I'll be very clear with you, Saverio: all of Art's *mates*, us and the others, want to find out what happened to him, and we are far more pleasant than the others. You show us goodwill, there could be something in it for you. But if word gets out that you didn't help when you could, me suing you is not the worst that could happen.'

'I'll keep an eye out,' Saverio says.

Fabio wipes his forehead with the palm of his hand. He is dripping. 'Who is…' He stops, then tries again, 'Who is that young woman?'

He points at a framed picture on the wall, showing a woman who is maybe in her late teens, if that. She has dark eyes, a dark complexion, and curly black hair making a halo around a lovely face. Her smile is so bright and open it seems to embrace you. She is not beautiful, no; she is much more than that. She is *enchanting*. She looks as if she could walk out of the picture any moment, take your hand, and start dancing with you. She makes you long for that to happen.

'My little sister,' Saverio says. 'She's nothing to do with Art.'

The young woman is on the beach, fighting playfully with a dog for the control of a Frisbee. The young woman has one side of the Frisbee in her long-fingered hands, the dog has the other in his jaw. The dog is big, white, shaggy.

Like the one Fabio saw in the olive grove.

'Is that your dog?' Fabio asks.

'Yeah, why?'

'Can I see it?'

'I've not seen him in days myself,' Saverio says.

On the first day of Art's disappearance it became clear that we were suspected, not in a specific way, just in general. Everybody wanted a scapegoat and we were handy. We were with Art when he disappeared, we had been smoking weed, we couldn't agree on the nature of the cry Art was supposed to have let out from the olive grove. We were natural suspects.

On the third day, the media started talking about Art in the past tense, going from *Art is a sweet kid who is everybody's best friend*, to *Art was a sweet kid who was everybody's best friend*. A shift in consciousness had occurred. Every hut and every trullo in the countryside had been searched. Dogs and helicopters were on the hunt night and day; they would have found a living boy. A dead boy, though? That was far easier to conceal. The Carabinieri made us go through the events of the night more times than I care to remember. The olive grove was in a lonely spot. Did we really go there only to look at the moon? That wasn't your typical teenage behaviour, was it? And how was it possible that our friend just vanished, in such a desolate spot, without us seeing where he went? We didn't have any answers for them, which to overworked Carabinieri translated as: we didn't *want* to give any answers.

On the fourth day, the Virgin Mary spoke to Concetta.

Mary made an unscheduled appearance in the Blessed Vineyard, with the specific purpose of telling Concetta the truth about Art. The truth being, Art was safe. He was safe in Her mighty bosom. That is, he was dead as a doorknob and in

Heaven. *The envy of men*, the Virgin said, *killed the poor, poor boy, but he is in a better place now, far from suffering and danger*. By then the metamorphosis of Art from creepy weirdo to town's dearest was complete (with the only exception of Fabio's dad, who never strayed from his position that Art was an arrogant little brat who would return home when tired of playing hide-and-seek). Concetta said she didn't need to explain what the *envy of men* was supposed to be. The implication being, foul play was involved, and who else but Art's best friends could be the foul players? As for Art's earthly remains, the Virgin Mary assured they were to be found *in the shadow of a tree or beneath the weight of a rock*, which covered pretty much the whole of Salento.

Casalfranco lapped it up. Though only a minority actually believed Concetta's – *pardon*, the Virgin Mary's – words, they kept their options open. A dead Art, a bright young soul harvested before its time, with the Virgin Mary appearing to announce his fate, made for a moving story, and who doesn't like a moving story? With a sprinkling of the mystical, too. We couldn't compete.

To the surprise of many, Art's parents stuck with us; their son's disappearance was not a game to them. On the sixth day, Art's dad called me, crying, and said he knew we were good boys – like brothers to Art – and the things people in town were saying were vile, just vile. He made me cry, too.

But then Art came back, with his bullshit story, and he instantly became the most profoundly hated kid in Italy. Concetta found herself in deep water. All those who had half believed her, which amounted to almost the whole of

Casalfranco, felt like fools, and people will forgive many things, but they will *never* forgive you for making them feel like a fool. Our seer jumped to the front pages of the local papers, and the third or fourth of a few national ones, and not in a good way. Her blood-flavoured grapes became a national joke. She tried to spin the story saying that she had been misled by Satan, but that only made things worse. A famous comedian did a sketch with him as the Devil dressed up as the Virgin Mary, and speaking in the voice of an old man trying to pass as a girl. An instant classic – you can find it on YouTube. Concetta's credibility was in tatters, her business over.

One night, a couple of months after Art had returned, Tony and I ran into Saverio in the network of alleys by Don Alfredo's church. Saverio was off his face, and he started shouting abuse at us. 'That asshole friend of yours,' he said, 'why didn't he just fucking die?'

Saverio, who was two years older than us, had a reputation for enjoying a good fight. I made to ignore him and walk on, but Tony stopped and replied, 'Your mum was making money on our and our mate's ass.'

Tony had a reputation, too.

'Oh, and by the way,' he added, 'she's a whore.'

Saverio roared and lunged at him. Tony waited for him to come, and when the distance was just right, he kneed Saverio in the balls. *Hard.* Saverio stopped, doubled on himself, covered his crotch with his hands, gave a stifled whimper. A spasm moved through his body, from crotch to head, and Saverio retched a thread of viscous yellow mucus. It could have stopped there.

Tony hit him again.

And I cheered. The only reason I didn't join in was that I had never been in a fight (which is quite a result for a boy growing up in Casalfranco) and I didn't know where to start. It wasn't very nice of us, what we did, but I think we deserve to be cut some slack. Everybody else was mad at Art because they thought they knew what he had done, but we knew we didn't. All we knew was that bad things had happened. Art had confessed to us that he hadn't run away, and when we asked what had happened instead, he just kept saying, *I don't know.* That line terrified me. It still does.

Tony slapped Saverio, then pushed him to the floor, and when Saverio was there, Tony kicked him in his face, only once, but hard, with the scrubby Doctor Martens he would always wear, cutting the gash into Saverio's eyebrow. Then Tony spat on him.

Saverio was sobbing, his head in his hands, his leather jacket soiled with puke and blood.

'Fucker,' Tony said.

4

I am in my parents' basement, digging for my old guitar. It is a large, dark room, cluttered with boxes, old bicycles, broken furniture. A museum of family memories, though now we only use this house as a holiday home. With both me and my brother living in Milan, Mum and Dad bought a little flat and moved up north. They didn't want to miss their grandchildren growing up. It was sweet of them – that's what I tell myself when I resent them, which I do more than is healthy for a man my age. My big plan was to reinvent myself in Milan. That never happened, partly because it was difficult to do that with my family reminding me who I was supposed to be, and partly, I suppose, because I just didn't have it in me. I am what I am, and if I am not overly fond of that, there's nothing to do but suck it up.

'You haven't found it yet?' Anna asks.

'Not yet.'

She came down with two glasses of red wine, after putting Ottavia and Rebecca in bed. I love this hour of the day, when the work with the girls is done and I have an entire night to myself before the grind starts again. Sleep is my favourite pastime, nowadays. Anna places the glasses on an old, dusty table and asks, 'Can I help?'

I gesture at a large chest, on which three smaller ones are piled up. 'You could check inside there.'

We had a family BBQ tonight, in my parents' spacious back garden, lined with apricot trees, lemon trees and prickly pears. There is a stone-built wood-fired oven in the middle, which has not been used in a while. Dad knows how to make pizza, I don't. Regular al fresco dining is one of the things I miss about Casalfranco. Along with the simpler lifestyle, the amount of pure oxygen in the air, the sea, the food, the landscape. I would move back, if that made sense financially. Maybe one day. I might even learn to make pizza too.

Over dinner Anna asked the girls, 'Did you enjoy your time with Dad this morning?'

'He taught us how to shoot,' Ottavia said.

Anna made a mock shocked grimace. 'Giving guns to his own daughters!'

'They were *water* pistols,' Ottavia hurried to explain. 'He said we can only ever shoot those, and never at strangers.'

Meet Ottavia: no sense of humour whatsoever. Which is sweet for a little girl, but I pray, when I pray, that she will acquire some before she turns into a teenager, or life will crush her soon enough.

'Neve' to strangers,' Rebecca repeated. She believes that her older sister is the upper crust of sophistication, and so she apes whatever Ottavia says or does.

I love my little girls, but, oh, they bore me silly. They quickly spoiled the good mood I was in earlier today – the good mood that comes from a dead friend and a secret mafia party. How screwed up am I?

'Look what I found,' I say. A crate of old toys. I take out an action figure, a muscular blond man in fur underwear and a chestplate. '*He-Man and the Masters of the Universe*. Do you remember those? I was mad for the toys, though I didn't care much for the cartoon.'

'You boys are weird,' Anna says. 'You wouldn't be caught dead playing with a Barbie, but a naked body-builder called He-Man is fine.'

I chuckle. 'Help me out with these boxes.'

We disassemble a pile. My guitar has to be somewhere

around here. Mum and Dad would never throw it away. They are hardcore hoarders when it comes to family memorabilia.

'Curiosity is killing me,' Anna says. 'How did it go with Concetta?'

I give her a run-down of our meeting.

When I'm finished, Anna asks, 'And do you believe Saverio?'

'It's possible he was buying weed from Art, but the part about him taking Tony for a Carabiniere? Please.'

'What was he doing at Art's, then?'

'That's what I hope his sister will tell us.'

'The stunning young woman.'

'You like that detail, don't you?' I joke. 'I have to tell you that Fabio is first in line.'

'I don't play fair.'

'Of course you don't, love.'

'Is Fabio sure that the dog in the photograph is the same he saw in the olive grove?'

'They certainly look the same.'

Anna rummages through the boxes without talking for a while. Then she says, 'You must promise me that you stop this thing the moment you sniff danger.'

'I promise.' Anna doesn't know that moment is long past. She is right, we should stop. We should have stopped when we learnt that the Sacra Corona Unita is involved. I am not even sure I know what I am doing anymore. We won't find Art's killers. We won't find his body, either. This is not about him, it is about us, me. I should stop. I will. 'What about you? Any fun with Fabio?'

'Lots and lots.'

Something in her voice. I can't quite place it – but there is something. Guilt? It could be. I suspect Anna and Fabio slept together at some point. I never asked and I don't want to know. It is in the past, when we were all young and stupid. I've never cheated on Anna, but that doesn't make me a saint.

I say, 'Those photos will make your colleagues... talk.'

'That's the plan.'

I love this woman; there are many things in my life which I am not sure of, but I am sure I love this woman with everything I have, more than I will ever love anybody else, our little girls included. She's the most marvellous gift Art ever gave me. 'How did you find Fabio, anyway?'

'Not well. Even though, and I'm going to say something horrible now... perversely, this trouble with Art might be helping him. It gives him something new to focus on. Something unexpected, off-scale.'

'I know what you mean,' I say, after a pause.

'And how are *you* holding up?'

I scout around the basement with my eyes. 'Sincerely?'

'Go, man.'

'What we found out about Fabio bummed me out.'

'Care to elaborate?' That *something* again. I should find the courage to tell her, *It's okay, stop feeling guilty for things far away in the past*, but that would mean admitting to my suspicions, and I am not ready for that.

'I thought he had a perfect life. He followed his dream, and won it all! Success, money, a glamorous job which didn't

194

involve finding creative ways to let people get away with not paying taxes.'

Anna sighs. She's heard those lines so many times. 'You can quit your job whenever you want, Mauro. You *should*. We'll figure something out when you stop being a drama queen.'

How? I want to shout at her. *How can I possibly quit my job? We have two daughters, two balls-and-chains sucking away from us the best years of our life, and they need clothes and doctors and holidays and toys, and the money you make is not enough, and our savings would be gone in six months, tops, and in six months we'll figure out we're fucked.*

I say instead, 'Fabio followed his dreams, Hollywood-style, and he's not happy. I did the opposite, I acted responsibly, and I can't say I'm happy either. Either you go for it or you're a good boy and follow the rules, it's all the same in the end. Is there a way, *any* way, to win at life?'

'I *am* happy,' she replies after a bit.

'There,' I say. Hidden behind cobwebs and a row of old bicycles, the unmistakable shape of the instrument that failed to change my life. 'I found it.'

5

It is all about computers now, but to score in the nineties, playing guitar was still the way to go. Honestly, though, I got started on the guitar not because of the girls, but because of a song, Led Zeppelin's 'Babe I'm Gonna Leave You'. It spoke of adventure, rambling. It filled me with a longing for things I had never known; I was too young to have memories to be nostalgic about, and I couldn't wait for those memories to come. I had a longing for nostalgia, and I started playing guitar because I wanted to play that particular song.

I wasn't half bad, if I say so myself. The other kids stuck to the basic chords (E minor, C major), using them invariably for each and every song they were asked to play, from 'Wonderwall' to 'Lemon Tree', regardless of the actual chords they were supposed to use. I discovered that I liked music for music's sake. I put time and effort into learning my chords, and if the girls were impressed, that was great, but impressing them wasn't the point of it.

Notwithstanding that (or exactly *because* of that), it paid off. It was the night of the tenth of August, the feast of San Lorenzo, the summer after the table-football tournament when I'd embarrassed myself making a move on Rita. With a large group of friends, we lit a bonfire on a fine sandy beach. The plan was the same as every year: spend the night at the fire, drink beer, smoke weed, and look for the shooting stars that on the feast of San Lorenzo fill the sky like silver confetti. Southern kids still carry on the tradition, even though lighting bonfires on the beach is technically illegal, and if they catch you, the coastguard will fine you – or maybe accept a bribe to go away. Joyless bastards.

The main action was around the fire, with two guitar players, and a gaunt bongo drummer as awful as them, putting on a show. I was sitting off at a distance, facing the black sea, practising the chords for a Santana piece, I don't remember which one. I sound terribly pretentious, but I wasn't striking a pose, I was just playing.

'That's cool,' Art said.

He sat down next to me with a beer.

'You didn't bring any for me?' I asked.

'Nope. No time for booze. You have to keep on playing and entertain me.'

'I'm not your monkey,' I said, distractedly playing a few notes.

'You're really good, man. You could be a rock star.'

'As if.'

'Money, fame, girls, which part don't you like?'

'The part where I starve.' It was the summer before our last year of school. We were starting to think about what to do next, where to go. We were starting to worry that we would make the wrong choice. 'The part where I become a pathetic never-has-been and I hate the music that ruined my life, which is how 99% of wannabe rock stars end up.'

'You shouldn't focus on those who fail, but on those who succeed.'

'And how many of those are there, Art?'

'You only need one: yourself.'

'I'm the responsible type.'

'Fuck being responsible!'

'Even if I were a good enough guitar player, which I'm not, I just… don't have it in me.' It was painful to articulate what I thought. 'I'm the sort of guy who mums like more than their daughters do. The music biz is not only about the skills, it's about the attitude. You have to look the part. And I look the part of the reliable uncle, the paunchy one who gets drunk at Christmas and tells corny jokes.'

'You smoke weed.'

'And that's as far as it gets. Not very sex, drugs and rock 'n' roll.'

'Sex, drugs and rock 'n' roll, that's right!' Art laughed. 'Actually, you got the essentials covered. Weed is a drug, check. You're a natural born rock 'n' roll guitarist, check. And about the sex…' Art got to his feet with a flourish. 'Let me show you how cool your life could be.'

'Wait…' I tried, but he was already running back to the bonfire. That was Art for you: a force of nature, unstoppable and, as often as not, unintelligible. I wondered what had happened in the seven days in which he hadn't been with us. I wondered if I would ever know.

Art started a conversation with someone, hidden behind the flames, then pointed in my direction, and the second person started walking towards me. Her outline shone from the flames behind her, her hair waved in the night breeze. Anna was coming, looking like a spirit of the fire. She was wearing an extra-large sweater, covering her legs all the way down to her knees, with sleeves too long for her. She was the cutest thing I had ever laid eyes on.

'I'm sorry to intrude,' she said.

I couldn't even look at her. I looked at the sea, black as the night at the bottom of a cave, but full of the reflections of the stars. I didn't look at her and I didn't reply, because I was too shy. That, Anna would reveal to me years later, made me come across as mysterious and aloof, a moody artist to die for.

She asked, 'Will you play a song for me?'

'Why?' Which, again, was said out of awkwardness, and sounded kick-ass. We all have our lucky nights; we have to hold on to them, to survive the other ones.

'Art says you're good, and Art knows his music.'

Was there anything Art didn't know? 'Are you into music too?'

'Piano, not guitar. Mostly jazz.'

'You like Petrucciani?'

'My favourite.'

'Cool.'

'Are you playing or not?' she said. 'You get to pick the song.'

Without giving it too much thought, I started the chords of 'Babe I'm Gonna Leave You'. It would become a running joke with Anna, that a song called 'Babe I'm Gonna Leave You' was my soundtrack of choice for our first date. In my defence, I didn't know it was a date. The notion that Anna might have wanted to date me was as alien as a walk on the dark side of the moon, especially after my clumsy attempt, the previous summer, at kissing her friend.

She sat down, facing the black sea and the shooting stars. She didn't say a word; she listened to my tune, and I played on.

6

The cappuccino they brew in this bar is fabulous, and they bake their own brioches, fluffy and not too sweet. It's been the most famous breakfast in town since before I was born. Shame about the décor change; they recently refurbished the place with transparent plastic tables and chairs, giving it a look which would be fresh if these were the eighties and Casalfranco was New York. When I arrive, Fabio and Tony are already sitting in the small room in the back. At another table the bongo drummer from that bonfire all those years ago sits, with a plump woman who's probably his wife. He pretends he doesn't recognise us and I reciprocate the favour.

When they finally leave, Fabio takes his phone and shows me a Facebook profile. 'Silvana: Concetta's daughter. She's FB friends with half of Casalfranco.'

Tony grabs the phone to look at a picture, with me peering over his shoulder. I can't make out the background, only Silvana's halo of curly hair, her eyes like lullabies, her flawless skin. Even in such a crappy photograph, her beauty is almost painful.

'Wow,' Tony says. 'She's so hot she's burning away my awful condition. Rejoice! I will be healed any moment now.'

Fabio takes back his phone, selects another photograph. 'And that's the dog.' A white shaggy dog resting in the sun, eyes closed, an expression of delight on his muzzle. Who knows how much time he had left before being hung from a tree, to die slowly in a stifling hot olive grove.

Tony tucks into his second brioche, and says, 'We have *la Madama*.'

'This is a girl who would obsess anybody,' says Fabio.

An idea comes to my mind, and I start talking, to give it form. 'Listen: we took it for granted that Art's first and second disappearances were connected, but what if they *aren't*? Not directly. Let's say that Art comes to town to write his book, and he meets Silvana. She wants nothing to do with him. But he starts obsessing over her, calling her *madama*. Perhaps he stalks her.'

Tony stiffens. 'Art wouldn't do that.'

'Art is not the guy we used to know, Tony, *none of us are*. Anyway, Saverio finds out what Art's doing and decides to protect his sister. Maybe Silvana sends him, or maybe it is his initiative. Be that as it may, he gets mad, he gets out of control, and he… kills Art.'

'So why did he come back to Art's, the other day?'

'To be sure there was no evidence left. Prints. Stuff.'

'It's a good theory,' Tony admits. 'But it doesn't explain everything.'

'A lot of the details might just be because Art was being Art.'

Fabio says, 'You're saying it was Art who killed the dog.'

'Our mate set up a cosy little abattoir in his basement. Clearly things had got a little intense, towards the end.'

'What about *the other* dog?'

'What other dog?'

Tony slaps a hand on his forehead. 'Art's! The dog he treated like royalty, remember? I totally forgot about it.'

I open my mouth, ready to reply, and realise I have nothing to give. 'Fine, I don't know,' I admit. 'Maybe Saverio killed it too? Wouldn't be too strange. The best we can do for Art is to tell this theory to Michele, and forget about it.'

Fabio says, 'This doesn't clear Don Alfredo. It was *him*, twenty-two years ago, and he's got to pay for that.'

'One thing at a time,' I say.

'I'm not Saverio's biggest fan,' Tony says, 'but we need to talk to the girl first. Get a clearer idea of the situation, before pointing the Corona at him.'

'Saverio won't let us anywhere near her.'

Fabio shakes his phone. 'On Facebook, she says where she works.'

7

It is walking distance from the bar. In Casalfranco, everywhere is walking distance from everywhere else – another thing I miss, especially when I am stuck in traffic first thing in the morning. We stroll down the main street, passing by two different churches, a nunnery, and then under a stone archway named after San Gregorio. We reach a funeral parlour whose window showcases an oak coffin, a plastic floral arrangement, and a black granite gravestone watched over by a weeping angel. A sign assures customers that the sculpture is, despite all evidence, *tasteful and discreet*.

Casalfranco has a flourishing funeral industry, not because

people in Salento die more than elsewhere, but because they spend a fortune on funerals. When you die here, you die as lavishly as you can, so as to give the townsfolk one last chance to speak nicely about you. This shop is the oldest one in town. The owner, who happens to be my dad's cousin, inherited it from *his* dad, who started it just after World War I. He had seen enough death on the front to come back convinced that funerals were a solid business, and definitely better than agriculture. It wasn't seasonal and didn't involve breaking your back in the fields – what's not to like? The worst-case scenario, say, a new war, could only improve business. Given that fascism then happened, and then World War II, I guess you could say he was proven right.

I push the door open. Remo, my father's cousin, is sitting at a mahogany desk. He is the only person inside the shop, which is dark and subdued, as you would expect. I have not seen him in ten or more years. He still sports a thick black moustache, pepper with only a trace of salt, a prominent belly, and very little hair. He wears a dark suit and a white shirt, and is playing with a tablet, enthroned in a court of model coffins, headstones and funeral paraphernalia. He grew up among the gadgets of death, and maybe this is why he fits the environment so perfectly. He raises his head when we enter.

'Remo!' I say.

He frowns, then recognises me and says, 'Mauro!' He begins a smile and immediately recants. 'What happened?'

'Nobody died, Remo, don't worry.'

I see relief passing through his soft body. 'I'm sorry. Mine is the sort of business where you don't want to see family walk in.'

I answer with a smile. 'Do you know my friends, Fabio and Tony?'

'Are you Angelo's son?' he asks Fabio. 'Angelo, the teacher of Classics.'

Fabio says, 'The *retired* teacher. But yes, that's me.'

'I was taught by your dad. You look exactly like he did then.'

'Is that meant to be a compliment?' Fabio jokes.

'Angelo knew his way around the ladies,' Remo replies, good-humoured. 'I hear you know yours too, with your photographs.'

'It's only a job, really.'

'Best job in the world.' He gestures at a coffin, making clear he is just messing around. 'I spend my days with *dead* people, you spend yours with *drop dead* gorgeous girls. Does that seem right to you?'

Fabio laughs at the cheesy pun and says, 'I could teach you photography if you want.'

'It wouldn't sit well with the wife, bless her. Are you guys having coffee?'

'If it's going,' Tony says.

Remo chucks a capsule into a white Nespresso machine. 'What can I do for you?' he asks while the machine starts.

'Is Silvana here?' Fabio asks.

After a few seconds Remo hands me the first cup of espresso. 'Is she your friend?'

'Actually no, we've never met. A mutual friend showed me some photographs of her.'

'Don't tell the wife I said so,' Remo chucks a second capsule in, 'but Silvana's a real looker, isn't she?'

Something in his demeanour has changed. His cheerfulness is wary, skin-deep. Suddenly, he *wonders* – but about what?

'Exactly. I mean to ask her if she'd model for me while I'm in town, for a book I'm doing. I won't steal too much of her time, I promise.'

Remo hands Tony his coffee. 'Have you tried calling her?'

'We don't have her number,' Tony says.

'I do, but I'm afraid it won't do much good.'

Remo's good humour is faltering. I don't like this. 'I thought she worked here.'

'She quit. Five days ago.'

It takes a moment to sink in, and when it does, I realise a simple truth, and it scares the hell out of me. Art was a weirdo and a loner. Silvana is (or was?) a young, fetching, photogenic woman. The shit-storm we would be calling on our heads if we were implicated in her disappearance would be catastrophic. We have to get out of here before we hear a single word more, and forget about Art. It is not selfishness. It is self-preservation.

'Why is that?' Tony asks, his voice coming from another world.

Remo waits for the last cup of espresso to fill, and hands it to Fabio. 'In a way, it came out of the blue,' Remo says, 'though only because I couldn't see the signs. Silvana was a good employee. Hard worker. Never stolen a penny, wonderful manners with the clients, nothing to complain about. I paid her well. Good personnel are hard to find.'

'So what happened?' Fabio asks, impatient as always.

Remo shrugs. 'Last week Silvana came into the shop and said she was quitting, just like that,' he snaps his fingers, 'and could I give her the money I owed for the last month, immediately, please, in cash. That knocked my socks off. I asked her what the problem was, and she said she didn't have a problem, she was only quitting, and she was sorry, but could I pay her immediately, please, and cash. And, listen to me, the girl was *terrified*; she had an expression on her face I've seen on girls whose father has died leaving mountains of debt and no rope to climb them. Not *worry*, not *upset*, but unadulterated *fear*.' Remo pauses. 'She's an adult by law, though. I paid her and asked her to stay in touch, and she practically bolted.'

'Bloody hell,' Tony says. 'What was that? Drugs? Boyfriend?'

Remo doesn't reply immediately. He licks his lips, thoughtful. He turns to me. 'A boyfriend, *sì*. Silvana said it wasn't like that, but I'm old enough to see when it is exactly like that. Mauro, I know you guys were best friends when you were little, but… ah… Arturo Musiello, are you still in touch with him?'

A cold, cold hand takes a grip on my belly and doesn't let go. 'Not so much. I'm not much in town in general.'

'I'm afraid he took one or two bad turns. He's not…' Remo pauses, then whirls a finger at his temple. 'He's not *right* in his head. Do you know that he talks to his dog?'

'Yeah, I heard that.'

'And don't ask me where he makes the money to get by, 'cause I don't know. Can't be anything clean. I don't like him.'

'Silvana did?' Tony asks. We shouldn't be asking questions. We shouldn't be going near Silvana with a ten-foot pole.

'For the last few months she was *always* talking about him. *Art says this and that.* He was full of theories, that one. Full of crap. I'm sorry to say so about a friend of yours, but Arturo never was a good apple. What with all the pain he caused his poor parents when he was a boy.'

I glance at Tony. He keeps a smile nailed to his lips.

Fabio says, in a light tone, 'Art's a player now? He sure wasn't one at school.'

'He's... what? Sixteen? Seventeen years older than Silvana? He's got experience. And consider that Silvana isn't well; she's a wonderful girl, but she has history.'

'Of what?'

'Mental issues. Mood swings, some difficult episodes when she was little. She's fine now. On medication.'

I fight the impulse to run. Young, beautiful, on meds, in the thrall of an older man with a BDSM-equipped room in the middle of nowhere: Silvana is a boon to every last newspaper, magazine, blog, kid with a Twitter account in Italy – Europe, possibly. We should leave, but Remo goes on relentlessly. 'Arturo took advantage of her. The first time she mentioned him, she said he'd given her a *book* he'd written. A book, go figure. Arturo didn't go to university, so what business does he have writing books?'

'A book,' I say, despite myself, in a deadpan voice.

'Not a *real* book, mind, only a bundle of paper, typewritten, if you can believe that. *The Book of Hidden Things.* Silvana got crazy about it. *It changed my life*, she said. *It showed me possibilities.*'

'Bloody hell, that's a book I'd love to read,' Tony says, as if it were a joke. 'We could all do with some change, couldn't we?'

Remo smirks. 'Wait here.'

He goes to a shelf behind his desk, where he keeps, neatly ordered, stacks of black leather folders. He plucks one without hesitation. He opens it, takes out a slim bundle kept together by a bulldog clip, and returns to us. He hands the bundle to Tony. 'Here.' On the first sheet it reads:

THE BOOK OF HIDDEN THINGS

A FIELD GUIDE

Tony pages quickly through the bundle. 'A bit on the thin side, far as books go.'

'It's the introduction. Silvana insisted I took it, and said she'd give me the rest after I read that. But I'm not much of a reader.' He pats a headstone. 'I'm a busy man. Kicking the bucket never gets old.'

Tony laughs and waves the bundle. 'Do you know what this is all about?'

'Ravings about saints and drystone walls and I don't know what else.'

'Sort of a *Da Vinci Code*?'

'Yeah, but less fun,' Remo says.

'May I keep it? You made me curious.'

'Suit yourself.'

I open my mouth to say, *Thank you, we're on our way*, but Fabio speaks first. 'Was Silvana in touch?'

'Not her. The next day Saverio, you know Saverio, that no-good brother of hers? Came to the shop, looking for her. I told him she resigned the day before and I thought he knew. He said sure, he'd forgotten. When he left I tried to call Silvana. I've been trying every day since.' He walks to his shop's phone, and touches a button which starts a rapid call on speaker. The answer is the robotic voice of a disconnected phone. 'That's all I get.'

Not worry, *not* upset, *but unadulterated* fear.

None of us says a word.

'Do you reckon I should call the Carabinieri?' Remo asks, after a long, awkward silence.

'No,' Tony replies. 'I reckon you shouldn't.'

And Remo, being a local, understands, and asks me how long I am staying in town, and if I am having fun, and how my mum and dad are doing, and Silvana is as good as forgotten.

8

'This is what Saverio was doing at Art's then,' Fabio says. 'Looking for Silvana.'

I say, 'Good for him. As for us, this is where we call Michele, bring him up to date, and give our farewell to Art.'

We are sharing a bottle of ice tea and a cigarette, sitting between two columns in the shaded archway of a minor church, in one of the alleys at the back of Remo's shop. The alley is paved in slabs of white stone, and you would think it is too narrow for cars, but they manage to squeeze through anyway, temporarily suspending the laws of physics, their wheels skidding on the bone-smooth pavement. The shadows cast by the whitewashed houses keep the temperature in the alley below boiling point, only just. It is not midday yet, and Casalfranco is already a bubbling cauldron. The Sirocco is blowing, the wind from the sea, the hottest, muggiest, worst wind there is.

'Before tracking down Silvana?' Tony asks. 'No way.'

I promised Anna that I would go back home immediately after breakfast. Anna looks forward all winter to our few precious days on the beach, and I am ruining them for her, leaving her stuck with two little girls and unable to go for her endless swims. She hasn't complained once, and that makes me feel like even more of a shit.

I say, 'We found bad stuff at Art's place, and a young woman is missing. These two facts tie together in highly unpleasant ways.'

'What happened to *Art's only got us*?' Tony asks.

'Real life happened! We started with the idea of sniffing around for a friend who ditched us on pizza night. This is on a completely different scale.'

Tony is going to reply – harshly, from the look on his face. Fabio interrupts him. 'Why don't we PM Silvana on Facebook? Mentioning Art and *The Book of Hidden Things*. Maybe she'll reply to that.'

'Seems sensible,' Tony says.

'On what planet?' I snap. 'This is a story waiting to blow.

It'll blow *hard*, and when it does, the fewer connections we have with Silvana, the better. She's young, and beautiful, and we're three older blokes, four with Art – can't you see what that could turn into?'

After a moment of quiet, Fabio says, 'You have a point.'

Tony shoots me a morose look, but doesn't reply.

I say, 'Call Michele, will you?'

9

Tony leaves to have lunch with his mum and dad, promising to catch up later. He is curt, and angry. It will pass. Tony's bad moods never last.

'I'll walk you home,' I say to Fabio.

He asks, 'Do you need some headspace before going back to Anna? Now that it is all over?'

I sigh. 'Possibly. What about you? How's Angelo?'

'This morning he didn't remember that I was staying at his. He jumped when he saw me.'

'I'm so sorry, Fabio.'

Fabio takes off his sunglasses, wipes the sweat from them, and puts them back on. 'I can deal with it. With Don Alfredo, not so much.'

'Why, what's he doing?'

'He's taken control of the house. He's always there, and when he's not, he sends women from church. *The community is here for your dad*, he says.'

'Maybe it's true.'

'And maybe chemtrails are bad for you. No, he's in it for the kicks. Half of Casalfranco were my father's students. Don Alfredo wants the town to know that the two of them are tight.' Fabio kicks a rock. 'I'm not stupid, Mauro. I understand that Don Alfredo will likely get away with what he did to Art.'

'Honestly? I'm not sure Don Alfredo did anything.'

Fabio doesn't reply. 'Maybe you're right,' he admits, after a while. 'What the fuck do I know. I'm a loser worse than Art.'

It is disheartening to see Fabio so low. Since he left Casalfranco, he always irradiated this aura of self-assuredness – he gave the impression that he could face up to a platoon of mad mutants, and emerge on the other side with a smile, a good photograph and a hot girl on his arm. I say, 'You're not a loser, and Art wasn't, either. He was just strange, and unlucky.'

'And what am I?'

'Alive?'

We walk in silence for a while, then Fabio says, 'Tony told you, didn't he? About my problems.'

'Yeah,' I say.

'I left my father to rot. You always thought I was a bit of a dick to him.'

'I…'

'It's okay, Mauro, you were right: I was a dick. My father is a bigot and a bastard, but he does love me. And I left him alone, a widower in a house too big, his only son calling on the phone once a month. I suppose I thought I would make it up to him one day. Too late now.'

I don't say anything.

'I had this fantasy,' Fabio goes on. 'I would break big, any time now, and show everybody in Casalfranco what I was made of. Especially my father. I would show him that his expectations, all his principles, were bollocks. I didn't hate him, not really, I only wanted to rub in his face that he was wrong. Turns out he was right all along, wasn't he?'

I wait a little, then say, 'You know I like your father.'

'He likes you too. He'd be happier with you as his son.'

'But trust me, *you* wouldn't be happier if you were me.'

'I'm not counting your pocket money, but I'm sure you can afford better gelato than me.'

'Do you have any idea what it means to have not one, but *two* children?'

'Means that you're building a family. Something solid.'

I scoff. 'That's how couples with babies lie to themselves, in order to survive. The truth, though? The truth is that if you gave a choice to those couples, all of them, *all of them*, would go back to how things were before. Hobbies? Forget about that. Sex? Not much. Sleep? As if. You run all day, and run, and run, making a pause only to clean asses and wipe noses, and then you keep running.'

Fabio looks bewildered. 'That's harsh.'

'Sorry,' I say, after a while. 'I didn't mean... I don't want to be unfair to my girls. I love them. I was the one who insisted on having Ottavia, even before Anna and I got married. When Ottavia was born, and that didn't make me happy, I insisted again on having Rebecca, thinking that now that I was used

213

to all those sleepless nights, I'd learnt to cope.' I have to hold back tears. I am a grown man and I have to hold back tears. 'But sometimes I think. If it weren't for them, I could change my life, do something better, something *worthy*. I live off the rotten, nasty financial system of this country. I'm no better than Michele. And now it's too late to change, now that I'm responsible for Ottavia and Rebecca. They're wonderful, yes, and I love them to pieces.' I cross my wrists, one above the other. 'But they're handcuffs.'

Fabio looks at me and says, 'You're nothing like Michele. You don't kill people.'

'Yeah, I only help them to ruin each other.'

We reached Fabio's house, a small, two-storey villa with a wrap-around garden. 'Do you want to say *ciao* to Dad?' Fabio asks.

10

'This squid is amazing,' Anna says.

I nod without answering. I should tell her about Silvana – I *need* to tell her – but I don't have a chance, because the girls are all over the place.

'It's not,' Ottavia whines, prodding her grilled squid with a fork. 'It's all *squishy*.'

'Squishy!' Rebecca repeats, on the edge of tears.

We are having lunch at the plastic table of a beachside restaurant, which has been opened for no more than four years and is thus considered *new* by the locals. The sand underfoot is made compact by dampness. The Sirocco pumps up the waves into billows, and makes you sweat even when you sit still. Its mission is to make your day miserable. Art used to call it *Suicide Sirocco*, because it gives you bad thoughts. *It'd be a great name for a grunge band*, he would say. *Mauro and the Suicide Sirocco*. It is making the girls fractious. I can't talk to Anna with them present; Ottavia is old enough to pick up more than is good for her. Private moments between Anna and me, like last night, are rare.

Anna looks sternly at the girls and says, 'Don't make a scene.'

'It is revolting!' Ottavia elaborates while stabbing the grilled squid. Where did she learn that word, *revolting*? She's intelligent for a five-year-old. But she is still five years old.

'Eat what you have on your plate,' I say.

Ottavia folds her arms. 'No!'

'No!' Rebecca joins her.

'Very well. No gelato then.'

'But, Daddy, I'm *hungry*,' Ottavia says.

'Then eat your squid! You ordered it.'

'I don't want it!'

'I don't want it!' Rebecca echoes.

Welcome back to your life: little girls and Excel spreadsheets. I wonder what would have happened if I had followed Art's advice and tried my luck as a musician. A rock 'n' roll life with no space for kids, not before hitting, say, forty. Yeah, and where did Art's wisdom lead him? *In the shadow of a tree or beneath the weight of a rock.*

Look at me, I'm quoting Concetta Pecoraro now.

'I want gelato,' Ottavia says, bursting into tears.

'Ottavia…' Anna tries.

'Me too,' Rebecca cries.

When they throw a tantrum, they do it together, in stereo.

I stand up.

'Are you all right?' Anna asks.

'I need to go to the loo.'

I make my way to a small toilet in the back of the restaurant, a temporary structure made of planks and corrugated sheet-iron. I lock myself in. *What's my problem?* The girls are acting up because of the wind, but also because they picked up on my mood. Kids are like dogs that way. I want to keep playing cops and robbers with my friends.

I take out my phone, to look at Silvana's profile.

Anna would agree she is a dream made flesh. There is something in her eyes, as if they are openings into a wild, dazzling world. I can understand Art falling for this girl, doing crazy things for *la Madama*.

Everything on her Facebook is public: her profile, her smile. Such a trusting girl. Casalfranco being what it is, we have twenty-odd friends in common. Her last post, from six days ago, is a quote from Nietzsche: *If you stare into the abyss, the abyss stares into you.* It warms my heart. The same abused soundbite would be on every battered journal when I was her age – even though no teenager in Casalfranco had ever actually read Nietzsche (not even Art. He had pointedly refused to show an interest in him, just because, I suspect, everybody else pretended to).

Considering that Silvana went AWOL soon after posting that status, it might have a more sinister meaning. But it might not. Nietzsche is the go-to guy for teenagers who want to sound a bit dark. Scrolling down, I see Silvana shared some paintings by Klimt, another mainstay of under-twenties taste.

But she also shared, and this is more interesting, Orthodox icons: saintly figures on golden backgrounds, the fixity of their pose making them vaguely disconcerting. The saints, always the saints. She posted lots more quotes, from the obvious (J.D. Salinger, *Mothers are all slightly insane*, definitely appropriate for Silvana) to the puzzling (John Fowles, *The most important questions in life can never be answered by anyone except oneself*). And photographs of herself, too: in a winter coat, in an almost non-existent bikini, smiling, pouting, always beautiful in a way which leaves no hope for whoever looks at her. I scroll down quickly. Further back, Silvana used to post lighter content (games she played, food photos), but they slowed to a trickle and fell to zero last year, leaving space only for culture bits and naive sexiness.

This is a girl who wanted to impress; Art's shadow is all over her profile. I hope to God he didn't hurt her too badly.

All her posts have strings of likes, comments, smileys, almost exclusively from men. Some of the male names recur over and over again – friend-zoned buddies, I feel for them. In a detective story, one of them would be the suspected culprit, or a red herring, at least, leading to the real culprit in the end. I tap on *Message*, and the Messenger app pops up. Silvana's profile is open to messages from strangers. Should I or should I not?

> I know about Art and The Book of Hidden Things. And I
> know you're keeping yourself to yourself, but can we meet?
> I'm one of Art's best mates. :)

My thumb shakes on the *Send* button, without touching it. There is no rational justification for sending the message. I should press *Delete* and go back to my family. The best thing that could happen at this point is for Art's death to be ignored and forgotten. He won't receive justice, and maybe he doesn't deserve any.

My phone rings.

It makes me jump and lose the grip. I catch it just before its seven-hundred-euros weight takes a plunge in the WC. It is Tony.

I answer. 'What's up?'

'I messaged Silvana.'

'What the hell, Tony? We agreed that—'

'She replied,' he says.

11

'Why did you message her?' I ask Tony while he drives. The coastal road is deserted; this weather doesn't put you in a mood for partying late. 'We agreed to call it quits.'

'I read Art's introduction to his book.'

'And?'

'It changed my mind.'

'I thought we were over Art's ravings.'

'Read it and then we talk.'

We pull over by the roadside on the Litoranea, half a mile or so from the closest bar. We walk to the middle of this lonely stretch of beach. It is eleven pm. My shirt is plastered to my skin, *like a superhero costume*, to quote Tony. The sand cracks underfoot, and Suicide Sirocco plays its grunge tunes: tall, broad waves leap and break on the shore with beastly roars. Fabio didn't join us; it hasn't been a good day for Angelo, and Fabio wants to stay with him. I should be with my family too.

Tony shouts to make himself heard, 'This girl likes drama.' He has already forgotten that he is cross with me. 'The waves! The wind! The beach at night!'

'Fabio would like it too. It's a spectacular backdrop for a photoshoot,' I shout back.

'What you mean is, a spectacular excuse to make a girl drop her knickers.'

She is late. *Local time*. The Sirocco slaps my face with tiny drops of seawater. 'I visited Angelo today.'

'How is he?'

'He thought I was Art and told me off for running away from home.'

'Shit.'

'When Fabio told him it was me, Angelo's eyes watered. He apologised and said, *Forgive me, son, it is not me, it is this silly Alzheimer's.*'

Tony and I keep looking around, but we don't see anybody yet. 'Do you know what Fabio's planning to do about him?' Tony asks.

'He's not sure. He's staying in town for a little longer. He's thinking to ask Lara, his girlfriend, to come down for a few days.'

Tony points at the dunes separating the beach from the road. 'Look: is that her?'

A dark silhouette is moving in our direction. She's slim, not very tall, and seems to waver in the wind. I can't make out her features at first, but when she comes closer, I recognise her, even more beautiful in person than in the pictures.

Silvana glances at me and turns to Tony, with an angry scowl. 'You didn't say you'd bring a friend.'

'He's Mauro,' Tony says, as if that explains everything.

Silvana bites her lips, without answering.

'Was Art your friend?' I ask.

She says, 'Why do you talk about him in the past tense?'

'You know he's missing, right?'

'*Yes, I fucking well know he's missing!*' she replies. 'Why did you want to see me?'

I'm taken aback by the strength of her reaction. *Mental issues. Mood swings.* Two older men on a beach with her. Why did I ever agree to come?

'We want to help,' Tony says.

Silvana scowls. She puts a hand behind her back – and it comes back out again carrying a gun. I can't say if it's a big gun or a small one. I can't say if it's new or old. I can't even be sure whether it's the real deal or a replica. All I can say is that the metal of its barrel is made shiny wet by the Sirocco.

The world slows down and becomes strange. Guns belong

to gangster movies, not to my life. I know guns exist, I know the Sacra Corona Unita use them, but I have never had one pointed at me. I have to pee. A shivering, beautiful girl is pointing a gun at me, and I have to pee.

Tony says, 'Easy.' He is calm. He handles violence better than any of us. 'We're friends.'

'No, we're *fucking not*!' Silvana yells, waving the gun. 'It's too late! Stay away from me! Mind your own business or…'

'We're friends, Silvana,' Tony repeats, in his best soothing voice.

'FUCK!' the girl yells.

I don't see her pulling the trigger, but I hear the explosion, louder than the waves, louder than the wind, louder than my blood pumping through my veins. And I see Silvana's hand thrust upwards to the sky by the recoil.

And I feel a sudden jolt somewhere in my body, and pain everywhere in my body.

And I feel a gurgling sound rising to my throat.

And

I

…

THE BOOK OF HIDDEN THINGS

A FIELD GUIDE

I

When I was eight years old, I saw my grandmother die.
She had been in bed for a week or so. She coughed
in prolonged gurgling explosions which seemed to
come from a creature only halfway human. By night-
time her noises scared me, as if Grandma were not
Grandma anymore, as if she had changed, somehow,
into a harpy with talons and claws, and that was her
cackling. My mum and dad spent as much time as they
could with her – they understood she didn't have long
to live – but that Sunday afternoon they had had to
go to Portodimare, to sell the apricots from our
trees before they rotted. They left me the doctor's
number, for emergencies.

I had my nose in my books, drinking milk and
nibbling the sparsely sugared biscuits my mum used
to bake, when Grandma called me. 'Art,' she said,
between a fit of coughing and the next. I jumped to
my feet and ran to see what she wanted.

Her room (it would later become our living room,
but I will always think of it as Grandma's bedroom)

was in darkness, with the curtains drawn and the lights turned off. There was a smell of stale sweat, and a whiff of urine and faeces. When Grandma's coughing fits were particularly bad, she would lose control of her functions for a moment or two.

'Art,' she said.

I inched closer. Scary as the sight of her was, I couldn't take my eyes off her. She had aged a hundred years in seven days, like in a fairy tale. I didn't understand, yet, the very real havoc that time can wreak on a body.

Grandma coughed and shook, with her flimsy metal bed trembling beneath her. The fit went on. I had already turned my back to run to call the doctor, when suddenly the room went quiet. I cautiously turned my head again, to look at the bed. Nothing moved.

'Grandma?' I said.

'Art,' she said. And then, in a clear voice: 'Crisci Santu.'

In the three steps it took me to reach the bed, she was gone.

II

Crisci Santu: 'grow up a saint' is a common saying among peasant grandmothers in Southern Italy. From their point of view, it is common sense advice. When both your mother and your father toil in the fields, becoming a saint is still a viable option, whereas becoming, for example, a doctor or a lawyer, is not.

But the Catholic doctrine dictates that in order to be made a saint you must be able to work miracles.

Only the evidence of miracles is evidence of sainthood. You can lead the most blameless life and still will not qualify if all your actions, however commendable, turn out to be worldly. This means, in practice, that you are a saint only if you can work magic. Such was the wisdom of peasant grandmothers: they knew that only magic can save lowborn children from toil.

III

I am not a Catholic. I can get on with other religions. Buddhists are fine, Hebraism is fascinating, Wicca – the mystifying English cult of the witches – makes a few points I can very well relate to, but Catholicism? A religion based on (male and male only) authority, on notions of pain and blind obedience, which overtly compares its followers to sheep? I am no sheep and I have no patience with self-proclaimed shepherds; I would rather spend eternity in Hell than in a flock. And yet in order to understand the nature of the Salento landscape, the meanings hidden under its sun, we must understand how, and to what extent, the saints came to define it, in rocks, and dirt, and thorns, and lizards.

IV

My friends say that I change my interests as easily as a politician changes their mind. They have a point. I will study baroque this year and learn herbalism the next, but that is not because I am a fickle man, no. It is because we inhabit a vast, extraordinary universe, and I mean to embrace as much of it as I can before I die. Every day that goes by is one less day I have left to live, and every piece of knowledge that I miss is lost forever. My interests do not change, they grow, the pursuits of yesterday seeding those of tomorrow. Take drystone walls; as a child, I became fascinated by them, and that in time led me to my greatest insights into the Hidden Things.

In Salento, drystone walls are everywhere. You see them demarcating plots of land, private gardens, or, in their oldest incarnations, as prehistoric town borders. Wherever they are, they do one thing and one thing only: they mark boundaries.

The building technique can be explained in five minutes, and yet it is so essentially precise that it has survived the centuries and the millennia, scarcely changing in time. Or in space – in the Scottish Highlands, with their cold, dismal weather, I found walls built with exactly the same technique as used in Southern Italy, a land of unconquerable sun.

I was attracted to drystone walls in the instinctual way of bright children. I found it fascinating how the walls marked boundaries between different fields, and, in practice, created that difference. How come the land on the right of a wall was exactly the same as the land on the left, and yet, it was different, belonging as it did to another family? How come I was a prince on one side, a trespasser on the other? What happens if I move the wall? I asked my father, at which he laughed and replied, in dialect, nno ppuei spustari lu muru, 'you can't move the wall'.

Those words made the wall a thousand times even more magical to my eyes. Before, it was just a pile of jagged rocks, only a little taller than me, and now, it was an eternal barrier, with the power to decide <u>who</u> ruled <u>where</u>. It decided how much food my family would get that year, and therefore how many presents Father Christmas would bring me. Surely there was a great mystery there.

That mystery was revealed to me in the form of an adder.

V

Where there is a drystone wall, so too there are adders; it is a well-known piece of southern lore. But at the age of five I had never seen one. I lived with my family in the deepest countryside, in a smallholding lost in an expanse of fields, with nothing more than a narrow, unpaved lane as a bridge between humankind and my doorstep. I knew perfectly well that adders were plentiful, and yet, I had never seen one.

I knew the rules, of course. My father had impressed them on me. Adders come out when it's warm. They are shy, but will bite if startled. When you are in adders' territory, you have to stamp your feet, or beat on the rocks with a stick, so the adders can hear you coming and slither out of the way. If they <u>do</u> bite, my father assured me, you will probably die. (Which is not true. He lied to me in the name of prudence.) To have a chance

of survival, you have to tie two tourniquets, one
above the bite and one below, then say a particular
prayer to San Vito, and then run to ask for help
(strictly in this order – the saints, in Dad's view,
were better doctors than mortals). My theoretical
knowledge of adders was therefore pretty solid, but
no theoretical knowledge is solid enough to endure
the blows of reality.

The mystery of the adder was revealed to me one
day in July, when not a breath of wind, not a trace
of activity, moved the air. It was too hot for birds
to sing or leaves to shake. I was the only moving
point in the landscape, a child of five traipsing
alongside a wall, touching all its rocks, one by
one. I had made up a spell. For it to work I had to
touch all the rocks in the wall, and then I would
own the wall, and its magic powers would be mine. I
came to a spot where three rocks of a particularly
crooked shape met, forming a black hole in the
middle. My hand was resting on one of them, when
I felt a movement, a faint vibration transmitting
through the rock to my skin. I left my hand there,
hypnotised; was that the buzz of magic? I hadn't
really expected my spell to work, but could I
dismiss the possibility...?

A grey-brown reptile head snuck out of the hole.
I froze, in wonder, not in fear.
From Dad's description, and from the pictures
on a yellowed Reader's Digest book I'd studied, I
recognised the serpent for what it was, not one
of the many harmless snakes peacefully stealing
through the countryside, but a real adder, a real

228

danger – the promise of a real adventure.

It was beautiful.

Its head stayed there, amber-eyed and motionless, with that uncanny slice of darkness in the middle of each pupil. I felt as if the adder was the answer to my spell, a spirit I had summoned, and now controlled.

I lowered my head, fascinated by those reptile pupils, and for the briefest moment the adder and I, the spirit and the child, locked eyes. Then I said, ciao.

The adder struck.

It sprang out of the hole, thrusting its lips towards mine, as if it meant to kiss me. Instead it sank its teeth into my right cheek, just shy of my mouth, causing me an intense, stabbing pain. I cried and sprang back, and the adder sprang back too, disappearing into its hole.

I brought my hand to the bite. It was hot, oozing a syrupy mixture of blood and venom. And I thought, how can I tie a tourniquet above and below a bite on a cheek? I would surely die. I turned my back on the wall and ran towards the field where Dad was working.

I didn't think for a moment to say a prayer to San Vito.

I didn't pray, even then.

VI

Dad drove me to the hospital, where a tall doctor injected me with an antidote and a heavy dose of telling off. I was soon up on my feet, and on our way back, Dad gave me a box on the ear. 'Be careful next time,' he said. At home Mum made me my favourite dishes: pasta with fresh tomatoes, mozzarella and olives, and fried aubergines with olive oil and mint (melanzane alla poverella, they are called – 'aubergines the poor man's way'). The stick and the carrot – that was how my parents brought me up.

The next day I went back to the wall. I had learnt my lesson, and I was careful this time, but what had happened had sharpened, rather than killed, my fascination with drystone walls. The walls were crawling with life: spiders and worms hid among the rocks, feral cats slept on the top of them, and the mortally dangerous adder journeyed through them, occasionally making itself visible, to pit its wits against the humans. There was an inordinate amount of life – life I didn't see, life I didn't so much as glimpse – happening just beyond the reach of my senses. An entire world of things hidden to me. And if that world existed, how many more could exist? It was a kind of magic, or perhaps, it was magic as such.

That was my first peek into the Hidden Things.

VII

Like the adder, the Hidden Things do not exactly hide from us, they just mind their own business. Like the adder, the Hidden Things are with us at all times, unseen, unheard, stealing through walls, resting under rocks. Like the adder, the Hidden Things do not normally mind us, but will, in some circumstances, bite. And just as with the adder, when they bite it is no good praying to the saints for help. They will not give you any. Because the saints, too, are Hidden Things.

VIII

In Salento there are traces of the saints everywhere. They are as ubiquitous as drystone walls and, sometimes, as secret as adders. Locals hardly notice them anymore, because locals don't live in the countryside like they used to. Peasants rebranded themselves as farmers, and there are fewer of them, while newly made lawyers and small entrepreneurs drive their SUVs on well-paved roads.

But in this Age of Information, of satnavs and endless connectivity, secrets, far from dying out, are thriving. People drive through the countryside, don't wander inside it anymore, and the landscape is to them a backdrop, not a context. The folk are losing their connection with the land, and, as a result, new forms of wilderness are arising. Humans leave, so more space for others is left. Far from the sight of the crowds, the adders are taking over. Secret, hidden things, flourish.

Slowly but surely, the culture I was brought up in is dying out, and when a culture dies, it leaves behind a mystery. Think of the Maya, think of the Egyptians, think of what America will be a thousand years from now. And then look at Salento – and you will see.

Small chapels are scattered where you least expect them, unassuming white cubes that have been

there for centuries, resisting the wind, the heat,
the storms, a place for the faithful to fall on their
knees and pray to their jealous God. The countryside
is littered with such chapels, and shrines,
and statues, and other, less distinct traces of
forgotten lore: a spring which quenched San Pietro's
thirst, an olive tree made immortal by San Gregorio.
This deeply religious part of the world, harsh and
scorched by the sun, belongs to the saints. They are
junctions between the profane and the sacred, the
seen and the unseen. The Hidden Things, if you will,
and us. The saints and their places of worship mark
the boundary between two different lands - exactly
like drystone walls.

IX

When I was fourteen I disappeared for seven days.
The Carabinieri and the rest of the townsfolk did
their best to find me. Helicopters were deployed.
Volunteers combed the countryside. Highly trained
dogs were called in from as far away as Trieste. It
was all a bit hysterical, but sweet. It was useless,
too; when I came back I did it on my own, and at that
point all the love I'd received backfired on me. I
did not want to reveal what had happened, so I made
up the sort of lie that people would want to believe.
I said I had run away from home, and I said that with
such arrogance, such bravado, that my townsfolk
accepted it. I went overnight from victim to
villain, and my early success became in their eyes
only more proof of my arrogance. My lie, as all good
lies, was bait and hook at once and they all bit.

I had my reasons to do that. I'll leave you to
judge whether they were good or not. I promise I will
give a truthful account of those seven days, which
opened my eyes to the existence of what I am calling
the Hidden Things. After so many years, I finally
came to understand the message of the adder.

I will tackle my disappearance further on, where
it makes sense to do so. First I want to focus not
on the event, but on the space where it happened: an
ancient olive grove. That was where my friends last
saw me.

X

That olive grove is empty of chapels or shrines, but
that wasn't always the case. The grove (it doesn't
have a name on any registry) was bought by the
Diocese of Oria, to which Casalfranco belongs, in
1882. Before that, it had been part of the Mazziani
family estate. The family still live in the town,
and though they are not rich and powerful anymore,
their name still carries a weight of sorts. The heir
to what little is left of their fortune (an almost
barren vineyard and a house in dire need of repair)
is a young woman called Carolina. She was at school
with me. She is married, with a baby. I wish her
luck; the sins of the fathers should not be visited
upon the children.

In their day, the Mazzianis owned much land,
people, law, and other such goods which no one
should ever lay a claim to. In the mid-1700s a young
man from town was found dead, hanging from a tree in
an <u>olive grove</u> belonging to the family. There were

rumours of an <u>unholy</u> relationship between Vittorio Mazziani, the family elder, and this young man (a peasant who does not merit a name in the archives). The official verdict was that the young man had committed suicide. The priest was quick to point out that suicide is a mortal sin and the man would burn in Hell for eternity. Even prayer was wasted on him, and he was to be buried on unhallowed ground. Vittorio's reputation remained unblemished. Indeed, the men 'calumniating' him (the young man's father and cousin) were condemned to pay a fine they could scarcely afford.

There were other stories, before and after that – prostitutes, shady deals, land said to have been acquired by blackmail. I don't wish to make out the Mazzianis as a heinous line of arch-villains; dig deep enough in the past of any powerful or once-powerful family, and you will inevitably find similar episodes. You don't gain power by being nice. You gain power by lying and slaying and raping and stealing. It is not power that corrupts, but the road to it.

To return to the young man's death: the Mazzianis could not have a property of theirs cursed by the sin of suicide, and thus they called the priest to consecrate the olive grove. They organised a gathering in the very spot where the young man had died, inviting the entire town. The priest came in full regalia, with altar boys carrying consecrated water and enough incense to smoke a hog. He showed off his best Latin and sprinkled the trees with water and incense, while the Mazzianis offered food, wine and music. Whatever misgivings the townsfolk still harboured they drowned, and buried deep, and forgot.

Vittorio was devoted to the Virgin Mary. His second name was Maria (giving male children the indisputably female name of the Virgin was and remains a common quirk of noble southern families, and of families with pretences to gentility). To mark the renewed purity of the grove, Vittorio had a shrine to the Virgin built on its western edge. So now the saints were there, and the grove had, it seems, become part of the Hidden Things. Or rather, it was marked as such. Some places have a sacredness of their own, which might or might not be recognised by human beings, but is there nonetheless.

The nameless young man was not the last person to meet their end in the grove. Members of the Mazziani family continued to use it for their secret vices. In 1875 there is a report of a girl of fifteen who was found dead in a local olive grove, seat of a 'well-known' shrine to the Virgin. Her body had been violated, her throat sliced, and the blood from her 'exquisite neck', a contemporary paper reports, had blemished the statue of Mary. The victim had been so uncouth as to bleed to death on the shrine.

An 'inquest' found that the victim, Rosa, was a woman of ill repute, surely killed by one of her customers. Good Christians rightly condemn paying and butchering a prostitute, but they undoubtedly consider being a prostitute a more serious offence. She had it coming, so why waste time and money looking for the killer? The case was quickly forgotten, another sinner was burning in Hell, and there was nothing more to be said.

When blood is spilled over a Catholic altar or shrine, a priest must consecrate it again, but the sources I found don't mention whether that happened, or if the shrine was abandoned, spoilt beyond repair in the collective consciousness. Be that as it may, eight years later the Mazzianis sold the grove to the diocese. The fortunes of the family were dwindling, and in order to pay back the debts accrued at the gambling table, they had to sell more and more of their land. The diocese entrusted the grove to the parish of Casalfranco, and, with no fanfare, the place ceased to be used for worship, or for anything else. Today no one picks olives from its trees, and no trace of the shrine remains.

Men have left; the adders took over.

XI

This olive grove is an example of the sort of place you stumble upon when you start exploring the Hidden Things. The junctures between the Hidden Things and us brim with enlightening stories, and enlightening stories are rarely happy. Suffering, more than any other state of mind, allows us to glimpse beyond the obvious, the everyday, the expected.

The Hidden Things are slippery and changeable. My research brought me into contact with people as different as dancing masters and bogus psychics, and led me to act in ways which polite society frowns upon. But I cracked, I think, the message of the adder; I found an extraordinary key.

You see, everything goes back to what my father told me: you can't move the wall. I don't like to be told what I can and cannot do, yet I will agree that some actions are not practical. If I tried to move a drystone wall, rock by rock, I would be found before my work was done, and I would be stopped. It is true in practice, if not in theory, that you can't move the wall. It doesn't mean that you are stuck where you are.

A drystone wall divides and conjoins. You can't move it, but you have the option to study its innards, its mechanics, the microcosm of stone and biology which lies inside. The Hidden Things move inside the walls, so why shouldn't you climb over them? You can trespass. You can trespass to the next field; you can trespass on the side of Hidden Things. What's more, you have an intellectual obligation to do so. Wherever there is a boundary, wherever it is said that you are not allowed to walk any further, any intelligent person will be moved to do just that. Hic sunt leones? Here are the lions? Let me see them.

In this sense, then, this pamphlet is a 'field guide'. I will write down, in plain words, what I learnt about the Hidden Things, and I will explain how to get to their side of the wall. With the caveat that trespassing means breaking the law, which is a dangerous enough act.

But laws are made by men of power, and their jealous God; and I have no love, or respect, for either.

FABIO

1

I am standing in a dead man's room.

My father hasn't touched a thing since I left for university. My comic books are still stacked on the shelves. My posters still hang from the walls. A cheap portable fan Tony got me as a joke (*It'll help you to survive evil, evil summer*) rests on the small desk where I used to do, and not do, my homework. Even my Walkman is still there. A Walkman! I have seen a video on YouTube where a group of kids were handed one of those. They had no idea what it was or how to use it. My generation's adolescence has been wiped out quickly and thoroughly. It is not a big deal, I guess. The young man I was is dead, but he was a bit of a prick anyway.

I don't understand why my father left everything as it was in here. Is it a shrine? In that case, he loves me more than I ever gave him credit for. Or perhaps he just couldn't be bothered? In all likelihood, it is a statement: *You are still a kid*, this room

239

tells me, *and you are still from Casalfranco and you can do fuck all to change that. The person you were will never die, that awkward person always making excuses for himself, because time is not a river, it is a mountain – motionless, eternal, and you are not on the top of it, you are buried under it.*

The door opens and my father comes in.

I have to suppress a flicker of irritation. He never knocked. He never admitted, in his house, the presence of boundaries. I had to bury beneath the wardrobe the first portraits I made, because if I had left them in one of my drawers, he would have found them during one of his regular searches. *Do no evil and you will have nothing to fear*, was his refrain. *I wouldn't have to check on you continuously if you were a better son.*

'Where are you going?' he asks me now, in the tone of someone who has a right to know.

I am looking at myself in the mirror on the door of the wardrobe, buttoning up my shirt. I have bought a fresh pair of jeans and a white shirt; nothing that will get me in a fashion magazine any time soon, but a step up from the crumpled, sweaty t-shirts I have been wearing so far.

'I'm seeing Mauro and Tony.' Which is a lie.

'You boys must decide what to do about Arturo.'

Today is a good day for my father. He was energised by Mauro's visit, and hasn't slipped once since then. The Internet tells me that good days are to be expected, with early-stage Alzheimer's. Someone wrote on a forum, *Good days are the worst, in a sense, because they remind you of what you're losing*. I understand the sentiment, though I am not sure I agree. Good days are the worst because even when he is dying, even with his brain deserting him, your father still thinks he knows better than you. And you know what? It is possible he does.

'You must decide *soon*,' he insists, when I don't reply. 'Mauro agrees.'

'There are complications.' The mirror reflects a passable image. At least I look clean. I spent half an hour in the shower, making up my mind about tonight.

'It does not come as a surprise that Arturo was in bad company. Don Alfredo has known for some time that he was selling drugs.'

I feel a surge of anger. The fucking priest, always meddling, always judging, preying on the weaklings, *in saecula saeculorum*. 'Yeah? And how come he knows that?'

'He is a priest.'

I stop myself just before uttering *a cocksucker*. I am not fifteen and I won't pick a fight with my dying father. 'I have to go.'

He closes his hands and opens them again. It is a nervous gesture of his, which, I am not pleased to say, I have inherited. 'Listen…'

'I'm listening,' I answer. It comes out as more of a snarl than I would have wanted.

'I want to thank you, Fabio. The two of us don't often see eye to eye. You don't like me and I am not sure I like the man you have become. But you are my son, and that means something, no, *everything*, to me. I am grateful that you agreed to stay in town a little longer. Lord knows I need company. Thank you.'

I am taken aback. I honestly don't remember the last time he talked to me like this, if ever. 'Dad…'

He turns his head. 'It is not a ploy to keep you here. You went above and beyond what you consider your call of duty. I am simply giving credit where credit is due.'

And I notice it in his voice: a tremor, a stifled twitch.

He says, 'I enjoy our time together, Fabio. Soon, I might not be lucid enough to say it.'

He is holding back tears.

2

I walk through Casalfranco in a daze. My father just gave a roundhouse kick to my already shaky sense of reality. *I enjoy our time together, Fabio.* And he was crying. He taught me that crying is an act of self-indulgence, pointless, shameful, that it doesn't solve problems, it makes them worse. The only other time I saw tears in his eyes was when Mum died, and even then only once, when they closed the coffin after the funeral.

I wish I could convince myself that my father played a trick on me, that he concocted a story with Don Alfredo to make me feel this heart-wrenchingly guilty and miserable.

The town is oppressed by the Sirocco. But it doesn't stop holidaymakers and locals from filling the bars. There is a summer buzz in the streets, a merging of drunk voices and pop music and teenagers doing their *struscio*. I feel like a ghost. I could pass through them, through solid walls and flesh, and all they would notice is a drop in temperature. I envy each one of them for how *connected* to each other they are, for how much they *belong*.

I pass by the Carabinieri station, that yellow fascist monstrosity. I know very well that I didn't stay in town because of my father. Neither did I stay for Art. I stayed because at first the town forced me to, and then I stayed for an entirely different reason, one which is selfish, and wrong.

I knock on Mauro's door.

It was a half-hour walk from my father's place, and my once-crisp shirt is soaked in sweat. After a short wait, Anna opens the door. She wears shorts and a tiny vest, her nipples surfacing under the flimsy pale green fabric.

'Fabio?' she says, surprised to see me.

'Can I come in?'

She stands aside to let me in. 'Weren't you spending the evening with Angelo?'

'That was a lie.'

Anna doesn't reply, but she closes the door. 'The girls are sleeping,' she says, in a soft voice.

I whisper back, 'Can I get some water?'

She walks to the kitchen, barefoot, and I tiptoe behind her, following her through a dark corridor. There is no air conditioning, but the air is fresh nonetheless, between these thick white walls. A calendar from 2002 hangs on the kitchen's wall. The year when Mauro's parents moved to Milan, and this home officially became a holiday house. The past is everywhere in this bloody town.

'Water or beer?' Anna asks, opening the fridge.

'Beer, since you're asking.'

She takes out two icy bottles of Peroni, opens them, and hands me one. 'You guys didn't tell me everything that's going on with Art,' she whispers.

I shake my head. 'But this is the last night.'

'Is it? Mauro said the same thing. What he didn't say was where he and Tony were going.'

I swallow half of my bottle. 'The nitty-gritty is, we're done. It's over.'

'Well, as long as they're not doing anything stupid.'

'They're safe, Anna.'

'I don't like being kept in the dark.'

'I understand that.'

Anna leans with her back on the fridge, a smile on her lips. 'Why are you here, Fabio?'

'Because this is the last night.'

'And?'

I take a long breath. The better angels of my nature hurl insults at me as I say, 'And Mauro is not here, and when things go back to normal, I don't know if and when you and I will have another chance to be alone together. And I *crave* being alone with you, Anna. I don't... I don't know if I love you, I don't know. But I *want* you, I want you more than I ever wanted anyone, and this is our last chance. I...' I swallow some more beer. 'I'm making myself ridiculous.'

Anna comes closer. 'Not in the kitchen,' she says.

She takes me by the hand, and silently guides me out of

244

the room, through a short corridor, to the bedroom she shares with Mauro. Those better angels, those sanctimonious pricks, are shouting and rattling their wings, but I barely hear them, enchanted as I am by Anna, by her bum gently swaying with every step she takes, by her long, healthy legs. She pushes the door closed behind her. 'I'm in love with Mauro,' she says.

'I know.'

'Can you handle that?'

I don't reply; I don't have enough self-control left to talk. I put my hands on her shoulders, and kiss her on one cheek. Not on the lips; not yet. I remember vividly the only other time we fucked. I remember every moment and every gesture, and I remember she liked to play rough. I bring my mouth on her neck and bite, and she exhales happily as my tongue licks the skin I hold in my teeth, and the thought crosses my mind that Mauro might notice the signs on Anna's neck tomorrow, and I don't give a damn.

Anna pushes me back, and takes off her vest. In the semi-darkness of the room, her skin shines with sweat. She grabs my head and forces it to one breast, and I close my teeth around the erect nipple, and she whispers, 'Go.' I bite her hard while she fumbles with her shorts and her knickers, and I keep biting when she undoes my jeans, and grabs hold of my cock.

'Harder,' she says.

I slide my hand between her legs, and rest a finger on her clitoris, slowly tracing circles, my mouth filled with the salty flavour of her skin.

Anna slaps my ass, laughing.

'How dare you,' I laugh, under my breath, and slap her back.

'Don't stop biting, dude.'

I bring my lips to the other nipple and bite, as hard as I can, and she exhales again; not a moan, not yet, but almost there. I keep my finger on her clitoris, then I slide it further back, and I touch Anna's wetness, complete, excessive, as is everything about her. Nothing in this world is as erotic as the wetness of a woman; it means that she likes you, that you are worthy of her. Nothing is as erotic as the wetness of Anna.

I want to die here; I want to die while I fuck her, and forget my damn life.

My phone rings.

Anna jerks. 'It'll wake up the girls!' she whispers.

I fall on my knees, frantically fishing for my trousers, as the stupid phone keeps ringing. I finally find it. 'It's Tony,' I say, raising my head.

Anna is sitting down on the bed. She lies down on her belly, raises her legs behind her, and puts her chin on her cupped hands. 'Already on their way back?' she says. 'We should hurry.'

I turn off the phone, and hurry.

TONY

1

My ears ring. Silvana stares at me. Her fazed eyes say that she can't believe there's a link between her finger on the trigger and the man falling in front of her. Mauro's body hits the sand with a soft *thump*, louder to my ears than the gunshot in the crashing of waves. The girl snaps out of her daze and turns her back to us, and flees.

I make a start behind her, but Mauro starts yelling, and I stop in my tracks. *What am I doing?* That bitch can run all the way to Hell for all I care. Mauro comes first. I fall on one knee beside him.

'How bad...' he swallows, '...how bad is it?'

He's brought his hands to where the bullet hit the flesh – just under the ribcage, which could be good or very bad. 'Let me see.'

Mauro moves his hands away. If only all my patients were this obedient. I sink my fingers in the blood of the entry wound. The wound itself is no biggie, and there's no exit wound, meaning the bullet is lodged inside. I bring an ear to Mauro's heart, which is beating fine, and then focus on the sound of his breath. I've heard worse. I don't think there's major internal damage, and the bullet didn't touch the bones. 'It looks worse than it is,' I say, taking out my phone.

'Who are you calling?'

'Emergency.'

'No.'

'What?'

'Only if it's… absolutely necessary.'

'I know what you're thinking, but…'

'Is it necessary?'

My gut says – not at all. Not if I get the right tools. 'Are you sure?' I ask.

Mauro nods. He's losing a lot of blood, getting weaker by the second. There's no time for debate. I rip off my t-shirt and press it against the wound. I run to where we left the car, open the rear door, and run back. 'Still alive?' I ask.

'For now,' Mauro manages to say.

I push my arms under his body and lift. He's lighter than I expected. I drag him to the car, quick but not too quick, to cause minimum distress.

'Hold on,' I say. 'The best surgeon on this beach is on your case.' I don't know if he can still hear my words, but I can, and I need all the reassuring I can get.

I slip Mauro onto the back seat, as delicately as possible, and close the door. I run to the driver's seat, stick the keys in, and start the car. I'll have to go easy on the brakes. Or Mauro's body will roll off the backseat. That'd be a laugh.

I keep one hand on the wheel, speed-dial Elena's number with the other.

'Hey, big brother,' she answers.

'Listen: do you have a friendly doctor?'

There's a pause on the other end, then Elena asks, in a voice suddenly serious, 'You need one now?'

'I need his tools.'

'What's up?'

'I'm coming to yours if that's okay.'

'Sure,' my sister says, and there is no pause this time.

'Can we keep this between you and me? Rocco too, but nobody else.'

'Sure,' she repeats.

I close the call and immediately dial Fabio's number. I wait and wait, but he doesn't pick up. I try again. The phone's switched off.

What the fuck is wrong with that man?

2

Rocco helps me to carry Mauro inside. He holds Mauro's legs the right way, and does not let the body rock. He has done this sort of thing before. Mauro is still conscious, but he's not strong enough to talk. We carry him to a room on the ground floor, where a camp bed has been prepared, with a clean white sheet on it. Good thinking. *Professional* thinking. Elena is waiting for us with a brown medical bag. She appraises Mauro's condition with the coldness of a doctor, without saying a word – there'll be time to talk later. Rocco and I lay Mauro on the bed, and she hands me the bag.

'I hope that's everything you need.'

I open it and glance inside: yes, there's everything. Not that I doubted that. 'Leave me alone.' They can't help me. It'd take longer to explain what to do than do it myself.

Rocco and Elena leave, closing the door behind them.

And I'm on my own with a friend whose life I'm gambling. I took a beastly risk: Mauro didn't travel in an ambulance, this is not an operating theatre, and I don't have a team with me. I'm good though. More than good.

Silvana didn't know how to use a gun, and guns have this quality; if you don't know how to use them, they'll kill when you don't mean to, and won't when you're out for blood. I learnt that doing night shifts in the emergency room in Rome. People think guns are magic wands for killing, but you need skill to make them work, and luck, as with everything else in life.

I take a few more moments to clear my mind. The body on the bed is not a friend's, it's a lump of meat, an engine needing some tough love. It's an object that I am here to repair. Other doctors cultivate finely tuned detective skills. Other doctors think and discuss and have the leisure of time. But us surgeons? We are fixers, mechanics with a butcher's attitude. We don't debate the finer points of diagnostics. We get shit done.

I grab a disposable scalpel, rip its sterile bag open, and get to work.

An operation is an act of intimacy. The first time I conducted an operation on my own, from start to finish, I felt something disturbingly close to sexual arousal, and I ended up – I kid you not – with an erection. I was disgusted with myself. I thought it indicated something fucked inside me. I debated whether I should confess it to Dr Costa, the old surgeon who was my mentor at the hospital, and in the end, I decided to give it a go. When I awkwardly confessed my boner, he laughed. *It happens to many of the good ones*, he said. It took me some time to understand why. When you operate on someone, you must synch your rhythm to theirs; you must understand how their body works, and also, to some extent, how *the soul* in the body works. The ghost in the machine is still part of the machine. Take two patients the same age, the same weight, the same clinical history, with the same ailment, and they will react differently on the table. It's a lot like sex. And I poke and thrust and penetrate, and I've got to be completely *there*, all other thoughts forgotten. The main difference being, while in sex you can let yourself go, that's not an option in surgery, where you can't trust your patient, you can only trust yourself. Your patient is a machine with a sleeping ghost inside; you, and only you, are in control.

It's awkward to be intimate in this way with Mauro.

I get a cannula in and inject him with tranexamic acid, to stop the bleeding. He finds enough strength to give a yell when I pop out the bullet. I check for internal damage until I'm ready to swear there is none. I disinfect the wound and sew it closed.

As I stitch, I pray, using the stitches as the beads of a rosary. I appeal to the Santi Cosma and Damiano, patrons of doctors. I appeal to Sant'Anthony, my namesake. I appeal to Mary, and to Our Lord and His Son Jesus. Mauro is a good man; and yes, bad things happen to good people, but I'm begging you guys. I've seen enough of that.

Mauro flakes out while I clean the wound. Nothing to worry about. I take a chair and drag it to the bed. In the bag, there's everything I need for a blood transfusion. I am O−, the universal donor; *The ultimate blood group for a doctor*, Art joked. Probably Mauro won't need a transfusion, but it's good to know that's an option.

I use a sleeve to swipe the sweat from my forehead. I rip open a wet towel bag with my teeth, and use a few towels to wipe most of the blood off my hands. Then I fish out my phone and check the time. It's less than an hour since we got here. It might as well be ten minutes or ten years; time freezes when I'm operating, as it does when I'm having sex. I speed-dial Fabio's number. Nothing again.

I leave a voicemail. I've still got my phone in my hand when it vibrates and goes *bling* with a Facebook message.

It's Silvana.

4

How is he?

I stare at the screen. The nerve this bitch has. *Keep calm*, Mauro would say. *Keep calm and think.* Imagining being able to reach at her through the screen and kick her ass all the way to the Carabinieri won't help. I answer the message with my number – and wait, my eyes fixed on the phone as if it were a rabid dog.

The moment the ringtone goes off, I answer.

'What the fuck?'

Silence on the other side. Then, 'Is he alive? The man I… shot, is he alive?'

'The fuck you care?'

I hear sobs choked back, and Silvana's broken voice says, 'Please, please, did he die? Oh my God, did I kill him?'

'No,' I say, 'he'll be fine.'

'Jesus, thank you,' she whispers. The relief in her voice is palpable.

I breathe in and out. I shouldn't be too hard on her. She's young, and nuts, and a victim of Art. 'Why did you do that?'

'I don't know what you want from me.'

'We're Art's best mates. Tony, Mauro, and there's Fabio too. Art never mentioned us?'

'He didn't talk about his life. It wasn't my role to ask.'

My role. My mind flies to the BDSM dungeon in the trullo. 'Were you Art's… slave?' I ask. It's blunt, but this girl shot my mate. She can take it.

She hesitates, then says, 'Yes, I had that honour. I loved him. I… I still love him.'

Everything goes between consenting adults. Silvana's old enough to qualify as an adult, but she's also nuts enough *not* to qualify as consenting. I need to forget what this girl did to Mauro and think about what Art might have done to *her*, and muster some pity. 'How did you guys meet?'

'When he came to talk to Mum, he mentioned he was going to start selling weed to get by. He became my dealer.'

'Wait, wait. Art talked to your mum? What for?'

'His masterwork.'

'*The Book of Hidden Things*. I read the introduction.'

'You've got to read it all to understand.'

'I'd love to, but I don't have all of it. I heard you do. We could meet and…'

She scoffs. 'Is that a trap?' she says. '*Is that a fucking trap?*' she shouts.

I wish I'd specialised in psychiatry, so that I'd know how to deal with nutcases and wouldn't be swinging between wanting to head-butt this girl and give her the warmest hug I can. 'You know what happened to Art, don't you?'

'Yes,' she replies.

'And you're afraid because of that.'

She doesn't answer.

'We can protect you,' I say.

She forces a laugh. 'You can't even *see* them!'

'Who? The… the Hidden Things?'

'Sssst!' She pauses. 'Fuck off, twat,' she says. 'Come looking for me and I'll kill you all.' She ends the call.

I immediately try to call her back. Her phone is disconnected. I let out a cry of frustration and draw back my arm to throw my mobile at the wall. I stop just in time. This is not the moment to go haywire. I dial Fabio's number once more, but once more it goes straight to voicemail.

And I start worrying.

FABIO

1

Anna makes me come inside her. The feeling of connection is so intense it is almost an orgasm in itself. She laughs. She is too honest to pretend to be coming as well. I roll on one side, only for the space of a breath. Then I gather my strength, ignore the sleepy grip already sneaking up on me, and roll back on top of her, pinning her to the bed. I use every inch of my body, my tongue, my fingers, my knees, to pleasure and worship her. And finally, when my joints are shivering and my muscles are letting me down, I sense a tremor running through her body. I have buried my head between her legs; I look up to see her face, her teeth biting her lips to stifle a shout coming not from her throat, but from her entire being. I sink my head again and keep licking her, slow circles on her clitoris, and she shakes so violently that I have to grab her ass with both hands and hold tight to stay in place, and I keep going, and I keep licking, occasionally sucking her small lips, until her movements get slower, and I hear her breathe out, and she loosens up in my hands and under my tongue.

I am ready to go again. In five minutes, I will.

For now, I crawl next to her and let myself fall on her side, skin to skin, and I kiss her mouth, the merging of our sweat as exciting as the merging of all other fluids.

'Can you do that all over again?' Anna says, with a laugh.

I stick out my tongue. 'I can't feel it anymore,' I say, keeping the tongue out, so that my words sound all strange.

Anna grabs my hand, brings it between her legs. 'Use that, then.'

It is mad. The south is mad, with its lavish sun setting hormones on fire. We know that being in bed together is an awful, awful thing we are doing, and this is the last time we will ever do it, so we are dragging the moment out as long as we can. Tomorrow Anna and I will still be alive, as people, but *we*, the awesome entity we make with our naked bodies joined in fucking – that will be dead. We will be dead and we mean to burn bright before that.

So I stick a finger inside Anna, and I close her lips with mine, and stop her tongue with mine, to stop her crying out loud, to stop her waking her and Mauro's girls.

2

Time is a blur of kisses, skin, and the occasional drink of water.

Anna asks me, 'What time is it?'

We are getting our breath back, lightly stroking each other's body, not losing physical contact for a moment. 'I don't know.'

Anna frowns, hauling herself up on the bed. '*Do* know, then. They were coming back. The scene would be… awkward.'

She's right. She's always right. I roll out of bed and take my phone. I switch it on. 'It's past one.'

Anna jumps up. 'I thought it was midnight at most!'

Tony's call was more than two hours ago. If he and Mauro were not on their way back, why did he call me? The phone finds a signal, and receives the notification of a voicemail from Tony's number. I dial voicemail.

'Where are you, man?' Tony's frantic voice asks. 'We have a problem. It's Mauro. It's… don't get worked up, nothing's out of control, but come ASAP. We are at my sister's.' He gives the address. 'If Anna calls you,' he adds, 'tell her you didn't hear from us. There's a couple of things we have to work out.'

'Was that Mauro?' Anna asks. She is putting her knickers back on. Our night is over; we are already dead, me and her. 'Fabio? Was that Mauro?'

I don't know what to say.

TONY

1

Fabio rings at the door. Only, when I open it, it's not Fabio I see, it's Anna, and she is pissed off.

'What happened to my husband?'

'I...'

She puts me aside, gently but firmly, and steps in, repeating, 'What happened to my husband?'

'Where's Fabio?'

'Home, with the girls. Tony, tell me what happened to my husband. *Now.*'

Fucking Fabio. I told him to keep his mouth shut with Anna. If you can't trust your mates, then who?

'He's alive,' I say, and immediately switch from cursing Fabio to cursing myself. *He's alive* is only good news to doctors. For the rest of the population, *alive* is what you're supposed to be. 'He got shot,' I explain, 'but he's fine.'

'How can one *get shot* and be fine?' Anna is calm, like a calm ocean under which a kraken is curling its tentacles.

'The bullet didn't touch any organs, or bones. I stopped the bleeding, cleaned the wound, and stitched it. He's not at risk, Anna. He'll wake up just fine.'

She's pale, and her hair is a mess, as if she jumped out of bed and drove straight here, which is probably what she did, after that dick of my mate spilled the beans. Why did he have to do that?

'I want to see him,' she says.

'Sure.'

'Why is he not in a hospital?'

'Long story. It should be Mauro to tell it.'

She replies, glacially, 'And instead, it's going to be you.'

2

Mauro's asleep, and, like all people when they sleep, he looks young and helpless. I have noticed this at the hospital: in bed, an eighty-year-old man can look like a boy, the same childish expression on his face, the same trust that the world won't hurt him. Anna's eyes rest on the linen stained red. I open the window; the room smells of blood.

'You promise he's all right?' she whispers.

'I wouldn't take chances with his life.'

She knows me well enough to trust me on this. She leans over Mauro and pecks him on one cheek. Then she leaves the room, and I follow.

Elena and Rocco are in the kitchen, making coffee and panini with salami and gherkins (Sirocco makes bread flabby, so they are toasting it). Theirs is a large, modern kitchen, with chromium-plated appliances and cabinets made of solid oak wood, in a 'rustic' design that couldn't be more different from what you'd find in a *real* rustic household like Art's. The dining table is oak too, and the chairs. Bundles of herbs are hung to dry under the spice rack, the only detail that resembles our mum's kitchen. 'Thank you, sis,' I say.

'Don't mention it.'

They leave us alone with food and coffee. I sit on a high metal stool and pick at a panino.

'Tony…' Anna says.

'I know, I know. Give me a moment to gather my thoughts.'

There are not many. Her husband had a brush with one of the most dangerous criminal organisations in the world, because of me, and then got shot, because of me. I owe her the truth. As for Art's disappearance, reading the introduction to his book put a couple of ideas in my mind, of the barmy type, and those I don't have to share.

'I'll give you the whole story,' I say. And I do. I tell her everything since the moment when the story as she knows it started diverging from the story as it is – when we went to the Dance of the Swords and met Michele. I tell her of Silvana. I tell her that reading the introduction to *The Book of Hidden Things* made me want to meet the girl.

'Why?' Anna asks, coldly. 'What did you find in it?'

'It's not easy to say.' Bollocks. It's only that I'd sound

263

insane if I tried. 'There is something about it, which made me think…' I pause. 'In the chapter I read, Art promises he'll reveal further in the book what happened to him when he went missing, and Silvana read the whole book.' It is a half-truth, and half is better than nothing.

'And you wanted to hear what she had to say, whatever the cost.'

I bow my head. 'We had no reason to believe the girl would be dangerous. No reason at all.'

'Why, because she looks cute?'

That doesn't need an answer.

'I'm sorry,' Anna says, after a long silence.

'You have every right to be upset.'

'I feel for that poor girl, I truly do. She wasn't well before meeting *your friend*, and I can't imagine what he could have possibly done to her.'

Me neither. I suspect I've only skimmed the surface, during my brief call with Silvana. 'She says she knows what happened to Art.'

'I don't care, Tony. This story ends *now*. Are you sure that going to the Carabinieri is not an option?'

'The Corona said no. Means no.'

'Then call this *Michele*, please. Immediately.'

'I'll have to talk to the guys first. There might be a fallout, one way or the other, and…'

Anna says, 'Make the fucking call.'

FABIO

1

'Where's Mummy?'

The voice startles me awake. It takes me a moment to remember whether the older girl is Ottavia or Rebecca. 'Hi, Rebecca,' I say, tentatively.

She pouts. 'I'm Ottavia.'

'Of course you are.' The girl found me sleeping at the kitchen table. I'd sat here precisely *not* to fall asleep, but it is too muggy to stay awake. 'Mum and Dad went out for a walk. They left me here to watch after you.'

Ottavia yawns and glances at the darkness beyond the window. 'It's late. Where did they go for a walk *this late?*'

I'm not good with children. I raise both my eyebrows in what I hope will be a mysterious face and say, 'It is a *secret* walk.'

'Did something bad happen?'

'Of course not.'

'I want to call my mummy then.'

I could argue and try to convince her to leave Anna in peace. And she could burst into tears, and wake up her little sister. Calming down two crying girls is vastly beyond my capacities.

I dial Anna's number and offer the phone to the girl.

'Mummy?' she says.

They speak briefly, then Ottavia hands back the phone. I bring it to my ear and say, 'Anna? Still there?'

'On my way back,' she replies, and rings off.

Ottavia's mind is at rest now. She takes a cup of water, drinks it dry, then honours me with a goodnight peck on one cheek and goes back to bed. Her economy of movements would be the envy of a CEO; she is an almost too-perfect blend of Mauro and Anna.

I should feel guilty. The moment I close my eyes, though, I am back in bed with Anna, or I am picturing in my mind what might have happened to Mauro, or, disturbingly, the two things together. Desire and anxiety, that is all. I have no space left for guilt.

I hear the front door click open, and Anna's steps.

'Anna…' I say, standing up.

'Tony promised Mauro will be fine.' She goes to the fridge, takes out a carton of orange juice, and drinks with an expression identical to her daughter's.

'What's the situation?'

'Silvana shot Mauro.'

'*Silvana?*'

'Tony patched him up and promised he will be fine,' she repeats.

I don't need to ask why they didn't go to a hospital. 'I'm so sorry.'

Anna puts the carton back and closes the fridge, with the calm gestures of someone who is making a great effort to keep her gestures calm. 'What were you thinking? Getting involved with the Sacra Corona Unita, like a bunch of bloody teenagers!'

'We were carried away. It was very… gradual.'

'That's how you screwed up your life, Fabio: gradually.'

That is spot on, and it hurts. 'You're right,' I say, after a split second.

'I'm not blaming you more than I blame Mauro. I want to be clear on that. And I see how you all could get caught up in this little game. But it was stupid.'

'A little.'

'The three of you, under the spell of Art, even after he's dead.' Anna shakes her head, and puts her car keys on the table. 'Go, they're waiting for you.'

'What for?'

'Michele is coming.'

2

At the sight of Mauro's body, guilt finally starts to creep in. I was fucking his wife while he was being shot. He was fighting to stay alive, with Tony at his side, and I had my head between Anna's legs. Now he is a small thing in another bed, not his own, surrounded by blood, his own. Even though my rational mind knows there is no connection between the two events, between full sex and near death, my gut begs to differ.

Tony rests a hand on my shoulder. 'Mauro's all right, considering.'

We seek asylum in the kitchen, drinking ice tea and waiting for Michele. The night is giving way to a hazy dawn when we hear a car outside. He has arrived. When Rocco opens the door for him, Michele pats Rocco on the cheek with a patronising joviality, and then hugs Elena. His hair is perfectly combed, his corduroy trousers crisp and clean. He acknowledges my presence with a swift movement of the chin, then turns to Tony. 'Who died?' he asks.

'Nobody. Mauro got shot.'

'The Serious One?'

Tony nods.

Michele asks, 'Was it one of our boys?'

'It's more complicated than that.'

'We'll need a coffee, *sì*?' Michele says with a genial face. 'Elena, if you please…?'

Elena is already heading to the kitchen. 'Of course.' Rocco follows her in silence.

Tony, Michele and I sit down at the dining table, where Tony tells the story, succinctly, but leaving no details out. As a shadow, Elena comes in, leaves a tray with three cups of coffee and a pile of homemade biscuits, and leaves.

Michele sips his coffee, thoughtfully. 'It's a pity things went this way.'

'Indeed,' Tony concurs.

'Do you have Art's book with you?'

'The introduction, yes.'

'I'd love to read it.'

'It's yours. But, Michele, you won't… like it.'

'Why?'

'When he wrote it, Art was even less keen on our Lord than I remembered.'

'Art is a complicated man,' Michele concedes. 'What's your take?'

'I don't have one.'

Michele finishes up his coffee, puts the cup back on the little plate and the plate back on the tray. 'Don't insult me. Please.'

Tony doesn't reply.

I open my mouth. 'I think—'

'Did you read what Art wrote?' Michele interrupts me.

'No.'

'So be a good boy and shut the fuck up.'

I wish I could hit this *dancing master*, but even I am smart enough to be scared of him.

Tony is fiddling with his hands, nervously crossing and uncrossing his fingers. He says, 'You are a believer.'

Michele makes the sign of the cross, and tops it off by kissing his own fingers. 'That I am.'

'I think Art was too.'

'You just said a different thing.'

'No, I didn't make myself clear. When we were kids, Art was a sceptic through and through. From what I read, though, I'm under the impression he went through a… how can I say… *experience* that changed his mind. He *did* believe, in his own way, though.'

'And what sort of experience would that be?'

'Whatever happened in the olive grove, Art implies it was something mystical, supernatural. Mind, he never spells it out in the section of the book I read, not openly, but it feels like that. You'll understand when you read it. Silvana is a young girl with a history of mental illness. Art must have been spinning her all sorts of balls, to sleep with her, or… I don't know.'

'You're not a teenage girl, and you're convinced too.'

Tony shrugs. 'Not *convinced*.'

Michele looks at him for a little longer, as if to make sure those are the last words he will extract from Tony, then he claps his hands once. 'Right,' he says. 'I appreciate that you young men did as you were told. From this moment on, you don't have to worry about a thing. I'm taking matters into my own hands.'

'Don't be hard on the girl. She's not well.'

'Don't worry about a thing, Tony.'

He nods and says, 'Thank you.'

'You're Elena's brother,' Michele says. 'You're family.'

3

As I drive back to Anna, my hands shake on the wheel, and I don't know whether it's because of the inordinate amount of caffeine which I have pumped into my bloodstream in the last twelve hours, or from the relief. Whatever happens from now on, we're out.

Saints and Virgins and Jesus Christ. The level of craziness of all-things-Art has risen exponentially. We should have stopped investigating a long time ago, before anybody got shot. Before I betrayed a friend. I feel like Tony and I just gave our real farewell to Art. Mauro should have been with us. When he wakes up, we will make a toast to our mate, the three of us. This is the end of the Pact, the undoing of the last threads connecting me to the wide-eyed boy I was.

I try not to dwell on Silvana, a girl with mental issues who was used by our friend, and then left, by us, in the hands of the Corona. Michele's definition of *not too hard*, I am sure, is not ours. I tell myself there is nothing we can do, and I hope I will convince myself, at some point, that it is true.

I leave the car with Anna, reassure her that our game of detectives is definitely over, and walk back home. The sky is heavy with clouds this morning. I smell a storm coming. It will start any minute – thunder is rolling in from the distance. Sirocco likes to end with a bang. After that the air will be clean, the wind will be gentler. I will return to real life.

Reality hits me jab after jab. I will have to talk to Lara after having cheated on her; I will have to understand my feelings for her. I will have to work out how to pay rent four months from now. I have to decide what to do with my life. But first, I have a friend to mourn. My generation got old fast. I did, at any rate.

I steal inside my father's home and into my room. Its

mementos feel more fake and wrong than ever. I tear off my trousers and my shirt, on which I smell not only my sweat, but Mauro's blood, too, and Anna's perfume. In my underpants, I crash on the bed. Lightning shines through my window, and, on cue, the storm begins. Heavy rain starts beating on the window glass, each drop as fat as a worm. I used to love storms. It was something Art said: *They are perfect power*. We felt like we could control that power, when we were young – harness the storm. We felt like we were immortal. I toss and turn, once, twice, and it is like a fairy-tale spell; I am certain that, at the third turn, I will fall asleep.

4

'Fabio,' my father's imperious voice jolts me awake. His hand shakes me.

'Can't you bloody *knock*?' I protest.

'Come down. Your friend is at the door.'

Art! my half-asleep brain thinks. I have been so obsessed with him that I automatically associate the word *friend* with his name. If only. Art is dead, Mauro in a bed; it is Tony.

Two in the afternoon, and the storm outside is over. The sky is bright clear again, the air, thankfully, a little better. It is still hot, but not as oppressive. I slap on a pair of shorts and a t-shirt and descend the staircase to the ground floor. My father could be gracious enough to let Tony in, but no, my only friend deserving his respect is Mauro. I open the door.

Art is there.

Art is there.

It takes me a long, breathless moment to recognise him – his prominent nose, his sticking-out ears, his glasses. He is thin, as he always was, and slightly stooping, as he always was – healthy, too, in good shape. I reach out to him. I touch his arm. It is flesh and bones, warm and sticky. Flesh and bones, what else?

'Art?' I ask. My voice is like a child's who can't tell whether he's amazed or terrified.

Art beams at me. 'Fabio, man,' he says. 'I'm back. I've come back to save you all.'

TONY

1

Storms are pure power, Art used to say. Or was it *perfect power?* He was something of a storm expert. He went through a phase in which he studied the shapes and names of clouds, and from there, he graduated to extreme weather conditions. He found out (and we found out with him, because when Art got himself a new hobby, he *had to* share every last detail with us) that storm-spotting was a thing, and a network of storm nerds existed, communicating mostly through amateur radio, fanzines and, for the lucky ones who lived in *America Online* land, newsgroups and e-mails – science-fictional gadgets to us. Storm-spotters would travel hundreds of miles just to see, and take records of, the most magnificent tempests. Art couldn't afford to travel, and there were no other storm-spotters in Southern Italy to exchange notes with, so he contented himself with enlightening us on the delights of rain and thunder, and watching our local storms. Which are, if I may say so myself, not too shabby.

Lightning cracks outside. The rain is drumming on the large concertina door giving onto Elena's garden. I've left the door slightly ajar, so as to let in the delicious smell of rain. It reminds me of when I was a boy and summer was an endless sequence of first experiences and shenanigans with my mates. I like where I am now – the only thing I miss is a steady boyfriend, and that, I am sure, will come. I like where I am, but I'd be lying if I said I never miss how it was then. Before two of my buddies got miserable and the third died, before my baby sister moved into a home built on blood money. I sit on a wicker chair, looking outside, all my energies spent. I *loathe* every minute I've got to stay between these walls.

The best storms come in summer, as a goodbye gift from Sirocco. Art's favourite spot to watch them was the Sea Star, a bar on a beach in Portodimare. It shut long ago. It was tiny, painted blue, and erected without the least trace of planning permission. Its best feature was a veranda overlooking the sea, from where you could see the clouds making their way over the waves, cancelling the sun, huge and awe-inspiring as a rumbling mountain range. And you could see the lightning, not only its light, but its shape, sparkling magic blue light marrying the sky to the sea, both dressed in black. Not many people stayed at the Sea Star when a storm came; most went back home and waited for the weather to improve. The few who were too lazy to go moved inside, rather than linger on the veranda, where, you know, you could catch your death. The veranda was left as a private place for the four of us – and it was fantastic.

It was during a storm that Art did the only thing I ever saw him do which was authentically crazy, by any definition of the word. It was the end of August. The lightning cracked open rifts of light in the sky, and the raindrops were so big, and fell so heavily, they felt like hailstones. When you looked across the sea it seemed as if the giant drops were squirting out from the water, instead of falling into it, like small seeds the sea was shooting up to the sky. Even Fabio was impressed, and Fabio was rarely impressed when no girls were involved.

'You know,' Art said, his eyes on the sea, 'there is enough energy in a single bolt to power a house for one month.'

I asked, 'And?'

'And that means that, in terms of money, the amount of cash a storm generates is enormous. Nature can afford to burn billions. Nature doesn't care for our cash, our rules, for *us*. It doesn't care. We are insignificant.'

'That's a bit gloomy,' Mauro said.

'Why? I'm not planning on *staying* insignificant.'

He brought his hands to the hem of his t-shirt and took it off.

Fabio asked, 'What are you doing?'

Art took off his glasses and put them in a pocket of his trunks.

'Are you going to *swim*?' I said.

As an answer, Art took off his trunks, folded them with his t-shirt, and left everything on a chair. He stood there naked, his hands on his hips like a slightly too old Peter Pan, inviting us to Neverland. 'Are you guys coming or not?'

Mauro turned his head towards the bar, and I turned mine

too – thank God there were no clients left, and the only person inside, the guy at the till, was watching TV.

'I'm not coming anywhere near your dick,' I said. 'Faggot.'

Art raised his hands to the sky. 'You've got to be naked if you want to feel all of it.'

'All of what?' Fabio asked, amused.

'The *power*. The… the… *potential*.'

Mauro said, 'You'll feel it and then you'll die.'

'Maybe.'

He jerked around and started running towards the sea. Fabio, Mauro and I exchanged a glance and ran after him, to stop him, tackle him if necessary. Water conducts electricity. Lightning could strike Art. Or lightning could strike *away* from Art, and the electricity would whizz like a shark, and Art would still be dead.

But he was quicker than us.

He ran like a man possessed, ignoring our calls and our shouts. His feet hit the shoreline, and the next moment he dived in and went underwater, invisible.

'Art!' I called.

There were only the waves and the storm, and then Art's head came out of the water, laughing like mad. 'I feel it!' he cried. 'I *am* it!' He stood up, raising his arms and his head and his eyes to the sky, immersed in the water up to his belly. '*I am it!*' he shouted at the top of his voice, while waves and lightning crashed all around him.

And I envied him a little.

2

'Art had a thing for storms, if I remember,' Elena says.

Her voice snaps me back to the present.

She is sitting down in a wicker chair identical to mine, next to me, folding her bare feet under her legs. The women of my family are notoriously beautiful. The men make do.

'Once he went swimming in the middle of one,' I say. 'Naked.'

Elena chuckles. 'I don't know that story.'

'I've got a ton of Art stories, but I've got to make them last now there won't be any more.'

I see real love, real pity, on my sister's face. 'Michele will find him.'

'Not alive, I don't think.'

'But he'll find him.'

I take my head in my hands. 'I don't like it, Elena. No, I'll be honest with you: I *hate* it. I hate it with a passion.'

She frowns. 'What are you talking about?'

'What you've become.'

She lets my words linger. She doesn't take her eyes from me, and the expression on her face doesn't change, but she doesn't speak.

I say, 'You married a *criminal*.'

'Did Mum put you up to this?'

'No, *I* put myself up to this. Look, I know he's your husband…'

'That's exactly it, Tony: he's my husband.' Elena takes a

hand to her round belly. 'The father of my son.'

'Do you love him?'

'Very much.'

'What Rocco does…'

'Rocco is a businessman.'

'Don't do that, Elena. You were at the Dance of the Swords.'

'You were there too.'

'Because I had to be!'

Elena looks at me, her expression darkening. 'I *had to* as well. I live in Casalfranco, Tony, and that's how business works here.'

'Mum and Dad had a shop for decades.'

'And for decades they paid their fees.'

'Why can't you guys do the same? You pay and get on with your life, without… mixing with that scum?'

'In this world, Tony, there're people who pay, and people who get paid. What would you rather be?'

'I'd rather not be a crook,' I say, struggling to keep my voice even.

'That's rich. *You* introduced me to Rocco.'

'When I was young and stupid.'

'Oh yeah?' Elena says, in a flat tone. 'And now that you're all grown up and smart, what did you do the moment you realised Art was in trouble? You came *here*, you came *to me*, begging for help.'

'Only because Art…'

'You begged me to put you in touch with my people, and I did that.'

My people.

'Then, when Mauro got shot,' she goes on, relentlessly, 'what did you do, oh my tall and mighty brother? *You begged for my help*, again.'

'Mauro was *dying*, Elena!'

'You could have taken him to a hospital, *sì*? To do the right thing. And told the Carabinieri that a mentally ill girl is at large, with a gun. But no, you chose to come to *my* house, and I took you in, no questions asked, and you didn't give a fuck for the girl, as long as you and your mates were safe. How does that work? Your goody-goody rules don't apply to you?'

I close my eyes and take a breath. 'I'm not looking for a fight.'

'Me neither.'

'Just try to put yourself in my shoes, sis. It's all so very difficult to swallow. I had no idea you were so involved.'

'Of course I'm involved with my family business.'

'I am your family.'

'Yes! And here we are, with one of your mates bleeding all over my best linen.'

'Is it Rocco? Does he beat you? Are you afraid of what he could do?'

She stares at me with her deep black eyes, and takes a hand to my cheek, as she did when she was little. 'Oh, Tony. You really don't get it, do you?'

'What?'

'I call the shots, not Rocco.'

I try and find the words but I find I have finished them all.

I can see it at last. I can see the full extent of the woman my little sister has become, and what's worse, I can see how that happened. It could've been me, if I'd stayed in Casalfranco. Honour, camaraderie, a sense of belonging to a large, powerful tribe – these are all things I am attracted to as much as she is. Elena and I are very similar people who took different roads.

In the last few days I haven't only lost one of my best friends, I've lost my sister too. Or I lost her somewhere in the last few years, but it is only now that I realise that she's slipped far beyond my reach. It's too painful to bear, but I won't start crying in front of her, so I concentrate on the weather raging out of the window, and try to remember Art's voice saying that storms were power, that he was power, that he was the storm. After a while Elena leaves, without a goodbye, and I stay on the wicker chair, alone, looking at the storm outside, until Mauro enters the room.

MAURO

1

I limp out of the bedroom, trying to find my bearings in this unfamiliar house. There was a storm in my dreams, and it made its way to the real world. It darkens the day, occasionally brightening it with flashes of blue light. I stumble into a large room with wicker furniture. A concertina door takes up the entire back wall, giving a perfect view of the storm. Art would enjoy it.

Facing the door sits Tony. He jumps to his feet. 'Mauro! How are you?'

'Alive.'

'Hungry?'

'I don't know.'

Tony pushes another chair closer to me. 'Sit down.'

I let myself fall into it, grateful. 'How long did I sleep?'

'Fifteen hours. A little more.'

'And nobody thought I was dead?'

'*Hoped*. The word is *hoped*.'

I make a faint grin. 'You saved my life.'

'Yeah, I'll take the blame.'

'Does Anna…'

'She knows. Every detail.'

'Shit.'

Tony looks embarrassed. 'I tried to buy time, but…'

'No need to apologise. I know my wife.'

Tony says, 'Fabio and I did another thing too.'

'What?'

'We called Michele. Anna was *adamant* she wouldn't accept anything less than that.'

The game is over, and it was high time. 'I see her point.'

'Me too, honestly.'

'How long do you think the Corona will take to find Silvana?'

Tony says, 'They'll have her by tonight, tomorrow at most. She's no Art.'

Lightning strikes outside. It is one of the last numbers in the show; the raindrops are getting smaller, the thunder more distant. 'That poor girl. This storm must be terrifying for her.'

'Why do you say so?'

'Because she was haunted, Tony. Afraid of her own shadow. She will be squatting in some godforsaken hole in the countryside, listening to the thunder, imagining God knows what. That poor, poor girl.'

Tony leaves a moment before saying, 'You're a good man.'

'Do you reckon Michele will go easy on her?'

'He'll do what he thinks he must do to get to Art,' Tony

answers, without looking me in the eye.

Art. Our friend. The genius, the liar, the dealer, the bastard. 'He was really screwed up towards the end.'

'Screwed up, yes.'

'What was it in his book that made you want to meet Silvana?'

Tony looks out of the window, at the dying storm. 'The pages I read were ramblings on the saints and the Virgin Mary, and I found it odd, *very* odd, that Art would get in Silvana's knickers by feeding her some mystic crap. Silvana's mother practically *invented* that sort of scam in Casalfranco. Would you expect her, of all people, to be susceptible to it?'

No, I wouldn't. 'What do you think, then?'

'Art was sincere. He meant what he wrote, and he happened to strike a note with the girl. Or maybe…' Tony makes a frustrated face. 'It's Art,' he says. 'Impossible to the end.'

The storm outside is over, except for one last spray of light rain. Give it another hour and the sun will shine; it will be beach weather. 'I've got to call Anna,' I say.

'Not looking forward to that conversation, are you?' Tony grins.

'Take pity on me, Tony.'

2

Tony drives me home. We try to call Fabio, but his mobile must have run out of battery. I leave him a voicemail to let him know I'm fine. The storm has given way to a cool day. Bright colours and pleasant aromas and a light breeze on the skin – I couldn't ask for any better for a new beginning.

'How's the pain?' Tony says, when he stops the car.

'Bearable.'

He fishes from a pocket the bag of weed he took from Art's car. 'Here. A tried and tested painkiller. All natural, too.'

'I'm obliged.'

'I'm not kidding. If the itchin' gets bitchin', roll a joint. You've got your doctor's blessing, so, go for it.'

The front door opens and Anna appears. Tony waves at her, kicks me out of the car, and leaves.

'Hey,' I say.

Anna frowns, as if unsure what to do. Then she throws her arms around my neck and hugs me tight. I let out a cry – more for the surprise of feeling a stab where my wound is than for the actual pain it causes – and she springs back. 'Sorry,' she says, embarrassed. She's been crying.

'I'm here,' I say. 'I'm good.'

Anna guides me inside. Ottavia and Rebecca are in the back garden, which, after the rain, embraces me with a wonderful smell of herbs and ripe fruit. Ottavia sits on the swing hanging from a lemon tree, with a Donald Duck comic book, while Rebecca is cross-legged in the shade of a peach tree, playing with Lego bricks. 'Daddy!' Ottavia says.

'Daddy!' Rebecca says.

Anna briefed me over the phone; she told the girls I fell down a staircase at Elena's while I was with my friends, and

I had spent the night there to recover. It is still easy to lie to them. They still trust us.

'Don't hug him,' Anna advises them, with mock severity. 'He's hurt.'

Rebecca purses her lips in a serious expression. 'May I hug your hand?' she asks.

My heart breaks a little. I reach out with my hand, and hers closes around three of my fingers, the most she can hold, and squeezes them with what must be all her strength. I love this girl. I love her and her sister and their mother. It only seems like yesterday that Ottavia was born, that Rebecca was born, or that I married Anna, and my friends got me a beautiful Stratocaster, which I played for the first and last time on my wedding day. If I turn my head, I can see those moments; they are just around the corner. They are precious. And I was on the brink of trashing them for good.

I start shaking. Anna notices that and says, 'Daddy's tired. I'll get him to bed.'

'But, Dad...' Rebecca starts.

Ottavia stops her. 'Can I see your Legos?' she says.

So young, so wise.

Anna takes me inside just in time, before I start weeping, tears flowing to my cheeks. I am shaking so hard that the suture itches again.

I could have died on that beach.

When I woke up earlier today, and realised I was alive, I realised that, too: *I could have died.* But only now, safe with the woman I love, I allow that simple, bare fact to surface. I could have been killed by a sick girl – a crime with no culprits. And now she will be dealt with by real villains, folks who don't think twice before dissolving children in acid just to send a message. All that, because I was bored. Other lawyers, when they have a life crisis, get themselves a bloody sports car. Other lawyers, though, never met Art.

'I'm sorry,' I say. 'Anna, I'm sorry, I'm so sorry…'

'Hush.'

I crash on the sofa in the living room. 'I didn't mean for things to go this far. It just… happened.'

Anna nods. 'I know,' she says. 'I'm not mad, Mauro.'

'You're not…?'

'We all make mistakes.'

And I am sure now, I am sure that something happened between her and Fabio, years ago. I would love to tell her that it is ancient history, and I will, when we are both strong enough. 'What I did is enormously bigger than a mistake. I put my life at stake. No, it's not even that. I put at stake…' I swing my index finger between Anna and me, 'us.'

'You're unhappy.'

'I'm not. I'm…' I stop. My wife deserves honesty. 'Yes, I was unhappy. My life turned out different to what I expected, and I wasn't coping well with that.'

'I'm not sure I ever understood what you were expecting.'

'*Meaning*, I suppose.'

Anna says, in a gently teasing voice, 'You should've done as Art said and become a rock star.'

'Big fat good that did for Fabio.' I shake my head. 'No, Anna,

I have a good life, different from what I thought, but good, and I should count my blessings. What I did is unforgivable.'

'There is nothing to forgive, my love.'

'Thank you for being awesome. Thank you for sticking with me. Thank you for making my mates call Michele. Thank you, thank you, thank you. I just don't know what came over the three of us.'

'You guys were being loyal to a friend. It didn't end well, and probably the person himself wasn't worth it. But, your sticking to him? That was admirable.'

'I...'

My phone rings. It's Fabio. Must have heard my voicemail.

'Take it,' Anna says.

I smile at her and take the call. 'Hey, Fabio.'

'Mauro, are you all right?' Fabio's voice is strange. Spaced out, as if he has been sampling a generous share of Tony's *painkiller*.

'Dandy,' I say.

'Good. Good. Listen... uh... Christ.'

'What's the problem?'

'Art,' he says. 'He's back.'

FABIO

Art has lit a small fire at the mouth of a cave facing the sea. His lanky figure has the air of a lonesome cowboy. Like a cowboy, he lies on one side, eyes on the fire, or on something that the fire shows him; and he has a satchel bag which could easily be swung onto a saddle. The only detail missing is a blade of grass dangling down from his lips. Not much grass to go around, in this corner of the world. When he sees us, he smiles and waves.

We call them *caves*, but they are little more than tiny niches at the bottom of the tallish rocks which line this part of the coast. In a country as flat as this one, every rock is a mountain and every hole is a cave. I reckon that half of the locals have lost their virginity in one of these. I did. They offer no actual protection from prying eyes, but they allow you to tell yourself you are safe.

It is a mellow night, the finest we have had this June so far, and the sky is heavy with stars and the shape of the Milky Way, rolling overhead like a friendly white serpent.

'Bloody hell, it really is him,' Tony whispers.

It is.

When he knocked at my door, Art was in a hurry. I gave him a rundown of what we'd been doing, and he arranged to meet us all here, promising he would explain his side of things. I was half expecting not to find him – that I had imagined him, or that he would vanish for the third time. But no; he is here.

'Looking good, Tony,' he says.

I put the grocery bag I am carrying down on the sand, and Tony does the same. We brought sandwiches, snacks, and beer, as Art had asked.

Tony plays along with Art's poker face, and says, 'We come with supplies.'

'You guys are the best.'

I ask, 'Are you sure the fire is a good idea?'

'It's cosy.'

'I was thinking about the coastguard.'

'The beach is empty,' Art says, opening the bag with the sandwiches. 'We hear them, we run. Which one is mine?'

'The brown paper.' We had the fat cut off the Parma ham in Art's sandwich; his taste in food is a five-year-old's.

'I'm not going to ask how much I owe you, sorry,' he says, grabbing the parcel with an air of triumph. 'I happen to be skint.'

'It's on the house.'

Tony uses the bottom of a lighter to open the bottles of Peroni, while I open a jar of pickled gherkins and a bag of crisps.

Art tucks into his sandwich, and asks, with a full mouth, 'Where's Mauro?'

'Home.'

Mauro was furious over the phone. When he knew that Art was physically intact – again – and refused to give clear explanations – again – he told me he had to stay with his family, and killed the call.

'He couldn't spare a night for a mate.'

Tony says, 'He spared a lot, actually.'

'That came out wrong, sorry.' Art bites into his sandwich. 'I was only hoping there would be all of us, that's all, considering that we've now missed the Pact two years in a row.'

'Not my fault,' says Tony.

Art tips his sandwich at him. 'A tad nervous, are we?'

'No, just curious to hear which brand of bullshit you're selling this time.'

'A tad nervous,' Art confirms, washing down his bite with a gulp of beer. 'But that's fair enough. I didn't play it straight with you guys. You'll understand that I didn't have a choice.'

'How deep in trouble are you?'

'Trouble?' Art is surprised. 'Not one bit. How on earth did you get that impression?'

'Then why are we meeting here, and not somewhere civilised?'

Art opens his arms to embrace the beach. 'I'd rather Michele not know I'm back.'

'Back from *where*?' I ask.

'Ah, and that is exactly the question, isn't it? It is the question now, and it was the question twenty years ago.' Art looks at the fire, his face adjusting to a serious expression. In my mind, he remained the scrawny kid I met when I was eleven, at the new, scary school. But I can see he is long past being a kid; his face is beginning to be lined, his hair streaked with a touch of white. 'When I told you that I didn't know what happened during the seven days I went missing…'

'You were lying.'

Art makes a disappointed face. 'I was not. I didn't know. I couldn't know.'

'Are we talking of amnesia here?'

'I remembered every detail, but I needed time to process, and understand. What good do facts do by themselves? No good! Okay, without further ado, here we go, the truth: when I left you guys with the telescope and went into the olive grove – I was kidnapped.'

'Don Alfredo,' I say.

Art whips his head to look at me, with a puzzled expression. 'Don…' he starts chuckling. 'Don Alfredo! No, Fabio, it wasn't Don Alfredo. The person who took me… she wasn't from Casalfranco.' He pauses. 'She wasn't *human*.'

There is a moment of complete silence.

Tony asks, 'How do you mean?'

'What do you think I mean? She was – she *is* – not human. She doesn't have a name you could understand. She's… she's… I won't claim I can tell you what she *is*, because I still can't. I can say what she *isn't*, though.'

'Which is *human*,' Tony says, his voice steady.

Art points an index finger at him, with the thumb cocked, in a pistol gesture, as if to say, *Dead on target.* 'She was a Hidden Thing.'

We have a trick of the trade, us photographers, which some jokingly call our *special sense*. It is a particular gaze, a way of looking at things: you strip your subject of everything that is *you* and not *them* (your preconceived notions of what *good lighting* is, your instinctive reactions to certain colours), so that you will see their nature, their intimate *truth*, emerge. You need the truth. You can choose to portray it as it is, or to change it beyond recognition, but you have to know what that truth is. I use my special sense on Art. I clean my mind from everything I know about him (decades of friendship, gone), everything I believe about the existence of non-human beings (common sense, gone), everything my mind tries to tell me, and in those few, precious moments of silence, I look at Art and his truth.

He is insane.

It is all over him, from the twitch in his eyes to the way he doesn't stop moving his fingers; he is way past the stage when he was charmingly quirky. He needs help, lots of it, and well qualified.

Tony says, 'I thought all that stuff about *hidden things* was, like, a metaphor.'

'Why?' Art asks.

'Because that would mean you're sane.'

'Who cares whether I'm sane as long as I'm right.'

'What are they, then?'

'They are… something else entirely. A different aspect of

the world. The place where they live, it is a real place, as real, no, infinitely *more* real than this one,' he says, stomping his bare foot on the sand. '*La Madama* took me there when she kidnapped me.'

I say, '*La Madama*? We thought that was Silvana.'

'She's a lovely thing, for sure, but not a patch on the one I love.'

I do my best not to catch Tony's eye: Art would be sure to notice, and I don't know how he would react. I am glad I am not alone with him. There is not one shred of sanity left in the space between his ears.

Tony says, wearily. 'Art…'

'You think I'm crazy. That's why I didn't tell you before. I knew you'd think that. And I haven't even got to the best part, yet.' He stops to produce a Cheshire cat-sized grin, and announces, 'The part where I get *magic powers*!'

'Because you have magic powers,' I say.

Art laughs and claps his hands. 'Sure! How else do you think I lit this fire?'

'Matches?' Tony suggests.

'Magic! And that's how I came back, too; I was riding the storm! I was *being* the storm. I somersaulted with beautiful thunder and gorged on luscious raw electricity.'

Art's voice has gone up one octave. Tony doesn't show any reaction. 'Can you show me?' he asks. 'Can you do some magic now?'

Art shows us the palms of his hands. 'I could but I won't. I'm not a show-off.'

'Dude, you're the biggest show-off I ever met.'

'When I was younger, yes.'

Art is scaring me. I let Tony do the talking. I want to get this over with, tidy up as much as possible my relationship with my father, and go back home, to London, to Lara. I am not strong enough to survive the place that broke Art.

He takes a swig of beer and wipes his mouth with the back of his hand. 'But let's start from the beginning, shall we?'

'Sure,' Tony says.

'Where was I? Oh, yes: that night. When I entered the olive grove, I smelt an intense fragrance of violets. *Violets, in January?* I thought. And then I *heard* something. It was… not a natural sound, not a sound of this world. It was the sound water would make if water could have an orgasm, you know what I mean?'

'Actually, no.'

'Right. Right. Well, I can't explain it better than that. I saw a light, of an eerie, delicate shade of sapphire. And a voice said, *Good evening, Arturo.* There was a woman there with me, the most beautiful woman I'd ever seen.' Art winks at us. '*Naked.* I let out a cry and then stood there gaping at her, and she laughed. She eased closer, walking, though the way she did it, it was more like *gliding*, and sealed my lips with a kiss. *You are coming with me*, she said, not like a question, or an order, but like a statement. I swallowed and asked, *Where?* and she – honest to God – put a hand on my crotch, and squeezed lightly, and said, *With me.* She turned her back to me and started walking. And her ass, Good Fucking Heavens, her ass! It was the roundest, most perfect thing that ever graced this land. Large, fully formed and perfect. I couldn't help but follow it.'

'And you call *that* a kidnapping?' Tony says.

'You stick a hook into a worm and dangle the hook in the water. When a fish takes the bait, can you say, in all honesty, that the fish *wanted* to become your dinner?'

'Point taken.'

Art shoves a few more logs into the fire and says, 'I followed her, and the olive grove grew bigger, and stranger. I… it's beyond words, literally; the language we have is not made to describe what I saw and did. Suffice to say *la Madama* brought me to the other side, the hidden one. As soon as we got there, she jumped on me, and started fucking me like there was no tomorrow. Then she fed me some fruits, vaguely similar to figs and prickly pears, but with a spicy aftertaste – like jalapeño, you know? – and sweet wine. And then we talked. That became our pattern: we would fuck, eat, drink, and talk, and fuck again.'

'Yes, but where?' Tony asks. 'Was it a house, a field…?'

I see what he's doing. Good man.

'Not a house, no. We were always out of doors. The only structure I ever saw on that side were drystone walls. I asked *la Madama* why, and she replied, *They mark the boundaries*. As for the rest, it is a place of trees, and grapes, and shrubs. It is always warm, but not too hot. Like late May. Call it Arcadia, if you want.'

I ask, 'And what did you talk about?'

'Art. Philosophy. Magic. Name it! And between the fucking, the feasting and the talking, I realised something obvious, a simple truth, the simplest truth there is. *Before* la Madama *took me, I was dying.*'

'I seem to remember you weren't.'

'We all are! As soon as you're born you start dying. Children talk of getting big, they can't wait for it, but actually, no, as you grow up, you get *smaller*. When you are young, you are *immense* – then you shrink. Everything is possible at five, but what is left for you at forty? With every choice you make you renounce all the choices you could have made instead, and so you become smaller and smaller, each choice consuming you a little, burning your *possibilities*, until nothing is left of you. Death is a progressive shrinking that brings you from vastness to nothingness.'

Tony makes a vulgar gesture with his hand. 'And you had this insight while…'

'Yeah,' Art laughs. 'Best way ever to become wise.'

Tony says, 'Seems a bad vibe to get, while being all blissful and such.'

'It wasn't bad at all. It was like, you're rich, you realise other people are poor, and you feel for them, but that doesn't change the fact you're rich, right? I wasn't dying anymore, Tony; the Hidden Things are changeless, pure enchantment, beyond time and space. On their side, I would never grow small.'

'But you didn't stay.'

Art pushes two gherkins into his mouth. '*La Madama* kicked me out. We had one last, glorious fuck, and I fell asleep with my head snug between her breasts. When I woke up, I was back in the olive grove.'

'She didn't explain?'

'She didn't need to; she got bored with me.'

'Harsh.'

'She's *la Madama*, isn't she? On our first day together she said to me, *Arturo, I was attracted by how bright you shine*. When you shine as bright as she does, though, other lights dim fast.'

'That's when you came to me?' I ask. 'Soon after she dumped you?'

'I walked all the way to your place. I could've stopped at a phone box and made a call, but I needed to walk, you see. I had to *think*.'

'About what?'

'How to get back there.'

Tony says, 'The chick kicked you out the first time…'

'But surely, *la Madama* would appreciate a human being who found a way to get there on his own,' Art interrupts him. 'Now, *that* is a light shining bright! After school I left Casalfranco. I travelled. I studied whatever I thought might help: quantum physics, mindfulness, fairy tales, most of it rubbish but here and there some good stuff. I came across powerful magic, Marvel Comics-level powerful. You know I can levitate?'

'Can you do it now?'

'Yes, but I won't. I'm telling you, it was the most frustrating endeavour. Quite a few people have met the Hidden Things over the years, but it was always by chance, or because someone from *there* took them. Getting there from *this side*, though, and willingly? That was different. That was trespassing – *against the law*. You know me; I couldn't stand that. It became an intellectual challenge as much as a practical one. Who had decided that humans should be confined to one side and one only? I wanted to trespass, and not only that, I wanted to enable other people to do the same, in the face of whatever metaphysical bore took it upon himself to write the laws and mark the boundaries.'

These words make me smile. With all his ravings, Art remains Art. 'Was your return to Casalfranco part of the research?'

Art claps his hands. 'Yes! Yes! Precisely! For a while, I'd understood that I could finish my… *apprenticeship* only here. But I resisted. The change would be enormous. When Mum died, it made me realise it was time.' He makes a dramatic pause, moving his eyes from me to Tony, back to me again. 'Ten days ago, I managed to trespass. *La Madama* was impressed, and promised that I could stay with her forever after.'

Tony laughs, 'Seems to me she gave you the boot once more, with feeling.'

'No! I decided to come back, temporarily.'

'What for?'

'To get you guys.'

I inch closer to the fire. The night is getting chillier, and it has been ages since the last time I felt the warmth of a bonfire on the beach. It is a unique sensation, water and fire not trying to outdo each other, but coexisting peacefully. 'You want to bring *us* on the… side of Hidden Things?'

'I want to save you. You're brilliant! It's not right that people like you must die. I won't have any of that. You have already shrunk so much, Fabio, it's painful to see. Come with me and you won't shrink any further. You won't end up in nothingness.'

'That is…' Tony clears his voice, '…very kind of you.'

Art raises an eyebrow. 'Are you taking the piss?'

'Just a little bit.'

Art chuckles. He reaches into his satchel bag, and extracts three bundles of paper, each kept together by an elastic band. 'Here. My book. It explains how to trespass and everything. Read it and then we talk, okay? I'd be grateful if you could swing by Mauro and leave his copy with him. And hurry up, guys.'

I take mine. *The Book of Hidden Things*, the magnum opus revealing all Art's secrets in one handy package. 'Silvana had one of these,' I say.

'I know.'

Tony pinches his nose and sighs loudly. 'You also know the Corona is after her.'

'They already got her, actually.'

'What the…?'

'Fabio told me they were looking for her, and I ran to where I knew she'd hide, a hut in a field near Portodimare. She wasn't there.'

'And you don't give a damn.'

'Michele has no reason to hurt her.'

'Aren't you guys chums? Go tell him you're back and he can let that poor creature go.'

'It would be a waste of time.'

'It'll take all of five minutes!'

Art looks at Tony with an expression I know – the expression he has when he's trying to make you understand something, and you are too stubborn or stupid to get it. 'The Time will last only until tomorrow.'

'I sense a capital T in there.'

'It's in my book. It explains it all. There is only a small window of time during which you can trespass. If we miss it…' He shakes his head. 'It'll take more than five years for the next window to open.'

Tony is looking for words. 'Right,' he settles for. 'Even so, why should Michele want to waste your time?'

'It's obvious, Tony: the Corona wants to exploit my magic. You heard I healed a boss's daughter? They know what I'm capable of, and they want it for themselves. They left me in peace while I kept a low profile, observing my moves. But now? They won't take the risk of having me run off again. They'll nab me and keep me trapped.'

'Michele speaks of you as a good friend.'

'I've got no illusions about how far that friendship stretches.'

He is right. In practice, it doesn't matter that what he is saying is a huge pile of bollocks – if a mafia boss thinks it isn't, then it isn't. Fact: Art needs medical help. Fact: we take him to a doctor, we are handing him over to the Corona. Fact: we hide him from the Corona, we are dead meat, and Silvana with us. 'Art, you son of a bitch,' I say, under my breath. 'You've screwed us *royally*.'

'On the contrary,' Art proudly stabs his index finger at the book I hold in my hands. 'I'm giving you a chance to be whole forever.'

MAURO

1

If Art was here now I would hit him. Or not. I don't know. This is history repeating, or rhyming at least: Art vanished again, he made us worried sick again, landed us in trouble again, and again came back, apparently safe and sound. This time, though, I don't have the resilience, or the trust in life, that I had at fourteen. I am drained.

Tony texted me:

> We have the book. Art's not with us. Can I drop by yours quickly?

I replied: *Sure*. I told Tony to come to the garden gate, so as not to wake up the girls.

It has been a good evening. We ordered take-away pizza and watched *Frozen*. The girls sang along to 'In Summer', the song in which the little snowman dreams about what summer would be like (forgetting that in summer he'd be dead, which everybody finds a laugh, but I find a bleak commentary on the life of us all). They are in bed now, and Anna and I are in the garden, waiting for the guys.

'Hey,' Tony's hushed voice says, from the other side of the gate.

'Where's Fabio?' I ask, opening it.

'I dropped him home on my way here.'

'Come in.'

'Only five minutes. I'm knackered.'

He has a bundle of paper in one hand, which he places on our little table. '*The Book of Hidden Things*,' he whispers, 'for your enjoyment. Art got us a copy each. He said he kept them for us since he finished writing.'

'How is he?'

'Not well.'

'Can I get you something?' Anna asks.

'Ice tea would be awesome.'

She takes a bottle and three glasses, and we sit down, drinking, while Tony tells us Art's story. A mysterious woman (gorgeous, *ça va sans dire*), magic, sex; it has it all. It makes my heart sink.

'An adolescent fantasy,' Anna sums it up. 'The sexy woman, the supernatural, a dream of… empowerment?'

'Psychogenic amnesia.' Tony shakes his glass slowly, making the half-melted ice clink. 'That's the name. It is when a memory is too bad to cope with, and you build some fantasy to… hide reality from yourself. Art needs a psychiatrist, before he…'

his voice trails off. 'I was giving a chance to the supernatural. Honestly, I was. I'm open-minded, you know that, and I said to myself, *I believe in God, why not something else?* But a *flying Art?* That stretches it too far.'

I say, 'Do we have a clue what really happened?'

'Might have. I'll have a look at the book, and once we're cleared with the Corona, I'll give it to a couple of shrinks, buddies of mine. There must be some hint there; memories don't come out of thin air. Perhaps the person who abducted Art really was a woman. I bet she wasn't naked, and she wasn't magical, but the sex part?' Tony shrugs. 'Why not. It's common for abuse survivors to turn their abusers into figures of awe.'

'About the Corona,' Anna says, 'I owe you guys an apology.'

'*You* owe *us* an apology?' Tony says. 'I nearly had your wuss of a husband *killed*.'

'Yes, but I insisted that you had to get Michele involved.'

'Anna,' I say, 'we involved him in the first place. He's a professional. We'll find a solution.'

'Leave it to me.' Tony checks his watch and stands up. 'I need to get going. I'll get some shut-eye before I get cracking with Art's ramblings. You two carry on with what's left of your holiday. I'll keep you posted, and, you've got my word, I won't bring a mafia party to your bedroom.'

Anna kisses him on the cheek. 'Thank you, Tony,' she says.

2

I'm sitting on the toilet, the seat pulled down, in my boxers.
I gasp a little as I take off the gauze, ripping out a good deal
of hair in the process. I do my best not to tear out the surgical
thread with them. The wound itches as if I had chickenpox.

Anna knocks at the door. 'Are you okay?'

'Still alive.'

I sprinkle on a generous dose of disinfectant, wrinkling my
nose at the hospital smell. Then I carefully apply a fresh gauze,
and secure it with four stretches of adhesive bandage. I feel
badass, like Arnie in *Terminator*.

I hobble to the bedroom. My side aches; it is cross at me
for how I handled it. Seeing Anna lessens the pain. She is
on the bed, naked, reading a novel. She keeps the massive
volume in balance just beneath her breasts, in a lovely pose
which Fabio could transform into the best cover ever seen on
a literary magazine.

'You're pale,' she says.

I let myself fall on the bed, and bring my hand an inch
above the gauze, without touching it. It doesn't give off heat.
It's basically fine. 'It hurts.'

'Painkiller?'

'That's my girl.'

I take Art's weed from the side table, a pouch of tobacco
and a paper.

'I can roll it if you want,' Anna says.

'Let me see if I remember how it's done.'

There's a lot of coke around in my line of work (I snorted once or twice – not my thing), but marijuana? That's not a drug for a lawyer. Since the end of university, I've only smoked occasionally, either here in Casalfranco with the guys, or at parties with Anna's colleagues (philosophers, as opposed to lawyers, smoke vast quantities of weed). The joint I end up with is lumpy and misshapen, but it'll do fine.

I take a long drag, letting the sweet-flavoured smoke travel all the way down to my lungs. I make an appreciative face.

'Any good?'

I pass Anna the joint. 'It's so strong it's illegal.'

'Weed *is* illegal,' she laughs, accepting it.

'This is extra-illegal.'

She takes a drag and hands me back the joint. 'You need it more than me.'

I close my eyes and take another long drag. Art was never a man of compromise. This weed is hard-edged as everything else about him. It kicks me hard and sends me high into space, fuels clarity, heightens my senses. From above here I can see Art, studying different strands of marijuana, cross-pollinating them to create the ultimate strand, one strong enough, strange enough, to keep him interested. Marijuana elevated to an art form. *Art, art.* There's a pun. It makes me laugh. We've been seeking art! Art is our best friend! A college student would make an art film with that. Art again!

I turn my head to look at Anna, her lovely shape draped on the bed. I close my eyes again and inhale, deeply happy now the weed is putting my head to rest.

Or not.

'What are you doing?' Anna asks.

I bury my nose in the pillow and inhale again. With my drug-induced super-senses, I pick up a smell, which is not mine, or Anna's. A stranger's smell; no, not exactly a stranger's. I force my head to turn to Anna. Is that a bite mark on her neck?

'Fabio,' I whisper.

'What…?'

'Did you sleep with Fabio?'

'What? No!'

The key of her voice, the way she moves her shoulders, defensive, attentive. 'You slept with Fabio,' I say, and I pray she will get angry at me for insulting her.

She lowers her eyes.

And I…

…I don't know what to do. I would jump on my feet and make an exit. *Bitch!* I would yell. *Whore!* Or I would weep and say it is my fault, it is all my fault, and beg her not to do it anymore; I will be a better husband. I would, I would, I would – but I am tired. I let my head fall on the pillow, and take one last drag, before smothering the end in a glass of water on the side table. Nothing good could come from Art's weed. I should have known that.

'You didn't even take the trouble to change the sheets,' I say.

'I was more troubled by the fear you might die.'

'Do you love him?'

'I love *you*.'

I gasp for air. I feel a pressure, on my chest, as if Fabio was

310

sitting on it, laughing at me and giving me the middle finger. I ask, 'When was the last time we had sex?'

'Before Christmas.'

'It can't be that long.'

'It is.'

I pass a hand across my face. 'Jesus.'

'I'm not going to lie and tell you I didn't want to sleep with Fabio. I did want it. I had a *great time*, too. I thought I would feel bad afterwards, but no. But that doesn't change what you mean to me.'

'You were fucking one of my best friends while I was risking my life, and you don't feel bad?'

'Don't you *dare*, Mauro! You were doing as you wished, following your ego, ignoring your responsibilities to me. To your *children*.'

'You slept with another man!'

'So what? It was only sex, and I'll take sex over death any day of the week. I enjoyed it – yes, I did – and I don't feel guilty, not in the least. I thought I would, but I don't. Sex is sex. It doesn't change… *us*. I love you, Mauro, you know that, and I know you love me.'

I scoff. '*Us* has a lot of problems.'

'Some. We can fix them together.'

'How would you feel if I slept with someone else?'

'Try,' she says, dryly. She means it too.

'This is,' I say, fighting to keep my voice light, 'this is the worst apology I have ever heard.'

'I'm not apologising.'

My body begs me to lie in bed, but my senses are still high, and Fabio's smell comes at me from all sides, and I have visions of him in bed with Anna, and Anna is not apologising, and I dive into rising tides of paranoia (does Fabio have AIDS? Did he make her pregnant? Does he have a bigger dick than me?). Strong weed and bad news don't go well together. I stand up slowly. Anna doesn't ask where I'm going. She said what she had to say, and now she will give me time to digest it. That's how she rolls.

I put on a short-sleeved shirt (white linen, one I use for the beach) and walk out of the room. I get a cold beer from the fridge, grab Art's book, and go out into the garden. I feel calm, not in a mature, let's-talk-about-this way. *Shell-shocked* is more like it. It is a cool night – cool enough for me to go back inside to fetch a jumper.

I slump in a chair, start drinking, and start reading.

CHAPTER 3
On Trespassing

I

I badly wanted to go back. You would too if you had
been there. Getting to see the kingdom of Hidden
Things only to be exiled is like knowing that the
most fabulous party is happening in town, with loose
women and men, sweet wine, the best music, and you
could get in if only you could find your way there.
You can either go out and look for it, or stay home
and watch TV. What would you do?

Crashing the party has been my life mission; it
took me all over the world – and some would say that
it made me waste my golden years – but I'm convinced
that a life spent on an obsession is a life well
spent. Give me joy, or give me sorrow, just keep me
away from blandness.

I never stopped hearing the buzz of the
party, a ceaseless soft music at the edge of my
consciousness, taunting me, calling me. The kingdom
of Hidden Things is different from our own, as the
sky is different from the land, but I was sure that,
as you can fly up in the sky, so there had to be a way

313

to get there. And I was right.

Finding the way was not easy. I had to work against not only the laws of nature, but its very Constitution. Whereas land and sky are contiguous, we and the Hidden Things are divided, as if, so to speak, a drystone wall were between us. I cannot say whether this 'wall' has been put there by some spiteful god or it just is. Be that as it may, it is there, and thus we must climb it. It took me a while to learn how to do that, but once learnt, the system is comparatively easy.

All you will have to do is follow my instructions. In order to fly a balloon, you need some sturdy fabric, a wicker basket, and a source of hot air. In order to trespass on the kingdom of Hidden Things, you need a unity of Place, Time and Action.

Let me explain.

II

La Madama took me from a specific olive grove. She didn't take me from home, she didn't take me from the field where I was messing around with my friends; she lured me to the olive grove and took me from there. Why? The place had to matter somehow.

In my first, clumsy attempts at trespassing, I simply went back to the olive grove and waited.. Nothing happened of course, but I could feel the atmosphere of that particular place in a way that I could not put into words. It was a poetic, not rational, understanding, but an understanding nonetheless.

Years later I came to see how in some places the Hidden Things come closer to us. Think of a winding country lane, getting now closer, now further away from this or that specific field. I have visited many of these points of closeness; Glastonbury in England is one of them, the island of Crete is another. In Salento they often become places of worship of the saints. A topography of the saints, then, is a topography of Hidden Things. Follow the saints and you will find where to trespass. It is as simple as that.

III

It is only possible to trespass at certain times. The seasons change, equinoxes and solstices run after one another, old things die and new things are born; there is a secret rhythm to the Universe, and Time is the name of that rhythm.

I took my first hints about the importance of Time from astrology. Scholars like Marsilio Ficino and Girolamo Cardano were masters of Time. Tying together art, science and magic, they gained an amazing understanding of the secret rhythm. A good astrologer can calculate the best month, day, hour and minute to take any action. Some moments are better suited to war, others to love, others yet to study. If you force peaches to grow out of season, they will be almost flavourless. If you rush a relationship, it will end in disaster. Either you dance to the secret rhythm, or it crushes you.

In the astonishingly complex dance of the stars, some specific alignments only come every once in a while, and it's only then that you can trespass.

In order to get on the other side I had to learn how to be both a topographer and an astrologer, to calculate the right Places and Times, where and when the journey was possible. This pamphlet is an exploration of such Places and Times as they occur in Salento, Italy. By using the information in Appendix 1, you can work out the equations yourself, and apply them to any other corner of the world.

IV

I still lacked something: a propeller of sorts, the equivalent of hot air in a balloon. At the right Time and Place, it is easier for the Hidden Things to visit us at their pleasure – but how can we get there at our pleasure? How can we climb the drystone wall? I refused to believe that I was condemned to be at the whim of other forces.

To get my answer I had to piece together a million figments, undergo a million life experiences, and commit, I regret to say, more than a fair share of mistakes, some of which would be truly horrific had they not been made in the name of research. I finally found what I sought thanks to an unlikely source: Concetta Pecoraro, a Casalfranco woman widely considered to be a charlatan. The townsfolk here will remember her name, and some might as well remember that my disappearance as a boy caused, more or less indirectly, her ruin.

Starting in 1987, Concetta made a flourishing business out of visions of the Blessed Virgin Mary, peddling clichés to the local peasantry. When I disappeared, she announced that the Virgin had revealed to her that I was dead, and implied that my friends had killed me. When I returned alive and well, the locals had to decide who to blame for having lied, Concetta or the Virgin Mary, and they picked Concetta.

Concetta was without doubt a fraud, but good lies are built upon foundations of truth. Two years ago, shortly after I moved back to Casalfranco, I went to talk to her. Concetta agreed to sell me her story, in exchange for almost all of my savings (little more than 4,000 euros), in cash. When I left her house I was broke, but also the happiest I had been since I was fourteen.

Concetta had never seen the Virgin Mary, but she had once caught a glimpse of La Madama. It had happened many decades ago, when Concetta was twelve. It was a different time for the south, harsher, crueller. Concetta's father was a brute of a man, uncivilised and uncouth, quick with his hands and partial to wine. He was, in short, a typical man of his time. Always beware of typical people.

On a stifling late summer day Concetta was helping her father with the vendemmia, the grape harvest, in the vineyard of a local doctor. It was just a tiny patch of ground, and the responsibility of the vendemmia was entirely on the shoulders of Concetta and her father. Although, in practice, it was on the shoulders of Concetta alone; her father made her do the plucking, while he lounged in the shade of a fig tree, feasting on wine and the figs he picked.

That summer a change had happened to Concetta;
her figure had become fuller, her lips more red.
Womanhood had arrived, and that day, as he drank,
her father noticed it.

At around midday (the hour of demoni meridiani),
Concetta's father stood up, tottered over to her, and
pinched her bottom. When she recoiled, he made coarse
jokes – which I'd rather not report – about her curves.
The jokes gave way to more serious words, until
the man grabbed his daughter, and pushed her to the
ground, shouting at her to stay quiet, obey, and let
him do as he wished. He started unbuckling his belt.

Concetta refused.

Young, in her prime, and not afraid of work, she
was much stronger than her father, and she was not
drunk. She kicked him in the shins, and when the
drunk man doubled up, she picked herself up, and
started hitting him savagely with her fists.

He did not offer any resistance.

I will gloss over the gratuitous blow-by-blow
account Concetta gave me, cackling like a frog at
every word; suffice it to say that she did not stop
until her father was on the brink of death. And while
she was pounding him, something wondrous happened.
Concetta saw the vineyard 'change'.

She could not describe how it 'changed' – no
better than I could ever describe the kingdom of
Hidden Things – she only said that it became bigger
and 'taller'. It 'stretched' and the colours became
brighter, as though 'the colours were on fire'. A
woman passed through, draped in a see-through blue
veil. Concetta thought the woman must be the Virgin

318

Mary, for in a corner of that field sat a small shrine to the Virgin, and everybody knows that blue is her colour.

The woman in blue didn't lift a finger, either to help Concetta or to hinder her. She just stood there, watching, watching, without the smallest trace of emotion on her face. And when Concetta finally had enough ('Just because it was hot and I'd been working my ass off all day,' she remarked, justifying herself for not having beaten her father to death), the woman disappeared, and, with her, the sense of awe was gone from the vineyard.

Concetta remains convinced to this day that the Virgin Mary appeared to her, to praise her for what she was doing. 'The Virgin eats no shit,' Concetta said to me. Years later that encounter would inspire her to start her own seership scam, reckoning that if the Virgin was offended by that, she could come down and speak her mind.

Strip this story of superstition and you will see that the otherworldly lady was la Madama. I had seen her draped in a sapphire veil, as I told in Chapter Two. I knew exactly which veil that was. La Madama and I had sex on it more than once.

I came out of Concetta's house with a precise idea of how to return to the other side. Her story chimed with theories I had been working on. It was only a matter of putting them to the test.

V

Life is all about action. Trees take action in growth, animals by feeding or procreating; even

319

thinking, done right, is but a highly sophisticated form of action.

Action was the fuel I needed. I simply had to go to the right place, at the right time, and make the right action, and I would climb over the wall.

You see, Concetta had caught a glimpse of la Madama when she had found herself about to commit an outrageous act – killing her own father with her bare hands. By means of this action she opened the gate. To trespass on the side of Hidden Things is to break laws which go far deeper than the normal laws of nature. Trespassing is, and thus requires, a transgression.

I will leave it to you to figure out the practicalities. For understandable reasons, I cannot spell them out. I strongly advise against whatever mild images of transgression might be coming to your mind; in the best case, a small mischief will allow you a quick peek of the Hidden Things, lifting the veil for a fraction of a second, but more probably it would bring no fruits at all. No – if it does not hurt body and soul, it does not work. A near-kill is good enough – for a girl of twelve.

The word sacrifice comes from the Latin sacrum facere, 'to make sacred'. Trespassing is a sacred transgression, and thus it requires important sacrifices. The traveller must be ready, then, to crack many, many eggs, to make this particular omelette.

FABIO

1

What if he is right?

I lay down the last page and massage my eyes. It's eight in the morning. The night has gone and I haven't had any sleep.

What if Art is right?

It is a testament to how messed up I am that I even entertain the notion. Art's book reads like a serial killer's memoir, a cunning one, who never speaks openly of his kills, but teases you all the way down to his lair. *Be ready, then, to crack many, many eggs.* What the fuck?

I walk to the kitchen to find my father having breakfast. 'Good morning, Fabio,' he welcomes me, uttering each word as if it were a command. He is *ordering* me to have a good day, while drinking his tea (someone from church once told him it is healthier for his heart than coffee). He has forgotten to take out the teabag; the liquid in his cup is ink-black and Dad doesn't notice, just as he doesn't notice the soggy parcel of tea leaves, not even when it floats to his lips and makes some tea drip down his chin and white shirt.

I can't stand to look at this. I turn my back and hurry to my room, trying to outrun my reason. I dial Art's number. He picks up at the second ring.

'Hey, mate,' he says.

'I've read your book.'

'And?'

'You're out of your mind.'

'Never denied that, but I'm also right.'

'Yeah? Heal my father, then.'

Silence at the other end. Even in these circumstances, it gives me some pleasure to take Art by surprise. 'What from?' he asks.

'Alzheimer's. Early stages, advancing fast.'

'You should've told me immediately.'

'You *can* heal him, right?'

'I can,' he says, after a pause.

I should laugh, but I feel relieved. If someone can work a miracle, it's Art. I should be ashamed of myself for buying into this sort of superstition.

Art says, 'We'll have to put him to sleep.'

'Sorry?' I ask.

'The… healing process will require me to take certain *actions* which Angelo would object to. Strongly. I have to be in a room with him to heal him, but he must not see what I'm doing.'

'Art, I won't *drug* my father!'

'I have what we need,' he rambles on, in all seriousness.

'The risk of death is very slight, less than 1% if I remember. With Alzheimer's, it's 100%.'

For a moment, a brief, stupid moment, I think to myself, *sure, it makes sense, numbers don't lie*. I will allow Art to drug my father, and then to bring him home (down to that cosy little abattoir?), where Art will *take certain actions which Angelo would object to*, and then my father will be restored, the same old sharp-witted, tight-arsed man I knew. I'm on the verge of trusting Art with his drugs and his magic and this crazy new world of saints and violence which is his latest obsession, when someone rings at the door. I don't want my father to open it, in the state he is in.

'Gotta go,' I say, and terminate the call.

I go to the door. It's Mauro.

'Hey,' I welcome him.

I see him bunching his fists. I don't get it. *What's that all about?*

Then I get it.

'Mauro…' I say, pulling back.

His arm has already lifted. I try to dodge; I fail.

Mauro hits me, hard, in the face.

2

I let out a cry of pain and Mauro lets one out too. I fall on my shoulder, the impact hurting me more than the jab. I taste blood, and I feel it, viscous, in my mouth and down my nose. Mauro shakes his hand with a grimace. Tony always said, *Don't*

punch a guy if you don't know how to. You'll hurt yourself more than him.
Slap him instead. Ah, the good counsel of a friend.

'What seems to be the trouble?' Angelo says. He stands in
the doorway to the living room, his white shirt stained with tea
and breadcrumbs.

'He slept with my wife,' Mauro says.

My father looks at me, narrows his eyes, and then shakes
his head. 'Will you ever cease to disappoint me?' he asks. He
turns to Mauro. 'I apologise for my son. I hope you will find it
in yourself to pardon him. He is weak, and impressionable. He
needs examples the likes of you.' He makes a brusque gesture
of salute with his head, and goes back where he came from.

My eyes are filling up and I let them fill. Tears merge with
the blood running down my nose. Sitting on the floor, like a
baby, I start weeping, my body shaking with the sighs. I bury
my face in my hands and cry, cry as if Mauro wasn't here, cry
as if I was alone, and I could freely show what a wimp I am,
what a little, broken thing I am.

'Hey,' Mauro says. He rests his other hand, the one he
didn't hit me with, on my shoulder. 'Hey, man.'

'I'm a fucker,' I manage to say.

'Can't argue with that,' Mauro says.

3

'*Sorry* doesn't cut it.' I am making liberal use of a tea towel
folded around a bunch of ice cubes, pressing it on my nose,

on my lips and cheek. Mauro presses another on his hand. He sits on the bed, cross-legged, under a *Dragon Ball* poster, its colours still bright. When I was hanging that poster on the wall I never thought I'd grow up to be the guy who sleeps with his friend's wife.

'You always liked Anna,' he says, 'and she liked you.'

I look at his side, where he was shot. Tony's handiwork has held. 'She likes me, yes, but she loves *you*. She told me, even when...' I let my voice trail off.

'She told me the same. Excuse me if I have my doubts, after she fucked one of my best friends. And excuse me if I doubt what a good friend you are too.'

'I'm not a good friend. I love you, Tony and Art to bits, but I'm a selfish, egotistical wanker, and selfish, egotistical wankers make for very poor friends.'

'Go on, I'm liking this.'

'When I saw Anna, at the shoot, I...'

'Are you in love with her?'

'I don't think so.'

'And you slept with her only twice, right?'

That caught me off guard. 'How long have you known?'

'Long enough. Only twice?'

'Only twice.'

Mauro shifts the ice on his hand. 'She accused me of being selfish.'

'She was...'

'She was right,' Mauro interrupts me. 'I don't mean only for the troubles with Art, no, it started before that. I was obsessing

325

over what *I* wanted and did not want for my life, and I took for granted that everything was fine with hers. She doesn't whine like me, but that doesn't mean she doesn't have needs, or problems of her own. I was horrible to my wife. She and you were horrible to me. Let's call it even and leave it at that.'

'It's not even,' I try to joke. 'You didn't do anything to me.'

'I just have,' Mauro says, arranging his face in a grin.

I am trying to think of a witty reply, when both our mobiles ring at once. A collective text from Tony. He's giving us access to his Find My Friends app. *I'm going somewhere with Michele*, he writes. *I don't know where. No reason to sweat, but just in case.*

Mauro and I look at each other. He starts to stand up, moving slowly, so as not to open his wound. 'I've got to see my family,' he says.

TONY

1

Michele waits for me in Elena's garden, sipping iced coffee under the scented canopy of the wisteria. Elena told me over the phone that he wanted to talk to me, immediately, but she didn't say about what. My little sister, the mafiosa. Her presence makes me physically sick.

I managed no more than an hour of shut-eye last night; I couldn't wait to begin Art's book, and once I started, I couldn't go back to bed. Even though the meat was all in the introduction and in the third chapter, the whole thing must be a hundred thousand words long. Art does ramble a lot. We thought he was far gone, but we hadn't grasped just how far. Same mistake I made with my sister.

'Didn't get much sleep?' Michele greets me.

'I had a PlayStation night.'

'A waste of time, if you ask me.' Michele stands up. 'Come, I've got something to show you.'

'I just need to pop into the loo, first.'

It might be Art's rantings that made me paranoid, but there's a tension in Michele's manners. He's a friend; I don't have a reason to be afraid. Do I? He's Corona first, a friend second, and I'm not sure I trust even my own sister anymore. I lock myself into the bathroom and text the guys, just in case. If they've read *The Book of Hidden Things*, they'll be paranoid too.

I say *ciao* to Elena and Rocco and follow Michele to his car. He asks me to ride shotgun, which relaxes me; Rocco told me once that when dangerous guys want to do dangerous things to you, they make you sit in the back, with a huge *someone* at your side. Only hearsay, Rocco clarified, nothing he knew first-hand. Michele's car is a blue, unassuming Fiat Punto, the ride an accountant would choose.

'Where are we going?' I ask.

'To meet Silvana.' He puts music on, some *taranta* tunes, and I take the hint and shut up. He lights a cigarette, without offering. We drive beyond the sign that warns tourists they're leaving Casalfranco, site of ancient history, strong wine and perpetual sunshine, on the road that connects the town to the sea. A little after that we take a left into a lane, and then another, and we stop at a small two-storey house with a shaded porch, almost entirely hidden behind a tall hedge of prickly pears. Their green cladodes reach out to the street, like thorny hands eager to pierce you through.

A young man with a bleeding heart tattoo on his neck sits on the porch, in a rocking chair, playing with his phone. He wears knuckledusters on both hands. When he sees Michele, he jumps on his feet and opens the front door for us. We enter and go through a bare kitchen and down a short staircase leading to a small cellar, from where come the excited voices of anime characters on TV.

The only light is a naked bulb dangling from the ceiling. It is a very small room, almost entirely occupied by an ancient TV set on one wall and two wooden chairs. Silvana sits in one of them. The chair is orientated towards the TV, but she's not really watching, only staring at the screen. In the other chair sits a wiry man in a white vest, skin burned black by the sun, a gun prominently in his lap.

'That's her gun,' Michele says. 'Saverio, her brother, bought it from us years ago. She stole it.'

Silvana keeps staring at the TV set. Michele makes a gesture to the wiry man, who turns the TV off. Silvana still doesn't turn her head, her eyes now on the dead TV set.

'Do you want five minutes with her?' Michele asks.

I say, 'Excuse me?'

'The girl shot your mate. I can give you five minutes with her, but you promise you don't kill her. And you don't rape her either,' he adds, as an afterthought.

'No,' I say, 'thanks.'

Michele shrugs. 'Hey, beauty,' he calls to Silvana. 'Smile a little.'

She still doesn't look at us. Michele walks to her, calmly, and takes her chin between his thumb and index finger. He forcefully turns her head towards me. 'Do you remember this man? He's Art's friend.'

'*Sì*,' Silvana says.

'Tell him what you told me.'

Silvana shrugs. She jerks her head free of Michele's grip, in a gesture which makes her long hair wave around her head. She turns her head to look at me. She looks fine, no bruises or anything. These men don't use more violence than they think necessary; the trick to getting on with them is making yourself scarce *before* they decide violence is necessary. I have to take this girl out of here. Everything she's going through is Art's fault, and ours. We believed Art was in love. Wrong, wrong, always wrong about him. I ask, 'Is this what you were afraid of?'

She looks at the ceiling, then at me. 'I'm afraid of *them*. The Hidden Things. Those who… came after I killed Sam.'

'Who's Sam?'

'Sam is my dog.'

Her dog. 'Did you leave him hanging in an olive grove?'

'Michele told you.'

'No. Fabio, another friend of mine, saw him before you took him down.'

She shakes her head. 'It didn't work. It wasn't enough. Art's gone and I'm not able to follow. He trespassed and left me here, *to rot*.' Her words are suddenly brimming with hatred.

'I'm not sure I understand,' I lie, for Michele's benefit.

'He trespassed and went to live with the saints.'

'She had Art's book with her,' Michele says. 'The introduction was missing, but the rest was full of notes and underlined passages. You take it seriously, don't you?' he says to Silvana.

'Mock me as you like. Every word is true.'

330

'Why did you kill your dog?' I ask.

'To trespass! You've got to break many, many eggs to make this particular omelette. But it wasn't enough, it wasn't. All I did was mess me up.'

'What do you mean?'

'I didn't make it to the other side, but I *see* it now. The Hidden Things, I see them all the time.' She pauses. 'And they see me too.'

'Who are *they*?'

'The saints, and the Virgin, and all the others who live there. They're angry at me because I see them but I'm not supposed to. It's either there or here, I can't be on the border, I can't sit on the wall, no I can't, I shouldn't. They're angry at me.' While she talks, she keeps looking beyond my shoulder, as if someone were there. It makes my skin crawl.

'Are they here in this moment?'

'They're always with Michele. They dance with him.'

'That's enough,' Michele says.

2

'I guess you can let her go,' I say.

We're taking coffee in the field at the back of the house, in the omnipresent humming of cicadas. Prickly pears are the only thing growing in this field, wild, their thorny fruits violet and orange. We are standing up, which is Michele's way of telling me that my visit is over. He doesn't answer.

'She's nuts,' I press on. 'Nuts and harmless. I don't see the point of…'

Michele looks at me, and I shut my mouth.

'I have a theory,' he starts.

'Go on.'

'It's about bodies. It goes like this: there are easy bodies and difficult bodies. Some bodies might create trouble, so you look for alternative ways to handle the people that are attached to them. Others, they're no trouble at all. Silvana is an easy body. A lowlife's daughter, she kills herself with her brother's gun? Burying the enquiry will be a walk in the park.'

My heart is pounding. 'Why should you kill her?'

'I've skimmed Art's book. It is blasphemous. I understand why he didn't want me to read it. A man, or even a woman, under the influence of that book could make some noise. And around here? We like calm and peace round here. Silvana is alive only because I want to be sure she has nothing else to tell us.'

'She's a girl. She only needs a cuff on her ear and…'

'Have you seen Art?'

It takes all I have not to jump. 'What do you mean?'

'Word in the street is that Art might be back. They caught a glimpse of him in Casalfranco. Might be my boys being overzealous, might be true. I'm asking you what you think.'

'I think it's bollocks.'

'Do you?'

Time slows down. I feel every drop of sweat on my forehead, and I pray that Michele and his *saints* will believe that I'm sweating because of the heat. 'Michele, I'm not an idiot. If Art was back and I knew it, I'd have told you.'

'And your friends, are they smart too?'

'Smarter than me.'

'You're difficult bodies, all three of you, but you must know, Tony, that we're not afraid of difficult bodies.'

I say, in my firmer voice, 'You don't have to threaten me.'

'Me, threatening Elena's brother?' Michele laughs, and pats me on my cheek. 'You got it all wrong. Relax. I'm Art's friend too. You remember that, *si*? No one will harm him, or any of you guys, if you don't make it absolutely necessary. We're all buddies here. Now, there's buddies higher than me, who, in light of recent events, are dying for a chat with Art, and they'll want it even more badly after reading his book. They are not inclined to touch a hair on anybody's head. Let's keep it that way, shall we? I'm not *threatening* you, Tony, I'm helping you to see the situation for what it is.'

'I appreciate that,' I say.

Michele says, 'Good for you, son.'

MAURO

'What's going on here?' Tony asked, after a glance at Fabio's face and then at my hand.

I didn't intend to tell him; he will hate Fabio more than I hate him now, probably more than Fabio deserves.

'I slept with Anna,' Fabio said.

Tony made a face as if he were expecting a punch line. When it didn't come, he spat at Fabio's feet. 'Scumbag.'

'Later,' I said.

We are taking a meandering route through secondary roads and country lanes to make sure nobody is tailing us. Art agreed we need to have a serious chat, and I can't sit this out, not with a girl's life at stake; Fabio is having a breakdown, and Tony is too soft when it comes to his mate. Even Anna agreed I couldn't just ignore it all. 'Don't get shot,' she said.

'Don't fuck passers-by,' I replied.

The guys and I have never been so tense in each other's

company; the car is full of ghosts. I pull in at a small white chapel at the edge of an olive grove, bigger and tamer than the one Art disappeared into. He said that he used this grove to trespass the second time, to prove his theory about the existence of many 'Places which are right'. I would give half my savings to be able to read between Art's lines and understand what is really happening. A moped is parked beside the chapel. I wonder if Art rented it or stole it.

Stop wondering.

We didn't come here to hear more of Art's stories. We are here to convince him to talk to his friends in the Corona. Only he can clean up the mess he created, and save us, and Silvana.

His head peeps out from the chapel's door. 'So you deigned to come,' he says, in mock seriousness, as I get out of the car.

'Only because we're all going to die.'

'Not in the kingdom of the Hidden Things.'

Tony says, 'I'm not in the mood.'

I didn't know this chapel – not even old folk know all the chapels dotting the countryside. This one is in better shape than most. The outside recently received a fresh coat of paint, and on the inside, on one of the walls, is the painting of a man hugging a book (the golden writing underneath assure the faithful that he is San Gregorio). The artwork is of the quality you would expect from a local chapel, but the room is clean. A vase of fresh flowers is at the saint's feet, as are a bag of weed, one of tobacco, and a paper with a mixture of the two.

'Isn't it a bit early for that?' I say.

Art taps his index finger on his ear. 'This world. It's so loud, after you get used to the Hidden Things, and the music is so crass! I'm better when I tune it down.' He sits on the floor, his back against the wall, and returns to his task. 'It's only until tonight anyway.'

He is barking mad. Fabio and Tony couldn't prepare me for his jerking movements, the way he keeps shaking his eyes, the trembling in his hands. He licks the paper. 'What's going on with your face?' he asks Fabio.

Tony says, 'Art, this is serious. The Corona has Silvana.'

'Told ya.'

'They're going to kill her.'

'As if.' Art brings the joint to his lips and lights it.

'Art…'

'Did Michele give you his easy-bodies-versus-difficult-bodies bullshit?'

'Didn't seem bullshit to me.'

'It's not, to an extent. The truth is, all bodies are difficult. The Corona are not as powerful as they make out, nobody is, without magic, and they have none. Michele's using Silvana to impress you. With me gone, with *us* gone, he won't have a reason in the world to harm her.'

I chose to ignore the *magic* part. 'We're not going anywhere. *You* are going to Michele, and you are going to talk to him.'

'Why?'

'Because that way we'll all survive.'

Art offers me the joint. I refuse it, so he passes it to Fabio, who takes it. Art says, 'Didn't you read my book?'

'Yes, Art, we did.'

337

'So why wouldn't you want to come with me? Mauro, you can bring Anna and the girls if you want. They'll love it.'

Tony, Fabio and I exchange a look. 'Art,' Tony says. 'You need help.'

'You guys think I'm crazy?'

'To sum it up, yeah,' I say.

'And you won't give your buddy a fighting chance.'

Tony says, 'Michele promised they won't harm you. We can go through Elena to be sure it's safe…?'

'What, you think I'm *afraid* of Michele? Come on! I know they won't touch a hair on my head. They're after my magic. If I had more time, I would go and have coffee with that fellow, for old times' sake. But we must go back to the Hidden Things in the next,' he checks his plastic wristwatch, 'fifteen hours, give or take, or the Time won't be right anymore. The next good window opens in no less than five years. Did I tell you that? And I won't spend five years in this dump, nope, not me.'

Fabio offers the joint to Tony, who refuses it, so it goes back to Art.

Tony asks, 'Why did you even get in touch with someone like Michele?'

'Duh, to learn the Dance of the Swords.'

'Which you wanted to learn because…?'

'When danced properly, it attunes you to the things Michele would call *saints*. It brings you to the edge of sanity, and makes you feel their presence.' Art lifts the marijuana cigarette to show it to us. 'All part of my research project.'

'The weed too?'

'Dealing was a no-stress day job.'

I say, 'You met Silvana when you talked to her mother.'

Art nods. 'Bright girl, that one. She was curious, and I satisfied her curiosity.'

'We saw your gear,' Tony says.

'The trullo or the basement?'

'Both.'

'It was a long research project, requiring more than a few experiments.'

'You got a stockpile of posh dog food too.'

'That was for Ged.'

'Where's Ged, then?'

'Ged!' Art sighs, and shakes his head. He stands up. 'Come.' He leaves the chapel, with us on his tail, and walks round to the back. He stops at a dog-sized mound of dirt in a small spot surrounded by wild prickly pears, a recent mound, the sort of mound we prayed not to find when we searched his fields. 'Ged's a cracked egg,' Art says.

The wound in my side throbs. It feels as if a swarm of small living creatures are trying to undo the stitches to escape. I bring a hand to my stomach. I won't get sick here. 'You need help,' I whisper.

Art puffs out a cloud of smoke. 'Listen to me, guys. Give me a chance to show you I'm right, and if I fail, I promise I'll go and talk to Michele, and to a shrink, whatever.'

'Art...'

He says, 'Did I ever let you down?'

Nobody replies.

'*Did I ever let you down?*' Art repeats. 'An answer, guys, I deserve that.'

Fabio says, 'No.'

'Humour me then. Or you'll have to hit me, physically I mean, and drag me to Michele, kicking and screaming all the way down. Your choice.'

Fabio takes me by surprise when he says, 'All right.'

FABIO

1

I say goodbye to my father with something akin to guilt, as if I wasn't coming back. It is just after eight, and the sun is setting – in London I would still have a few hours of light. I Skyped Lara earlier, and though I didn't tell her about me and Anna, it felt like a farewell call. She picked up and asked, laughing, if I'm planning to fly to the moon and never come back. I hope I made a good job of my pretend laugh. I'll have to be honest with her, and tell her what I did (with the guys, and with Anna), if I go back to London.

When.

When I go back to London.

Art might be many things, but he didn't forget how to be convincing. Here we are, three grown-ups following him to another, better world, in this role-playing game of his gone out of hand. I wish his fantasy were true.

If I have to be honest, I am not entirely sure it is not. Art said it himself: he never let us down. I suspect that Tony, and even Mauro, agree with me; but the idea that Art could be right this time is too strange, too *wild*, to speak aloud.

The meeting is at the olive grove. *Right Time, right Place*, Art said. Was it a surprise? Certainly not, considering the sick romantic logic our friend has spiralled into. Mauro drives Tony and me there, following, as he did this afternoon, a complicated route. Only when we are sure we have nobody on our tail, we take the road to the olive grove.

'I can't believe what we're doing,' Tony says.

'It was the easiest way. Or did you want to start a fight with Art?'

'You know what freaks me out?'

'Yes,' I say, 'the action.'

'I won't break any eggs. I won't start killing dogs.'

I don't reply and neither does Mauro. Tony offers us a cigarette, and we all light one. It shouldn't feel like a last one. It really shouldn't.

We leave the car at the side of the road, where we had left our mopeds that night twenty-two years ago, and we walk to the olive grove. The moon is smaller than it was that night, the countryside much darker. We didn't think to bring a torch. I'm terrified. I'm like a kid who got lost in the woods and knows that wolves, and stranger creatures, are after him.

My mates are with me, and the entire thing won't last very long – I assume – but the sort of fear that grips me goes deeper than rational thoughts. Once we accept that Art didn't trespass into another world that night that means we *still* don't know what happened. The bad people are still out there, and are they watching us? Or is a hidden world of promiscuous saints spying on us?

Art's moped is nowhere to be seen. Orange light flickers from inside the grove. It gives me a scare, before I notice it is candlelight. Tony enters the grove first, then Mauro, and I get in last. We follow a trail of tea-lights leading to the centre of the grove, where Art waits for us, standing in a dignified pose, as a bishop at the end of a church nave. There are four pillar candles on the bare earth in front of him, delimiting a square. The thick chatter of crickets fills the air, and perhaps magic is real, tonight, magic will happen.

'Is this a fucking black mass?' Tony laughs.

Art says, 'I wanted to create a modicum of atmosphere.'

'That's *so* gay.'

'I did it for you, my fairy.'

I ask, 'What are we doing, exactly?'

With a conjurer's skill, Art produces an immense joint. 'We shall relax, to begin with.'

2

Tony and I met on the first day of secondary school. Mauro was in class with us too. Mauro and I had been in class together since first grade, never becoming friends, for no specific reason. In Italy, you pick a desk on the first day of school, and that will be your desk until the last day; you never change class, and you only change place when some teacher feels especially daring and forces you to.

On the first day of school Tony sat next to me. 'You have a funny face,' he said, which was the highest praise anyone ever paid to me. The boys from Casalfranco found me too bland to be fun, and girls hadn't entered my horizon yet.

Tony was the first friend I ever made. It was with some pride that I invited him for dinner by the end of the second week of school. Having *friends for dinner* seemed almost too cosmopolitan to bear, the sort of thing country gentlemen did in the English novels I had already started reading. When he said, 'May I bring another friend?' my heart sank. Tony needed a sidekick to waddle through an evening with me. I asked who he wanted to bring, and Tony replied, *Art*.

I'd heard of Art – me and every other kid at school. He was a very small kid with very big ears in our year. The week before, a boy three or four classes above us had called him Dumbo. Art had replied, *Better to have big ears than a small dick*, and when the other boy jumped on him, Art had *bitten* him on the neck. The viciousness of the bite varied wildly, depending on who told the story, but Tony was there and assured me it wasn't as big as some of the kids said (Art definitely hadn't taken a chunk of flesh out of the other boy's neck and munched it). Tony had put himself between the two, separating them before anybody was seriously hurt. It had only been a scrap; an unusual one though.

I told Tony that, sure, he could bring Art, the more the merrier, though jealousy was eating me from the inside out. When they came *for dinner*, as I kept repeating, my father took an immediate dislike to Art. Even before we sat at the table he overhead Art telling a dirty joke about a nun and a penguin, and he stormed amongst us, saying he wouldn't have that sort of thing under his roof. Art politely apologised. But when Art apologises, he looks like he's taking the piss, which is exactly what he is doing.

That way, Art and I became friends.

So now I had, in one stroke, an entire crew of two. I couldn't believe my luck.

Some months later (I remember it was the first warm day of the year, so probably March), Art brought Mauro in. He had single-handedly decided that Mauro and I were *more like each other than any of you realise* and thus we had to be friends. I strongly disagreed, not because I had anything against Mauro, but because two friends were already a treasure beyond my wildest dreams, and I was superstitiously afraid that any change in the balance of our little group would ruin it. Art didn't give me a chance to choose; he invited Tony and me to play at his place, and, without telling us, he invited Mauro too. I was suspicious, at first, and Mauro was even more suspicious of me.

'Then I mentioned the X-Men,' Mauro says. We all laugh.

We are towards the end of the second joint, telling stories we've told a thousand times. I don't know if it is the marijuana or the familiarity we share, but I can easily forget what we are doing. I can forget that such a long time has passed (where has it gone?) and that Art is sick and vicious. I can easily go back to that spring day when I discovered that Mauro knew the X-Men too, which was outstanding for Casalfranco in the early nineties. We bonded over four-colour rejects.

'How long ago was that?' Tony asks.

'Long enough for people to die in the meantime,' Art replies. 'Do you remember Carla? Curly hair, not the sharpest tool in the box?'

'Yeah.'

'Lung cancer, last year.'

We receive the news in silence. I haven't seen Carla since school, and I wasn't even her friend on Facebook; this feeling in my stomach is about me, not her. We are old enough to have friends dying of lung cancer. When did that happen?

'Spoilsport,' Tony says.

'That's what I'm saving you from.' Art turns to Mauro. 'Last chance here. Do you want to call your family, or are you leaving them behind?'

Mauro makes a sad sigh. 'We're not going anywhere.'

'As you wish,' says Art, jumping to his feet. 'I'll go get the tools.'

He disappears between the gnarled olive trees. This is not a four-colour world anymore. We were happy, life was easy. I wonder if everybody slips that far from their golden years, or if it is just us.

Tony sees something and brings his hands to his head. 'Oh, no,' he says. 'Oh, no, no, no…'

I follow his gaze. Art is coming back. The candles, illuminating him from beneath, give him the appearance of a demon. In one hand, he has a kitchen knife.

In the other, a kitten.

Knowing that this moment would come hasn't made us ready for it. Tony scrambles to his feet. 'No way,' he says. 'No way, dude.'

'You read *The Book of Hidden Things*; you know what we need to do to trespass.'

'Sick fucker…' Tony's voice is not angry. It is disappointed.

'Easy, Tony, I won't ask you to sacrifice this little treasure.'

I have smoked too much, or Art's stuff is stronger than I thought. I wobble. I am unstable on my feet. As if coming from afar, I hear Tony's voice say, 'I won't let *you* kill it either.'

The kitten is a small, marmalade affair purring in Art's arms. Pets are supposed to pick up the emotions around them. This one is far too comfortable for one who is going to be slain. He might be under a spell.

'Have you even *read* what I wrote?' Art says, annoyed. 'I made it clear that the sacrifice required depends on the person making it. When I trespassed the last time, I had to offer my own dog, a pet that I had been treating as a friend, as a *peer*, for months, grooming myself for the sacrifice as much as him. The entire notion of *sacrifice* is that you are renouncing something of yourself, shedding old skin to get a new one. This cat? I got it today. I could break his neck without feeling anything at all. It wouldn't hurt.'

'Then, what…?'

Art points the knife at me. 'Fabio has to do it.'

'No way,' I say.

'I'm not the person to do it,' says Art. 'Tony? You're a tougher cookie than you give yourself credit for. And Mauro, well, Mauro is a lawyer,' Art chuckles. 'No: to trespass, the best of us, the weakest, the dreamer, must push his boundaries.' He offers me the kitten and the knife. 'Please, Fabio, do the honours.'

I feel sick. The floor underfoot is unsteady.

What if he's right?

'If nothing happens I'll come with you straight away,' Art says. 'But think about it! Think if it were true! An entire new world, where you will live and fuck, immortal, forever young. Forever *big*. In the kingdom of Hidden Things, life can't chip away at you.'

'The real world doesn't work that way,' Mauro says, in a soft voice.

'Reality is overrated.'

I reach out to Art. I have to take the knife and the kitten from him – he could strike at any moment, just to make a point. Art smiles, and hands them over. 'All yours.'

I hear Tony breathe out, now that the kitten is safe. I see Mauro shift on his feet, coming closer.

What if he's right?

What if Art could save my father, could save us, could save me? It wouldn't be the first time. He made us the men we are, for better or worse. And sure, what he is saying now, those are things no sane person would say. But what if he is right? Am I ready to refuse this last chance at doing something big, something wonderful, with my life? At *being* big and wonderful? In a magic kingdom where time can't chip away at me.

It is only a kitten.

Art has folded his arms, looking at me expectantly.

'What's your problem, dude?' Tony asks, watching my face.

My problem is that I am a fucker, and I am tired of it.

I take the kitten in one hand. He is so small I barely feel his weight. I lift the knife.

'Go,' Art says.

I sink the knife into the kitten's warm body.

4

The shadows shift; a better world opens for me. My body – somewhere, somehow – is falling to its knees, and my throat is screaming so loudly that it burns, but it doesn't matter, because I am calm. Deep inside, I am happy.

A familiar flavour fills my mouth, one I haven't tasted since I was a boy: it is pasta, Mum's secret recipe. It would take an entire day to make, with ragu sauce, prosciutto, tiny meatballs, and I don't know what else. The last time she made that pasta, she already had her diagnosis, and she hadn't told me yet. She would die three months later. I didn't savour the pasta as much as I should have. I didn't keep it with me. She should have told me it was *the last time*. I had a right to know. The flavour brings tears to my eyes. Only Mum knows how to make that pasta. That pasta is hers, it is *her*.

I feel so safe, so *loved*, that it is almost too much, overwhelming. Grown-up life is never this wonderful. I remember Sunday visits to my parents' friends in the country, smoky old houses, Mum walking through olive trees like these.

Is it just a memory, or am I seeing her now?

Not right now, but I will see her soon.

The shadows are shifting, and one of them will be Mum's. I am perfectly clear, as I fall to my knees and I scream with blood on my hands, that she is dead but not gone, that she is *somewhere else*, with the Hidden Things, and I can't really see her yet, but I remember her so vividly, the sense of her presence is so strong that she can't be far, she is coming, and I will see her in a moment. I can scent her in the wind, the inexpensive cologne she liked so much. She is drawing closer.

Yes. I will see her in a moment.

5

I realise I am kneeling and the kitten is dead. I have never taken a life before. I couldn't imagine it was so easy. The blood is flowing freely from the cat to my hand. The creature didn't let out a whimper, and if he did, I covered it with my cry. I throw its body on the ground, disgusted. I let go of the knife too.

My cry dies out. The olive grove is the same as always, and my friends too. Mauro and Tony are petrified. Art is furrowing his brow.

'It didn't work!' he whispers. 'Why didn't it work?' He crouches, to look me in the eye. 'I misjudged!' he says. 'What happened to your face, Fabio?'

I bring a bloodied hand to my face. *I killed a living being. I killed a living being because I thought it would take me to another world. Did it?*

'WHAT HAPPENED TO YOUR FACE? What have you done that has changed you?'

'I slept with Anna,' I whisper.

Art is taken aback. 'Life has hardened you,' he says. 'I get it. I get it! *Killing* a kitten wasn't enough for you. I thought it was, but no, I should've made you *torture* him before, and then, oh, then surely we would've trespassed.' He turns to Tony. 'We'll try again. I know where to get other kittens. All the kittens we'll need!'

Tony steps forward. 'That's not going to happen.'

'The window will last only a few more hours!'

'I swear to God, Art, this ends here.'

Art looks afraid. 'I see,' he says. With a jerk, he takes the knife and stands up. He points the knife at Tony. 'You ungrateful bastards. *I came back for you!* I had *everything*, and I risked it all for you! And you want to trap me here now? Oh, *that* is not going to happen.'

Tony steps forward. 'Art…'

'Don't move another step, or I swear, I'll jab a hole into your prissy face!' He whips round. '*I won't let you trap me in your miserable world!*'

He turns his back, and starts running.

TONY

1

Art starts running and I set off after him, choking down the impulse to stay and beat Fabio to a pulp.

Art runs deeper into the olive grove, far from the candlelight. It's hellish terrain, with surfacing roots and jagged rocks. I've got to mind where I'm going, but Art is too crazy to bother; he runs and jumps like a gnome on cocaine, pulling away from me. When I get to the end of the grove, he's a silhouette in the distance, barely visible against the countryside. He runs towards a narrow lane. I force my legs to a final sprint, but I still have to mind rocks and bushes, and Art skims them. He gets to his moped, and I put all of myself into my legs, praying for them to run faster, faster yet. The engine roars.

When I get to the lane, Art is gone.

'Fuuuck!' I shout to Art, to the sky, to the unmoved fields.

There is an emptiness, in me, I don't know I'll ever fill again.

2

Fabio leans against a tree, bug-eyed. The kitten's body is at his feet, where he shoved it as if it were on fire.

'Hey!' I shout.

I'm ready to have a go at him, but Mauro stops me. 'Let him be,' he says.

'He fucking killed a...'

'It's all right, Tony. It's all right.'

I look at Fabio. Blood has stained his hands and his face and his t-shirt. He doesn't care. A fog is lifting from my brain. Yes, what Fabio did is unforgivable, and he knows that as well as I do. But Fabio's falling apart, and when a mate falls apart, you be there and keep him together.

'I'm sorry,' he whispers. 'I thought...' he stops. 'I don't know. I just did it.'

I close my eyes and take a few long breaths, with the diaphragm, as I do before an operation. 'It's Art. He's good at making people do things.'

'I just did it,' Fabio repeats.

Mauro says, 'We should go.'

I ask, 'Where?'

'To find Art. In his mind, he has only a few hours left before this window of *Time* closes. Killing a cat wasn't enough, and he

354

doesn't have other pets that he groomed. So: what's he going to do next?'

Shit.

3

We drive by Art's place. We know it's chancy – Michele could have someone on it – but it's a risk we must take. Art's not there. That was our only idea. We go back inside Mauro's car, but we don't start the engine.

Mauro says, 'We need to regroup and think.'

Fabio says, 'We must call Michele.'

He's slowly coming back to life. The blood on him is drying, and some colour is returning to his skin. 'How're you holding up?' I ask.

'Better than I deserve.'

'Don't be too hard on yourself,' Mauro says. 'We're all looking for a way out.'

I'm not, I'd like to say. *I was fine before all this, and I thought my mates were too.* It's been a non-stop reality check. Instead, I say, 'Calling Michele is precisely what we *must not* do. He gets the picture that we've been keeping information from him, he'll do unpleasant things. To *us*.'

'What do we do then?'

'Let's go to Elena's. We need to bring the tension down a notch, and you need a shower.'

Mauro says, 'Is that safe?'

'Fabio's covered in *blood*. Do you want your girls to see him like that? Or my folks, or Angelo?'

'Yeah, I know.'

'I trust my sister.'

Mauro hesitates, then turns the key. 'If you say so,' he says, as the engine comes to life.

FABIO

You don't realise how easy it is to kill until you do it. It doesn't take courage, or skill. It only requires you to stop thinking for one moment – and there, the deed is done. As long as you have a tiny patch of *nothingness* inside you, you will find that killing is as easy as breathing. Human beings are not the guardians and masters of earth, we are its alpha predator.

Water, boiling hot, pours over my body, in one of Elena's many shower rooms. *I killed a living being.* It was only a kitten. I have seen local kids doing far worse. I eat meat every day. Every day someone kills for me: chickens, pigs, fluffy little lambs. *Someone* – not me, though, and that is the key. This is not about reason, this is about the visceral feeling of blood on my hands, of a warm body becoming stiff and lifeless because of an action I committed. I wonder what sort of actions Art committed. I wonder what sort of actions were committed *on him*, to propel him so far from the boundaries of everything we consider decent, and proper, and normal.

God, am I jealous of him.

How free he must feel. How invincible. Beyond the rules of men, beyond the vile shackles of this *reality*. In his mind it all holds together, the magic, the wonder. For a heartbeat, he managed to make it true in my mind too – and I will be damned if that heartbeat wasn't the most beautiful of my life. I did *believe*. Of course I would sacrifice a kitten to hold on to that. Who wouldn't? A life of beauty, enchantment and freedom, all that we strive for when we are children, all that we think will be ours one day, and then, invariably, one day we find does not exist. A life resplendent with all the colours we used to see before our world turned the hue of a charcoal-grey suit.

I turn the water off and ease myself into a fresh towel Elena has prepared for me. There is no way out. Photography doesn't matter; sex doesn't matter; all artistic endeavours are pathetic; there is no intuition, no blessing to be had. We live and then we die, and some of us are better players than others, but that is all there is: a poorly designed game. Mum died and she's not singing happy hymns, in Heaven or with the Hidden Things. My father has Alzheimer's and no wizard will cure him. I am a zero, and not even Art, a mad genius, could make me better. I killed a living being and magic didn't happen.

Didn't it?

I put on some clean clothes of Rocco's and head downstairs. Tony, Rocco and Elena sit in the kitchen, with lukewarm coffee they will never drink. Tony's phone is on the table, and Tony doesn't move his eyes from it, as if he were in contemplation of a sacred icon. His face is the darkest I've ever seen it.

'Where's Mauro?' I ask.

'He couldn't reach Anna,' Tony says. 'He went to check on her.'

'You don't think…'

'I don't know what to think tonight.'

The phone rings.

MAURO

1

The front door is open.

The front door is open.

I storm inside, calling at the top of my voice the name of my wife, of my girls. Nobody replies. I call Art's name. The ground floor is empty. I run to the upper floor, where the bedrooms are.

Anna is lying on our bed, her legs akimbo, her face turned on one side. Not a natural pose. 'Anna?' I call. 'Anna!'

I touch her skin. It's warm. I put two fingers on her neck. There is a pulse, albeit slow. A new surge of panic. I rush to the girls' bedroom. *Oh my God, thank you.* They are both here, in their beds. I turn on the light.

No.

Only Ottavia is in her bed, and I distractedly register how strange it is that she didn't wake up. The bundle in Rebecca's bed is crumpled linen. Rebecca is gone.

I have to grab the doorframe so as not to tumble down. My

eyes fall on a note, on the floor, in Art's handwriting.

Don't call the Carabinieri, it says. *Call me.*

I take out my phone. It slips and falls down. The screen cracks, but the phone still works.

I dial Art's number.

2

'Art, you're a fucking psycho.'

'It is perfectly normal that you're mad at me right now.'

'Where's my daughter?'

'I want you to understand the context. I want you to understand it perfectly. I'm tougher than any of you. The things I did… I did things, let's leave it at that. Every time you commit an Action to trespass, you toughen up, and the next Action will necessarily need to be tougher in turn, do you understand that?'

'Cut your crap, Art.'

'No, the context is important, the context is everything indeed. You *refuse* to listen to me, even though I never let you down, I *never* let you down. Why do you refuse to listen to me? I tried to have one of you guys open the way, so that we wouldn't have to do anything too horrible, but it didn't work. You have to understand, Mauro, that killing animals is not enough anymore for me to trespass. Not *remotely*. I'll tell you more. I wouldn't say that just any girl would work, not after what I've been up to. My mate's daughter, though? A girl I love as if she were my own? The thought alone gives me goosebumps. That's just what we need.'

'You're going to kill my girl.'

'I'm going to *make her sacred*! I *have* to leave, I have to; this world is too small for me. And it is too small for you too. How can you accept this travesty of a life? Find a job, sell your time, and then retire, in silence, and die. Isn't that horrible?'

'Art…'

'You guys are the only reason I find myself in such an ungainly predicament. Do you think that taking Rebecca's life doesn't fill me with dread? It is exactly because it *does* that it will work. You will understand, Mauro. I promise you will understand.'

'You're at the olive grove.'

'Mind, I want only the three of you here with me. No, wait, you can still bring Anna and Ottavia, if that makes you happy. If I see anybody else, I will sacrifice Rebecca and trespass all alone. But I'd rather go with my buddies, you see that? I'm sorry it had to go this way. When we're on the other side you'll come to see things my way. We'll laugh about this, mate. One day we'll laugh about this.'

Art rings off.

3

I sit on the sofa, and wait. My legs slightly opened, my arms resting just above my knees, my back bending forward, I wait. I look at the wall behind the TV and wait. After a century or two, I hear Tony's car, I hear the front door open and my mates' steps rushing in.

'Upstairs,' I say.

Tony runs, and I still wait, sitting on the sofa. Fabio clears his throat. 'Dude…' he tries, but he knows better and stops. I have no interest in whatever he could say. I wait; I wait for Tony to come down, and tell me if my life is over or not. Another century goes by, then another, and I wait, on the sofa, looking at the switched-off TV.

At last, Tony's steps climb down the stairs, and I lift my head.

'They'll be fine,' he says in a clipped voice. 'Art injected them with anaesthetic. He knows how to use it.'

I take a few moments to ensure I didn't make up his words. 'They'll be fine,' I repeat. 'They'll be fine?'

Tony nods. 'The anaesthetic will run its course and they'll wake up.'

'Good.' I stand up; I am done waiting. 'Let them sleep through this.'

I wish I could do the same.

FABIO

1

It is dawn when we get to the olive grove. I have not seen the sun rise in a long time. It is a red sphere between the red sky above and the red dirt below, in one of those dawns so common in southern summers – the air still retains a small measure of coolness, which is only there to tantalise you, and will be swept away in the next few minutes. Many things will be swept away in the next few minutes.

Tony is packing a gun. He asked one of Elena, and she produced a small selection to take his pick from. We don't talk about what he's going to do with it. He said he's not going to do anything at all – but.

'Jesus,' says Tony now.

The olive grove is on fire. I make out trees burning. Each tree is a different flame, red as everything else is red, with smoke billowing up in long, long spirals.

Then I move my eyes to the side of the lane, and what I

see there frightens me even more. We were expecting to find one car parked – Art will have stolen one to come here with Rebecca. But there are two.

Sitting on the boot of a blue Fiat Punto is Michele, smoking a cigarette.

Tony swallows. 'Fuck you, sis,' he mutters. Friends and family are what he lives for, and friends and family are letting him down one after the other. This is the worst thing that could happen to him, worse than financial ruin, perhaps worse than a terminal illness.

Tony pulls in and we get out of the car. Michele has a gun stuck prominently in his jeans. He jumps down from the car with the agility of a man thirty years younger. '*Compari*,' he greets us. He takes out his gun.

Tony spits. 'Thirty pieces of silver? Was that the price you paid to Elena?'

'Elena did the clever thing, for her family. Means for you too.'

Tony marches towards him, with a stride I have seen him taking in the past, when he was going to deliver his idea of punishment on some would-be bully. 'Elena is a bitch.'

'That girl is the one reason you will probably get to live after disrespecting me. Do you hear that? The only reason, son.'

'You're not coming with us,' Mauro says. 'Art was clear: only us, and my family if I wanted. He's going to *kill my girl* when he sees anybody else.'

Michele waves his gun. 'I'll do what I please.'

'You'll do what's clever,' says Mauro. 'We can take Art. Then he's all yours.'

366

Tony says, 'A little girl is a difficult body.'

Michele points his gun at us. 'Go. I'll follow you at a distance.'

Mauro sets off towards the olive grove, and Tony and I go behind him.

'Oh, and, Tony?' Michele calls. 'Don't be smart. The shooter Elena gave you: it's unloaded.'

2

I smell petrol. Art has soaked the olive trees, one by one, and set them on fire, in an amped-up version of the candles he lit earlier tonight. It's not all the trees, but enough of them to make the grove hotter than the beach at noon. The trees burn like uncanny torches, stuck in the soil, reaching deep underground. Each of them is hundreds of years old. Such a squandering of life. Such a boost, in Art's troubled mind, to his spell.

We walk through trees on fire. The thick smoke makes it almost impossible to discern the shape of objects and people. The scrub will catch fire any moment, and then the entire grove will burn and it will be an inferno. But for the moment, I don't feel an immediate sense of danger. What few animals dared to tread this grove have fled the fire; the only sound comes from the crackling flames. It is not silent in here, but it is very quiet, in its own way.

Wading through the mist-like smoke we finally come across Rebecca. She is lying peacefully asleep in the lap of the root of a majestic tree, which the fire has spared so far. I did not notice this particular tree the other times I was here, and I wonder how that's possible, considering how tall and thick it is. It has seen centuries upon centuries; its trunk seems to be made of numerous smaller trunks winding around each other and reaching to the sky with a forest of arms and fingers. Rebecca could be a creature of the wild, a changeling, more in her place here than in a city. Art sits beside her, with the kitchen knife. Tidy as always, he's wiped it clean of the kitten's blood.

When he sees us, he jumps up with a broad smile. 'You came!' he says. 'Oh, I knew you'd come!' He's excited like a boy who just robbed Santa. 'This is going to be *epic*, guys!'

'Let her go,' Mauro says, advancing towards him.

Art's expression darkens. He swiftly kneels down and brings the knife to Rebecca's throat. 'Don't.'

Mauro stops in his tracks.

My eyes are welling up from the smoke. I wipe them. Art's eyes are filling too, but they are real tears. 'Don't you understand?' he says. 'After you've danced with the Hidden Things, being trapped here,' he beats the soil with a foot, 'is *miserable*. It is… I can't take it, dude. I can't take it.'

'You're right, it sucks,' Tony says.

Art lifts his head to him. 'You understand, then.'

'I do. It sucks and it's unfair. The Hidden Things are all you ever wanted, and you renounced them for us, and we've been much too big sissies to get back on their side with you. That's unfair, and it's unfair that we didn't trust you.'

'Yes…'

'But you know what? Life's unfair. Deal with it, man.'

'I can escape. *We* can.'

Tony kicks a stone, lazily. 'At the price of a mate's daughter? Seriously?'

'You still don't believe me.'

'No, Art, it's not that I don't believe; *it's that I don't give a fuck*. Mates come before anything else. Your crew, your family, that's all that matters. So when life is unfair, and it is, more often than not, you *do* fucking take it. Not for you, for *them*. I'll forgive my mates almost everything. Letting me down, though? That's where I draw the line. Open me the secret gates to the universe! Show me wild magic, show me your *Madama*, show me a horny Lord for me to shag forever after, and I still won't give a fuck, because you're a sell-out who'd double-cross a mate to get what he wants. I won't say *thank you* and I won't have a laugh and I won't come with you, and I swear, man, I will *never* forgive you. So. Your call.'

Every muscle in Mauro's body is tense. Mine, too. We are ready to jump on Art, to try and disarm him before he can hurt Rebecca.

But Art's grip on the knife releases; he bows his head, his eyes streaming, and lets go of the blade.

'Pick it up,' Michele says.

He comes out of the blazing trees, pointing his gun at Art. 'Come on, pick it up.'

Art looks at him. 'You're the last person I was expecting.'

'Show me the saints, Art,' Michele says. 'Pick up the knife and show me.'

Art shakes his head.

'I believe you, son! I feel them with me when I dance. *Show me their faces!*'

He is not looking at me. I move a step in his direction.

Michele turns. 'I never liked you,' he says, and fires.

A burst of pain in my knee, fierce and sudden, the bones shattering and cutting flesh like shards of glass. My leg gives way and I plunge, yelling as hard as I did when I killed the kitten.

How graceful Michele's movements are: his gun returns to Art immediately after he fires, with the ease of a little wave coming ashore. He is a dancing master, and dances as well with guns and sinners as with swords and saints.

Another person is yelling. Behind veiled eyes, on the point of losing consciousness, I see Tony draw his gun to point it at Michele's head.

'It's unloaded, *coglione*,' Michele says.

Tony pulls the trigger.

It is not.

MAURO

1

Thank God Rebecca is sleeping.

I turn my eyes too late. I catch a glimpse of Michele's head being suddenly thrust backwards, drops of blood and chunks of bone zipping by like tiny insects in the smoke. When I look again Michele is in the dirt, a huge hole in his skull, blood soaking the earth, almost invisible, red upon red. Tony has stopped yelling, and Fabio too. It is a strange moment of bonding, the four of us silently watching the corpse of a criminal we just killed. And Rebecca is sleeping, thank God, and she will never know any of this happened.

See? We didn't *trespass*. I am mad at myself for the pang of disappointment surging inside me. I was silly enough, or enough in the thrall of Art, to believe that possibly, maybe, who knows. But Tony killed a man and no magic happened. There is no escape from this world. You can only face the music and dance.

And what a dance we have here.

I bring my hands to my face. It is a little secret ritual I go through before a difficult day in court: I join my open hands on my face, and then I let them slip sideward, one right and one left, as if I could wash away all fears, all worry, from my brain, and keep inside me only the useful bits. I forget the guitar player and leave space to the world-weary bastard. As my hands slip, I smell smoke and petrol, and think, *we need to get out of here*. The fire is spreading fast.

It is a tight corner, but it could be tighter.

I take a quick look at Fabio's leg. His knee is shattered into a million pieces; I doubt he will ever walk again without a cane. The man who did that is dead.

Good.

'Take Rebecca to the car,' I say to Tony.

He says, 'I killed a man.'

'Yes, and we don't have time to talk about that just now. Take her to the car.' I turn to Art. 'Are you helping me with Fabio?'

Without a word, he walks to Fabio. Fabio lets out a cry while Art and I carefully lift him to his feet. I cry too – my wound hurts. From the corner of my eye I register Tony scooping up my little girl. We make our way out of the olive grove, and every step is like a hammer blow. From the fields outside, I can appreciate how much smoke the fire is giving out. It will be noticed, even in this desolation, if it has not been already.

'Do you have any petrol left?' I ask Art.

'In the boot.'

Some things don't change: Art would always be sure to stock spares, whatever his project was. He doesn't take chances. Art and I help Fabio into the back of Tony's car. Tony rests my beautiful Rebecca in the front. While he gives Fabio first aid, I walk to Art's car and open the boot. There are two red petrol cans. I pick one and walk back to the olive grove.

I am a tax consultant; hiding traces is second nature to me.

Being alone in this grove gives me an eerie feeling; a whiff of my escape fantasy hits me again. If only it were true. If only another world existed, where you can be forever young. I squint to see if I can make out eerie shapes in the smoke – a half-seen enchanted woman, a glimpsed ghost – a trace, at least, if not proof. But nothing is there.

While I walk I open the can, and when I reach Michele's body, I empty the contents on it. It has to burn quickly; when the fire brigade arrives, the easily recognisable parts must be gone. They will identify him in time, but not tonight.

The root of the immense olive tree on which Rebecca was sleeping caught fire. I kick the body towards the root, and the fire, hungry as it is, spreads from wood to petrol to flesh. I am sorry for Tony, who killed a man, I am sorry for Fabio, who will lose his leg, I am sorry for Art, and I am sorry for myself. I have no tears left for this small-town mafioso. I hurry out of the olive grove. I have my friends waiting for me. Michele had his friends too.

Therein lies the problem.

Tony pulls into Elena's driveway, Art follows in his stolen car behind us. Fabio managed not to pass out, but he's getting weaker by the minute. Tony won't fix him as he fixed me; Fabio was shot by a professional who meant him harm. And yet we can't take him to the hospital. After what we did to Michele, we'd be condemning him, and ourselves, to certain death.

'Come in,' Elena says, opening the door. 'I made coffee.'

Behind her is Rocco, who doesn't even pretend anymore to be in control of this household. I scoop up Rebecca, while Art and Tony help Fabio in. He is biting his lips hard enough to draw blood. Elena shows me the room where I rested only two nights ago. The linen on the bed is clean. I lower Rebecca onto it, and kiss her forehead. The scent of smoked olive wood lingers on her skin. It smells good, like the aftertaste of a bonfire with friends.

When Elena and I get back to the living room, we find Art sitting on a wicker chair, Fabio slumped on the sofa, breathing hard, and Rocco standing with his hands buried in his pockets and the face of a man who is in over his head. Tony shouts at Elena, 'You *fucking sold me*!'

Rocco says, 'Chill out, man.'

Tony whips his head in Rocco's direction, and Rocco moves a step back.

He's laid out the coffee on the table in front of the sofa. Calmly, Elena picks a cup and sips. 'I put you in touch with Michele, and Michele told you what to do, and you didn't do it.'

'I'm not Corona.'

'So what, Tony? Are you too much of an idiot to realise the danger you put my family in? I did what I had to do, for *all of us*.'

'Selling my ass was what you had to do?'

'Your gun was loaded, wasn't it?'

Tony hits a wall with the side of his fist. '*You made me kill a man!*'

'I didn't *make* you do anything. I was praying you'd be smart, that's all.'

I shoot a look at Art. All his energy has left him; he has a tired face, ten years older than his age. He is looking at the light of the morning outside. He must still be thinking of his *Madama*, of his hidden world, and though that world might not exist, his longing for it is all too real. I can relate to that. I don't hate Art because he tried to kill my daughter. I love him because he couldn't; even the promise of eternal pleasure could not make him harm Rebecca. Buried deep inside the lunatic he has become, there is still the good man I knew. I hope that goes for the rest of us too.

'But now we have a problem,' I say. 'We killed a Corona man.'

'And *Fabio's leg* needs to be seen to!' Tony snaps.

Elena says, 'There might be a way out.'

Silence. Then Art scoffs and says, 'Was that your plan all along?'

Elena shrugs.

Art shakes his head slowly. He does something I have rarely seen him do – he looks at Elena with respect. 'Go on, then. Make your call.'

Elena stands up and exits the room, shadowed by Rocco.

'What?' Tony says. 'What's going on here?'

Art says, 'The King, Tony, the head on which the Corona sits – he has more use for my magic than he had for Michele. I'm giving myself into his hands.'

'For fuck's sake, Art, I *killed* a man and nothing happened! Your Hidden Things, your magic, *none of that is real.*'

But Tony knows as well as I do that's beside the point. Reality belongs to those with bigger guns.

'He's a reasonable man,' Art says. 'I'll ask him to give you no grief in exchange for my services, and you'll see – no sane doctor will ask what happened to Fabio's leg. Oh, and the Corona won't have a reason to hurt Silvana. I give myself to the powerful man, to the King, and it's win-win.'

Sure, in a world where win-win means you and your families are not going to die in the next forty-eight hours. On the sofa, Fabio struggles to keep his eyes open. I think he is still awake, but he can't, or won't, talk. I look at him. I look at Tony. *It is funny. Art's magic will save us after all.* 'Are you sure?' I say. 'If I understand how this works, once you're in the hands of this man, you'll be his... servant, basically.'

Art smiles, a trace of his energy returning. 'I'll find a way out when the Time is right. Meanwhile...' He pauses, and rubs his hands together. 'I'll play court wizard to the King. It's not going to be too bad after all. No, no. It is going to be fun. A whole lot of fun.'

TONY

I will never get tired of American Pizza. The pizza is good, not the best in town, but good. It could be kneaded with rat poison for all I care. I come here just to be here. Outwardly this place has changed a lot since tourists discovered Casalfranco, but its soul remains the same. For many, many years, me and my mates would meet here, once a year, the only fixed point in the carousel of our lives. There would be four of us; now there's three.

I am the first to arrive. I sit down at our table, order a glass of Pinot Grigio, and start on the bread. I'm as nervous as a sixteen-year-old on a first date. It has been two years, exactly to the day (of course), since Fabio, Mauro and I came here, and Art didn't. It has been almost two years since I killed a man. I came to accept that I don't feel bad about that. Michele was a monster. I pulled the trigger, but he forced my hand.

A German couple sit at a table not distant from mine.

They are extremely proud of greeting the waiter by name and ordering food in heavily accented, but clear, Italian. Retirees, I bet; Salento is turning into Europe's Florida. A lot of local people complain, but I say it is better now than it used to be back in the good old days, when fifteen minutes of hailstones in August could destroy your crop and make your family starve for the next year. The couple seem happy. They cheer me up.

'Best shirt ever,' Mauro says.

Two years can do a lot to a face. The last time I saw Mauro, his hair was starting to go grey; now it's definitely in salt-and-pepper territory. It suits him; it makes him appear wiser.

'I knew you'd like it.'

My short-sleeved shirt sports Disney characters dressed up as the Avengers. Uncle Scrooge makes for a wicked Iron Man, while I'm not that convinced by Mickey Mouse as Captain America.

Mauro sits down and clears his throat. This is supposed to be the Pact reborn. Not *exactly* the Pact, because we did have to be in touch to organise it, and because it can't be the Pact without Art, but the closest we could get. We couldn't do it last year: our wounds were too fresh. This year is an experiment, a let's-do-it-and-see-how-it-plays-out. I wasn't sure I could sit at the same table with Fabio.

'Boyfriend,' Mauro says.

I grin. 'You saw Sergio on Facebook?'

'Yup.'

'He's hot, right?'

'I'd know the answer if I were a faggot.'

I purse my lips in a kiss. 'Come on, be my fuck buddy. We're open-minded, Sergio and I.'

Mauro twists his face in pretend disgust. 'What does he do?'

'He's an actor.'

'Aren't they all?'

'He's for real. He does Shakespeare and all that.'

'Cool.'

'I get a lot of free tickets.'

Mauro picks at some bread. The conversation languishes, which is a first, with Mauro or Fabio. Too many elephants in this room. I'll make away with the biggest.

'I don't have a clue what Art is doing,' I say.

'I wasn't asking.'

'Yeah, but you were wondering so loud I could hear you thinking. I'm not in touch with Elena. I saw her for the baby's christening, and last Christmas, but we talked just enough to keep Mum and Dad happy.'

'You still haven't made up your mind about her?'

'No.'

Elena gave me a loaded gun. Was it out of a last-minute sense of sisterly love, or because she hoped I would dispose of Michele? I don't know and, sure as Hell, I can't ask her; I won't sit down to be spoon-fed her bullshit. I can only rely on facts, and facts don't look good. When I shot Michele, I knew I was saving Rebecca's life, but I also knew that the Corona wouldn't take it well. By pulling the trigger I was making dead meat of us all.

Except, Art saved us.

He gave himself to them, via Elena, and this time everything went according to plan. The King let us go, hushed any question about Fabio's leg, freed Silvana.

And also, he lavishly rewarded Elena with influence and power.

Rocco's firm is now the biggest in town. My little sister's career got a serious boost out of me killing Michele. The question is, when she loaded my gun, did she do that to help me, or to double-cross him? I will never know. Mauro says it doesn't matter, but of course it does.

Just like I will never know what happened in the olive grove, twenty-four years ago, that was bad enough to send Art off his rocker. There were moments in which I almost bought his story. That was just a reflex. We always listened to him when we were young. But if I need any proof that Art's story is a sad case of self-delusion, there we go: I killed a man, in the right place, at the right time, and we didn't trespass. Am I such a bastard that *bumping off a guy* is not enough for me to do magic? Please. I'm rough sometimes, but I'm not Elena.

No, I will never know what happened in the olive grove. All I can do is accept and move on. I lift my glass. '*Alla salute di Art*,' I say, 'the King's wizard.'

Mauro smiles, clinks his glass against mine. '*Salute*.'

I ask, 'Is Anna here?'

'No.'

'Are things between you guys okay?'

'Brilliant. But she says she had a revelation two years ago.'

'That is?'

'Casalfranco is a sexist shit-hole and she'll never come here again.'

'She joined Fabio's club,' I say, and immediately I wish I could take it back.

Mauro laughs. 'That was awkward.'

'Sorry.'

'Lots of water under lots of bridges. I'm fine with Fabio. Are you?'

'I'll know when I see him.'

'I was the one who made it to the end in one piece. I refuse to hold grudges.'

That day in the olive grove, when we stopped our clever friend Art from doing a very stupid thing, Fabio lost his leg. The bones and ligaments and muscles were fucked. They had to cut the leg above the knee. He'll have to wear a prosthesis and walk with a stick for the rest of his life, which I suppose is worth a lot of forgiving.

'You're a better man than I am,' I say.

'You're an *awesome* man, the best of the best. What you did for Rebecca is… I'll never repay that debt in full.'

'Paying for dinner tonight would be a start.'

'Let's not get carried away.'

'I hear banter happening without me,' Fabio says. 'That, my friends, is unacceptable.'

He wears a clean white shirt and has some stubble on his chin. He looks like a film star, more than ever, one that should be in front of the camera and not behind it. I am curious to learn how he is making ends meet; far as I know, he didn't manage to sell his book. He will fill us in. He walks to our table, beaming.

He walks. Without a stick. Without a limp.

'Your leg!' I say.

Fabio sits down. He says, 'Art.'

ACKNOWLEDGEMENTS

I have a fraught relationship with acknowledgements. By saying thank you to the people who made a book with me I am implying not-so-subtly that there is something to thank them for, and thus, that said book is pretty good. No one would say, 'thank you for cooking this stinking hotchpotch with me'. By acknowledging others, what we are in fact doing is congratulating ourselves.

Though I like congratulations as much as the next guy (scrape under the skin of the most reserved of writers and you shall find a smug bastard), I really want this page to be about those other folks, the hidden ones, who gave time, soul, and sweat to make this book the best it could be.

Starting with Piers Blofeld. Piers, you are far braver than I would have a right to ask. You are not only patient with my oddball ideas about stories and wonder, no, you actually *defend* them. To misquote the immortal Bluto Blutarsky, when goings get tough, you get going. Thank you for that.

Ella! *Ciao*, Ella Chappell. You were kind enough to believe in this book and clever enough to see the work that needed to be done. Every last comment you made was precious. Your sense of rhythm and your sense of poetry have been huge assets, and a joy to behold. So: thank you.

To my friends in Salento: thank you for refreshing my memory when it needed to be refreshed.

My dear Bloomsbury crew: you know who you are, and you know what I am saying thank you for.

Vassili Christodoulou and Susan Quilliam, your enthusiasm for the raw manuscript energised me and saw me through the many rewrites that brought it from there to here.

And before anything happened, before I wrote the very first word on Hidden Things, before I took the very first note, there was Paola Filotico. Paola, you were certain that I could learn, as an adult, to write fiction in a second language. I thought you were bonkers.

Fine. You win.

ABOUT THE AUTHOR

Francesco Dimitri is an Italian author and speaker living in London. He is on the Faculty of the School of Life. He is considered one of the foremost fantasy writers in Italy, and his works have been widely appreciated by non-genre readers too. A film has been made from his first novel, *La Ragazza dei miei Sogni*. *The Book of Hidden Things* is his debut novel in English.

THE RIFT

Nina Allan

Selena and Julie are sisters. As children they were closest companions, but as they grow towards maturity, a rift develops between them.

There are greater rifts, however. Julie goes missing at the age of seventeen. It will be twenty years before Selena sees her again. When Julie reappears, she tells Selena an incredible story about how she has spent time on another planet. Selena has an impossible choice to make: does she dismiss her sister as a damaged person, the victim of delusions, or believe her, and risk her own sanity in the process? Is Julie really who she says she is, and if she isn't, what does she have to gain by claiming her sister's identity?

The Rift is a novel about the illusion we call reality, the memories shared between people and the places where those memories diverge, a story about what might happen when the assumptions we make about the world and our place in it are called into question.

THE RACE

Nina Allan

A child is kidnapped with consequences that extend across worlds… A writer reaches into the past to discover the truth about a possible murder… Far away a young woman prepares for her mysterious future…

In a future scarred by fracking and ecological collapse, Jenna Hoolman lives in the coastal town of Sapphire. Her world is dominated by the illegal sport of smartdog racing: greyhounds genetically modified with human DNA. When her young niece goes missing that world implodes… Christy's life is dominated by fear of her brother, a man she knows capable of monstrous acts and suspects of hiding even darker ones. Desperate to learn the truth she contacts Alex, a stranger she knows only by name, and who has his own demons to fight… And Maree, a young woman undertaking a journey that will change her world for ever.

The Race weaves together story threads and realities to take us on a gripping and spellbinding journey…

CLADE

James Bradley

On a beach in Antarctica, scientist Adam Leith marks the passage of the summer solstice. Back in Sydney his partner Ellie waits for the results of her latest round of IVF treatment.

That result, when it comes, will change both their lives and propel them into a future neither could have predicted. In a collapsing England, Adam will battle to survive an apocalyptic storm. Against a backdrop of growing civil unrest at home, Ellie will discover a strange affinity with beekeeping. In the aftermath of a pandemic, a young man finds solace in building virtual recreations of the dead. And new connections will be formed from the most unlikely beginnings.

THE RIG

Roger Levy

Humanity has spread across the depths of space but is connected by AfterLife – a vote made by every member of humanity on the worth of a life. Bale, a disillusioned policeman on the planet Bleak, is brutally attacked, leading writer Razer on to a story spanning centuries of corruption. On Gehenna, the last religious planet, a hyperintelligent boy, Alef, meets psychopath Pellonhoq, and so begins a rivalry and friendship to last an epoch.

An astounding SF thriller for fans of Adrian Tchaikovsky, Neal Stephenson and David Mitchell.

NOD

Adrian Barnes

Dawn breaks over Vancouver and no one in the world has slept the night before, or almost no one. A few people, perhaps one in ten thousand, can still sleep, and they've all shared the same golden dream. A handful of children still sleep as well, but what they're dreaming remains a mystery. After six days of absolute sleep deprivation, psychosis will set in. After four weeks, the body will die.

In the interim, panic ensues and a bizarre new world arises in which those previously on the fringes of society take the lead. One couple experience a lifetime in a week as he continues to sleep, she begins to disintegrate before him, and the new world swallows the old one whole…

HEKLA'S CHILDREN

James Brogden

A decade ago, teacher Nathan Brookes saw four of his students walk up a hill and vanish. Only one returned – Olivia – starved, terrified, and with no memory of where she'd been. After a body is found in the same woodland where they disappeared it is first believed to be one of the missing children, but is soon identified as a Bronze Age warrior, nothing more than an archaeological curiosity. Yet Nathan starts to have terrifying visions of the students. Then Olivia reappears, half-mad and willing to go to any lengths to return the corpse to the earth. For he is the only thing keeping a terrible evil at bay…

For more fantastic fiction, author events, exclusive
excerpts, competitions, limited editions and more

VISIT OUR WEBSITE
titanbooks.com

LIKE US ON FACEBOOK
facebook.com/titanbooks

FOLLOW US ON TWITTER
@TitanBooks

EMAIL US
readerfeedback@titanemail.com